To: Sebastian & Selena

BAD BOY

With love

Dad / Stephen.

BAD BOY

Stephen Gray

Book Guild Publishing
Sussex, England

First published in Great Britain in 2005 by
The Book Guild Ltd
25 High Street
Lewes, East Sussex
BN7 2LU

Typesetting in Times by
SetSystems Ltd, Saffron Walden, Essex

Printed in Great Britain by
CPI Bath

A catalogue record for this book is
available from the British Library

ISBN 1 85776 977 5

CONTENTS

PROLOGUE

October 1979, The City

There is no plaque on the sandstone walls outside Stephen Hamilton-Davies's club, no number on its Georgian door. The club is, the Chairman of Lloyd's believes, an oasis of sanity secreted away from the high-flying low-life of the market. A place to think in peace; a place to talk in private.

'Thank you, Tompkins,' the Chairman says to the wizened man in morning dress who places the bone china onto the occasional table.

He turns his attention back to his guest.

'All I'm saying', Michael Darrett resumes, 'is that, drummed out of Lloyd's, people like Mac and me end up scouring the back pages of the *Standard* for jobs at half the salary.'

'And all I'm asking is for you to tell me the whole story. Would you mind starting at the beginning?'

Part One

Bad Boy

Chapter One

August 1960, West Sussex

Ten-year-old Michael could murder a meal. Good or not. His blue eyes are pools of black as he stares at the ripe cheeks of the peaches perched on the stand outside the greengrocer's. Feet planted astride his bike, Michael lifts a hand to take one. Mac, his best friend, has halted three shops along. Michael can see the juice dribbling from the corners of Mac's off-centre grin. Michael's stomach rumbles, and his fingers touch the velvety surface of the fruit.

'Oi!' a jagged voice shouts.

Michael looks through into the shop. A lanky assistant and the ruddy-faced greengrocer peer out at him intently.

Startled, Michael races away. From over his shoulder, he sees the Keystone Kops of the greengrocer and the assistant clamber into their van. Overtaking Mac, Michael points to a narrow alley ahead of them. The cycles disappear under the overhanging trees that cover the twisting passageway.

As Michael reaches the end, he is aware that Mac is no longer close behind him. His sense of foreboding is increased by the darkness of the alley. Speeding out into the fresh air, he sees the trap too late. Grasping Michael's handlebars, the assistant sandpapers Michael with insults and accusations.

'It-it was only a peach,' Michael stammers. 'I did-I didn't–'

'You're a thief,' the greengrocer rasps. 'Who are you? Where do you live?'

The unforgiving rays of the morning sun highlight Michael's pallor.

'My na-name's Michael. Michael Darrett.'

* * *

3

The granite floor of the derelict car-repair workshop is tarred by oil stains. Clumps of cobwebs hang from the racks that once held proud tools. But, since his Mum's death, Michael prefers to camp there than spend time in the family flat above. Lounging on the coarse blankets on top of the wooden pallets that serve as beds, Michael runs his fingers through his ruffled locks.

'Did your Dad get the belt out?' Mac asks.

'No,' Michael replies. His shoulders go into spasm. He could have taken a thrashing, but it was much worse than that. Saying only, 'I can't cope with you any more,' his father had gone back and sat in his chair.

'It'll be alright,' Mac says.

No, Michael knows, it won't be. The day after Michael heard his father utter something similar – 'I can't manage the business' – he nailed a closed sign across the workshop door. Michael comprehends that they're living on credit, on borrowed time.

Mac extracts a packet of Player's from his shorts, puts a cigarette to his lips, lights it, takes a long draw and blows a smoke ring. With his straight black hair, strikingly handsome features and powerful dark eyes, Mac looks to Michael like the general of a children's army. One that has never tasted defeat. After inhaling deeply again, Mac nods encouragingly and passes the glowing cigarette to Michael.

'Might help,' Mac says. 'But you don't have to–'

'Who says I don't want to?'

The end of the cigarette is damp from Mac's saliva. It feels strange, weightless between Michael's fingers. He puffs at it, filling his virgin lungs with smoke. Nicotine nausea makes Michael's head swim and he splutters.

'Let's talk about your Mum,' Mac says. He plonks himself down on the pallets and puts a hand on Michael's forearm. 'That always makes you feel better.'

The tiny kitchen of Mac's chocolate box cottage is rustic bordering on rusty, cluttered with battered pots and drying washing. It harbours the smells of Bovril, Brillo and double-fried fat. To Michael, three days after touching the forbidden fruit, it reeks of rejection.

4

'Come on,' Mac's mother says. 'Not so sad. Your father just needs a break. He'll be back in a few days. You'll see.'

Michael looks up at Mrs MacIntyre. What he sees is a buxom woman with a sun-dried face which seems at home in the country. What he sees is that she knows too: his father has abandoned him.

'I'm so sorry, dear,' she admits.

The word 'sorry' rattles around Michael's mind. His father always took it as evidence of guilt. It is a word Michael is very careful about using.

'We're having roast chicken tonight; we're going to feed you up.' She steps over to the butler's sink and fills the kettle from the cold tap. 'Your Uncle Jim and Auntie Kathy are coming all the way down from London just to say hello to you.'

A loud bang, followed by a whooshing noise, enters the kitchen. Mrs MacIntyre flings open the kitchen window.

'I found a wasps' nest,' Mac shouts out, happily.

'When's Michael allowed out?' Josie, Mac's eight-year-old little sister, calls.

Laughing, Mrs MacIntyre opens the back door. 'You run along.' She pats Michael's posterior fondly. 'Those two will bring you out of your shell.'

The rear garden is Michael's Eden. Unlike the front there are no flowers to harm, and the grass has been chewed away by a thousand footfalls. Best of all are the three sturdy ropes, hanging from the branches of a horse chestnut.

Josie swings high into the air on the middle rope, lets go and crashes to the ground in front of Michael. She brushes dust from her knees and produces a princess smile which belies her tomboy appearance.

'Hello, Michael.' Her green eyes gleam. 'Do you want to come and play on the ropes?' Mac emerges from the shrubbery and pulls a face. Josie sticks out her tongue. 'Michael can play with me too. And he's going to fix my bike. Mum said! Anyway, your flame-thrower game is just stupid.'

'You got a flame-thrower?' Michael asks, agog.

Retrieving an oilcan from under a bush, Mac grins. 'You gotta be really careful with this stuff,' he enthuses in his unbroken voice. He rocks the can to and fro carelessly. 'I found it in the garage,' he explains while fishing some matches out of his pocket. 'Dunno what it is, but it really goes up.'

'Your Mum will go mad, won't she?'

'Only if we get hurt. Let's find something else to blow up.'

A fortnight later, summoning up another brittle smile, Michael waves back at the forlorn faces of the MacIntyre family. From the kerbside, Mac throws a thumbs-up sign at odds with his down-in-the-mouth demeanour. The Ford Anglia chugs forward, and Michael's rear window view slips away.

'You alright?' Jim Darrett asks, turning round, leaving the driving to its own devices. His uncle's voice resonates with empathetic emotion.

'Yes.' Michael's little body trembles.

Sitting with him on the back seat, his aunt – his brand new Mum – lifts a hand out to touch his face. He nestles his blond head against her arm; he recognises love. And its limits.

'They're going to miss you terribly,' Mr Darrett says. Michael notices that his uncle's hat is touching the car's roof. To Michael, he is a big man in every way.

'I wasn't always a good boy,' Michael says.

'They think the world of you,' Mrs Darrett soothes. 'And so do we, Michael.'

He leans further into her body, and she wraps her arms around him. Her blouse smells of Persil; Michael likes it. His natural mother was a devotee of detergents.

'Your father didn't leave because you were bad,' Mrs Darrett continues. 'After your Mum died, he gave up. On his business. On you. On himself.'

A gust buffets the car. The reminder of the cold external elements makes his new Mum's embrace all the more warming.

'Your father left you because he didn't know what he'd got,' Mr Darrett interjects. 'He's my brother; I feel ashamed at the way he's hurt you. But that's not why we're so thrilled that you're coming to live with us.'

Gulping, Michael swallows the reassuring words greedily. They think of him as an injured innocent, but he knows they are wrong. They weren't there when he had screamed 'Mummy would have', or thrown 'I hate you' into his father's face. They weren't there the evening Michael decided he didn't like baked beans and hurled his

6

plate away. If they knew about all the terrible things he has done, they would see the balance of blame differently.

The car brakes abruptly, then jolts forward.

'We've wanted a child for years,' Mrs Darrett is telling him. 'And you're already family, our flesh and blood.'

There was no blood, Michael reflects, sucked straight back into the purgatory of his thoughts. He was sitting on the living room mat, holding his natural mother's unnaturally cold hand. Propped up by pillows, she rested against the armchair next to the coffee table. A grey skin covered the cup of tea that Michael had made to try and rouse her. Soft music filled the air. The Light Programme was his mother's favourite.

The room was full of people in uniforms. Perry Como started to sing of 'Magic Moments', and one of them turned the wireless off. Numb, Michael watched his father talking to the man with a stethoscope. Michael could hear his father's voice, but the words he heard were spoken earlier: 'You shouldn't have moved her. You should have called an ambulance.'

Michael wakes from his memories and fights back the marauding tears that fill his eyes. 'If the doctors–'

'They couldn't have saved her,' Mrs Darrett says, as if reading his thoughts.

'What your father said to you that day was unforgivable,' Mr Darrett adds, wrestling with the steering wheel. 'She died of a massive brain haemorrhage. Instantly. And you made her comfy. After.'

Michael's head droops. His new Dad means well, but he doesn't want a furious defence against any self-criticism. It was almost a year ago; he was just a kid then. He has done a lot of growing up since; he is old enough to admit his mistakes.

A light drizzle descends, and Mr Darrett flicks the wipers on. Insects' innards smear across the windscreen. Michael curls himself into the corner of the back seat and glances out of the side window. His spirits rise. A festive cordon of cones welcomes them into the forbidding traffic of London's North Circular. Not far now. A real smile pastes itself onto his angelic face.

He is still happy when he reaches the house. Unlike the cramped flat over his father's workshop, or the confines of the MacIntyres' cottage, the living and dining areas are separate rooms. There are even three bedrooms. He has stayed here before, but now it is his home. Providing he behaves well. And he can; he knows he can. Grinning, he puts his bag down on the kitchen lino.

'Hold out your hands and shut your eyes, Michael,' Mrs Darrett says.

He opens them when he feels a wee bundle of warm fur tickling his palms. A snow-white mouse with tiny pink feet peeps up at him from between his fingers. Handicapped by the lump lodged in his larynx, Michael mutters a feeble thank you.

'He's the first of many new friends you'll make,' Mr Darrett says.

Clearing his throat, Michael has another try: 'Thanks, Mum. Thanks, Dad.'

'You don't have to call us Mum and Dad unless that's what you want,' Mr Darrett says, beaming paternally. 'Be honest with us.'

'It's what I want,' Michael says. It is.

Chapter Two

October 1979, Lloyd's of London

Michael Darrett leans against the aluminium rail, alone amidst the market's muted mayhem. Slipping a palm into his inside pocket, he retrieves his Lloyd's ticket. Without this little square of coloured card, he won't be able to enter Lloyd's again. Taking it in his hands, he tears it into tiny pieces.

Devoid of apparent emotion, Michael gazes at the nearest hub of congestion.

'I couldn't care what the amounts are in Guatemalan gizmos, Western Samoan washers or Hungarian hula hoops,' Michael overhears. 'What's it in Christian money?'

To Michael, the building's colossal pillars contrast with the little-Englander attitude of its dumber denizens. Swathed in Lloyd's surreal light, his dark thoughts fester. By rights, he should have handed the ticket in a month ago. But he won't be intimidated or bullied. Michael has drunk from that ditch before.

He turns on his heel, paces over to the double doors and makes his way out onto the street.

Chapter Three

September 1960, North London

Michael trudges past the tidy gardens of the semi-detached houses towards his new school: St Mark's. Because his blue eyes are so striking, the swelling under the left one barely shows. But the abrasion on his right cheekbone is pronounced, as if someone has run a cheese grater over his face. The gold crest emblazoned on his blazer is circled by the school motto: 'Forward with Zeal'. Daunted by the familiar prospect of being alone amongst so many unfamiliar faces, he drags himself round the last corner and walks up the hill to the yellow-brick school buildings.

The classroom is too hot. Miss Jennings, prim in her plaid skirt and embroidered blouse, chalks up equations on the blackboard. Michael watches the clouds drift through the sky outside.

'Michael, wake up,' Miss Jennings says, prowling over to his desk. 'I know you understand equations, but you must try and pay attention.'

Adrian Jones stares at him. Freckles span a heavy-set face that hints of his playground pleasures: impaling daddy-long-legs and carving expletives into benches. Michael knows that Jones hates him all the more for finding schoolwork child's play.

Michael laces his fingers together. 'Yes, Miss.'

'Michael, what's happened to your face?' Miss Jennings asks softly. Her eyes swim with concern. 'How did you get those bruises?'

A child at the front drops a pencil. It echoes.

'Perhaps I could help,' Miss Jennings says.

'I'm okay,' Michael replies. He looks down at his lap. In his view, accepting the first aid of her cloying pity would turn his chances of forging friendships septic.

Without knocking, the headmaster enters. Many of the children jolt upright in their seats. Michael focuses on the specks of dandruff that have fallen from Mr Raistnor's silver-streaked hair onto his grey flannel suit. Miss Jennings and Mr Raistnor speak in hushed tones, and then he steps in front of the blackboard.

Bayoneting Michael with his eyes, Mr Raistnor straightens to stand taller than his six feet. 'All of us, especially you children, benefit from St Mark's reputation. And we owe the school a duty to maintain it. I'm deeply disappointed to have received a note from a lady in Elmwood Avenue about a fight yesterday, after school, between six boys of your age. Right next to her house. Those involved will stand up – now!'

Swallowing, Michael looks around. Miss Jennings bows her head, and Adrian Jones shoots him a warning look. Ticked off that the marks on his face make admission unavoidable, Michael rises.

The drone of a distant plane cuts through the barren quiet of the classroom.

'Ah yes, Darrett. In view of what your...er...parents have told us about you, I will at least listen to whatever excuses you can offer if–' Mr Raistnor snaps his sentence short and bares his teeth. 'If you tell me who else was involved.'

A girl leaps to her feet. 'It's not fair.' Michael is stunned to see her strawberry blond locks flail indignantly. He has never talked with her, but she carries on speaking for him: 'You can't expect him to tell in front of–'

'Sit back down, Lisa. I'll deal with you later.' He scowls at Michael.

'Someone hit me, sir.'

'Do you seriously expect me to believe that you weren't fighting?'

'No, sir,' Michael replies, jutting his chin forward.

Mr Raistnor leads Michael from the classroom.

In the study, Michael looks pensively at the faded photographs of long-forgotten football teams, while Mr Raistnor retrieves a bamboo cane from the top of a glass-fronted cabinet.

'I wondered when we'd see the same delinquency that your old school warned me of. Let me make this clear: I won't tolerate any

11

trouble from you.' The headmaster flexes his cane. 'Bend over the desk, Darrett.'

Michael does as he is told. Whack. His slender frame shakes. Whack. Levering his head round, Michael sees Mr Raistnor's nostrils flare with bullfighter compassion. Whack. Michael grips the far edge of the wooden desk. Whack. Whack. Whack!

'I don't do this for pleasure,' Mr Raistnor says.

Without permission, Michael rises. He turns around and gapes; Mr Raistnor's trousers point forward. In evident disgust, Michael sucks air through his teeth.

After school, as Lisa Carter is passing through the parade of pushchairs and posh hairdos outside the school gates, Michael steps up beside her. His bottom still smarts, but the way that Lisa meets his eye makes him feel as if he has earned his stripes.

'Which way you walking?' she asks.

He puts a slight hop into his stride. 'This way.'

'Very funny,' she replies, sarcastically.

But she smiles at him so hard that her nose wrinkles up. They stroll along side by side, talking happily, saying nothing, bathed in the sunlight that filters down through the ranks of crab apple trees. When they reach the churchyard, he turns to face her.

'Thanks for trying to stick up for me,' he says. 'You get much of a telling off?'

'Not really. Except he went off at the deep end when I told him you were being bullied. He wouldn't listen. You should have heard him: "There's no bullying in this school, young lady." What did he mean when he said that stuff about what your parents told him? Did he mean about your real Mum being dead and that?' She winces. 'Oh, I'm sorry. I guess you don't want to talk about it.'

'No, it's okay,' Michael says, walking on. 'After her death, I used to get these icy rages. I just like went mental. Adrian Jones wouldn't have picked on me then–'

Propelled by a pushy little boy, a pram hurtles between them. The pursuing mother's heels miss Michael's foot by an inch.

'Adrian Jones lives just over there,' Lisa says, pointing at the only house in the road with a porch. 'He's a pain.'

A milk float, heading back to the depot long past its bedtime, sails past.

12

'Strange,' Lisa says. He casts a glance at the milk float. 'No, not that,' Lisa says. 'I've never seen you on the way to or from school.'

Michael laughs. 'That's because I live in the other direction.' They enter a cul-de-sac; she stops at the first driveway.

'I'd better get back,' he says. 'I've got Cubs tonight.'

'No, come in. You must know Peter, my brother.'

Michael simulates a smile; he would never have guessed that Lisa is related to the Cubs' football coach.

'I don't think he likes me,' Michael says. 'He's never chosen me for the team.'

'He only seventeen, but he thinks he's such an adult.' They wander up the garden path. 'He's nice really; I'll tell him that we're friends.'

Friends. Michael greets Mrs Carter with a huge grin. Unfortunately, Peter is out.

Smidgely, Michael's snow-white mouse, darts round the wounded Airfix aircraft and dismantled dynamo which are part of the patchwork of play in progress in Michael's room. The mouse skids to a halt by Michael's hand, sniffs it and climbs aboard. Michael pops his playmate back into the cage and continues to get dressed.

On each previous Cubs' night dressing was a prolonged process. As a recent recruit, he is the only boy in his school year not to become a sixer: a patrol leader. Tonight, he hurries into his seconder's uniform. Mrs Darrett looks on.

'You don't have to go,' she says. 'You don't like it there.'

She opens her arms to him, but he doesn't want to hide in her cuddle.

'Haven't you noticed? I want to. I've told you: I might get into the team–'

'I've noticed that you're pretending; I've noticed the bruising to your ribs; I've noticed the weal on your upper thigh. For God's sake, stop lying to me.'

Michael bites the inside of his lip and looks at her. Her alabaster skin radiates honesty: an honesty Michael shares. He has never lied to her. Not once.

She reaches out and strokes the back of his hand. 'I'm sorry; I shouldn't have said that. I know Cubs was Dad's idea, but you

13

don't have to try so hard to please us. We'll always love you. You could set fire to the house–'

Michael laughs. 'I promise not to do that.'

She smiles. Michael sees it as a rainbow smile, one that makes the warm sun and cold rain yet more noticeable.

'Later tonight, when Dad's returned from the City,' she says, 'I want all three of us to sit down and have a long talk.'

Michael swallows a frown. They want him to tell them about the cuts and bruises he carries home with his satchel. So they can go and speak to the teachers. And make things worse. He wants to talk about why his real father abandoned him. He is ready to confess everything, but they don't want to listen to that. They just try and shut him up by telling him not to blame himself.

Wrapping him in the cotton wool of care, Mrs Darrett drives him the two miles to the old church hall in the family Ford Anglia. Bought ten years earlier, three years before the price wars of 1953 made cars more affordable, the Anglia doesn't have the style of the new Ford Popular. But Michael knows his Mum is proud of it. Most of the other mothers can't drive, let alone own a car. They call it The Crate. Mrs Darrett joins in with the joke herself; she tells Michael it is harmless.

Outside the hall, Peter Carter stands with a group of Cubs. As his Mum drives off, Michael sees Peter whisper to the Cub next to him: Adrian Jones. Same old, same old. A wave of disappointment washes Michael's optimism out to sea.

'Crater! Crater! Crater!' a chorus of unbroken voices chants at Michael.

'Good to see you, Crater.' Peter's voice is ladled with teenage sarcasm.

Guiding the other Cubs inside, he shunts Michael round to the back of the hall. There, in the half-light, Peter sprays spittle into Michael's eyes.

'You told my little sister that I don't like you.'

Peter's acne scars make the proximity of his face all the more unpleasant. Michael backs away until he bumps into a scooter secreted in the shadows.

'You don't get into the team because you're not very good at football.' He lowers his voice and sticks the needle of rejection further in. 'Or anything else.'

Michael feels his aggrieved anguish turn into anger. Not heated

14

anger. More a dispassionate determination that manifests itself in a complete change to his facial features which are normally symmetrical, pleasing in their handsome ordinariness. His alter-face has thin lips, pinched cheeks and an opaque, eerie glaze that obscures the blue in his eyes. Running his fingers over the polished Italian design lines of the scooter, he grips the tank.

'Get your grubby mitts off my scooter,' Peter blurts out. But his voice is somewhere north of nervous.

Cold to the core, Michael glares at Peter and his machine as if they were insects in a jar.

Chapter Four

October 1979, Lloyd's of London

Nine o'clock Monday morning. Stephen Hamilton-Davies, the Chairman of Lloyd's, pushes his feet further forward under the mighty desk. On his knees, garbed in a red costume like some courtier in a period drama, a man completes his early morning duty: buffing the Chairman's brogues.

Raising his palm, the Chairman commands another forelock-tugging functionary to open the doors and let his visitor in.

The room is normally all high ceilings and low voices, but the pinstriped visitor oozes aggression as he marches in and, without ceremony, takes a seat in front of the desk.

'I don't care whether he has left the market. I want Michael Darrett's entrails gouged out, fed to his own sort,' the visitor snorts. 'They'll eat anything if you put it in a burger. Darrett, Mac and that damn Lisa girl...they're nobodies.'

'That's most intemperate language,' the Chairman says in a voice as bright as his shoes. 'The press conference will calm things down. Everything will turn out roses, you'll see.'

Chapter Five

October 1960, North London

A sound comes from the undergrowth leading down from the lake in Woodlands Park. Branches, crushed underfoot, crack. Michael pays the noises no heed. He continues to lean on the rickety bridge, watching the lazy stream meander through the rocks and breathing in the earthy smell of autumn.

The Saturday morning has a special, almost Christmassy, feel to Michael. Only 20 minutes until he gets his chance on the lopsided field beyond the swings. He has made the football team. He is goalie. He knows that he is no Gordon Banks, but it isn't what he will do on the pitch that makes him feel so pleased. It is what he didn't do. Unlike all previous times, he didn't lose control when that cold anger swept through his body. He just argued his case. To Akela, the pack leader. To Lisa. And to Mrs Carter. In the end, Peter had no choice. Michael is counting his other blessings when the first blow lands.

The assault is a blur. He doesn't know which boy's knuckles crash into his temple, or whose fist buries itself in his stomach, or whose hands rip at his hair and tear at his clothing. Clouted by anonymous arms and legs down onto the wooden slats, Michael can't see who drags his football boots from his feet, or which child's foot kicks him savagely in the kidneys. But, just before he loses consciousness, he hears Adrian Jones's laughter.

Tuesday evening and Mr and Mrs Darrett appear on the Carters' doorstep bearing a recovery room request from Michael: that Lisa looks after Michael's mouse, Smidgely. Mrs Carter wobbles her perm in palpable pleasure; Lisa's nose wrinkles up in delight. Lisa had worried that Michael would find Peter in some way to blame, and that Michael would find her guilty by proxy. Lisa will spoil Smidgely rotten.

'If there's anything else we can do...' Mrs Carter assures the Darretts.

As a matter of fact there is.

When Lisa returns from school the following afternoon, she finds the two children that the Darretts have deposited while they go and talk with Michael's teachers. Mac and Josie are sprawled on her living room carpet in front of the unlit hearth. In front of them, five storeys high, is a house of cards. Mac dismisses Mrs Carter's offer of barley water and biscuits without a word and, using his fingers as tweezers, removes another card after rolling a die. It collapses on Josie's turn.

'I won. I won,' Mac taunts.

'We were supposed to be working together,' Josie tells Lisa. Josie rises and tucks in her blouse – no, Lisa notices, a boy's shirt. Josie looks at Mr and Mrs Carter, who are hovering over their charges clucking inconsequences.

'We made ourselves some tea before we came up on the coach,' Josie says.

On their own, Lisa presumes. Although Josie is only eight, her green eyes are those of a worldly wild child. It is evident that she doesn't feel in need of babysitters.

'We're going back tonight after we've seen Michael,' Josie continues. 'Mum and Dad don't like us to miss school.' She smiles at her brother; it is obviously an in-joke.

'School's important,' Mr Carter says. 'Lisa might go to university – imagine that.' Oh, no. Her father has made this comment every day since the letter confirming her place at Hinchley Grammar landed on the mat. Worse still, he has framed the letter and hung it – for all to see, in splendid isolation – on the Sanderson wallpaper in the dining room: the 'best room'.

Lisa responds with a lukewarm gaze, an ill-concealed plea to leave her be. She knows that her father is not piping her praises to embarrass her, but she wants Michael's friends to like her. Garbed in his codger's cardigan and slippers, her Dad appears older than her peers' parents; his childhood is just too far back for him to remember pre-teen protocol.

18

Mrs Carter glances at the nicotine stains on her fingers.

'Let's get a cup of tea,' she says to her husband. The parents depart.

'University – imagine that,' Mac sneers.

He raises his black eyebrows at Josie, but she rebuffs him with a girls-on-top remark: 'Jealous?' At least Josie is friendly.

Lisa trots upstairs to see if her house guest is awake. He isn't; but mice do a lot of sleeping. That is good. If Michael isn't out of hospital before she goes off to Brownies' camp that weekend, it will be easy for Peter to look after Smidgely. It is kind of Peter to play foster parent, but she hasn't informed Michael. He might object.

Downstairs, grinning off-centre, Mac conjures a knife from his shorts and presses the silver button on the handle. A three-inch blade flicks up. It comes as no surprise to Josie that her brother has a flick knife. But she finds it odd when Mac picks up the charity box that sits on the mantelshelf. The animal welfare box, in the form of curly-tailed pig with a bandage round its head, doubles as a decoration.

Upending the injured pig, Mac slips the knife under the seal covering the bottom, empties the contents, takes two shiny sixpences, puts the other coins back, licks the seal, sticks it down, and returns the box to the shelf. Just as it was.

Mac tentatively proffers Josie one of the stolen coins. Accepting it, Josie slots the silver piece straight back into the box.

'And the other one,' Josie says. 'She's Michael's friend.'

'You won't snitch.'

'James,' she says, using his real Christian name like their parents do when giving him a warning. She will tell. Michael.

Mac obeys her command.

Cartoon giants in the undersized chairs of the children's ward, Jim and Kathy Darrett sit by Michael's bed. He hears the rain pattering against the tall windows and smells bleach and bandages. Row upon row of beds; an ocean of illness.

'It wasn't a fight, Michael. It was a beating,' Mr Darrett says.

19

'You've lost a kidney; four of your ribs are broken. They could have killed you. Whether you like it or not, we must deal with it. We need to protect you.'

Michael pushes the semolina pudding aside. After ten days, he has had a bellyful of food that would give a billy goat gut ache.

'Your teacher's taken a shine to you,' Mrs Darrett says, 'and your head, Mr Ratnor...Raistnor, says the school will do all it can to help.'

Michael feels an onrush of outrage, but he bottles up such bouts of bolshiness. Brat-like behaviour is behind him. 'Mr Raistnor canes me,' Michael says, sticking to the unvarnished truth. 'He started that time my cheek was cut. He knew I'd been attacked, and he still gave me a hiding.'

Mr Darrett's lips quiver. It is the closest Michael has seen to his Dad being angry. Wearing ties even at weekends, Mr Darrett is a model of middle-class moderation.

'Mr Raistnor will never lay another hand on you. You have my word on that.'

A knot of spotty medical students troop across the ward and surround Michael's bed. Their mentor, a consultant with an abundance of nasal hair, follows his flock. After a cursory nod to Michael's parents, the consultant gestures to a buck-toothed nurse who proceeds to pulls the curtains around Michael's bed.

Michael sees the consultant pucker his face into a rictal grimace of patronising importance. 'And how's our little warrior today?'

'Bog off,' Michael doesn't say. 'There's nothing wrong with me,' he parrots, as usual during the ward rounds.

And, for the second day running, the thermometer agrees with him.

'I can go home,' he yells, leaping out of bed. Images of Smidgely nibbling seeds from his fingers play through his head. It crosses his mind that he hasn't heard from Lisa since Friday. But he banishes the thought that something is wrong.

His new Mum and Dad are in his corner for keeps, Mr Raistnor will be warned off, Adrian Jones will stay away from him, Peter will pick Michael for the next match, and Smidgely will chase happily round his bedroom. Everything is wonderful.

* * *

20

Michael sits so deep in the Carters' maroon armchair that his bare legs are straight on the cushion, and his little socks stick over the edge. His mouth is fixed in a huge smile; he has dropped in to collect Smidgely. But Lisa is taking a long time to come down from her room. And, towering above him, Mr and Mrs Carter are talking in riddles.

'She was at Brownie camp,' Mrs Carter says.

Mr Carter fumbles an Embassy at her, but she already has one alight.

'I'll just go and find her,' Michael says.

He knows the configuration of the house. It is, like Michael's, a semi. When Lisa visited him in hospital, she called her house a 'Samey' and told him that she dreamed of living in a flat 'smack in the centre of London'. But he loves these houses; he wouldn't like footsteps on his bedroom ceiling. Come to think of it, he hasn't heard any noise coming from above: Lisa's bedroom. He bounces out of the chair.

'She'll be down any second...' Mrs Carter starts.

He can't make out the rest of what she says. Instead, already in the hallway, he is drawn towards the sound of scrubbing which comes from the back garden. He finds Lisa by the dustbins on her hands and knees, cleaning the bars of Smidgely's cage. She pulls herself to her feet; the stiff brush hangs limply in her hand.

'I don't know what to say.'

Neither does Michael. Bending down, Michael opens the cage door, teases the straw away from Smidgely's sleeping box, and feels the mouse cold beneath his touch.

Her eyes are bloodshot. 'I'm so sorry, Michael.'

Caught in the climbing roses that overhang the bins, newspaper pennants flutter in the chill wind.

'It's not your fault,' he says, comforting her in his loss.

'Please don't blame Peter.'

The Carters' comments about Lisa having gone camping plunge into place. Peter was supposed to be caring for his mouse. There is no anger, but he knows it will come later. He can't reply.

Michael picks Smidgely up and, using the tortoiseshell comb that belonged to his deceased mother, combs the soft fur. When he has finished, he drops the comb – and the unhappy memories stuck between its teeth – into the dustbin. Lisa says a prayer, but he doesn't join in. He wraps Smidgely in a clean handkerchief, and slips him into the pocket where the happy-homecoming seeds are.

'I'll try,' he says. 'I'll try not to blame Peter.'

'Thank you,' she says. She moves inside his personal perimeter and, to Michael's astonishment, puts her closed lips to his. He has always thought that kissing a girl would be revolting, but it isn't. Not with Lisa.

Chapter Six

October 1979, Lloyd's of London

The Chairman's smile of contained confidence weathers the cameras' volleys as the press conference reaches its climax. Bright white flashes and phosphorus questions are aimed at the podium where he stands, alone.

'That will be an internal inquiry, will it?' a reporter calls out.

'Yes,' the Chairman answers cheerfully, 'the inquiry will be internal.'

A chorus of excited disapproval fills the crowded room. The Chairman watches the reporters dip their heads. But he doesn't see them as just jotting down notes. He sees a forest of sharp pencils scribbling sharper words. And Stephen Hamilton-Davies isn't prone to whimsy.

'The findings will be published,' the Chairman adds. 'If Lloyd's has any bad apples, we will throw them out.'

'Unless they're one of your own?' a woman with strict hair accuses him. 'You won't just find the nearest pair of brown shoes and throw their owner on the bonfire?' she shouts.

Fighting back a desire to take issue with her temerity, the Chairman holds his head high. 'We accept that there's been wrongdoing. And we'll get to the bottom of it. There will be no whitewash.'

Chapter Seven

November 1960, North London

The pervasive smell of untreated athlete's foot in the church hall is nothing to the malodorous excuse for an apology that Peter greets Michael with on Cubs' night.

'Before you say anything, I didn't kill your mouse. It just died on me, okay?'

No, it isn't okay. He has tried not to blame Peter, but Smidgely's death seems to lack the random roll of chance. This teenage tormenter cares nothing for Michael, and neglected his mouse. If it looks like a toad and it croaks like a toad then it is a toad. Michael's eyes become opaque, his lips grow thin and his skin tautens.

He squints at the clock as Peter appoints Adrian Jones and another sixer, Patrick Coughan, as team captains for a softball match. Flicking his mop of dark curls out of his eyes, Patrick chooses Michael first.

Jones' freckled face erupts into a smirk. 'Reverse order is it today, Patrick? You expecting me to pick the next worst player?'

Something inside Michael tells him that this time his anger won't ebb away without an outlet. And swearing at Jones won't solve squat. He needs to answer Jones in the language Jones understands: violence. Gritting his teeth, Michael calculates the repercussions of immediate retaliation. Jones is a third heavier, and has two inches on him; Michael won't necessarily even win. And he would be pulled off before he could inflict enough damage to ensure durable deterrence.

'You've gotta deal with him,' Patrick mutters.

'Don't I know it,' Michael replies.

* * *

On his way home, Peter stops off at the Jack of Spades. It is one of the few local venues where the Venture Scouts are not required to verify their ages. The tables are empty save for two men in raincoats playing cribbage. Propping up the bar, the under-age boys tell tall stories about daring deeds and willing women. When – built too high by their imaginations – the tales topple, they fall around laughing. And get another round in.

Sometime after ten, Peter says goodbye to his friends. The half-moon glistens in the night sky, protesting innocence of the earlier rain which has doused his machine. Wiping the seat with his sleeve, he mounts it. With four pints of Best inside him, he revs the engine, enjoys its noise, and imagines himself as James Dean on a motorbike.

When he brakes at the first junction, the machine makes a grating noise. It troubles him, and he tests the brakes several times. They function perfectly. He relaxes. He has told his parents that the scooter's maximum speed is 30 mph. At 40 mph Peter turns the throttle full on and leans into the curve to approach the hill on which St Mark's school stands. As he reaches the brow, a gust carries the cold under his coat. He watches the wind whip ripples across the patchwork of puddles as he races onwards.

And then he looks where he is going, and draws in a massive gulp of air. A BMW Isetta bubble car is parked, 3 feet out from the kerb, directly in his path. The car is about 50 feet away. His mouth dries and the roots of his hair tingle. The Isetta looms closer. He pumps the brakes, but it seems to him that he isn't slowing. He tilts to the side and tries to steer round it, but there is no time left. Almost on top of it, he clamps the brakes hard. They lock. He careers onwards, out of control.

As his scooter ploughs into the Isetta, Peter hears the surreal sounds of glass and metal mash into a twisted mess. He feels himself fly clear over the bubble car and, sickeningly, hears his forearm break on impact. The noise is muffled, like the tearing of a wet branch. Alcohol offers no anaesthetic. His scream rends the air.

It surprises Lisa that the policeman who arrives the following afternoon is not much older than Peter. Peter has only just wandered into the world of work. She knows – he has told her – that

25

he is so junior that the surveyors he works for won't pay him if he needs time off. Propped up by cushions on the sofa in the front room, Peter faces the high-backed chair on which the boyish officer perches. Rain lashes against the bay window. Mrs Carter stands, arms akimbo, behind the officer.

'You're very lucky,' the young policeman tells him.

Peter squints. With his arm plastered from his wrist to above his elbow, Peter doesn't look very lucky to Lisa. She runs her teeth over her bottom lip.

'Lucky,' the officer repeats. 'Being inside, I mean.' A drop of water drips from the end of his nose. 'It's filthy out there.'

Peter shifts forward on his sickbed settee, moves his arm and hisses with pain. To Lisa, it looks like stomach-churning pain. The type that breeds resentment.

'We had a police motorcyclist look at your scooter. There's a lot of damage to the bodywork, the tank's dented, and the front wheel's buckled. However, he didn't find anything wrong with the brakes.'

'Told you so,' Mrs Carter tells Peter.

Hovering by the door, Lisa sees Peter drop his eyes and chase the fingers of his good hand down his cheek.

'You've made a very serious allegation,' the policeman says. 'There's no evidence whatsoever that Michael Darrett, or anyone else, caused your crash.'

'Have you spoken to him?' Peter says.

Mrs Carter tuts, loudly.

'You weren't there, Mum.' Peter's tone is bitter. Bitter as bile. 'He gave me this look. His eyes were like something out of a horror movie.'

'Michael is a minor; we don't feel it would serve any purpose to interview him.' The policeman's lips curl into a wry smile. 'This sinister look. At Cubs, wasn't it? Meetings end at 7.30. Your accident was at 10.15, after you'd been to the pub. We've made some enquiries. And I've a few questions to put to you. The degree of damage suggests that you were speeding. Were you?'

'Shall we take that as a "yes"?' the policeman continues, without waiting for an answer. 'And, according my notes, you'd also been drinking.'

'I only had two pints,' Peter argues.

'Oh, really,' the policeman replies, slipping a slight laugh between the words.

26

Seeing Peter pale, Lisa throws an acid look into his face. Peter is lying there in more ways than one. And Michael isn't capable of such an act.

The dawn is still bleary-eyed when the alarm clock orders Adrian Jones out of bed on Sunday morning. The air is freezing; the cocoa he makes himself is tepid. And, unless he gets a wiggle on, he will be late to start his paper round. By law, he is too young to be a paper boy. But, five-foot tall, six-stone heavy, Jones looks much older than ten. And rules are for other people. Slipping his podgy feet into his lace-ups, he lumbers out of the front door and closes it behind him.

The light isn't on in the porch. That's odd: his mother always leaves it glowing overnight. He stares at the fitting and runs a hand through his ginger hair. It is difficult to be sure in the semi-darkness, but it seems like the bulb has been removed. A shudder sprints down his spinal cord. But if he goes and wakes his parents, his father will give him merry hell for lousing up his lie-in.

He steps out of the porch. Jack Frost has painted the silent avenue white, and Jones feels he can almost hear the slugs munch-ing the winter pansies that border the path. Certainly, his senses are on edge. And he imagines footsteps coming from behind him. As if someone has followed him out of his house. He stops by the gate. His heartbeat climbs as he turns round.

'Aargh!' Jones' stomach ties itself into a knot; the blood drains from his face. Michael Darrett snarls an incomprehensible insult at him. Dressed in his goalie outfit, his features fizz with twenty-four-carat hate. And his eyes are opaque. Ghoulish.

'You bastard,' Jones says backing away. 'You scared the shit out of me.'

A boot slams into Jones's shin, and a rock – it feels like a rock – crunches into his jaw. Raising his arms, Jones tries to ward Michael off. But a fist smashes into his nose, and a foot hammers into his midriff. Winded, he drops to his knees. He can smell his own blood and see the blackberry-coloured blotches melt the frost beneath him. Lashing out, he hits nothing. Michael's studs bang on his ear, and two fingers stab into his eyes.

Wrapping his arms around his injured face, Jones flops into a foetal ball on the ground. But the attack continues. Knees press into his back, and hands close around his throat. He tries to wrench them away, but the pressure is that of an anvil. He chokes. Pins and needles prick every nerve in Jones's body as panic sets in. Gurgling hideously, he fights to gasp what he thinks may be his final breath.

'Don't...' he hears Michael start to say. He sounds on the verge of tears, but Jones hasn't landed a punch. 'Don't come near me again. Ever.'

The vice-like grip eases.

Part Two

Something in the City

Chapter Eight

Six Years Later, October 1966

The inhabitants of Hell would, Michael believes, feel right at home in Colney Hatch hospital. With dark stone walls and window bars, it is a prison for those sectioned within it. Zombies hang onto Zimmer frames; catheters protrude from pyjama fronts, and staff cling to the walls like timid bouncers.

Alongside Michael, on the chairs where the springs have sprung, the broken man is lucid. 'Don't go, son.'

Michael lifts a hand to part his Viking-like blond hair. He doesn't know what to say, or even what to call his real father. Because he's not a real father. A real father wouldn't have– Michael throttles the thoughts. Aged sixteen, Michael doesn't want to be sour. The letter from his father that lured him here was sweet, different to the cards that clout Michael round the head each birthday. His father had asked Michael to visit so he could apologise. But, in person, the only thing his father appears sorry for is himself. Still, he is ill.

'I hope they let you out of here soon,' Michael says.

His father grips Michael's knee with a hand bleached like driftwood.

'I've got to be off,' Michael repeats. 'Mac's Mum is coming up, and I don't want to miss seeing her.' He takes the bus back to where he is loved.

Don't get Julie MacIntyre wrong: she admires the Darretts' new kitchen. It's just not right that's all. The stainless-steel draining-board glistens, and the new Formica worktops gleam. Amongst the matching units the built-in Kendrick oven has pride of place. That must have cost a pretty penny.

'Oh, Kathy,' Mrs MacIntyre says, 'I can't get over this kitchen. It's stunning.'

It is stunning to her that Jim Darrett has spent all his remaining redundancy money on Kathy's new kitchen before finding a new role. Losing his job wasn't Jim Darrett's fault; whenever there is a takeover middle managers get it in the neck. Even she knows that. But, at Jim Darrett's age, finding a plum position is no cakewalk; you have to face facts.

'Thanks again,' Mrs Darrett says. 'Now, where were we?'

'Mac's not even seventeen yet; he's too young to leave home.'

'Julie, I've told you. He can stay here. Michael will be over the moon. They're like brothers those two.'

Julie's ample breasts heave. True, the boys spend holidays in and out of each other's homes. And the families crowd together to unwrap Christmas presents. If Mr Darrett was in work, she wouldn't fret. But giving them another mouth to feed at this time smacks of selfishness.

'Mac's not doing anything at the moment,' Julie MacIntyre says, seeking an acceptable excuse, 'apart from arguing with Josie. I know he should get a job. But this one. It sounds fancy – you know, working for a Lloyd's broker – but it's only a tea boy job. It pays terribly, and it's in the City. In London.'

'There aren't many advantages of having a husband with time on his hands, but Jim has been speaking to lots of people in the City,' Kathy Darrett soothes. 'He says it's a good time to start in Lloyd's. There was a gigantic hurricane in the States – last year I think he said – Hurricane Betsy. Lloyd's lost millions and millions.'

'That's good?'

Kathy Darrett isn't deterred. 'It's great. Apparently, the market will build up again. Lots of promotions. Jim calls it reverse gravity. You know, what goes down must come back up; he thinks Mac should grab the job. "Fortunate lad to get the offer," he says.'

'Will you let us...' Julie MacIntyre says, 'pay towards his keep.'

Kathy smiles warmly. 'Ah, that's what you're worried about.'

Sitting on Michael's bed a fortnight later, Mac taps his knees to the beat of 'Eleanor Rigby' which blares from the transistor radio. Michael's wallpaper is hidden by posters of Bobby Moore, Geoff Hurst and other heroes of July's World Cup victory. As they talk above the music, Michael throws dust-laden mementos from his wardrobe to clear space. Even Mac's meagre possessions won't all fit into the tiny spare bedroom.

Still, Mac has got a bedroom to himself. It could be worse.

'In fact,' Mac tells Michael, 'it could hardly be better.'

Mac lounges back on the bed, grinning off-centre.

'What a first week. It's just one huge adrenaline buzz. In the rush hour there's a whole sea of people – vast shoals of 'em swimming in and out of the stations. And the traffic – at night it's like some giant headlight laser show. Girls everywhere: on the tubes, on escalators, in skirts so short you can see their panties when you look–'

'When you look,' Michael corrects him, emphasising the word 'you'.

Michael watches Mac's eyes, powerful behind the hoods of his black eyebrows, dance excitedly around the room. Six foot tall, with the build of an athlete, Mac has an aura about him: like a young military commander.

'It's not just the girls,' Mac continues. 'Pinstriped men with bright-coloured shirts edged with bleached white collars and cuffs, old boys with bowlers and bespoke brollies, security guards in fancy-dress versions of police uniforms, chauffeurs in peaked caps, top-hatted doormen – the whole thing, it's just so–'

'So it's okay,' Michael teases. 'And the job?'

'I'm just a pen-pusher, but I know – really know – I'm going to be a player in Lloyd's. I can almost taste the blood of some of the wankers there. Not quite clever enough to go to university; not quite clever enough to do up their shoelaces. And they throw away opportunities like confetti – the sort of chances I would die for–'

'Well, I'll bet they missed out on metalwork at school,' Michael says.

'The brokers in my office don't know what work means, let alone metalwork. They dribble in just before ten, read the paper for an hour or so, chat about some rugger match, say they're "off for coffee" and then reappear, drunk as skunks, around five o'clock. Ten minutes' gossip about some deb's party and they piss off home.'

'I could go for a job like that,' Michael laughs.

'And they're all so alike. Jesus, I can't tell half of them apart. They've got those plummy accents and right-wing views that would embarrass a Nazi goose-stepper. They even look different to normal people. You won't believe this, but some of them wear garters, fob chains, monocles – the lot.' Mac picks up a cricket bat from Michael's floor. 'There's this man at work, Archibald Bufton-Tufton or something. No...Timbo, that's his nickname. Anyway, he says the London Market's like a club.' Mac hits the bat against his hand. 'This is a club.'

'My Dad reckons,' Michael says, 'that before the war, all the second sons of the gentry would have been out on the coffee plantations in the Happy Valley – Kenya that is – or whipping coolies–'

'I like your Dad,' Mac says, reaching down to pick up an aluminium catapult. He fondles it, as if it were a soft toy. 'Does he know you saw your real father?'

'No. Mum and Dad would give me layers of lectures about how I shouldn't chew over rotten memories. I'd put up with that, but I don't want to upset Dad. Being out of work's knocked him for six.'

'I'll tell you, Michael: you keep everything locked up inside, and you'll bloody start exploding again.'

The comment lands like a stone; Michael bites his lower lip. 'I haven't lost it for years,' he replies.

'Talking of not losing, you up for a game of snooker tonight?'

Michael shakes his head. 'Tomorrow. I'm seeing Lisa this evening.'

'Oh, her.'

Lisa likes the refuge the Wimpy Bar provides to teenage romantics on cold nights; it allows for conversation that the cinema can't. Sitting squashed together with Michael on the vinyl seat, she smells the hamburgers frying on the griddle and listens to Michael telling her that he loves her in a myriad of different ways.

Half a bap remains from the Wimpy they ate an hour ago. Breaking off little pieces, Michael places them into her mouth. She makes kitten bites at his fingers.

'This is more fun than feeding the ducks,' Michael says.

'It's like drowning in treacle,' the waitress with the lazy eye interrupts, collecting their empty cups. 'Are you two going to sit there till closing?'

'We'll move along when the rush begins,' Michael laughs. To

34

Lisa, the few tables that are occupied all seem set on winning the slow consumption contest.

'Ha. Ha,' the waitress replies and wanders back behind the counter.

Playtime over, Lisa toys with her strawberry blonde locks. She often feels the need to touch her hair when she is with Michael.

'How's your Dad doing?' Lisa asks, blushing. The stigma of unemployment smites its suburban victims, but Michael has stayed shtum on the subject long enough.

'He's written hundreds of letters, been to dozens of interviews. Nothing. Still, he's really positive. It's better than it was. I heard him crying the evening after he got laid off. I never thought I'd hear Dad cry.'

'He'll find something soon,' Lisa says. It isn't a lie; she hopes it for Michael's sake. And no one wants to be kicked in the teeth by the truth at every corner.

'He shouldn't have been forced out. My economics teacher gave me an 'E' and an earbashing for my paper on toxic takeovers. I argued that the market knows best. Those companies big on takeovers ten years ago are now worth less than those who didn't throw their weight around. He called it claptrap and said that takeovers clear away economic dead wood. My Dad's not dead wood.' His voice see-saws. 'If ever I get the chance to change anything... Stuck at school it's–'

'Calm down. You'll get your chance.' She kisses the tip of Michael's nose. 'Don't leave school. You'd have to get your hair cut. It looks great at the moment.'

She must be back before ten-thirty on weekdays, and he walks her home along the sleepy streets of semi-detached surburbia. As usual, she pulls him closer before they reach her house. She wouldn't want their snogging sessions outside her front door.

The place is always the same: opposite Adrian Jones's house. It is like she is drawn there. She had seen the souvenir indents of a strangler on Jones's neck, and she had watched Michael's wrath erupt when one of Jones's gang didn't get the message. The mauling Michael meted out had shocked Lisa.

Their lips melt together, and his hands slide inside her coat to touch briefly on her bottom and breast before wrapping themselves round her waist. The other girls complain of octopus-armed boys with one-track minds. But Michael is patient, gentle. The doubts drilled into her by her brother's conviction of Michael's guilt vanish again. Michael couldn't have caused Peter's accident. Anyway, it was all eons ago.

The green felt table-tops glow under generous lighting, but the edges of the snooker hall in Green Lanes are dark. And it is from those shadows that Michael hears two leary lads making snide comments about him and Mac. Fair enough, Michael knows that his long hair might make him seem like a tame hippy. And Mac's baggy pinstripe has given him a Mafioso makeover. But Michael isn't going to stand there and let these maggots take the mickey out of them.

'All that's missing is the violin case,' a North London accent jibes.

Mac sighs and rubs chalk onto his cue. Missing the reds entirely, Michael sends the white ball straight into the pocket. It is his third dreadful shot in a row.

'If you want a game,' Michael says to the interlopers, 'we'll give you one. Otherwise, just push off.'

'Minimum bet's a quid. Each,' Mac chirps up, as Michael expects him to. But a pound is money that neither boy can afford to lose.

The rude intruders strut into the light. The taller one has adolescent fluff masquerading as a moustache.

'Let's make it worthwhile,' he says. 'Two quid. Each.'

'You're on,' Mac replies. Michael hasn't got the money, but he knows Mac will sub him from the loan Mac's parents have given him until his first pay day.

The four of them ferret in their pockets and place the £8 on the corner of the table in a single pile for the winners to collect.

Michael tries to ensure that each of the balls he pots seems lucky; he clips the top of the white ball and bobbles the black down rather than despatching it cleanly. But there is no disguising the scoreline at the end of Michael's first turn. Forty-eight to nil is an emphatic start, and the taunting teenagers are trounced in short order.

'You fucking bandits,' the boy with the manky moustache says.

Mac snatches up the money and stuffs it into his suit. One beaten boy grabs Mac's lapels; the other boy prods the fat end of his cue at Michael. Leaning forward, Michael jerks the stick away.

36

'Don't be silly,' Michael says to the three of them. 'I gave up fighting years ago. Who wants to get into a ruck over a poxy snooker game? Put the money back on the table, Mac.' Mac scowls. 'You grabbed it too quick. Gotta offer them the chance of double or quits, eh?'

Obviously pleased at the prospect of doubling his winnings, Mac returns the money to the corner.

'Sod off,' the boy with the moustache complains. 'We can't get hold of eight pounds.' He steps into the spot where Michael is standing. Michael doesn't move; their noses almost touch.

'Tough,' Mac intervenes.

'Tell you what,' Michael says. 'If you stop interrupting our game and make an early night of it, we'll pretend you didn't up the ante and give you back two pounds.'

After a short argument with one another, the interlopers accept the peace offering and edge away. Supping the pint he couldn't afford fifteen minutes earlier, Michael smiles.

'I don't know what you're so happy about,' Mac simmers. 'We could've bought another five pints from the money you just gave away. Each.'

'That two pounds was an investment,' Michael says. 'They're greedy and stupid. There'll be another time. Guarantee it.'

But the prospect of further free beer isn't what makes Michael feel giddily good: he can keep the ghastly genie of his hideous rage locked up. And still show bottle. School's out; the important lesson is learnt. It is time for the ugly duckling to swan into the City.

Chapter Nine

Shorn, and feeling somewhat sheepish, Michael steps out of the barber's chair. Patrick Coughan, Michael's friend since Cubs, interrupts his inspection of the naked women in *Men Only* and laughs out loud. But, to Michael's relief, the other customers don't seem to share the joke, and stare at Patrick's flowing locks. The red and white pole outside, and the smells of Old Spice within, are as timeless as the traditional short back and sides that the regulars require.

'You here to get your split ends done?' Michael asks Patrick with a grin.

While Michael tips the barber, Patrick cleans the dirty magazines off the seat next to him. Michael sinks into it.

'You lined up any interviews yet?' Patrick asks.

'Yeah, first one's tomorrow with a Lloyd's broker. Like Mac. Different firm though; my Dad's pulled in a few favours.' Getting a boy a break is a man's work, but Michael just wishes his Dad could have found himself a post instead.

Patrick smiles wanly. Everyone knows his Dad is out of work.

'Best of luck, mate. And say hi to your old man, will you?'

Two weeks later, clinging onto the aluminium rail of the gallery, Michael faces his first storm at sea. He is a long swim out, having left school and accepted a job at Wetthards, an esteemed firm of Lloyd's brokers. Despite the tailored arm draped patronisingly round his shoulders, he stifles his doubts and soaks in the atmosphere. In amongst the swirl of suits rushing through the melee, he can pick out only two women. A powerful air of masculinity pervades the marbled halls. The noise is of bantering men and the smells of paper and marble; Michael is surprised marble has a smell.

Simon Jenkins has a watch chain. To Michael he reeks of cucumber sandwiches, regattas, nannies and a left-luggage childhood in cold school dormitories. He keeps his hand hanging loosely over Michael's shoulder while he slices through the air with his upper-crust accent. Michael feels even smaller than on his first day at St Mark's school when his Mum came into the classroom with him. For this occasion, a tour of Lloyd's, both his parents are there. All dressed up.

Using incomprehensible terminology, Jenkins warbles on about the activity in the 'underwriting room'. Even the simple word 'room' has a different meaning. The underwriting room is split into two open floors and is the size of an aircraft hangar.

A liveried gentleman walks past them with a dignified calm.

'That's a waiter,' Simon Jenkins says.

The man in the resplendent uniform appears to be delivering papers into cubbyholes at the end of large oak tables. He certainly isn't a waiter as Michael understands the term.

'And that', Jenkins adds, pointing to a young man with a carrot-top haircut who is obviously a clerk, 'is a scratch boy.'

Michael breaths in the aroma of money, of the polished leather of handmade shoes and of subtle colognes; his ears try to tune in to a confusing white noise, a chanting sound being broadcast over speakers which hang onto the mighty marble pillars. Here and there, pink blotting paper balls lie on the floor. He is about to ask what they are when he sees a scratch boy hurl one thirty feet at what Michael presumes to be a friend. It reminds Michael of a St Trinian's food fight he has seen on television.

'This is very kind of Wetthards...and you,' Mr Darrett says.

'It's a pleasure,' Simon Jenkins replies with blatant insincerity.

The four of them stand at the far side of the gallery, looking down at the bustling activity on the marine floor. Squeezing Michael's shoulder, in what Michael knows is mock affection, Jenkins points downwards.

'See...there. The grey-haired distinguished gentleman. That's an underwriter called Stephen Hamilton-Davies.'

They peer down over the rail at a dapper man with a pink silk handkerchief displayed from the top pocket of his suit. 'He's known in the market as "Diddy". Many underwriters have nicknames.'

'Mr Hamilton-Davies must be six foot tall,' Mrs Darrett says. 'Does he like being called Diddy?'

Jenkins gives her a plastic smile. 'His nickname's rarely used within his earshot. Over the years it's been abbreviated from its original form, "Diddy Heck", which was earned by his rigid underwriting approach. "Did he agree it? Did he heck." So, yes, he's proud of his sobriquet. Nothing wrong in being a tough underwriter.'

Mr Darrett beams, but Mrs Darrett can only manage a hint of a smile. Michael suspects she is uncomfortable in her specially bought shoes. But it could be her nerves. He twists his shoulder as if he has an itch. It works. Simon Jenkins removes his arm.

'What are underwriters and brokers?' Michael asks.

Jenkins ignores the question. 'Coffee?'

On their way to the nearest bank of lifts, they play human dodgem cars; Lloyd's people seem to Michael to be unaware of pedestrian precepts. Squashed amongst the suits, Jenkins takes them up to the Captains' Room where delicious coffee is served by white-suited waiters.

Eyes twinkling, Michael asks, 'What are these real waiters called?'

'Waiters, Michael,' Jenkins replies, as if talking to something stuck to the bottom of his shoe.

'This isn't just impressive,' Mr Darrett says to Jenkins. 'It's awesome. Michael's joining Wetthards, starting on the clerical side of...reinsurance broking?'

'Reinsurance underpins the financial community. Banks don't lend money and companies are loath to invest unless they have insurance. Insurers themselves need to lay risks off, like bookies. When insurers unload risk, that's reinsurance. That hurricane which struck last year cost Lloyd's over £34m. Hurricane Betsy, you must have heard of it.'

'Yes,' Mr Darrett confirms.

'One of our clients, a regional American insurer, was badly hit by Betsy. Over a tenth of the properties they insured were damaged. When you consider what you pay for house insurance, you'll understand that – without reinsurance – they wouldn't have been able to settle all the claims. When Betsy blew, our client's reinsurers – including Lloyd's, of course – paid up. A goodly proportion of Lloyd's business is reinsurance.'

Michael repeats his earlier question, 'What are brokers and underwriters?'

'Lloyd's is a market,' Jenkins says. 'The shoppers are the brokers. Expert shoppers. They know where to look and how much they should pay. The stallholders are the underwriters. The goods they're selling: protection. The shoppers come to the stallholders, and then they haggle.'

'It's like a pinstripe souk,' Michael whispers to his Dad.

'I beg your pardon?' Jenkins asks.

'I'll like it here,' Michael says, and downs the dregs of his coffee.

'May I ask what you do for a living, Mr Darrett?'

Michael's heart stops. Mrs Darrett bursts into a smile.

'I'm deputy head of sales of Kendrick's Ovens,' Mr Darrett says, sounding as pleased as Punch. 'Well, as from next month. We're going to take Michael out to lunch to celebrate afterwards.' To tell me, Michael thinks, glowing inside. Deputy head of a single department is a couple of steps lower for his Dad, but he has climbed the mountain back to work. 'Don't suppose you'd care to join us, Mr Jenkins?'

Mr Darrett supposes right.

'Oh, I see, oven sales,' Jenkins says and makes a half-baked excuse. For which Michael is truly grateful.

Working in the streets paved with promises, it takes Michael over a year to save the money for the ring. Each month he struggles to hold onto £3 of his salary. It's hard. Even so, the Hatton Garden jeweller is sniffy. But it's the best, the very best, Michael can afford. The little jewel-box contains a year of sacrifices, his heart and his hopes.

Two sentinel suitcases, one at either end of the sofa, guard Michael. Wearing a Carnaby Street miniskirt that hides less than it displays, Lisa scurries around the house rushing to and fro the carrier-bag city that she has built in one corner of her living room. Her parents are asleep; they have to wake early tomorrow to take Lisa on a six-hour journey north to university. The thought of her leaving is terrible to Michael.

When she goes to dash past again, he links his little finger into hers and guides her to sit next to him. Looking down at her thighs, he fumbles in his pocket. He takes out the velvet box and slides off the sofa onto one knee. In front of her.

'Please, Michael...don't ask.'

41

Her words sting. 'I must. Will you marry me?'

He presses the little box into her hand and waits. On his knee.

She holds onto his hand and the box. He looks at her. Little boy lost. She has explained that she will be on her own at university. Explained that she will be lonely. Explained everything. Except that they can still have a future. Except that she feels like he does: there could never be anyone else.

'I can't give you an answer,' Lisa says.

Joining him on the floor, she lifts his fallen face with her hands.

But he has another, unspoken, question. And that she seems to answer with a murmur, 'Lovely Michael', and by a kiss which he translates as 'Yes, I love you'.

He feels her tears wet his lips, and her tongue push into his mouth. Wrapping her arms around his neck, she tumbles him to the carpet and moulds her body into his. She is, he believes, hoping that desire will bandage his wound. So he breaks the kiss.

'I can visit every weekend.'

'Michael, it's over two hundred miles.'

He would respond, but she doesn't let him: her lips attack his. Pulling him over so that he lies above her, she reaches under his shirt and chases her nails up and down his back. Her miniskirt rides up further. He senses her enjoyment of the primeval rhythm of his movements as, through his trousers, he grinds into her. With one hand she kneads his bottom; with the other she brings his hand to her breasts. He gropes at the front of her thin pullover, runs a hand up her thighs, and smoothes his finger along the vee of her panties. And still the kiss lasts.

It stops when she pushes his shoulder in a half-hearted way. He isn't sure what she means by it, but the ache between his legs is becoming too painful. Interpreting her action as a message, he rolls off her to lie on his back on the living room carpet. Propping herself up on one elbow, Lisa stares at the fireplace. He follows her eyes and sees the soot from other days' fires that stretches upwards into the chimney void.

Waves of doubt surge across her face. 'I love you so much, but...'

She stops talking. He doesn't interrupt her. His crotch bulges inside his trousers and Michael can feel, in detail, the contours of his fly. As well as his face, his chest is flushed. His short hair is wild.

'Lisa...?' He looks at the heat marks above the bulbs of the hanging light, and hears the 'gub-gubbing' noise of a distant helicopter intrude from outside the closed curtains. Trailing his fingers across his chest, Michael feels his damp shirt pumping up and down. He brings himself to sit on the floor, extends his feet out in front of him, and looks at the unblemished skin of Lisa's legs. Snuggling against her, he sees her run her tongue along the inside of her lips and, encouraged by a faint crease of a smile, tilts his neck. Their lips meet again. As one, they topple over.

Michael is intoxicated by Lisa's smell. She makes no attempt to stop him as he fondles her breasts again, moaning gently when he reaches underneath her to release the clasp of her bra. Helping him bunch up her pullover, she presses his head onto her breasts. He toys his teeth around her erect nipples, and then sucks them hungrily. She gasps, paws his chest, and grabs his buttocks. Moving a hand between her legs, he rubs her, feels the wet panties and her openness beneath, and pushes her underwear to one side. His fingers tremble through the downy mass of curls; he enters her alien wetness easily with a finger. The smell of her passion floods the living room. Urgently, he slides in and out.

'Michael, stop. No. Stop it.'

Taking a firm hold of his head, Lisa raises it up and looks at his face. With sweat glistening on his brow, his tormented eyes implore her. But he withdraws his finger.

And – he doesn't understand why – she changes her mind, pulls his face back onto hers, nips his upper lip with her teeth, drags him back on top of her, and eases a hand underneath the material at the back of his trousers. Under the elastic of his Y-fronts. She strokes a finger around the rim of his bottom, and he sighs. Using both hands, Michael pulls her panties halfway down her thighs. While he explores her, she clasps at the front of his trousers, opens his flies and buries a hand inside. He throbs.

'Turn out the lights, Michael.'

As his eyes adjust to the darkness, he watches Lisa rescue her bra from inside her pullover, stand up, unzip her skirt and let it fall. Despite yearning for her, Michael makes no attempt to get undressed himself.

'You're sure?' he forces himself to ask. She nods.

He stumbles as he pulls off his socks and rips his shirt from his body without undoing the cuffs. One of the buttons flies off.

43

Both their bodies feel cold to him when they lie back down on the carpet. Lisa glides her palm down his body and takes him in her hand again. He feels her playing a fingertip over the satiny skin. Michael gasps and probes between her thighs. She parts them, allowing him to penetrate her. Seemingly unhurried this time, he twists his thumb to rub against the top of her sex. She pumps him in her fist. As he touches her, he breathes in his own pungent manliness. Removing his hand, he caresses her tangled hair and kisses her. He tastes the salt from her sweat.

She lifts her hips, reaches down and brings him inside her. And his head implodes. God, no. This isn't what he wants; this isn't what he has waited for. This a Judas fuck. They aren't having sex for the first time. She is saying goodbye. And the rejection is somehow worse than his real father's flight.

White pain sears him, and he loses control. He lunges into her, rupturing what seems to be several barriers with his first thrust. Then he plunges into her again, deeper. Digging his nails into the cleft of her bottom, he hammers on. Up and down, hard. In a frenzy, he can't stop. He claws at her breasts. Beads of perspiration fall from his tortured face. With one final exertion, he punches into her. Too late, he spills the rest onto her stomach. His wet fluid and her blood stick to her skin.

In the dark grotto of the room, he hears her weep.

Coming to his senses – if she does betray him now, he is to blame – Michael turns on the lights. Her clothes are one pile, topped by a white hat. Her pants. She recovers them and dresses quickly, saying nothing.

He takes her in his arms. 'I'm sorry,' Michael tremors. 'Next time it'll be–'

'There can't be a next time. I'm not ready for this.'

She ushers him out into the dark Sunday night with the little box in his pocket.

Chapter Ten

The weekend is over, and the fun begins for Mac. At Holborn the sliding doors of the Central Line tube close, and he is forced back against them. The edge of a parcel is jammed into his side; its corner prods under his ribcage each time the tube jolts. A bovine woman presses against him, burping garlic breath into his nostrils. He turns his nose away, only to be harried by a waft from her armpits.

The October wind, wet with drizzle, rushes into his face as he clambers up one of the narrow back exits of Bank station. Inside two years Mac has been promoted three times, rising from tea boy to senior broker. Or, as one of his colleagues puts it less charitably, 'from tea boy to barrow boy'. He is paid enough to start looking for a place of his own. Somewhere to take girls, to entertain them. Striding to the office, he whistles a merry tune.

Piles of paper sit unevenly on two corners of his desk; the littered contents of an open file cover his telephone. On his chair there are half a dozen letters, some with foreign stamps on them, a clutch of telexes and a bird's nest of scribbled telephone messages. Oblivious to the clatter of typewriters and gruff Monday morning voices, Mac looks at the debris. The whistled tune returns to his head.

A man in shirtsleeves appears from behind a glass partition and passes him a telex. Mac holds the thin paper in his hand. To him, telexes seem to resemble greetings telegrams at weddings. Except the messages aren't always as welcome.

This one is, though. Mac peruses it, puts it down on his desk, picks it up and studies it again. It relates to a small piece of business from a big potential client, Pacific Sea Quake Consortium. It reads, 'Congratulations, Mr MacIntyre. You have a firm order. Please proceed with all haste. Yours, Donald White, Chairman PSQC.'

'So you've won your first piece of business,' the man in shirt-sleeves says. 'Well done. I'd love to know how you got it though.'

'I won it in a raffle,' Mac says. Then, seeing the man's frown, he modifies his sarcasm, 'No, not really. I made that up.'

What Mac does not invent, nor speak about, is the importance of this business to his career. This single order creates his credentials as a producer: someone capable of winning business. A lion to bring meat back to the den. From now on, he will be able to gallivant around the world. And as for the client itself, Mac feels sure that at some future time he will be given all PSQC's business. Enough commission to start his own company.

The man returns to his glass foxhole which leaves Mac to contemplate how he did win it, laughing inside. It had all been so easy.

The previous month, Megan, the 16-year-old daughter of PSQC chairman Donald White, came over to London for a two-week stay as part of a European tour. And, as a favour, several broking firms – those either involved in PSQC's business or with ambitions about it – were asked to show Megan how Lloyd's worked. An everyday request treated in an everyday way by everyone. Everyone but Mac.

Tall, dark and handsome, with a fire of a smile, two years younger than him, Megan would have been easy to pluck. He'd watched her eyes on him; he knew. But he kept his hands to himself; a proper gentleman, he'd been. And a splendid host. Using his own money, rather than face an inquisition about the expense, he wined and dined her, took her to the theatre, escorted her to the opera and even toured her round boutiques. All that despite his loathing of the 'prissy ponces in the theatre', his detestation of the 'pretentiousness of the opera' and his abject horror at shopping in haughty halls where the prices are higher than the baroque ceilings. Not, he could tell, that cost mattered much to her. His own finances were more precarious; funding these outings necessitated a trip to the manager of Williams & Glynn's Bank in St Mary Axe. But he knew it would be worth it. On her last night, the opportunity he'd worked for came, oddly enough, at the least salubrious place: the Royalty nightclub in Southgate.

'Do all the Royal Family come here?' she joked in her Australian accent, 'Or just the Queen and Phil?' Her smile was incendiary.

He laughed above the music of the Flowerpot Men. On the dance floor, gangs of girls danced round handbags, whilst leering solitary wolves in ill-fitting Friday-night jackets swilled beer. When the music changed to a slow record, she quickly wrapped an arm around his waist; but he used the contact to shepherd her to the main bar, upstairs.

Palpably hurt, she asked, 'Why won't you dance – or kiss me? I see how you look at me. You fancy me too.'

'Are all Australian girls so pushy?'

'I'm not all Australian girls; I wouldn't know. Why won't–'

'Because it wouldn't seem right. Your Dad asked me to–'

'He didn't ask you to bring me here tonight. None of the other brokers spent any more time than they had to with me. That broker I was with yesterday – Roger something or other – even made me pay for my own coffee.'

'Oh. Roger!' Mac replied, without a clue as to who she was talking about. 'He handles part of your Dad's account, doesn't he?'

'How did you know?'

'Everyone knows,' Mac bluffed. 'He keeps going on about your Dad – about how difficult he is to deal with. "Dishonest Don", that's what he calls him...'

'That's disgraceful. You should have his business.'

Mac allowed his face to agree. 'Do you think so?'

'Are you going to ask me to dance?'

And that was it. He knew then that he would get his order, knew the knee-capped broker who lost it wouldn't understand why. They danced. And later he gave her a proper kiss, but even then he was careful not to break the spell.

Mac forages through his papers, recovers a transparent folder from his desk, and saunters out of the building. Fifty yards from Lloyd's, on the fringe of the London Market, he enters a ground-floor underwriting office. Inside, straight-leafed plants in china pots compete with nondescript prints on the walls to attract the least attention. The sterile office has a neutral smell and no taste.

'Sean in?' he asks the receptionist.

She spits her chewing gum into a soiled paper hanky. 'Dunno. Fink so.'

Strolling round the partition, Mac tries not to smirk when he finds Sean Collins, stretching his six-foot-three body, pivoting on his chair. Sean's haircut with its lopsided fringe makes every day a sad hair day.

Sean blinks behind his black plastic glasses. 'You're early.'

Grinning, Mac sits down on the visitors' chair alongside Sean's desk. 'I thought you might be bored. I was sitting in my office daydreaming about your soft skin. I thought I'd come in early, make your day special.'

'Yeah, yeah. The day you dream about anything but your next promotion, or an even bigger pay rise, will be the same day I suddenly find boys attractive. Even if I did, I'd look for one less ugly than you.'

Still smiling, Mac opens his folder and unfolds a concertinaed document made of soft card: a slip.

'Firm order,' is the only comment Mac makes about the slip.

'I never thought you'd win this, Mac. How'd you do it?'

'Some people find me irresistible.'

Taking a rubber stamp from the rack on his desk, Sean thumps it down on the slip. 'DBL have offered me a job in Bermuda,' Sean says. 'Paying no income tax is one thing, but the thought of avoiding you gives me just the reason I need to take it.'

Mac winks and stashes his papers back into his folder. 'I'll bet you say that to all the boys. I'm not that easy to leave. The reinsurance world's the same size as a golf ball. Hang on – DBL own your company, don't they? Doesn't that stop them poaching you?'

'You'd think,' Sean replies.

'You know, DBL are a funny firm,' Mac says seriously.

'You're telling me.'

'You'll never believe this, but I queried their activities in my first week in the market. They've got tentacles everywhere. Underwriting shops, broking companies.'

'Yeah, they don't even care whether it bleeds or not,' Sean says. 'If it's got a balance sheet, they want to fuck it.'

'I asked my boss how DBL handled all their conflicts of interest. Do you know what he told me?'

'To their own advantage?' Sean suggests.

'Yeah. Bang on the button. Of course, now it's all so easy to understand. DBL don't let their left hand know what their right hand's doing. One hand pats your back, while the other empties your pocket.'

Michael's morning is gritty. Lisa has left for university, and he is stranded in the middle of the floor facing three men sitting behind the boardroom table perched forward on their chairs like vultures. The room is stark, utilitarian. Harsh fluorescent light dissects him. All three have manicured nails and wear thick silk ties, but the cut of Cedric Richards-Riley's Saville Row suit marks him out as the most senior. Michael sees his most striking feature, the glint of gold in his mouth, when Richards-Riley feigns a smile.

He looks over his half-rimmed glasses at Michael. 'Since you joined us on the clerical side, Mr Darrett, you've certainly made an impression. Particularly with your seniors. Simon Jenkins says that you're expending copious amounts of time on a hare-brained scheme that no one but you understands.'

'No, sir. It's true I'm working on a new product, but Simon spoke to me about it back in July. Since then, all the work I've done on it has been at home.'

'Really?'

'Yes, really.'

Richards-Riley takes a deep breath. 'Simon also tells me that you intentionally made him look a fool. Apparently, he had to go back and personally apologise to over thirty reinsurers. Well?'

Michael moves his feet apart and press-gangs his shoulders to relax.

'Simon borrowed an idea of mine; he forgot to ask how it worked. For years, he's prided himself on his fail-safe methods of monitoring the work of his clerks. If there's a hole in the net and it's been found without any harm being done – except to his pride – then he should be grateful.'

One of the vultures pecks, 'Grateful?'

'Yes. I didn't make Simon do anything. If he feels a fool, perhaps he has good reason. Much of the work I do is unnecessary, dull. Everything has to be read through three times. I measure the typescript of the longer legal clauses with a ruler, checking the position of the end words only. If it measures up, I read it once. Just once. Half the work.'

49

The three men swap bright-eyed glances. Michael isn't sure if they are admiring his bravado or, sadistically, just having a good time.

Richards-Riley digs his talons in, 'So if I get rid of you, we don't even need to hire a replacement.'

'Yes, sir. You can fire me.'

'Simon's right.' Richards-Riley's golden glint returns. 'You're a shocking clerk. Disrespectful. "Lippy": that's how he describes you. We don't need you as a clerk.' Richards-Riley pauses. 'Let me tell you something. The word "broker" comes from the Middle East – sort of an Arab pedlar. In its original form it had an unpleasant whiff to it. Of course, here in Lloyd's today, it's not like that. Brokers are upright, truthful people. Still tough dealers, mind.'

Bemused at this irrelevance, Michael looks at his tormentors carefully and, anxious not to show any self-pity, forces himself to smile at Richards-Riley.

And Richards-Riley smiles back. 'What we want are decent brokers – people who can argue, without lying. You're a bastard, Michael. Congratulations on your promotion and welcome to the broking team. You start tomorrow.'

Chapter Eleven

'Are you staying in, washing your hair again?' Mac asks. 'Come on, it's my last weekend here and there are girls to fu-fu-find.'

On his bed, Michael sighs and casts an empty look around the room. Only corners of Sellotape remain where posters of his boyhood football heroes used to decorate the walls. Mac's possessions litter the coarse weave of the carpet, hiding the swirled pattern. Not that Michael minds, every time he looks at the carpet he feels seasick. He'd been allowed to choose it himself, as he had the curtains. Then, back when he was fourteen, the drapes were fantastic. But now their 'magnetic blue' irks him. Lisa's absence drags his spirits down; she doesn't let him visit. Writing, nearly every day, makes him feel closer. But the few lines she scribbles back once a week dispel any illusion that she still loves him in the way he thinks she used to.

'Forget her, Michael. We have to celebrate.'

Michael uses tight-lipped silence to ask Mac to change the subject.

Mac raises his eyebrows. 'What's Wetthards' relationship with DBL?'

'You know I can't tell you about business,' Michael parries, wincing.

Mac grins disarmingly.

'Our firms are competitors,' Michael adds.

'You're just as ambitious as me, Michael. I tell you stuff...'

'They're Wetthards' largest shareholder, that's all. I'm told their interest is just financial: DBL like to spread their bets around. But then again, DBL's big cheese, Professor Dietrich, has some reputation – corporate piranha. Not that I've met him.'

'Do DBL give Wetthards much business?'

'Mac, I can't...'

'Course you can. Never mind,' Mac huffs.

'You get that trip to Amsterdam agreed?' Michael asks in an attempt to placate Mac, expecting him to fantasize about the red-light district, acid trips and dope-induced highs in the cafés by the canal.

'No, Timbo spiked it.'

'Timbo?' Michael asks.

'Yeah, my director. Bastard. Timbo's his nickname; he's five foot nothing. Tiny Tim with an elephant's weight. It's time he found a new job; he's in my way. Don't you know him? He's set to do a bit of joint broking with Richards-Riley soon.'

'My chief executive?'

'You know anyone else called Richards-Riley?' Mac pooh-poohs.

'What's joint broking?'

'God, you're green. Joint broking is where two broking houses work together on a single piece of business. It's supposed to be cooperation in the client's interest, but sometimes it's a bit hairy – lots of back-stabbing. What's Richards-Riley like?'

'Old, snooty, but don't be fooled. He's sharp and vindictive.'

'Vindictive, eh?' Mac grins. 'Let's hope Timbo doesn't upset him.'

Sitting on a bench, in the square outside the university's halls of residence, Lisa watches a majestic crow land on the lawn and hammer its beak into the grass. She sees it as dishing out death to the blind worms. The bright morning sun melts the November frost and silhouettes the bare trees against the skyline, brave wood ready for another winter. Lisa lets the healing tears out.

The tears talk to her; they tell her she can't go on like this. Without Michael she feels unloved and, unable to raise a smile to make friends, a foreign coin mixed in the purse of university life. The other students ride bicycles and take buses; she walks. They spend hours in the library, talk politics and listen to Pink Floyd. She swims, reads magazines and cooks for one on a hotplate. Loneliness is a cold companion.

But she can't let Michael visit; he'd expect to stay with her. In her bed. She had wanted the memory of his tender body to remember him by in case, just in case, their love didn't graduate.

Sure, it had been his first time too. But the mechanical pounding that Michael administered to her wasn't an act of love. The numb morning-after fear of being pregnant gave birth to twin doubts.

If he really loved her, he wouldn't try to pressure her into a marriage she is unready for. And if she really loved him, she wouldn't suspect him of causing Peter's scooter accident. Michael's refusals to even acknowledge the allegation fly through her mind like trapeze artists. In silence, he doth protest too much.

So she tells Michael, honestly, that she doesn't have a phone in her room and, less truthfully, that her weekends are spent working. She can't bring herself to read most of his letters; his upbeat words and tender poems don't hide his own torment. And she won't allow herself to feel guilty; it is more Michael's fault than hers.

She can see Giles, over the other side of the square, watching her like always. She isn't attracted to him, not physically, but his ardent interest has compelled her to ask around about him. In his second year of an economics degree, Giles, like her, seems out of place. His parents have bought him a car. A little flat too, four miles from the university. After all, they have money; they are being kind; they want to help. The car makes him different from the other students; the flat keeps him apart.

Giles isn't handsome; he has a full nose, wiry hair and sideburns. She doesn't like facial hair, but she likes the cutting comments about him less. 'You could lose a dozen cats in those tufts and no one would ever find them,' one bitchy fashion-follower told her. He would be grateful for friendship; he wouldn't expect anything more. Lisa is sure of that.

She dabs her eyes with her fingertips, brushes her shampoo-advertisement hair back with her hand and crosses the lawn.

'You're staring at me,' she challenges him. Lisa sees the same hurt and need in his face that she sees in her mirror every day. 'I don't mind,' she adds.

Mac knows only too well that December is a hectic month in Lloyd's; most reinsurance business must be cleaned and polished by the first of January. But he must make time for the most important thing of all: his career. On Wednesday morning he surreptitiously joins the same queue as his director, Timbo. To amuse himself, while he waits for the right moment, Mac pilfers a newspaper from under the arm of a sleepy broker and reads an article about President Nixon's appointment of Henry Kissinger to the office of Security Advisor – some dyslexic diarrhoea about peace and reconciliation.

The underwriter they are waiting for has a presence, a power about him. His voice booms above the more muted conversations in the haphazard queue of brokers that trail from the box like dolphins behind a ship. Mac knows that Timbo finds this particular underwriter daunting. The familiar Lloyd's scents of antique wood and aftershave surround Mac. But that morning the only smell he can sense is blood.

Mac makes his first move by tapping Timbo on the shoulder. 'Timbo! Didn't see you there,' Mac lies. 'You look like a penguin carrying firewood.'

Timbo clamps his slipcase, a thick leather folder open on three sides, beneath his arm and frowns. 'I'm snowed under. Top of the heap is that damn joint-broking with Wetthards. Richards-Riley's a nightmare. He's insisted that we have one file between us, so I've got all his papers. That would be fine if he just let me get on with it. But no. Five or six times a day he calls me up, as if I'm going to lose his precious documents. Idiot. He doesn't know what the word "cooperation" means.'

'Tense?'

'A bit. Going to be a long wait. Could stretch over lunch,' Timbo says.

'Is that my paper?' the once-sleepy broker butts in.

'Sorry,' Mac says, handing it back with a grin.

'Fancy a swift half?' Mac asks Timbo, certain of Timbo's nervousness.

'What, during broking hours?'

'We'd only be waiting in line,' Mac says. Seeing Timbo's creased brow, Mac adds a flattering untruth, 'I need your advice.'

'Alright, just this once,' Timbo replies. 'After all, it's nearly Christmas.'

'Hold our places?' Mac asks no one in particular.

'Look,' the now awake broker grumbles, 'I'm quite happy to hold places while people make phone calls or go to the loo. But I heard you; you're going for a drink.'

'Who asked you?' Mac laughs. He turns to the others in the

queue. 'We're only going to The Grapes; it's just round the corner. We'll be back in fifteen minutes.'

After obtaining grudging murmurs of agreement, Mac and Timbo leave.

At one o'clock, twenty minutes after their return, the underwriter rises and marches off. So they can keep their same places in the queue after lunch, the waiting brokers make a list on a piece of paper. Timbo paper-clips it to the top of the underwriter's blotter.

As normal, many of the brokers deposit their slipcases around the box they will return to after lunch. Timbo puts his on the underwriter's seat. A scarecrow to deter early brokers seeking to worm their way to the front of the queue. Mac, whose barometer of suspicion is permanently stuck on rain, never leaves his own slipcase lying around. He resists the urge to point out that brokers mark out their territory in the same style as dogs.

Mac meets Michael just outside the main entrance, as agreed.

'The Ship?' Michael asks.

'Meet you there in ten minutes. Could you take my slipcase?'

'Sure,' Michael says, looking perplexed.

At lunchtime, the underwriting room resembles an out-of-season holiday town. When Mac re-enters, he sees the room in a way which is never possible during the bustle of broking hours. The massive indoor market is filled with boxes. Each box consists of two church-pew wooden benches with a solid oak table between them. In the middle of each table, rising to head height, oblong pigeon-holes hold the metal-rimmed books which are the main underwriting-records of each box. In total there are perhaps two hundred of these boxes – Mac isn't sure; he has never counted them. A few clerks remain, heads bowed, marooned in drudgery, trying to catch up on the record-keeping before the market comes alive again. The box they were waiting at is deserted. Vulpine vigilant for would-be witnesses, Mac snatches up Timbo's full slipcase.

Measuring his pace he weaves round a marble pillar, strides along the length of the underwriting room, barges through the double doors and climbs the marble staircase leading towards the gallery to where hundreds of slipcases, left by junior brokers with nothing of value to peddle, carpet the floor. He removes the transparent file, checks it contains Richards-Riley's documents, and pushes the captured slipcase deep into the flotsam of the others.

55

With the stolen file in his hand, he returns to The Grapes. The smoke-filled pub throngs with tight clans of brokers swapping market gossip and jokes.

After shuffling the papers to bring Richards-Riley's to the fore, he attracts the attention of a bottle-blonde barmaid.

'Found this on the floor,' Mac shouts above the hubbub.

He tries to hand her the file, but she doesn't take it.

'So,' she replies, nasally.

Mac flashes his eyes at her and lights up his face as if she were an old friend.

'I'd never have thought', he says, 'that the word "so" could be made to sound sexy. You have an amazing voice.'

'Get off with you,' she says, smiling broadly and tentatively raising her hand to take the folder. 'You brokers, you're all the same. Why do I want that folder, uh?'

'Come on, whoever's lost this will be worried sick. Oh, look! There's some headed paper. Just telephone...who's that? Mr Richards-Riley. Let him know it's safe. He'll come and get it. I wouldn't be surprised if he gave you a big tip. I'd phone myself, but I really must be off.'

After a swift lunch with Michael, Mac makes a pit stop at his office. His chairman collars him in the foyer. They stand under an indoor tree.

'I've had the CEO of Wetthards, Richards bloody Riley, spitting fire at me,' his chairman froths. 'Apparently, Timbo's fouled up big time – left some papers on a pub floor. I understand he's presently running round Lloyd's like some baby elephant chasing its tail. Did you see him this morning? Was he sober?'

'Sir?' Mac fences, badly.

'Don't try and protect him.'

When Lisa returns home for Christmas, Michael rushes to her house. The strawberry locks have gone, replaced by a severe hairstyle reminiscent of a Cromwellian helmet. She still looks beautiful to Michael. Just different. Her words seem guarded but, as she pecks his cheek goodbye half an hour after he arrives, her smile welcomes his dinner invitation.

Well-to-do extended families enjoying protracted conversations surround Michael and Lisa in The Norfolk Room. Tinsel winks at them from over the mistletoe, inviting them to share a kiss. They don't. But there is something that turns Michael on even more. Michael has known Lisa since he was ten; he knows her every nuance. That shine in her eyes, the irregular way her nose crinkles up, lots of things tell him. She is in love again; he is certain. And she hasn't mentioned anyone else.

'Oh, while I think of it,' Michael says over coffee. 'You remember my friend Patrick.' Lisa looks blank. 'Course you do. Patrick Coughan. Massive mop of dark hair. He was the one who put together the school magazine: *My Pen Leaks*. He's a journalist now. Anyway, he's having a party on Boxing Day. If you're free...'

'I'm not sure. Besides, we'll see each other well before then.'

That reply tastes sweeter to Michael than the complimentary Turkish Delight.

Michael works the morning of Christmas Eve until chinking glasses replace slipcases as business tools. After one sherry, drunk with love, he races back to North London, to Lisa's house, to surprise her. Having divorced all thoughts of an early marriage, he will give her the little jewel box as a present – not an engagement ring. He will pace any number of platonic miles with her.

As she greets him, the pinks of her cheeks turn the colour of snowdrops. Seeing this, he keeps his hand in his pocket and holds onto the little box for support.

'Michael, there is someone I want...'

Wearing jeans and a gold watch, now clean-shaven, Giles steps into the hallway. Awkwardly accepting Lisa's invitation to come in, Michael makes his way through into the living room where the three of them endure a cardboard conversation. Giles offers him a winter warmer.

'No. No, thank you.'

Giles leaves them to get himself a Scotch. Watching the hearth, alive with the glow of embers, Michael's memories of the last time he saw the fireplace burn into him.

He whispers, 'Do you love him?'

'I'm fond of him,' she replies. 'I meant to tell you, Michael.'

Her eyes are moist. Giles returns and, glancing at Lisa, tilts his head and pinches his lips together as if he has toothache. Noticing, Michael offers gratefully accepted excuses and rises.

In front of Michael, on the doorstep, Lisa says to Giles, 'He's my best friend – apart from you.'

Michael doesn't go straight home. The air is dry; Christmas trees cheer windows. Passing a group of carol singers, he puts a pristine ten new-pence piece into their hat.

'God rest ye merry gentlemen,' they sing, 'let nothing you dismay.'

Josie can see the funny side of most things, but watching her brother make out has never topped her Christmas list. Still, it tickles her that Mac is pressing himself against a pliant girl to the Hollies' harmony, 'He Ain't Heavy He's My Brother'. And a party – any party – is a better way to spend Boxing Day night than being bored witless by the board games that Darrett and MacIntyre parents unearth every year. She's sixteen; Michael and Mac are eighteen. Honestly, sometimes parents haven't got a Cluedo.

From where Josie stands in the hallway, she can see into all of the darkened downstairs rooms of the terraced house. Patrick Coughan's cavalier curls toss from side to side as he deposits cans of pale ale into 'gimme' hands. He stops deliveries to share a joke with Michael. Josie would join them – it was Michael's idea that she came along tonight – but a boy with a flower power shirt buttonholes her with a bunch of flattery.

'I like your hair,' he says. 'It's sort of pixie style, isn't it? Like that model–'

'Twiggy?' Her green eyes sparkle.

'Yeah.'

'No,' Josie laughs. 'Twiggy doesn't wear her hair that way.'

Josie glances at Mac and the girl who wears a leather shoelace tied across her forehead like an Indian squaw. They are squatting on the floor, and Mac is running his hand up her yellow jeans. It is Patrick's girlfriend, Theresa. And Mac is moving in on her in front of everyone. Manoeuvring a battered tin from his pocket, Mac puts his lips to Theresa's ear. She giggles and nods. He opens it, pulls out some cigarette papers, and starts to roll expert joints on the upturned lid. Josie decides that Mac needs protecting from himself and interrupts the flawed flirting of her suitor.

'Not here, Mac,' she calls. 'OK?'

Grinning a lewd thank you to Josie for advancing his seduction attempt, Mac takes the stolen squaw by the hand. Upstairs. And Josie goes over to talk with Michael. Just talk. That's all. She hasn't got some silly crush on him. And even if she did find him attractive, she wouldn't dream of going out with anyone who didn't treat her as an equal. And Michael sometimes behaves like she is younger than him. Nineteen months is nothing.

When Mac returns downstairs, minus Patrick's girlfriend, the Christmas party is down to its last mince pie. In the kitchen, Michael is discombobulated by Josie's princess smile. She is standing so close; her pert breasts touch against his arm. And her questions are too personal. No. She's his friend, Mac's sister, still a child; his sexual antenna is badly storm damaged.

'Lisa's got people staying,' Michael says, explaining her absence, giving himself an alibi of a girlfriend. He hasn't told anyone about Lisa's new beau.

Mac drifts out of the kitchen door, into the rear garden.

'He's really bombed,' Michael tells her. 'I'd better...'

'My brother needs a lot of keepers,' Josie agrees.

They venture out in time to see Mac back into the studs of a leather jacket, jolting the bearded man who hangs ape-like from the washing line drinking stout from a bottle. The man drops the bottle onto the concrete. With the neck broken off, the base of the bottle is a crude weapon. The bearded man picks it up and, dripping with aggression, turns the inanely grinning Mac round to face him.

'You figure you can take me on? Come on then.'

Michael steps between them. 'He didn't mean it.'

The man raises the weapon to Michael's face and touches his upper lip with the broken shards. A Procul Harem song drifts softly out from the party on the evening air. Pulling at his sleeve, Josie shouts something at Michael. He doesn't hear what.

'I could slice you up,' the bearded man says.

Michael locks his eyes in optic combat; his pupils glaze over; his heartbeat rises; his veins pump the icy anger through his body. A sliver of glass nicks his chin which juts forward, turning the nick into a cut. But all Michael feels is a detached indifference as he watches himself throw a smile at the thug.

'But you won't,' Michael replies. Lifting his arm, he wards Josie away. He wishes she wasn't there.

59

His skin tightens and control of his actions switches over to the autopilot of his anger. With the sudden swiftness of a samurai, Michael clamps the man's wrist in his and brings his knee up into his groin. 'Coz I'm not gonna let you.'

Despite his broader build, the man doesn't stand a cat's chance. He is felled, unarmed, and sat on inside three seconds. Michael's conscious mind clicks off. The screen is blank.

He has no idea how many minutes are missing when he finds himself with both hands around the man's neck squeezing very hard. The man is ripping, desperately, at Michael's hands. Mac is pulling at his shoulders; Patrick is rampaging out of the back door yelling, 'You're killing him.'

And Josie is looking directly into his eyes. 'It's enough,' she is saying.

Open-mouthed, Michael lets go. Hand to lips, shaking his head, Michael tap-dances through a series of denial actions. Meanwhile, the bearded man crawls onto the rockery and gurgles vomit over the alpine azalea.

Blood drips from Michael's chin. His anger curdles into horror. Michael feels truly frightened. Of himself.

Part Three

Utmost Bad Faith

Chapter Twelve

Ten Years Later, October 1978

'Him...he'd bring out the animal in me,' says the pretty teenage clerk.

'Your cat?' replies the brunette broker leaning over the box.

'Shush. You're so crude,' the clerk laughs. Her dimples become prominent.

'Well, you are a scratch girl.'

'Scratch girl,' says the clerk. 'I wish people would stop calling me that. Why doesn't anybody use proper names round here?'

Michael, who waits by the aluminium rail on the gallery, hears the exchange. His eavesdropping powers would put the CIA to shame. Obviously though, she doesn't mean him. For a start, he's twenty eight; she is just a teenager. Still, he does feel a success; he has been a director of Wetthards for five years. Slim, with short blond hair, tanned in October, dressed in a suit on which the cuffs can be unbuttoned, Michael looks the part.

The underwriter, Jeremy Templeton, returns from lunch, dispatches the brunette broker simply by his arrival, takes his corner seat and rests an arm along the side of the pew as if sunbathing in the busy noise around him. Thirty years Michael's senior, Templeton is an autocratic man whose puritanism Michael finds irritating – 'teetotally' extreme. The clear skin on the bridge of his predatory nose testifies to the resolve behind his mantra: 'clear head, clear conscience'.

However, while Templeton's syndicate happily accepts premiums, it takes a metaphorical knife to get claims paid out. That, to Michael, is unconscionable. It is also the reason the syndicate used to be nicknamed the 'Piggy Bank'. And it still would be if Templeton had not put an end to the use of the term by crucifying the career of the broker who coined it.

Templeton's arm touches the neck of his scratch girl. Seeming put out, she shifts forward.

Michael advances. 'You wanted to see me, sir.'

Michael relishes using the term 'sir'. It saves the embarrassment of forgotten names and ensures everyone is addressed equally. Such socialism, at the heart of the world's greatest capitalist enclave, amuses Michael.

'Michael, I want you to explain your new methods to me.'

'New methods?' Michael asks, feeling the blood drain from his face.

'Don't be obtuse. Alright, so you've been working on them a long time.'

'A long time. Yes. Ten years, sir.'

'Then it's about time you told me about them. The IV deals.'

'The concept was called Inherent Value before I sold the first one a few years back. Then, Home & Life used the methods to swallow a competitor whole. Using an IV deal, they paid a price that didn't upset the fickle spoon-counters in the stock market. Home & Life said the product was a life-saver so I abbreviated Inherent Value to IV – as in intravenous drip,' Michael says, patting his slipcase as if to leave.

Templeton scowls. 'Don't waste my time with anecdotes, please.'

'I thought you wanted an explanation,' Michael says. 'In their basic form, IV deals are simple. Reinsurers group together to buy the future profits on blocks of business; they milk the future profit-stream. Because they pool the risks, no one reinsurer stands to lose too much if things go pear-shaped.'

'Go on,' Templeton says.

'By using an IV deal, I reckon Home & Life saved over two hundred jobs,' Michael continues. 'The alternative would have been one of those takeovers where the winners – if you can call them that – get hounded by the loan sharks that masquerade as merchant bankers. And in go the butcher accountants to hack the defeated firm apart. With respect, sir, I can't see why you're interested.'

'If you don't mind,' Templeton says, 'I'll be the judge of what should interest me. Thank you for telling me about a deal you did years ago, but I think you're being rather modest.' He turns sideways to his scratch girl. 'Can I have that memo?'

Extracting a metal-rimmed book, she snaps open the ring binders and passes a mini-sized photocopied page over to Templeton.

'This memo's from you to the management of your company, isn't it?'

'Who gave you this?' Michael asks.

'I'm afraid I'd rather not reveal that, but you can see I know about that deal you did last month. To stop a takeover, that one, eh? With a management buyout. The management themselves only had a paltry £50,000 between them. So, rather than surrender their limbs to the venture capitalists, they came to you.'

'Yes...but...' Michael splutters.

'Virtually all the money was coughed up by the reinsurers', Templeton says, firmly drowning out Michael's attempts to interrupt, 'in return for a chunky, ongoing interest in the profits of the business. And those reinsurers will make money too. Everyone was happy. Especially you, I'll bet. The thing is, I know what you've done. You've turned money into a liquid. You can splash liquid around and make a pint seem like a gallon, or soak it into things and make a gallon seem like a pint. What I want is to understand the inner working. The plumbing.'

'Why?'

'Because I want to buy. I need a magic wand waved over my syndicate's underwriting results – so to speak.' Templeton smiles. 'I'm just too profitable.'

'I've never turned down business before, but – sorry, sir.'

'There are better brokers than you who'd auction their children to be offered business by my syndicate,' Templeton says.

'Ten years it's taken me, sir. An entire decade to mould these IV concepts into shape. If you've been told about them, you'll know that. And what you want me to do, sir, risks throwing all that away.'

'I need this arranged. Come on, Michael. You pick my fleas; I'll pick yours. It was only last week that I paid fifteen thousand to that interior designer girlie of yours.'

Michael frowns. 'She's not my girlie; she's married. Your wife was thrilled with her work. How many estimates did you get – ten? Who did who a favour, sir?'

'If you fucking "sir" me once more...' Jeremy Templeton hisses. His face flushes. Behind an intentionally bland expression, Michael battles back thoughts of trying to appease Templeton. To suggest a compromise would be like throwing meat off the back of a sleigh. The wolves would circle. And anyway, Templeton's purposes are undoubtedly doubtful.

'I don't understand why you won't accept my business,' Templeton says in a more rational voice. 'You're misunderstanding my intentions.'

'Perhaps it would be best...' Michael says. He moves back from the box in an unspoken end to the sentence: 'if we leave it there for now.'

'Have another think about it and come back, will you?' Templeton says.

Michael doesn't hear it as a question, but an instruction.

'No hurry,' Templeton adds, drumming his fingers on the desk.

'Thank you, sir,' Michael replies, choosing to accept Templeton's words at face value. 'Have a good weekend.'

From her seat at her mother's dining table, Lisa sees the paint flaking off the inside of the bay window and feels a bare patch in the carpet under her foot. Wafting through the air, the smell of Brussels sprouts assaults her nose. Her mother struggles into the room, wobbling a joint of lamb on a carving board. Mrs Carter looks her age; older. Her hair is thinning; her gait is unsteady. She puts the meat in front of her son-in-law and points a shaky finger at the carving knife. Staring at the overcooked joint, Giles picks up the knife and runs a finger along the blade.

'I hope this is going to be sharp enough,' he says.

'Try and do a better job of it this week,' Mrs Carter replies. 'I'll just put the vegetables into serving dishes.' She shuffles back to the kitchen.

'Giles, please,' Lisa says.

He downs his gin and tonic with a single gulp.

'Every bloody Sunday,' he says, hacking at the lamb.

'It's not every week. Mum's lonely since Dad died.'

'A spectator of stamp collecting has more fun,' Giles grumbles.

The Sunday lunch conversation is as dry as the meat; at least the meat has gravy. Mrs Carter isn't hungry enough to eat any of her home-made trifle, which is a shame because, even Giles has to agree, she makes the best trifle.

'I just feel so tired lately; I can't seem to get anything done,' Mrs Carter says. 'Those antidepressants make it worse. They've done a lot of tests, but no one seems to tell me anything.'

'We'll make another appointment with Dr Farlane,' Lisa says. 'That's the cure, Mum. I'll come with you if you want.'

'Oh, would you, dear?' Mrs Carter says brightly. 'How lovely.'

Sipping tap water, Lisa watches Giles pour the dregs of the red-wine bottle into his glass. Lisa exchanges knowing glances with her mother.

'I did bring it,' he defends. Yawning, he looks at his mother-in-law and adds, 'Seems your tiredness is catching.'

'When are you two going to start a family?' Mrs Carter retaliates. Giles cringes.

Michael's Monday morning is ragged. Too much business; too little time. And even though the City Flogger is only a slipcase's throw from Lloyd's, Michael is late for his lunch date. After clambering down the stone steps, it takes him a minute to adjust his vision to the dimmed lighting in the vault. Loud conversations echo around him. Although new, the City Flogger has beams, tankards, mottled paint and the smells of Olde England.

Edging through the busy throng, Michael finds Lisa guarding two stools in a candle-lit alcove to the side of the wine bar. He kisses her cheek and, noticing that as usual she wears no perfume, basks in the faint smell of her skin. Passing him a glass of wine, she tells him she has ordered food for them. He bites his lip.

'It's the least I can do,' she says.

'He paid you, then?'

'Yes, in cash – eventually. He made a fuss about the invoices, had me do them several times. Mrs Templeton's really nice. But him...'

'Templeton's property – Mayfair isn't it?' he asks.

'Um. Apparently, it's an investment. The Templetons don't live there. Where did he get the money?' Michael shakes his head. 'Still,' she continues, 'now it's renovated, it must be worth a fortune.'

'Thanks to you,' Michael says.

He enjoys the melody of her voice but, as she witters on about her work, his thoughts drift back to what might have been. Her degree is history – bunk; it has nothing to do with interior design. Within three months of leaving university she had borrowed money from her in-laws and, using her beauty rather than her BA to procure interior design work, started her own firm.

When she abruptly changes the subject, the edges of her lips slope downwards and her voice rises an octave.

'My Mum's ill. She's permanently tired, just like Dad was. She's had some tests. I'm going with her to the GP tomorrow. I think it's cancer.'

Michael reaches out his palm towards her in mimed empathy. When she leans towards him, though, he lets his hand fall, steps back to a proper distance and holds himself steady. He listens, drawing her out of herself. She breathes unevenly as she talks, and he sees tears form in her eyes. Dabbing at them with a handkerchief, she is obviously pleased to be interrupted by a waitress who brings a finger bowl and two half-pint mugs overflowing with unpeeled prawns.

'It's just such a horrible way to die: cancer,' she says. 'With my Dad, it got into his back. He was drugged up to the eyeballs, but still in such awful pain.'

'Oh, Lisa. I wish I could help.'

'Just talk to me. About anything – Lloyd's. I don't really know what you do.'

Michael picks a prawn, snaps off the head, peels back the outer shell, and uses the water of the finger bowl to remove the last pink eggs before biting in.

'Interesting place, Lloyd's. The individual investors are called Names – apt that is, some are household names. Minor royalty, businessmen, barristers and baronets, even the odd showbiz celebrity. And some of them are a bit off the wall. Anyway, these Names group together to invest in syndicates like Templeton's. He accepts business for his Names – he has a stake too.'

'And you don't want to be a Name?'

'No fear – not even sure I'm rich enough. There's a joke doing the rounds in Lloyd's about the investors herding into the market: "God gave us the cows; it's our job to milk them." But actually,' he says, reaching down to touch his wooden stool, 'the results are fine – at present.'

'If you wanted to be a Name, wouldn't your firm – Wetthards – sponsor you or something?' she asks.

'Yes, they've already offered. But to me it's like gambling on the horses with money you owe the mob. You'd better be certain you'll win. If I lost money, Wetthards would own my soul – what's left of it.'

'But you work inside the market; you can see problems coming. You could...'

'No,' Michael says. 'Not really. Lloyd's has a peculiar system of accounting: three-year accounting. By the time you know there's a problem, chances are you got three years of problems. That's big bananas in anybody's money.'

'But what do you do?' she asks.

'I'm a broker; I put deals together. I persuade underwriters to agree to take shares of risks by stamping their acceptances onto pieces of card: slips.' Michael retrieves a slip from his slipcase and unfurls it in front of her. 'Slips are curious things. Look at this one. Those coloured stamps with an anchor sign in the right-hand corner – those are Lloyd's syndicates. The others are companies. This is a Canadian catastrophe risk – a hundred million dollars.'

'Wow. Some of these are just written in without a stamp,' she says. 'Hang on, that one there is in your handwriting. Er?'

'Yeah. That's an agreement from an overseas reinsurer I've written on the slip. There's a telex on file,' he explains. 'That might sound odd, but what's much stranger is that this whole document isn't legally binding.'

'What?'

'It's all based on trust.'

Savouring the last of her prawns five minutes after he has finished his, Lisa chides Michael for eating his too quickly. He produces a theatrical look, as if he has just stubbed his toe.

'Trust – um,' Lisa says, continuing the previous conversation. 'Yes, everyone trusts you.'

Michael slips his tongue between his lips and raises his head.

'Oh, Michael. Let's not get into that. I think you wanted Peter to believe you'd dented his scooter. He only broke his arm. Anyway, I never doubted you. Not for an instant,' Lisa says, looking straight into Michael's eyes.

'No, I mean you're trustworthy,' Lisa goes on. Michael smiles.

69

'Not like Mac. I wouldn't trust him as far as I could spew. How can he operate in Lloyd's? Some of the stuff he's done...'

'I've done some things too,' Michael says impulsively, somehow feeling his masculinity threatened.

'Like what? So you lost your temper after Adrian Jones and his gang put you in hospital. You lost a kidney. You were brave.'

'When I was eleven, I broke the headmaster's windows – well, window.'

'You told me about that. At the time. He deserved it.'

'It was still wrong,' Michael says. 'After I'd done it, I just stood there by this white picket fence, holding my catapult, smiling.'

'What happened when what's-his-name phoned your Dad? You never really said.'

Michael pauses before replying, 'Mr Raistnor had no proof; all he knew is that I hated him. I didn't care if I was caught; I'd left St Mark's. Besides, I'd just tell it like it was. You know about his erections when he caned me and that – I told my Dad about them. When I owned up Dad just said, "Well." I guess he understood; he never told Mr Raistnor. And he never mentioned it again.'

'You haven't commented on my hair,' Lisa says out of the blue.

'It looks great; I prefer it long. Fishing for compliments?'

'No. Giles doesn't like me growing it. Just wanted to hear what you thought.'

'Well, I like it. How is Giles?' Michael asks, feeling awkward.

'He's...okay.'

Michael has just finished his last sip of wine when she asks, 'Are you seeing anyone at the moment?'

He hears Lisa's voice trail at the end of the question, as if she regrets asking it. He recoils, drawing his body inwards to protect himself.

'I must be going,' he says, gently touching her forearm goodbye.

Waiting is Mac's least loved task. That afternoon, up in the Lloyd's gallery, he waits to see 'Diddy': Stephen Hamilton-Davies.

'Once a Lloyd's man, always a Lloyd's man,' Diddy says to the broker he isn't listening to.

Diddy's voice combines gravitas and geniality in equal measure. But the good-natured tone of such rally-to-the-flag remarks doesn't fool Mac. Diddy means them. To Mac, Diddy's giant belief in the institution of Lloyd's goes too far. Diddy sometimes mutters dark platitudes about Lloyd's hand-in-till miscreants being pond life that should be flushed from the market. And yet, Mac muses, he trusts a system which allows those of Mac's rank and above to be innocent until proven – not guilty.

Behind Mac, in the queue, two ferret-faced brokers swap jokes following the death of the third Pope within a year.

'Andy Warhol says everyone will be famous for fifteen minutes. The Vatican says every cardinal will be Pope for a month.'

The broker with Diddy gathers up his slipcase. Mac steps forward and, flourishing two inches of cuff, Diddy raises both his hands in mock surrender. They exchange gossip, while Mac brings out slip after slip from a slipcase so full that he can't close the brass poppers on the open sides. Every few minutes, asking cursory questions, Diddy bangs his rubber stamp down, dips his quill pen into an ornate inkwell and signs a copperplate signature.

Mac inhales deeply, then pulls out the reason why he has waited: a slip on which there is already a rainbow of different coloured-stamps.

'I don't like to beg,' Mac begs. 'I know you've said no once...'

Diddy produces a finger gun and shoots, 'No.' He laughs. 'Said no twice now.'

'At least look at it,' Mac persists.

After a deluge of technical arguments, Diddy sighs and hammers his stamp down on Mac's slip. Agreement by attrition.

'Don't bring this back next year,' Diddy says.

'I owe you,' Mac concedes, digging down to the bottom of his slipcase to produce a tastier bit of business. 'And by coincidence, I just happen to be carrying the sweetie to make your grazed knee better.'

Diddy displays his cuffs and wets his quill. 'This is jam. I'll take it all.'

'Er...um,' Mac flusters. 'It is jam; I've got to spread it thinly; I can't give you the whole jar. I can let you have half: 50%. Even then I'm making my job hard; any other underwriter who sees I've given you that much will want the same generous treatment. And I've got a whole bunch of favours to repay. Could you pencil it... er...not on the slip?'

Smiling, Diddy tears a strip of white paper off his batch and pencils his agreement onto it. Unusually, although he marks up his own records, Diddy doesn't write onto the paper the details of the piece of business to which the promise refers. It is, Mac knows, a minor oversight, just an uncrossed 't'. But Mac looks at the open cheque of the unheaded promise and grins, off-centre.

Chapter Thirteen

London rain falls on the ranks of pinstripe warriors later that afternoon. Reacting as if it is napalm, they flee to their bunker – Lloyd's. The Billiter Street side entrance is like a magnet. Michael jostles past the huddle of brokers shaking golf umbrellas into the puddle in the foyer, pushes through the swing doors into the room, stops by the rostrum and inhales the odours of damp slipcases and drenched overcoats.

'Hey,' Mac calls from just behind him.

'Keep that brolly away from me,' Michael says.

'I heard about that. Some Bulgarian dissident murdered at a bus stop. That reminds me, how was lunch? How's the ice queen? Lisa could be a contract killer; she wouldn't need a poisoned umbrella. The girl with the lethal glares!'

'She loves you too,' Michael replies.

Jeremy Templeton marches past. Without breaking his stride he says, 'I'm still waiting for my explanation, Michael.'

'What explanation?' Mac asks once Templeton is out of earshot. 'You look like you've lost a pound and found sixpence.'

'You know my IV treaties. Some orifice in my office hasn't just told him about them – they've given him copies. I'd love to know who did it.'

'I'll tell you how to find out,' Mac says. 'His scratch girl, Jules.'

Flummoxed, Michael rubs his chin.

'It's Lisa, isn't it,' Mac says. 'You just don't notice anyone else. The bin-by-date on that romance is long gone. Wake up, look around. Jules hates Templeton and couldn't give a toss – or whatever girls give – about her job. I see one of Jules's friends, Veronica, on and off. I'll see if I can set something up, if you like.'

'Sure.'

'Great, I'll give you a buzz. Should be OK,' Mac says. 'Favour for a favour? I hear Wetthards is having a bit of trouble doing the latest DBL deal. To be honest, I'd like a poke at it. What's it about?'

'You'd like a poke at most things.'

'Come on,' Mac persists. 'Tell me.'

'Alright,' Michael says. 'It's in Wetthards' interest that I try to unload this. We've wasted hundreds of hours on it; we're getting nowhere, slowly. But I don't expect my myopic masters to share my vision – so keep me out of it. The deal protects against movements between the Swiss Franc and Third World currencies. The premium's far too low, and there'll be a bloodbath of losses. Just to make it interesting, all Lloyd's syndicates are banned from accepting a share because the market elders – bless them – say any business of this type is "not suitable" for a Lloyd's syndicate to even consider.'

Mac makes a corkscrew motion with his hand.

'There's no way round the rules,' Michael insists. 'You can change a cat's name to Fido – won't make it bark. It's impossible, Mac.'

'Bye,' Mac says. 'I've got a new piece of business to win. Catch you later.'

Svelte in her sarong, the waitress walks upright with one hand behind her back, carrying the drinks tray in the palm of the other. Flashing a bright smile, she bends one knee and places the tray down on the bamboo table. In the Hilton, at Trader Vic's, surrounded by fishing nets, hammocks and make-believe Polynesian foliage, Michael's guest sits in a peacock throne opposite him.

'Mac only mentioned a beer, not this,' Templeton's scratch girl says above the Hawaiian music. 'Shame he had to leave early. My friend really likes him. She'd have stayed on, if he'd hung around. Mac said you wanted to ask me some questions. I don't think I can help much, Michael. I haven't worked there long.'

Jules smiles at him, showing off her dimples again. Smiling back, Michael looks at her. A few amber streaks liven up her curls, and the way her lips trace up slightly at the corners suggests she laughs often. She is pretty, but no older than nineteen. Perhaps too young. Or perhaps that is just another excuse to remain safe in his emotional garret, pining for love long ago lost. Whatever. First to business.

'You know my firm, Wetthards, and your syndicate are linked.'

'Sort of,' Jules says indistinctly, 'but I'm not sure how.'

Putting the straw to her mouth, she sucks more of her cocktail from under the pineapple and mango pieces. Michael takes a sip of his planter's punch.

'Wetthards own the company which manages the affairs of two syndicates: Diddy's and Templeton's.'

'Are you always so serious, Michael? I feel silly in this chair. Can I come and sit next to you on the settee?'

Laughing, Michael pats the cushion next to him.

'Well,' he continues once she has settled in, 'the broking operations of Wetthards are supposed to work at arm's-length from the underwriting biz of your syndicate. The rules are a bit flimsy, but whoever gave your boss that copy of my memo was out of order. Do you know who it was?'

'That's easy; why didn't you ask earlier?' Jules says with a slight slur. 'Your chief exec, Richards-Riley, brought it to the box. They're both Masons.'

'How do you know that? It's supposed to be secret.'

'Mr Templeton doesn't appear fussed who knows,' Jules slurs. 'He even puts the meetings in his diary: Secret meeting, Lutine Lodge, Cafe Royale. Remember to roll up trouser-legs and hop around singing the Horst Wessel Song.'

'I don't believe you.'

'I might've exaggerated a tiny bit,' Jules concedes. 'I overheard him talking with Richards-Riley a month or so back.'

Michael nods then toys his fingertips together, as if playing cat's cradle.

'I think I'm a little pissed,' Jules says. 'I haven't eaten.'

'We could have something to eat here.'

'I don't feel very well.'

'Do you want me to call you a cab?'

'No...I.' She rises and, holding her hand over her mouth, stumbles towards the ladies' toilets.

Michael finishes his planter's punch and makes a decision. She is too young.

* * *

75

Friday, and every chair in the surgery waiting room is occupied. Lisa studies the faces of the others who wait; they all look so well. A cough here and there, but fit. Tattered magazines litter the low tables around them. She hears a woman's voice call her mother's name and rises, slowly, matching her mother's speed.

When they enter the room, the woman, Dr Farlane, recovers a wobbly chair from the far corner. She places it next to Mrs Carter and gestures for them both to sit. The doctor's hair is tied in a neat bun; it bobs as she pulls out a brown envelope which is covered in concise notes. There is a stagnant pause as the doctor extracts some papers from the envelope, unfolds two letters and reads them. On the wall, behind Dr Farlane, is an anti-smoking poster. Lisa focuses on it and reaches out a blind arm to touch her mother's trembling fingers.

'Mrs Carter...I have the reports back from the X-rays, scan and from the specialist that you saw at the hospital. I'm sorry to tell you that the X-rays indicate a shadow on your left lung, and the scan shows two distinct areas of the liver which may be secondary growths. These, we believe, would explain your tiredness.'

Reaching into her handbag, Mrs Carter fiddles about before producing a handkerchief. No tears come.

'Oh, Mum.'

Mrs Carter's voice wavers, 'But I might just be depressed. I miss my husband, you see. You can't be sure.'

'You'll need some more tests. I'll be referring you to Mr Taylor, at St Sebastian's. He's a specialist, an oncologist – really nice man, very well thought of – you'll be in excellent hands. I'll also contact the district nurse.'

There is a bite in the wind outside the surgery. With an arm around her shoulders, Lisa carries Mrs Carter's weight. She isn't heavy. But, even with this help, her mother needs to stop to lean against a bus shelter where an old lady waits.

Mrs Carter's body shakes. 'Why won't they tell me what's wrong?'

'They have, Mum,' Lisa replies, cuddling her.

Mrs Carter's tears are infectious. Lisa nestles against her. By the time they have stopped crying, the elderly lady has gone.

* * *

From his foxhole, Mac has a commanding view. Eyes glinting, he surveys the panorama of ancient buildings and Friday-evening bustle. Swivelling round in his chair, Mac signals to Julian to enter. He has kept Julian waiting by the door for twenty minutes.

'Take a seat,' Mac says, casting a dispassionate look at Julian.

Julian is a newcomer to the business, a 'runner' who chases round the market on errands. His expensive schooling and silver-spoon introduction to the firm has brought him directly into the broking room, without the need to spend time with the middle-class oiks in administration. The seventeen-year-old drummer boy with a cherub face too young to be at work has gone straight into the front line.

Cornered, in the sunken film-director's chair opposite Mac's desk, Julian gushes, 'Sure, the underwriter said "no". And yes, I have to admit, it should've been straightforward. But for the life of me, I can't understand what I've done wrong.'

'Can't you?' Mac says, sinking his fangs into his agitated victim while simultaneously lighting a Marlboro with a Cartier lighter – a gift from a previous one. A discarded daytime lover, now poorer, now divorced.

Julian shakes his head. Much to Mac's inner amusement, he sees that Julian's chin is shivering and that his nose is starting to run.

'Alright,' Mac says. 'I'll go back to the underwriter and put things right. The mistake you made was to talk to the underwriter about the business. I know that sounds odd. But never – never ever – discuss any simple piece of business unless you have to. Nothing wrong with silence, often it speeds up the underwriter. If you must talk, try the weather. Football. Anything except the business. You must have seen he wasn't listening. All you did was to seem nervous – made it look as if there was something wrong.'

'Thank you,' Julian says, meekly.

Mac savours the moment; this mishap makes Julian yet more pliable – putty. And now Mac can move on to the real reason he has called Julian into his office: the new business from DBL, the risk that Michael has tipped him off about. The telephone call which secured the opportunity was delicious. Thankfully, Dietrich hadn't asked how Mac knew the details. And, not only did Dietrich agree to his request, he also invited Mac to a cocktail party at his London flat.

'There's only one way to become a good broker, Julian. That's getting out there and getting on with it,' Mac says, picking up a file. He flings it at Julian who catches it, just. 'New piece of business for you – a challenge. We've got a chance to impress the legendary Professor Dietrich, to break into the massive DBL account.'

'You're giving this to me?' Julian asks, swallowing.

'Look at it, carefully, over the weekend.'

Without comment, he passes Julian another file – one seemingly unconnected to DBL's. The one in which Diddy's unheaded promised line is.

'What do you want me to do with this file?' Julian asks.

'I'm not asking you to do anything with it,' Mac says. His voice is ominous; it demands that Julian work it out on his own. 'Close the door behind you.'

Stubbing out his half-smoked Marlboro into an ashtray the size of a cereal bowl, Mac runs his fingers over the ornate leather inlay of his desktop.

'Just be yourself, Julian,' Mac says after he has gone. 'Clever as a lamb chop.'

Deep in the Kent countryside, Mac cannons his Mercedes along the narrow lanes. The roof is off – in October. Megan, the daughter of PSQC's Donald White, screams happily when, hurtling over a bridge, the car seems to leave the ground. A mile further on, Mac pulls into a harvested cornfield. Scrambling out, he charges up the slope to the man preparing the hang-glider. They seem to argue for a minute, but then Mac reaches into his back pocket and passes the man something.

'Two hours. And don't you bend it,' Megan hears the man call out before he trudges off.

Megan's calf muscles tighten as she walks up the incline; it is steeper than it appears. More of a hill.

'What was that about?' Megan asks when she has completed her ascent.

'Oh,' Mac says. 'He just wanted to see my P1+, my pilot's certificate.'

'Can I see it?' Megan asks.

'Sure,' Mac says. He hesitates. 'I'll show it to you...in a while.'

Talking to her all the time, he helps her get ready. Fifteen minutes later, he fastens the second karabiner linking her to the

78

hang-glider. Inside the frame, Megan feels like a human kite. Colourful and fragile.

'Don't forget,' Mac says. 'Avoid pushing or pulling on the control bar. All the effort you put into tensioning the harness must come from your hips and legs.'

Droplets of perspiration run down Megan's temples as she trundles, birdman-like, down the slope. When she feels the air take the weight, she swings her legs backwards and pushes her head forward. Just as Mac has told her. She soars upwards in a prone position. Rising higher, her inner ears tingle. Vertigo. She looks down. Mac said she shouldn't fly higher than ten-feet off the ground, yet she is as high as a house.

'Look straight ahead,' Mac yells from somewhere below.

Hanging onto the bar with an alloy-crushing grip, Megan feels herself being drawn downwards. Her heart pounds, her muscles tense, her eyes bulge and she grits her teeth to await the inevitable impact. She can hear Mac hurtling along underneath. The sounds grow louder until, with a jolt, she stops in mid-air. It feels unreal, as if she is caught in a time warp. She peers down once more and sees Mac holding her and the hang-glider above his head, like a weightlifter.

'Phew,' Mac laughs. 'That was close.'

Gently, Mac lowers her and helps her get free of the harness. He stands over her while she gets her breath back.

'As knights in shining armour go, you're not bad,' she says. She finds a gap in the stubble and lies back, on the bare earth, smiling radiantly at him. 'It's strange, I can't remember ever feeling so safe as at this moment.'

He motions towards the contraption. 'Another go?'

'No way,' she giggles. 'It's dangerous, like you. You could've killed yourself. You told me never to step under a moving hang-glider. Come here, Sir Galahad.'

She tugs at his chunky pullover and, without a further word, pulls him to the ground. They kiss lustfully until, with a look on his face as if someone has taken a power drill to his kneecaps, he pulls away from her. She watches him writhe on the stubble, close his eyes, and shudder in self-imposed frustration.

'What do I have to do, rape you?' she laughs. 'Three weeks...'

'Doesn't seem like you've been here three weeks,' Mac says.

'Ten years ago,' she purrs, stroking his face, 'after I got back

79

home, I pinned a photograph of you to my bedroom wall. I was only sixteen. I told myself it was some childish infatuation, after all we'd only had one kiss. But, once a year, you came out to Australia to visit my Dad. Every time I saw you, I just...'

Mac blushes. 'Does your Dad know about us?'

'What's there to know?' she asks.

He strokes the bronzed flesh of her forearm. 'I love you; you know that.'

'Yes,' Megan says, tidying her hair. 'And yes, I've told Mum and Dad. He likes you. It's a pity, really.'

'What, that he likes me?' Mac asks.

'No,' Megan laughs. 'He's spent all his life building up PSQC. Now, his shareholders look like they're going to dump him down the dunny. Still, he'll find an escape route – he's talking about a management buyout. That's his dream. He's always wanted to...how's he put it...own the shop where he gets his lollies.'

'So, what's a pity?' Mac asks.

'I don't like to see him work so hard, and he keeps arguing. He's got this thing about professional fees. He thinks lawyers and bankers should be paid the same as gardeners.' Megan looks down. 'And also...'

'I'm going to lose the business he gives me, aren't I?' Mac asks sotto voce.

She sucks her bottom lip. It is her decision. Whether to tell him, that is. And she has agreed with her father that she can pick the moment. Mac's love for her is still too new, and there is no compelling business reason to blurt it out. So not yet. But if she is going to lie then better make it a large one. Little lies have short legs.

'Perhaps I shouldn't tell you this, but Dad says you're the best broker he's ever dealt with.' So far, so good. That is true. She glances at his face. You can't love someone too much. 'You'll get all his business, I promise.'

They see the hang-glider man returning. Hurriedly, Megan preens her clothes and dashes back to the car. She finds it unlocked and shakes her head.

In the evening, after dinner, Mac returns with her to the penthouse flat which she shares with six other Australians. Her flatmates are all female which adds, she recognises, to Mac's passion for visiting her. As usual, one of the girls flirts recklessly with him.

80

Whilst Megan doesn't mind, and Mac behaves perfectly, she is pleased when the last of her friends goes to bed.

'You free next Sunday?' he asks, apropos of nothing. 'I'd like you to meet my parents.' She moves next to him on the leather sofa, puts her arms around his neck and hugs him. 'Don't seem so surprised,' he says. 'I've already introduced you to Michael.'

'I enjoyed that evening; he's great,' Megan says. 'A sober influence,' she adds in a poor pretence of a drunken voice.

Mac clears a space on the glass-topped table in front of them and, conjuring a white sachet and a packet of razor blades from his pocket, smiles at her.

'I'm not doing *that* with you,' Megan says.

Seemingly unperturbed, Mac uses a razor blade to shunt the powder into a thin strip to create what he calls a sherbet line. But it isn't sherbet.

'Coke's really great, providing you control it. Not let it control you,' he says.

'I'm not stopping you, am I? I just don't want to try it. That's all. I know you're not addicted. I don't know how you do it – it's like the way you smoke on and off.' She moves to a beanbag, playfully imitating his off-centre grin.

'Do you have to go back next month?' Mac asks.

Megan smiles dazzlingly. 'No.'

'Good,' he replies, and snorts the cocaine.

Cut off from the administrative encampment by three sets of double doors, the sanctum of the brokers' room in Wetthards' offices allows free speech which is given free rein each Tuesday lunchtime. Over prawn sandwiches and cans of Skol lager, the brokers meet to discuss last week's events and that week's targets. Ten men – all present and all insisting they are correct.

Two-thirty comes and, pulling his watch out of his waistcoat, the vulture-like chief executive, Richards-Riley, signals lunch is over. Slipcases in hand, they file out.

'Not you, Michael,' Richards-Riley says. 'Jeremy Templeton's asked me to talk to you. He wants you to consider his request.'

'I have, and the answer's no. IV deals are a corporate banker's wet dream: hassle-free takeovers, defences, management buyouts.'

'What an interesting analogy, Michael. Your language gets more colourful by the day. "Wet", yes. Jeremy likens your IV methods to turning assets from solids into liquids. He wants to appoint you as his master plumber to fix him up with a tap. Then he can choose when to turn it on and off. You should be honoured.'

'If it were normal reinsurance, I would be,' Michael replies. 'Anyway, Templeton's not buying up companies; it's really not the best vehicle for him.'

'He believes it is,' Richards-Riley states.

'Look, the Revenue and the Department of Trade and Industry think IV deals are snow white. It's vital they're not tarnished; I'm inches away from real mega-money. Trust me.'

'Trust me?' Richards-Riley laughs spitefully. 'I never thought I'd hear anyone say that – except as a joke. Personally, I don't like these IV deals one jot. But, as you're spiriting money in and out of balance sheets for other clients, you can do a wizard job for Jeremy Templeton.'

'Selling profits isn't black magic. Let's say I come along and pay off your mortgage in return for an agreement to stay with you in your house rent-free. Your position would have changed. For one thing, you'd have a lousy lodger you couldn't get rid of who practised drum solos after midnight. But you'd also have no mortgage. It's the same with IV deals. Clients must tell everyone with an interest in the house about the new lodger and, yes, they can declare that their financial position has changed. That's reality. But Mr Templeton doesn't want reality. He wants a novel way to present fictional figures.'

'Jeremy wants your assistance. That's what he wants,' Richards-Riley says.

Michael snakes a hand into his slipcase and draws out a well-thumbed photocopy of an old, official-looking report. The Cromer report.

'You know what this is? Point 252's interesting. It recognises that when a broker controls a syndicate there's a conflict of interest that can't be ignored. Lloyd's commissioned–'

'I'm not going to rise to that bait, Michael.' Richards-Riley's voice is mellow. 'I don't know where you got hold of that report; it's supposed to be private. But no matter, in this case there's no conflict of interest.' His gold tooth glints. 'We should all be pulling in the same direction. Why won't you do as he asks?'

'Mr Templeton has made a large profit on one year and wants me to hide it. If he wants to roll profits forwards, there're ways to do it. But he wants to use the IV methods. And I hate rollovers. Thousands of new, vulnerable investors are joining Lloyd's each year. Templeton's profits aren't sustainable; they're dangerously high.'

'Many of those Names wouldn't know a sustainable profit from a profiterole. Mr Templeton wants to prudently keep some of the profit to one side. You do know the tax rate on unearned income, don't you? You don't do you? It's 98%...98%.'

Michael runs his fingers through his hair. 'Templeton's profits come from high-risk business. On that stuff when losses happen they spiral upwards, sucking all in their path into the vortex. If Templeton doesn't give the true figures to his Names, he paints a picture of a sunny day – encouraging the lemmings to take that cliff-side walk...'

'He's doing those lemmings a favour. They avoid the tax.'

'They don't avoid tax; they evade it – big difference.' Michael's cheeks redden; he has discovered the joy of releasing exasperation. There is nothing wrong with the occasional temperate show of temper. 'If Templeton succeeds in hiding this profit, then he's hiding the danger. These people aren't investing; they're sitting at a roulette wheel. Blindfolded. Worse, in that game all they can lose is the chips in front of them – in Lloyd's there's unlimited liability.'

Richards-Riley shakes his head. 'Don't preach to me, Michael. Every company makes efforts to present its financial results as it wants others to see them.'

'Presentation? This isn't gift wrapping; it's deceit. And Lloyd's system of three-year accounting means it's three times as deadly. Shareholders in companies which go belly-up lose the value of their shares; Templeton's investors stand to lose their homes, their children's educatio–'

'Shut up,' Richards-Riley bellows. 'You're being melodramatic; he just wants the results given a bit of nudge, that's all.'

'If it's that straightforward, then he doesn't need my services.'

'Your new type of deal suits him better. Why, is none of your business.'

'You don't get it. It's plain wrong. Ignore that – what about Templeton's audit? What will the auditors say? Or are we expected to tweak the transaction to make it look Persil white? What about Lloyd's itself? Is Templeton going to discuss it with them? No? Why not?' Michael rants rhetorically.

'Jeremy Templeton's one of us. It's got to be done, Michael. I'll leave it to you to sort out how to help Jeremy deal with the audit and Lloyd's.' Richards-Riley crushes an empty Skol can in his fist. 'I understand from Jeremy that you introduced him to some interior designer friend of yours. You've misused our time and our connections to get money for a woman you're having an affair with.'

'Look...' Michael's voice is raw. 'You've no idea how much pleasure I got from introducing Lisa to Templeton. I remember the shock on Templeton's face that I even knew an interior designer. It was just one of those supercilious questions the Lloyd's elite throw around, like "Should we send Tabatha off to Roedean?" As if some prole like me could even spell Roedean.' He decides to up the stakes. 'All this hassle has been caused by you passing Templeton – a fellow Mason – our broking secrets. I've a good mind to go and visit the Chairman.'

'If your mind was as good as you think,' Richards-Riley hurls the twisted can at the furthest bin, 'you'd have worked out that the entire main board already knows. The sand you're making a stand on is sinking. Think about our request – hard.'

Chapter Fourteen

The drab autumnal daylight outside Lloyd's is transformed by the swathes of frosted glass that cover the walls to create, inside, a sunny afternoon. Mac knows that for most others the atmosphere in the room is somehow compelling, beautiful yet functional, vast but compact. His own views are different.

'Some brokers think this market is dog eats dog,' Mac says to Julian. 'To me, it's hawks and budgies. If you can't convince the other birds to keep away from you, then you aren't going to spend much time alive in this cage.'

Extending from the corner of Diddy's underwriting box is a small oak seat on which brokers often perch. Knowing his footprint will end up on another broker's rear, Mac places one of his brogues onto the seat.

'I told you to look at those files over the weekend,' Mac says. 'It's now Tuesday, and you've done bugger all. Haven't even read them, have you?'

'I have,' Julian mumbles. Julian's shoulders are hunched up. His collar is at least one size too large; to Mac, he appears to be trying to hide himself inside his suit.

'The DBL business looks terrible,' Julian whines. A dab of tissue paper, a shaving souvenir, is attached to his chin. 'Am I missing something? I don't know much about economics, but it seems to me that the Swiss franc is bound to increase in value against, say, the Mexican peso. I've never heard of some of the currencies.'

'Just get on with it,' Mac snaps. 'I expect it done.'

'Mac, I can't. It's impossible,' Julian pleads.

'You'll do it, or find another job,' Mac says as if he is reading a lunch menu. His voice contrasts vividly with the threat.

'You h-h-have to h-h-help me. Give m-m-me some ideas.'

'Stuttering brokers are a liability,' Mac says unsympathetically.

'You know I don't normally stutter,' Julian begs after a few minutes of hollow silence. 'You could do it, and you would – even if you had to cut a corner. Just tell me how. I'd never let on, Mac. Please.'

'Work on the technical arguments,' Mac says, softening his tone.

'That won't be enough. Please explain.'

'If you ever breathe a word of this, I'll disembowel you. If you get caught, it'll be your own fault. Trying to blame me afterwards would just make things worse for you. Do you understand?'

Julian nods avidly.

Mac snatches Julian's slipcase and extracts the file in which Diddy's 50% unheaded acceptance lurks on a piece of paper. 'Remove Diddy's promised line from this file and paper-clip it to the front of the DBL slip you can't do. Other reinsurers, persuaded by Diddy's huge share, will be influenced. Believe me, they'll accept it.'

'Why?' Julian asks.

'It's like follow-my-leader; the lesser underwriters follow the judgement of the best respected. Stick to the company market; stay out of Lloyd's. If you muck up, and Diddy finds out, deny it. Say you misunderstood, simply placed the piece of paper in the wrong file.'

Julian sighs in palpable relief. Mac sees Diddy approaching the box with two clerks loping alongside him as if they were seeking his autograph.

'There are only so many hours in the day,' Mac quips to Julian, 'so why should any underwriter have to waste more than four of them by actually working?'

'I heard that,' Diddy says in a stentorian voice.

'Morning, sir,' Mac says, smiling expansively. 'You were meant to. Well, you do like to make your grand entrances fashionably late.'

Mac stands up, the clerks shuffle into their seats, and Diddy places his posterior into position. The process is a little ceremony: musical chairs, Lloyd's style.

'Don't you listen to Mac,' Diddy says sternly to Julian. 'As you'll learn, many facets of Lloyd's life are deceptive to the eye. As a stallholder, I have to sell my brand of fruit and veg personally. But we underwriters have awesome responsibilities – managing our businesses when not at the box. Of course, some things are just as they appear, like brokers sitting around all day, doing nothing but gossiping, swapping jokes and getting drunk – eh, Mac?'

Pasty, Julian fails to raise the required laugh and rushes off.

'New boy,' Mac explains, opening his slipcase.

'When I married Lisa,' Giles complains, 'my sister didn't even bother to try and rearrange her holiday. And that telegram she sent...'

'That was', Peter agrees, rolling his eyes, 'too much.'

Giles is explaining, as if his brother-in-law has asked, why he sees so little of his own family. Though the telegram that Giles's sister had sent was cruel: 'To Queen Lisa and Frog. Sorry the kiss didn't work. With love.'

Peter and Giles play squash on Thursdays. Up the hill from the 'squash club', as they refer to the squash courts next to the local swimming pool, is the King's Head pub where afterwards, to recover from the aches and strains, they sup pints. The pub isn't busy, its lack of music and tacky prints of hunting scenes see to that. There is no rush for Giles to get home; Lisa is spending the evening with her mother; they have been in the pub for well over an hour.

'One for the road,' Giles offers, and then shifts the conversation onto the subject of Michael; Giles knows he will find a ready audience for his views in Peter.

'He's obsessed; anyone can see it.' Giles bangs his glass on the bar. 'The way he looks at her, like a hurt puppy. It's not Lisa's fault, but...'

'He makes my skin crawl,' Peter agrees, rolling up his sleeve. 'See that. My left arm's still mangy. Ten fucking years old, he was.'

The scar on Peter's arm is barely noticeable, but the bones which show through the skin are flat. As if they have been ironed.

'Michael should've been sent to borstal for that,' Giles says.

'I told you what he said when I accused him, didn't I?' Peter says, rubbing his nose. 'Nothing. Not a dicky bird.'

They part outside the pub and walk off into the darkness, in different directions. They have agreed to leave their cars in the swimming-pool car park, but Giles's mile-long walk takes him back past it. Slowing on his way down the hill, he drags his teeth across his lower lip and, when he reaches the entrance to the car park, stops.

It was the sublime smell of the Jaguar's leather seats that persuaded Giles to buy the car. The heady aroma works its magic again, banishing caution. He reverses the car out of its parking space, slips the automatic gear into drive, edges forward towards the exit and purrs his machine into the road. In his wing mirror he sees a white vehicle. He realises it is a police car. His neck muscles tighten, his stomach lurches, and he turns on his lights. From behind him, the police car flashes its headlights.

'No,' Giles says out loud.

Pressing his foot down on the accelerator, he glides forward quickly. His hands are clammy on the wheel, and his eyes dart between the flashing blue lights in his rear mirror and the road ahead. Mouthing an obscenity, he pulls in.

'Would you step out of the car, sir.'

The policewoman's face seems understanding, but he expects her to ask why he didn't stop immediately. She doesn't; she just peers at him.

'I only forgot the lights for a sec,' Giles says, climbing out of the car.

'Can I see your licence, please?'

'Is this your car, sir?' she asks, perusing the licence.

'I can smell alcohol on your breath, sir. When did you last have a drink?'

Her frown is very real to Giles; he feels a film of sweat building on his forehead; his Adam's apple bulges, and the skin of his legs turns to gooseflesh.

'I had one pint of lager. Ages ago.'

'Wait here, please.'

While she speaks into her radio, her colleague, a policeman with a phallic nose, emerges from darkness holding out a breathalyser.

'Breathe, steadily and slowly, into the mouthpiece, sir.'

The breathalyser changes colour. So does Giles.

In Lloyd's, six days later, Michael is up against the wall. He faces the news board, reading the telexed reports. Greenpeace are fighting a rearguard battle to save grey seals.

'I like going clubbing,' laughs the wag standing next to Michael.

Michael looks at the stranger in the multicoloured bow tie. 'Rainbow Warrior,' Michael says ambiguously.

Chugging forward to the Lloyd's rostrum, carrying a slipcase, indistinguishable from the other brokers milling around him, Michael climbs the two marble steps under the Lutine Bell. Dressed in red, a man sits under an elaborate Victorian canopy with a four-faced clock above it. The liveried man continues reading into the microphone while Michael talks briefly into his ear.

A wry look crosses Michael's face when the name of his chief executive is called: 'Terence Wetthards, Richards-Riley.' Terence Wetthards was the firm's name ten years ago, since when it has changed twice. Lloyd's traditions might be under siege, but they are stoutly defended.

Drawn by the sound of clicking fingers from the gallery above, Michael hoists his eyes upwards and catches sight of Richards-Riley leaning over the rail. Michael doesn't take offence at being called the same way as a dog; it's normal. Lethargically, Michael wends his way upwards, to Richards-Riley, to Templeton's box.

'You're getting up my nose,' Richards-Riley hisses at Michael. 'Professor Dietrich tells me that we've lost that DBL Swiss franc thingy – your mate's getting a shot at it. You know, the one that looks like a Waffen SS officer, Mac. I know damn well that you fed this to him.'

'Good morning,' Michael replies, resting his slipcase on the rail.

'You bloody upstart. You and your ilk are wrecking our market; you've no decency about you – no sense of what's expected from one.'

'One what?' Michael interrupts.

Richards-Riley stares at him.

'We couldn't do the DBL deal,' Michael states, coldly. 'We tried. And we tried. It was really costing us.'

'I'm not into word games; asking if you were Mac's source is pointless.'

Michael ponders the lost point. Like everyone, he doesn't always run his fingernails down the blackboard of truth. Perjury has its place, but most lies are lazy. After twelve years in the trenches, Michael can dissemble in a dozen ways without uttering an untruth. He opens his hands to avow that the accusation is absurd.

89

'You think I can't fire you,' Richards-Riley continues, 'just because you produce some business. If I find out you've let one of our competitors eat our lunch, you'll be back where you belong, stacking the shelves at Tesco's. I'll put the word out; you won't get another job in the market. IV deals! Bloody rocket scientist.'

'So you're not a fan then?' Michael says calmly. 'Fact is, Wetthards need people like me – you know you do.'

'We may need you; I don't have to like you.'

'Let's get this over with,' Michael says as Templeton comes free.

Richards-Riley and Michael approach the underwriting box together.

Commanded by a flick of Cedric Richards-Riley's hand, Michael sits next to Templeton who, raised by a cushion, is three inches taller.

'Oh great, it's you, Michael.' Jeremy Templeton's friends-again voice sounds manufactured. 'Hope you don't mind Cedric joining us.'

Michael raises an eyebrow and a weak smile. 'Gave us a chance for a chat,' Michael says, enjoying the rare satisfaction of patronising his superior. 'I've explained; I can't arrange the deal you've asked me to. It would distort your accounts. You can see that, Jeremy.'

Tightening his club tie, Richards-Riley draws his chin inwards and snorts, 'With due respect, it's not our job to tell Mr Templeton how to present his accounts.'

Templeton pats Michael on the forearm. 'Look, your IV deals weren't a secret inside your offices. And I'm part of Wetthards. We're colleagues – family. Families share, Michael. You can't leave your toys on the floor and then complain when other children want to play with them.'

'Sorry, can't do it,' Michael recites.

'Won't, you mean,' Templeton says. Then he speaks to both Richards-Riley and Michael, 'I need Wetthards to dress up my reinsurance as an IV deal. I expect a teaspoon of cooperation; my syndicate gives you boys over two million of business.'

Michael's normal negotiator's face drops; his mouth falls open.

'I didn't know you were such a large client, sir,' Michael says and turns to Richards-Riley. 'I might not sit on the main board, but I'm a director of Wetthards. And this is the first I've heard about a two million pound account?'

Richards-Riley twists his thumbs upwards in the direction of

Templeton. For others the movement would be unseen, or if noticed as comprehensible as Urdu, but to Michael it is clear: Richards-Riley is horrified that Templeton has shared such specific figures with Michael.

Templeton points at Michael and fixes Richards-Riley with an unflinching, reptile-like stare.

'I will be,' Templeton says to Richards-Riley, 'how can I put this...displeased if you can't talk him round.'

At lunchtime, perched on a stool at the far end of the Wine Lodge pub's downstairs bar, Michael calls out, 'Mac, over here.'

Mac navigates a route through. 'Sorry I'm late, Michael. Bit of trouble at the office – Diddy discovered one of my people had been lying. And you know Diddy. I had the full sermon – utmost good faith. Pious bugger. One of my brokers – Julian it was. Do you know him?'

'Think I've seen him,' Michael replies. 'He's your runner, isn't he?'

'Was. Had to let him go. Diddy insisted. Shame really – only a boy. But he died on his sword; he almost finished that DBL deal you told me was impossible.'

'Got you a beer,' Michael says, passing Mac a pint of best.

'I should have got you one.'

'Yes,' Michael says, nursing his glass. He scuffs his shoe across the carpet thoughtfully. 'So, the DBL business still won't get done.'

'Yeah, it will. I'll get it finished. Most of what Julian's done will stay in place. Some of the underwriters will whinge a bit, but I can take it from there, luckily.'

'I won't ask how you greased luck's slide. Do you want a sandwich?'

'It's my treat. I owe you,' Mac says.

Standing at the counter, Michael watches the white-coated sandwich maker load his order: cream cheese and ginger in brown bread.

Mac grins. 'Bit embarrassing really, I suppose – for Wetthards that is. After all, DBL are your largest shareholder. I'll bet Richards-Riley's a bit put out.'

'You could say that. He's threatening to sack me; he knows I tipped you the wink. But so long as he can't prove it, he won't get board approval to elbow me out. He knows it; I know it. What did you tell DBL?'

Mac orders a sausage and anchovy sarnie before answering, 'Dietrich didn't ask. If you want, I'll use that stuff Jules told you about Richards-Riley being a Mason. Blame it on him blabbing indiscreetly at a Lodge meeting while chomping on a cigar – like Masons do. I could stitch him up for you.'

Michael whistles silently. 'No, leave him be. I'm glad you're on my side.'

After they have returned to their seats, Mac whisks a gilt-edged card from his inside pocket and places it in Michael's hand.

'It's an invitation – my engagement party. I'm getting married.'

Michael gapes at the card. 'Married?'

'I know it's a bit sudden, but she's...great.'

'Megan's a lovely girl – special.' Michael places his palm onto the back of Mac's hand. 'Mac, I don't wanna seem...are you sure?'

Mac sniffs. Their conversation stalls, stutters forward like an early biplane, then, short of the fuel of positive words from Michael, stalls again.

'How's tricks?' Mac asks.

'What, apart from facing the sack? I'm dropping all my juggling balls. You know, it's ironic. I spend my life trying to win business. Now I've got a client who wants to give me an order that, if I accept it, may ruin ten years of hard slog. What's more, I'm in trouble for getting Lisa that interior design work from Templeton.'

'I warned you to stay away from her. So you're not happy there. Wonderful.'

'Wonderful?' Michael asks.

'Yes, I want you to start a new broking house with me. I'm going to be given a major chunk of business – a whole truck load of money. I could just hand it over to my present owners in exchange for continued permission to come to work, but then again I'd rather like a new Merc. I'm going to need some money. The ring Megan wants costs more than all of Woody Allen's psychiatric bills put together.'

'Has your supplier got a sale on? First you tell me you're getting married, and then that you want to start a business,' Michael snipes.

Mac looks down, palpably stung. He replies in a hushed tone, 'It's just recreational. You listen to old love songs; I use a bit of coke from time to time.'

Wishing he hadn't made the comment, Michael troops off to the bar for refills as a way of saying sorry without using the word.

'Mac, I don't think I'm ready yet,' Michael says on his return, passing over a pint. 'I reckon I need another year or two at Wetthards. If you or I start our own show and it doesn't work out, there's no way back into the market. Not for us. Let me think about it. Where's the biz coming from?'

'The Pacific Sea Quake Consortium.' Mac fondles his glass. 'It's known as Cutesie in the market. Cutesie are one of the largest reinsurance buyers in the world. I've handled a piece of it for years now.'

'I know that.' Michael tilts his head. 'But why are they going to give it all to you – in a new firm?'

'Megan's the daughter of Donald White, the president of Cutesie.'

Michael gulps. 'I didn't know Megan had any connection to the business.'

Mac grins, off-centre. 'Oh, I did.'

Chapter Fifteen

Mingling is mandatory at Mac's engagement party. Navigating through the narrow entrance passage of the wine bar, Michael tries gamely to avoid the enforced frottage. Once through it, he takes a deep breath and looks around. The Five Lamps' low ceilings create a City cosiness which is enhanced by the soft-tone lighting. Obscure news-clippings, hanging in rosewood frames, stud the walls.

A girl in a leather skirt grabs Michael's arm and steers him into a corner where her friends boil a cauldron of the market's caustic wit.

'I've never seen Mac with the same girl twice,' a coiffured redhead says. 'He chain-smokes girls. I feel sorry for his butt-to-be.'

'I didn't know he was capable of it,' whinnies a horsey girl whose mane of hair looks to Michael as if it could do with a good brush.

'What, forking out for a ring or showing normal human emotion?' the redhead asks rhetorically. 'You're his friend. Perhaps you can explain,' she says to Michael.

'Excuse me,' Michael replies. Frowning, he tries to move away.

The redhead steps into his path. 'Come on, Michael. You must be as stunned as anyone; the only thing Mac knows about love is that it rhymes with shove.'

Michael winces. 'It's his party,' he says, manoeuvring round her.

From twenty feet away, he gazes at Megan. Her smile radiates warmth and her body, a shade under six foot, just shorter than Mac's, has gentle curves which are accentuated by the black cocktail dress she wears.

Piloting his way across the floor, towards Megan's smile, Michael stops. A slim girl with long hair, wearing a blue designer dress, catches his eye. Her back is to him; and the last time he saw her was eight years ago at her eighteenth birthday bash. But he would recognise Mac's sister Josie anywhere. Michael's cheeks flush and he rushes to her, kissing her on both cheeks. Stepping back, she touches the side of her dress and peers at him. Her face bursts into a grin.

'Michael!' They look each other up and down. 'My, my,' she says.

'You're all grown up, Josie.'

'I was all grown out last time we met,' she says, giving him a princess smile.

'I tried not to notice,' Michael laughs. 'Mac said you'd moved to London.'

'Yes. Came up to the big smoke with a friend. About a month ago.'

'A friend?' Michael asks.

'Female. She's nice; you'd like her.' Their eyes play hopscotch. 'I've got a job in a boutique in Hampstead – it's fun. My dress is from there.'

'I like it,' Michael says, flirtatiously running his tongue along his lips.

'The last time I was in a dress shop,' he says, 'this girl asked to try on the ball gown in the window. The assistant told her she could, if she wanted, but most people preferred to use the changing rooms.'

'You always were quick-witted.' Josie smiles mischievously. 'Quick-fingered too if I remember rightly.'

The comment cuts, but he can tell from the sparkle in her face that she isn't trying to taunt him. Just doing what she always did: opening up his emotions. Good and bad. He feels her hand touch his.

'I promise not to steal anything today,' he says. 'It's my day off.'

'And Mac? What's he stolen lately?'

Michael smiles. 'Megan's heart I think.'

'I hope he gives it back in one piece when he's finished,' Josie says.

'I've just left the warm embrace of those lovely maidens over there because of jokes less cruel than that.' Michael tosses his head towards the group of girls and edges as if to move away, but his eyes stay locked on Josie. 'Perhaps I should...'

'No, don't go. I'll behave.'

They squeeze through the party to congratulate the couple.

95

Holding a glass of champagne by its stem, Mac makes the introductions. His voice is louder than normal. After exchanging pecks with Josie, Megan takes Michael's hand. She lingers over the handshake, smiling into his eyes.

'Hi,' she says. 'Good to see you again, Michael.'

Michael bathes in the happy glow of her Australian accent. She holds her ring close to Josie's face. Dutifully, Josie 'oohs' and 'ahs'.

'Why do you think Mac kept us apart?' Megan asks Josie.

'Oh, he probably didn't want me to tell you about the things he used to do when he was a boy,' Josie says, grinning. 'Does he still dress up in women's clothing?'

'I told you that would come out sooner or later,' Michael says to Mac.

'It's a complete lie,' Mac says happily.

He puts his arm round Megan's waist and coos a compliment or two.

'Mac says you work in a boutique,' Megan says to Josie. 'Do you know anything about shoe shops in London? Size nines are so hard to find.'

Michael runs his eyes down Megan's leggy body; her feet don't seem large in proportion to it.

'Try Crispins in Chiltern Street,' Josie suggests. 'It's near Baker Street station.'

'When I go to the Baden-Baden conference, you can come with me,' Mac says, seemingly irrelevantly. 'It's easier to find large sizes in Germany.'

'I think you're very brave, Megan,' Josie interrupts. 'Marrying a man with a perverse interest in women's shoes. Did you meet Mac in a shoe shop?'

Megan laughs. 'No, we met years ago. Even then, I don't think Mac was looking at my feet.' She wiggles her body. 'Now I'm cobbled together with a Pommie with a shoe fetish. Life can be grim.'

'What do you do?' Michael asks her.

The question sounds stupid to him even as it leaves his lips.

'Handstands, monocycling and shopping,' she replies with a laugh.

'Your shopping – that's not funny,' Mac says, pinching her bottom.

Megan gleams at Josie. 'We've found a house. It's in Virginia

Water – pretty place. Only fifteen minutes from Heathrow, but it's not noisy. Great, long gravel drive, four bedrooms, amazing kitchen, chandeliers and a staircase like in one of those old films,' Megan enthuses. 'A staircase to die for.'

'A staircase to die on. The whole of the top banister is loose,' Mac says.

'Oh you, we can get it fixed,' Megan says, melting him with her smile.

'It's too expensive,' Mac stage whispers to Michael.

And, from Mac's expression, Michael knows she will get her house.

Megan and Mac leave their guests without saying goodbye, but none seem offended; Mac also leaves the bar bill open. Some time after nine, Michael and Josie climb up the steps into the alley and stroll along Fenchurch Street. They walk, as lovers sometimes do, a fingertip apart. Through the glass and steel of the buildings, a quarter moon shines down on them. By the empty newsvendor's stand, a black cab pulls up alongside them with its yellow 'For Hire' sign glowing. Neither have hailed it and neither acknowledge it; they look at one another awkwardly. Michael bends down to tighten an already tight shoelace, and Josie ferrets in her handbag. But the taxi, and its no doubt knowledgeable driver, continues to wait beside them.

Josie breaks the impasse: 'Well, I'll ask then. Shall we get something to eat?'

Wordlessly, he beams his acceptance.

'I've never done that before,' Josie says.

'I eat every day,' Michael replies, opening the rear door for her.

Frederick's, the Islington restaurant they ask the taxi to take them to, is full. They wander past the antiques market and, window shopping along Upper Street, Michael takes Josie's cold hand in the strong warmth of his. Her touch is tender. They stop outside a busy Italian restaurant and peer through the window at the menu. Inside, a waiter wields a large pepper grinder. This, to Michael, is a bad sign.

'The quality of the food and the size of the pepper mill are inversely related.'

Josie chuckles. 'The boy I remember wouldn't have used words

97

like "inversely related". Let's eat, Mr Inversely Related. Come on, the menu looks good.'

North from Upper Street, on the corner of a mews, Michael's mock Georgian house seems to Josie like a grown-up version of a doll's house. The outside walls are painted off-white.

'You told me you had a cream house. But it's a dream house.'

'That's a terrible joke, Josie.'

'The quality of the joke and the house are inversely related.'

'And that's worse,' he says, opening the front door.

Although the open-plan room is only half decorated and Josie can smell fresh emulsion, there are no signs of any work in progress. The beige carpet and cream walls overpower what she perceives to be Michael's forlorn attempts to relieve them with bright prints of modern art. In the middle of the room, a sunken settee faces a television sitting on top of an upturned packing-case – one of six such cases positioned randomly like rocks on a beach. Hanging from the ceiling, a single light bulb emits a faint hum. Against the far wall is a huge, antique bookcase from which books spill out onto the carpet. While Michael prepares coffee, Josie scans the titles in the bookcase.

'*Complete Mechanics Guide*?' she calls out to him above the gurgling noise of the percolator. 'Harper Lee. *A67/70 Actuarial Tables*. What's this? Virgil! I didn't even know you could read.'

'Prison was a real stepping stone.' He must be joking.

'I like men in uniforms,' Josie says, locking up the temptation to discuss Michael's temper. That is a taboo topic. For now. It would spoil the mood. Besides, Michael's anger doesn't fill her with angst. She likes him as he is.

'Any chance of some tunes?' she asks.

Michael runs upstairs. Elkie Brooks's music breezes down well before he returns, changed into casual clothes. Pouring two mugs of steaming coffee, he brings them over to the sunken settee. Josie takes off her jacket, sits down and leans back as if she intends to stay for hours.

'I should get back,' she says smiling. 'My flatmate will worry.'

He perches next to her, crouching forward. Resting their mugs on the carpet in unison, they turn to face one another. The sexual electricity shocks her as their fingers meet. She hasn't had a boyfriend for some months. By choice – she won't settle for silver. And because her timing is out of sync. She needs to trust a man before she lets him into her bed. The alternative, a groggy 'did I really do this' goodbye at three in the morning, is just depressing.

'It's very bright in here, Michael,' she says, ignoring her doubts.

Leaving the kitchen area downlighters on to provide half-light, he switches off the light in the room. When he gets back to the settee, her heartbeat has increased and her lips feel dry. Suddenly shy, they sit sipping their coffees.

Moving his knees sideways to brush against hers, he turns to kiss her. And, mouth-to-mouth, it is as she had hoped. He can kiss; the warmth of uncomplicated desire flows through her body. He explores behind her teeth, presses his chest against her and, before the kiss ends, despite their clothing, she feels her nipples harden.

Josie sips her coffee again and rubs her tongue around her lips, smiling.

'You've got lipstick around your mouth,' she teases.

'Wonder how that got there?' he replies.

'We should stop this, now.' What she would like is another cuddle, to leave, and then to see him again. But his pupils are dilated. Another male off-message.

He wraps an arm round her shoulder. Making no attempt to stop him, she sinks down again into the sofa. This time the kiss is more urgent, more immediate, and she pushes her tongue into his mouth. He places his hand on her right breast, cups it, fondles it and gently rubs it with his palm. The kiss continues. Undoing the buttons at the top of her dress, Michael moves her bra downwards and bends his head onto her. He sucks on her breasts; she is lost in lust. With a wisp of a moan, Josie reaches into Michael's lap and paws him. He is zip-breaking hard. Josie's head spins; she is skiing towards sex far too fast.

He lifts Josie's hand and kisses it. 'You're right. We must stop; it's not fair on you. I don't just want a one-night stand. Not with you. You're too...'

The next morning, resting in his cracked-leather armchair, Richards-Riley has his hands bunched into fists under his chin. His gold cufflinks would match the glint in his smile, but the smile is absent.

'Sorry I lost my temper the other day,' Richards-Riley apologises.

It sounds forced. Michael crosses his legs and nods, just once. He looks at the painting above Richards-Riley's credenza, a darkly forbidding work of a First World War battleground, in which a British stretcher-bearer is cutting the throat of a wounded German. The rich detail of the oil is displayed by the overhanging picture light that Richards-Riley now points to.

'Our role as brokers is to put things in their best possible light. That's all we're asking you to do for Templeton, Michael. It's not for us to say whether something is right or wrong. Come on, old chap. No one's asking you to murder your mother.'

Michael sits, silent in tight-lipped defiance, in the low visitors' chair.

'As you now know,' Richards-Riley continues, 'the Templeton syndicate's a very large client of Wetthards. Whilst you're a Director...'

Michael responds to the cold water of the thinly-veiled threat. 'Why wasn't I told about that, sir?'

'Not this again. There's nothing untoward; it's not like you to be paranoid.'

'I'm not paranoid,' Michael says.

'I'm not the only one to keep things private, am I?' Richards-Riley accuses. 'What about that Home & Life folder on your desk?'

'Have you been going through my files?'

'Your files?' Richards-Riley peers over his half-moons. 'May I remind you who pays your grocery bills?'

'Look,' Michael explains, 'it's just a file, OK? As you know, Home & Life were my – sorry, our – first client on the IV deals. It's hardly surprising that I keep files on existing clients, is it?'

'So the market rumour, that Home & Life is about to give you a big slice of their business, is wrong, is it?'

'That's right,' Michael answers in a way that could mean it was, or it wasn't. 'This is pointless. You don't understand. If all Templeton wants to do is move profit forward, he doesn't need our methods. He's hiding something.'

'I do understand, Michael...'

'Well, if you understand, why does he want to switch the funds through the hoops of several offshore accounts? Templeton says he'll bring all the money back, with interest, tax-free. But once it's out of sight...'

100

'This is the Templeton syndicate; they are linked to us. Are you suggesting one of our syndicates has a dishonest underwriter?'

'I didn't say Templeton's dishonest,' Michael says. 'This roll-over's dangerous. Templeton wasn't writing high-risk business when Hurricane Tracy hit in 1974. So his Names think he's safe. Say we arrange this deal and Templeton's unlucky. His Names will reach for their lawyers, and Lloyd's will string us up. It'll be Armageddon.'

'I've talked this through with the main board,' Richards-Riley says. 'We like to look at problems as opportunities. We've taken the opportunity to look at what you give us, and what we give you. When you've arranged Mr Templeton's deal, we'll increase your salary by £5,000 – you won't have to wait until April. You'll be promoted to senior director to get round the pay guidelines. And we'll also upgrade your car when it's due for replacement.' He pulls a sheet of paper from his inside pocket and looks down onto it. 'Next June.'

'I'm flattered,' Michael says. He hesitates. 'But I'm on the verge of a major breakthrough. I really don't want to...'

'We all have to do things we don't want to,' Richards-Riley says, breaking into a smile. 'Tell you what, I'll authorise a business trip. I know you're busy, but we can cover for you. Wherever you want to go – a few days.'

Richards-Riley rises, moves across to the antique globe to the side of his credenza and spins it. 'Grand Cayman's very pleasant this time of year – fantastic scuba-diving. You'll have to see some people, but there'll be lots of time. Travel economy and you can take a friend.'

'That's generous; I'm not inflexible; I'll talk to Mr Templeton. But arranged his way it won't even work. I can't promis–'

'So, then we're happy again. You'll talk with Jeremy Templeton and his people before you go. Relax on the beach, and when you return you'll arrange the business in a way which allows you to sleep at night. But he'll want the profit rolled forward. And not by normal means. Well done in advance.'

Richards-Riley clears his throat. 'Oh, Michael. Use my secretary. I don't want your colleagues–' Just put the expenses on the company credit card for me to agree.'

* * *

101

When they emerge from the rear entrance of the cinema on Sunday night, Michael links his arm through Josie's. They head off down Haymarket with Josie on the kerb side. Her attempts to mimic a dentist's drill are more reminiscent of a wasp trapped in a food processor. She keeps trying as they amble into Jermyn Street, but her laughter makes her efforts sound even worse.

'Is that the kind of film you usually take your girlfriends to on first dates?'

'Are you my girlfriend?' Michael teases. 'You said you liked Dustin Hoffman, and I know you liked the film.'

Josie prods his ribs. 'You're supposed to walk on the outside of the pavement. I thought you were a gentleman.'

As they switch places a man with whiskered jowls pushes past her.

'I should have stayed on the outside.'

'See, you don't want a gentleman. My chief executive's one and he's offering me a whole hat-full of money, £5,000, to do something he knows is wrong.'

'Sounds like the kind of problem I'd like. Personally, I'd take the £5,000 and say thank you.'

Michael blushes, he hadn't meant to tell Josie the figure. 'With that sort of attitude, Wetthards would be very interested in your services.'

'Seriously, if you really don't want to do it, why not talk to Mac? He'll have some ideas; he's a real expert at getting out of corners. Oh, Michael, while I think of it, I told Mac that we were going to the cinema tonight. He was fine, rather funny about it actually.'

'What did he say?'

'He told me to be gentle with you. The cheek.'

They reach Michael's Alfa Romeo, hidden in a gap between garages, just off St James' street. He holds his car keys in his hand, but doesn't unlock the car.

'I might speak to Mac, but I am tempted to take Wetthards' money. They've put a cherry on top of the bribe. A trip to Grand Cayman. I can take a friend.'

Chapter Sixteen

The crisps at Simpson's-in-the-Strand taste home made. Michael takes the last one from the silver bowl on the table in front of him. As he savours it, Mac strides through the upstairs bar. He rests his slipcase against the wall and plumps himself into the seat next to Michael, grinning.

'What's the mystery, Michael? Must be today? Away from Lloyd's?'

Twiddling his hands in the empty bowl, Michael jabbers on about an unspecified holiday. He interrupts himself in mid flow.

'You know I've being seeing Josie?'

Mac stays silent. The void forces a torrent of words from Michael, including 'nothing's happened'. Mac's grin widens until, finally, Michael unfurls his question.

'Wetthards have given me a long weekend in Grand Cayman – five days. It's a bribe; they want me to owe them. I'd like to take Josie, if it's OK with you. We could have separate rooms.'

Mac laughs. 'Why are you asking me? Separate rooms? It was you who went to Sunday school. I'm allergic to crucifixes.'

Michael takes a sip from a dented tankard and swallows.

'It's fine, Michael. Josie can look after herself. It's you I worry about. Anything is better than watching you continue to waste your best years of testosterone pining for Lisa. Anything, even the indignity of having my best friend going out with my sister – lying awake at night wondering what you're up to together.'

The corners of Mac's mouth rise further. 'I have a trip for you: Sydney in February. I want you to be my best man. I need to be back in London early March to arrange Cutesie's business.' Mac stops. 'Don't look at me like that; February wasn't my idea. It was Megan's father's.'

'Do you love her, Mac?'

'At first I didn't. Now, I don't know. I think so.'

Michael smiles wryly. 'Do you think you love me too? Is that why you say you need me in the new company?'

Mac pulls a sheaf of papers from his inside pocket, passes them to Michael and frowns. 'I need you, Michael.'

Entranced, Michael reads. Cutesie want a management buyout: a $200 million deal.

'It's perfect for your IV reinsurances,' Mac exhorts. 'With a fair wind behind you, you might be able to get a fifty million profit into the hands of the management. What's more, I reckon the commission will top a million.'

Michael finishes reading and stretches his palm out towards his friend.

'Sorry. It's too risky, Mac. This is one deal; you can't base a business on one deal. Anything could happen; Donald White's under the cosh. Even if I put together the perfect arrangement, it might get shot down. Let's say I leave Wetthards and set up shop with you. If it doesn't work, then I'm out the market. No one will touch me; I'll be as welcome as poverty. It's different for you: you'll still have the main Cutesie business. That would buy you another bite.'

'Think about it, eh?' Mac asks.

Michael grits his teeth.

'Are you sure there's no other reason?' Mac presses.

'I really can't join you,' Michael says, side-stepping the question, 'but I'll do everything else I can to help.'

They move from the upstairs bar across into the restaurant. Mouth-watering smells invade Michael's nostrils as they feast on the menus. Both opt for the beef from the trolley. A jolly waiter carves meat off the massive joint and serves it with a huge Yorkshire pudding, roast potatoes, cabbage and lashings of horse-radish. Between mouthfuls, Michael talks.

'I went to see Templeton in his office yesterday; he showed me the brochure that he gives prospective investors. Full of pie charts and photo-library pictures. It puts such a sheen over the downside that even the brightest investors would be blinded to the danger. I've got to come up with a way forward, but I'm not going to let him ruin my IV deals.'

Nodding gravely, Mac stops chewing, tilts his head sideways and holds the heavy, silver cutlery suspended in mid-air. 'I don't think there's much wrong with this Templeton deal.'

Rolling his fingers into a telescope, Michael puts his hand to his eye. 'I see no ships,' he laughs.

'I understand your motives,' Mac says. 'Even if you don't. You want to keep the IV deals squeaky clean for use in takeovers. So you can save the job your Dad lost more than ten years ago. You're too late.'

Raising his head Michael looks around the vast dining-room, taking in the portraits on the wall. As usual the restaurant is full, or very close to it. Michael surveys the slickers who, at the drop of a handshake, can decide who gets to work and who gets no pay. Perhaps, Michael admits to himself, he is carrying a torch. But his Dad was only unemployed for three months; Michael has got other grounds too.

'I'm not criticising you, mate,' Mac continues. 'It's just...'

'Do you know, on that deal last month, Wetthards picked up a cool hundred thousand commission. Happy as sandboys, they were. Short memories, they've got. I've only just begun. I can't believe Richards-Riley's gross stupidity.'

Mac finishes his beef and takes a sip of house red.

'A hundred K. You never told me that. No wonder they gave you a rise. If you ask me, it wasn't very generous. But the real reason you're so anti remains–'

'Your Dad was never on the wrong end of a P45.' Michael smiles. 'So lay off,' he quips, intending it as a joke.

'Sorry.'

'As you can see into my subconscious,' Michael says, finding Mac's doleful demeanour doubly amusing, 'then you'll also know that I believe Templeton doesn't want to use my IV methods; he wants to hide behind them. If I do what he wants, it'll go wrong – I can sense it. And if I'm the fall guy, my chances of pulling off another deal – that includes Cutesie – are zero. I'd feel like Neil Armstrong would've if Apollo had landed and he realised he'd left his helmet at home. Anyway, how do you know what my pay rise was?'

Michael pushes his knife and fork together. Repeating his question by raising his glass, Michael waits for Mac's answer.

'I could give you some ideas on Templeton.'

'Thanks, Mac. Back up a mo, who told you about my pay rise?'

'Josie did,' Mac says. 'Though it wasn't really her fault. She wanted information about you; I insisted on a trade-off.'

'How many of my sordid secrets did you sell her?' Michael asks.

'Er...nothing nasty. Just about how often you still meet up with Lisa and that. Look, there's no such thing as a free lunch.'

'Yes there is. For that, you're paying.'

A waiter in a chequered waistcoat whisks their plates away; another pulls up with the dessert trolley. 'Just coffee', Michael and Mac concur.

'So...about the help you're going to give me on Templeton.'

'Yeah. Say Templeton insures a tyre manufacturer, right?'

'Does he?' Michael interrupts with a smile.

'I don't know, do I? Let just say he does. This manky manufacturer sells his tyres for £1, but it costs him £2 to make them. When does the loss happen?'

'That's an old joke,' Michael says, nodding a thank you to the waiter for the coffee. 'And the punchline was "When's the fire?" last time I heard it.'

'No,' Mac says. 'The question is "When does the loss happen?" If you only spend £2 to produce a tyre, then those tyres are lethal. You'd get hundreds of deaths. So in which year do these losses happen? When the tyres are made, or when the accidents happen, or when the claims are paid? Who can say, um? What we do know is that Templeton's accounts must be prepared in a consistent way so that losses and premiums are treated the same way from year to year. That way he presents a true and fair picture.'

'Perhaps I'm being dim,' Michael says, 'but I don't see how that–'

'Well,' Mac cuts him off, 'what I suggest is that Templeton adopts a slight change to his accounting policy so that he personally judges which premiums and which losses belong to which years. And he applies this personal judgement every year. What', Mac winks, 'could be more consistent?'

'How could he justify–'

'I can give you a whole a laundry list of justifications for moving different types of premiums and losses around. And Templeton can choose the excuses he likes the look of. Not your problem. You can present this list in a hypothetical way, like a lawyer advising his innocent client what might happen if he pleaded guilty. You could rush off to the men's room and wash your hands afterwards. Come on, it's not as bad as what he wants to do.'

'I don't like being involved at all,' Michael says. 'But do you know what? If you give me that list, then I'm under an obligation to advise Templeton of the option. Could you jot down some notes?'

'Sure, I'll have them ready for when you've finished playing in the sun with my little sister.'

'Thanks, Mac.'

'I don't know why you're bothering; Wetthards are going to fire you. You're too...trusting. This trip to the Cayman Islands – it's a set-up. I can see it.'

'I've looked this gift horse in the mouth. Wetthards won't fire me. Richards-Riley would love to, but he'd have to convince the main board. And he'd need something pretty nasty on me to do that. I've every right to protect my IV deals providing I do my best to help Templeton another way.'

Instead of going straight back to the office, Mac takes a taxi to Harrods and walks round the corner to Hans Place. The Asian girl who answers the door to Professor Dietrich's London flat could be any age between 18 and 30. Brazenly lying, Mac explains that Dietrich has told him he should telephone from here if he has anything he wants to impart in confidence. Inscrutable, she isn't. Mac can see her balancing the consequences of letting him, a stranger, in – against the repercussions of shutting him, a confidant of Professor Dietrich's, out.

'He'll want to talk to me,' Mac repeats.

'The Professor will still be asleep,' she says.

'No, it's seven-thirty in California. He'll be in the office.'

She shows him into the lounge, a vast room with an acre of polished floorboards. The walls are decorated with Victorian display cases, like those used by butterfly collectors. But the insects in Dietrich's collection are mainly beetles, mostly large. Pointing to the telephone on the far table, the girl leaves him and shuts the door behind her.

He takes his kit out of his pocket and carefully arranges a line

107

of cocaine. After snorting it violently, he savours the sensation for a few minutes then, brimming with confident enthusiasm, picks up the handset.

'Thanks for letting me use the flat,' he says to Dietrich, as if Dietrich has offered. 'It's more private than my office. Thought you'd like to know: I've almost finished the Swiss franc deal.'

Dietrich is silent at the other end of the phone.

'The other good news is that I'm setting up my own business,' Mac continues. 'I'd like you to consider backing me; I'm preparing a business plan.'

'I'll certainly look at it,' Dietrich says in a clipped voice. 'I like brokers with a bit of spunk. Richards-Riley's furious about losing the Swiss franc business; he says one of his people gave you the inside rail. Is it true?'

'Yes,' Mac says. Pausing for effect, Mac counts, silently, to five. 'It was Michael Darrett, but I want him to be my partner in my new business. And he won't – not if he feels I've forced him to leave Wetthards.'

'However, you wouldn't mind if – this Mr Darrett you say – were to resign over something else. Is that what you're telling me?'

'I wouldn't have any control over that,' Mac says.

'I hope you complete the Swiss franc deal,' Dietrich says. 'And I look forward to seeing your plan. If I like it, I'll ask you to come over. Bring your new colleague; if he checks out, that is. I'll need to ask a few questions about him first.'

'Could you leave that for a few weeks, let the dust settle?'

'Yah, sure,' Dietrich says, revealing for the first time a hint of his native accent: the guttural Swiss-German of Liechtenstein. 'Could you put Susie on?'

Mac goes to get the girl and sits on the sofa while Dietrich talks to her. She only says a few words. Replacing the telephone, she slinks across to Mac, puts his hand on her bee-sting breast and says, 'The Professor tells me I should look after you.'

Hiding her surprise at his young age with a counterfeit smile, Lisa shows the Inland Revenue PAYE compliance officer into her office storeroom. The office itself is no larger than a bathroom, and the storeroom is too small to swing a malnourished kitten in. He gives her a, 'I've seen everything – twice', glance before looking down at his trouser turn-ups. In the confines of the storeroom, the man's aftershave assails her. Quickly, Lisa clears a space to make a work surface and squeezes a chair into the room. She points to the books and ledgers on the upper shelves explaining, in a fashion, where the records are.

Escaping the aftershave, she returns to her desk where she finishes her lunch, joins paper clips together and, after two hours, makes a phone call to cancel an appointment. She rereads the Revenue's form letter and the booklet they have sent her. When she phoned to fix the time and date, the compliance officer told her the routine visit might take an hour or so. 'Or so' is an upset client. Four o'clock should have been safe.

Adding another link to her paper-clip chain, she scolds herself. This inspection is normal, once every five years for a business of her shoebox size. Shoebox it might be, but Lisa enjoys it. Interior design brings her to meet people who interest her, to venture into their homes, thrill them with ideas and make dreams real.

Clean out of paper clips, with no more meetings to reschedule, she notices it is dark outside. Protected by the smell of tea from the cup she carries, Lisa ventures into the storeroom. The tea is meant to obtain the time when the man, and his scent, will leave. It doesn't. Following her out of the storeroom, he asks, with a politeness so pronounced it makes Lisa cringe, if he can take a seat. On her desk the paper-clip chain offers evidence of her boredom. Or nervousness.

'Thank you,' he repeats, 'we don't often get tea. Great timing – I've just finished. I've got some questions, if you can spare a few minutes. Mostly general questions to help me understand your business. It'll probably save time to try and deal with those you can answer now so I needn't bother you with them in writing.'

Lisa nods. 'It's a small company, just me and Jenny. Jenny works part-time. It's mainly private houses, a few small businesses. We get our work by word of mouth; one satisfied client tells another – that sort of thing. My husband does the books – deals with the pay. Well, not recently. Lately the paperwork's got a bit messy. I'll sort it out soon. I have to look after my mother at the moment.'

The young man scribbles notes onto his pad, turns the page and pulls out a typed list of questions.

'Your case was referred to us by our colleagues in another department.'

The triangular black marks under Lisa's eyes accentuate her pallor.

'My case? You said it was routine.'

'It is routine for us to follow up referrals,' he says.

'I think', Lisa says, 'I'd prefer you to put your questions in writing. I should leave now, visit my mother. You've taken much longer than you said you would.'

At St Sebastian's hospital, Lisa is surprised at just how hot her mother's room is. Just how bone dry the air is. And just how noisy. The room is filled with the sounds of other patients' televisions and the echoes of nurses' brisk footsteps. Still, it is a private room. It comes courtesy of her father's former employer, who agreed to keep up the health insurance premiums for a year after his death. Her mother thought little of it at the time. 'Wasting their money,' she told Lisa.

'Pure luxury,' Mrs Carter says as she looks at the little dinner menu. 'Chicken soup or melon? What shall I have?' she muses. Mrs Carter's head wobbles as she talks. 'That consultant, Mr Taylor, he's ever so nice. Such a handsome man.'

Examining the measurement lines on the pouch that hangs next to her mother's bed, Lisa touches the transparent tube that runs from the equipment to the bandage on her mother's wrist. Her brother Peter likens it to an umbilical cord that drips hope. Lisa sees it as pumping poison that will just prolong her Mum's pain. But it is her Mum's choice. She knows that children can't tell their parents how best to die.

'That's not the chemotherapy; that's just washing it through,' Mrs Carter says. 'They've told me all about it. I'm going to get better. Just you see.'

Lisa has seen it before, not long ago. By the third session, her father's hair started to fall out. And Lisa knows that her mother could remember it just as clearly, but somehow Mrs Carter has managed to shut it out.

Driving home, she sees images of her mother, her father, the drip, the compliance officer, but not, until ten feet away, the lorry in front. She brakes sharply, pulls the car into a bus stop by the

110

train station and sobs. The stream of passing commuters are invisible to her.

At noon the following day, Lisa's husband looks in the bathroom mirror. He pulls at his puffy cheeks and runs his fingers along the bridge of his nose. Minuscule red blood vessels criss-cross it. His wiry hair is uncombed, unkempt. Unshaven, in his dressing gown, he pads from the room, sees the brown envelope on the mat and picks it up. 'Magistrate's Court' is writ large on the front. It is the date for Giles's court appearance for drink-driving.

'So soon – so bloody efficient,' Giles says. 'Bastards. Tell the postman. Good old gossip with the neighbours.'

No one is in the flat to hear him.

Lounging in an armchair, he brings his briefcase up onto his knees, takes his diary from it and pencils the court date in. His case will be heard in two months; this is his first entry for next year, 1979.

'Happy New Year,' he says.

He uses both arms to bring himself out of the chair, fetches a glass from the drinks cabinet, weighs it in his hand and fills it a quarter full with whisky. After the warmth of the first mouthful, he picks up the telephone to let his office know he won't be coming in. The call with his secretary is brief.

'Good afternoon, Giles. We guessed earlier.'

On the patio of the Hyatt Regency Grand Cayman, hopping on the vacant table next to Josie and Michael's, a bird pecks at the breakfast crumbs. Josie watches the bird as it flits its head about, red eyes alert for enemy waiters. Michael holds Josie's hand across the table. Americans in bathers stroll past the patio to reserve their loungers. Inhaling deeply, Josie breathes in the lush fragrance of tropical plants and the heady smells of bacon and orange juice. Michael's plate is empty.

'You've got a big appetite,' Josie says.

'I can't cook Eggs Benedict. It's delicious–'

'Who's talking about the food,' she says with a dirty laugh.

To cover her whiteness, Josie borrows one of Michael's shirts for the short walk to the beach. As they stroll across, they share a smile brimming with intimacy. The breeze blows the scent of the aquamarine sea to them; the view is travel brochure beautiful. Standing at the water's edge, they wiggle their toes in the warm sand, feel the waves' ripples clean their shins, and watch a pair of jet skis dart across the surface, engines roaring. Her green eyes ask. Michael seems to understand the question.

Taking her hand, he leads her up the beach to a hut where a black man, with a mariner's skin crusted with salt, sits under the shade. Michael digs some dollars out of the back of his trunks. And, talking all the time, giving novice Josie advice, the man walks them to the cluster of glistening machines tethered in the water. At Josie's insistence, Michael drives. In yellow life-jackets, with her tucked behind him, holding him around the waist, they scud off, power through the water, speed over crests and dip down. The sea spray covers them. Full throttle, Michael cuts a straight line, crashing onwards and into the choppier waters further out. Clinging onto him, Josie screams as they hit one wave after another. A rip tide of 'this is too good to last' happiness washes through her.

Afterwards, they sit together on the sand playing footsie.

'I felt so alive on the wave runner,' she says. 'With anyone else, it would have been frightening. But with you it was thrilling...' She hasn't finished speaking, but she picks up a handful of sand. The last grains trickle through her fingers before she continues. 'There's only one thing about you that scares me, Michael.'

'I really make an effort to control my temper.' He reaches out, takes her hand and kisses it. 'I'd never hurt you; you do know that, don't you?'

'I know you'd never hit me.' And if he just let the lid off his anger from time to time, like everyone else does, it wouldn't build up so much. Then it wouldn't worry either of them. But that isn't the issue. What troubles her is Michael's ongoing obsession with Lisa. 'I do know about her.'

'It's nothing physical. It's just–' He looks out at the sea.

She's just...there. And the fact his feelings are sustained without the glue of sex makes it worse. But she has made her point, and she doesn't want to rain on the holiday. It is too soon to make demands; she must grant him time to cut the cord.

'Are you going to form a new company with Mac?' she asks.

'No. I feel bad about it; he needs me. I'll try and help him, but I'm not ready yet. And also– Josie, I don't have a choice.'

'"And also" what? I don't mind, Michael,' Josie says. 'If there's another reason, you can tell me. I won't repeat it.'

A girl in a baseball cap comes up to them. It takes them a minute to understand that she is a waitress. They order two lemonades, and she bounces away.

'Mac's way of doing business', Michael explains further, 'is different to mine.' He pauses. 'And if the new biz didn't work out, I'd be out of the market.'

'If you ever do leave Lloyd's, what would you do?' Josie asks.

'I dunno; I've got no qualifications, and I've got used to this lifestyle. It would be a long drop. Besides, I'm not going to leave; I love broking.'

She feigns a frown. 'Do you know what I want to do?'

'No.'

Chuckling, she reaches out to stroke his face. 'Sunbathe.'

Standing there, on his second day back in the office, Michael purses his lips together and curls his toes inwards inside his shoes. The impromptu meeting has a military feel to Michael, like a court martial. By the hatstand, to Michael's right, is a set of golf clubs in a battered leather bag which looks as old as its owner. It occurs to Michael that he is keeping his chief executive off the fairways. Richards-Riley sits behind the desk; his pulse is clearly visible in the veins of his temples. He doesn't seem to be blinking. Not at all.

'Don't you pretend to be some shy virgin. Your blood was on the sheets the first time you went out into the market and came back with a smile on your face.'

'All I did was to advise Mr Templeton of the option. He could achieve everything he wanted to at no cost. All he had to do is to change his own records, moving some losses and premium about. He could even pick and choose how to do it – so only he'd know where the bodies were buried. It was still wrong. And I told him that. Apart from anything else, he still wouldn't have warned his Names that their picnic of profits was taking place in a minefield. That aside, it was relatively simple and it didn't involve Wetthards, or me.'

'Jeremy Templeton tells me that falsifying the records would be fraud; he couldn't go along with your idea. I don't blame him.'

'Falsifying the records?' Michael says. 'Fraud? You've got to be kidding; it was a darn sight less dodgy than using the IV deals. It was an idea that was given to me that, as his broker, I was obligated to tell him about.'

'Jeremy doesn't need you any more,' Richards-Riley says, ungiving as illness.

But Michael sees Richards-Riley's wrist twitch. Polished though he is at concealing the truth, Richards-Riley has just disclosed that he is lying by suppressing a hand-to-mouth cover – the same one that children use when they deny eating the missing Smarties.

'Doesn't need me?' Michael asks. 'Look, I know I'm not indispensable. But when I spoke with Mr Templeton this morning, I accepted his answer; I told him I'd find another way. He took my hand in his and said he appreciated my efforts. What's going on? I can't do any more than I'm doing; I'll get there.'

'You're too late,' Richards-Riley says. He smiles a cruel smile loaded with malice. 'I've already spoken to the board. There are things I can't do too. I can't go back to Mr Templeton and say that a director of this company continues to seem unwilling to help him and expect him to remain a client, even if his syndicate is linked to our company. Resign voluntarily and we'll work out the details fairly.'

'I'm not unwilling to help him, and I'm not resigning.'

Richards-Riley takes off his half-rimmed glasses. 'If you don't resign, I'll fire you. For dishonesty. First, you misused our contacts to get private business for a friend. Then there's your trip to the Cayman Islands with yet another lady–'

'What?' Michael braces himself.

'There's no trip requisition form, and precious little business was done. You went on holiday, took a friend and billed it to our credit card. Theft. Resign or be fired. Either way, you're leaving. Today. You can make your decision as to whether you wish to resign after you've gone.'

Stunned, Michael sleepwalks from the room, along the corridors, through the guts of the building, to his desk where he finds a security guard waiting with a black bin-liner in his hands. Unspeaking faces blanch and look away as Michael takes the offered bin-liner, rifles through the drawers and drops books of business cards, his diary and some personal bills into the trash bag. Lastly, he removes the photograph of Lisa in her bridal gown from his desktop and puts that too into the plastic. The whole task takes two minutes.

He holds back the tears that well in his eyes, bunches his fingers and draws the skin of his face tight, ensuring the unseen tears retreat. Michael hasn't cried since Lisa's wedding day.

Chapter Seventeen

Michael's black rubbish bag weighs ten pounds; it is very heavy to carry when watched by eyes that have seen it all before. Out on the street a white-haired delivery boy, aged fifty going on fifteen, stops his conversation with the flower-seller and points at Michael. She cackles. There and then, Michael decides to go to his childhood home.

His Mum coddles him with teacakes; his Dad soothes his injured self-esteem with a compliment-coated lecture, and Josie leaves work early to air ambulance him back to Islington where she kisses his cares away.

Michael's morning-after mood is resilient enough to phone in his resignation. Ensconced in the sunken settee, he chases his hands along the brushed cotton of his flares as Richards-Riley gloats down the phone. Remaining calm, Michael ratchets Wetthards' meagre severance offer up to a golden goodbye.

'They still fired me,' Michael grouses as he replaces the handset.

The central heating is up high, protecting Michael against the ice in the December air and forcing Mac to remove his suit jacket. Unwatched, the midday news flickers on the television.

Mac paces up and down in front of Michael. 'They didn't fire you. You resigned. Wetthards couldn't fire you for dishonesty. It would bring into question all the stuff you did for them whilst they employed you.'

'Oh, like Julian wasn't fired.'

'Julian was a runner. We could have unravelled his big deals in the time it takes to boil an egg. Besides, every underwriter in the market would know that it couldn't be true – not Michael Darrett, patron saint of conscience above commerce. Look at the upside: you're free now. We'll form our own company; it won't just be fun; it'll be glorious.'

116

'What's that phrase...death or glory,' Michael says.

Mac stops pacing and sits down next to Michael. 'I feel guilty. Templeton told Richards-Riley that those proposals I gave you would be falsifying the accounts. Fraud. I was only trying to help. But in a way it's my fault, isn't it?'

'No,' Michael says, recovering his smile. 'Don't be daft. Anyway, Wetthards are paying me six months' money – no tax. It's the closest thing to a lottery win that you can get in England. I bet you wish your owners would fire you.'

'Too right,' Mac laughs. He leans forward. 'The Cutesie proposal. You can do it, can't you? And the business plan. We need cash-flow projections, a five-year plan, a complete analysis of first-year expenses...'

'The Cutesie proposal. Ah, yes. I can't promise – you do understand that, don't you? It's difficult – and large.' Michael's tanned face cracks into a canyon smile. 'But the business plan's done. Well, the draft is.'

'You genius. You shit – you got me to lick your ego. And you knew.'

'I didn't want them to fire me. But it was a possibility – just a possibility.'

Michael springs from the settee, vaults upstairs and returns brandishing two neatly-bound booklets.

'I don't expect you did much typing in Grand Cayman. Too busy playing your fingers across my sister – ugh. You've only been back four days.' Mac ravishes through his booklet. 'And you can't even type, can you?'

'Josie's coming over later on. We were going out, but all three of us could have a cosy evening in.'

Looking as though he has just been invited to watch a vivisectionist at work, Mac says, 'I'd rather see Megan. Are you going to answer my question, or what?'

'I started the day after lunch at Simpson's. I used a typing agency up by Aldgate – first new company expense, I guess. I did say I'd help.' Michael laughs raucously. 'Hate to say it, but most professional boxers could write a better business plan than you.'

Mac produces a pout, then grins.

They leaf through the Conqueror wove paper: the draft. Concise, detailed and complete, each subject, however complicated, is dealt with in a single page – twenty pages in total. With the promised

117

Cutesie business, the new company will make a profit in its first year.

Launching into a one-sided discourse on potential backers, Mac finally persuades himself as to the right company: '...their main operations are a string of insurance companies across the world – massive insurance interests in Europe and the States. Yes, DBL are perfect for us.'

Michael studies his friend; it seems to him as if Mac's suggestion of DBL as the backer is pre-planned. 'Last time I had an idea that bad, I had a hangover that lasted a week. DBL are Wetthards' largest shareholder – my employer until yesterday, remember?'

'It won't make any difference. I know the top man, Professor Ernst Dietrich. Although DBL are European, he's based in San Francisco. Keener than a bodybuilder's chest to expand. They'll crawl across broken glass to get involved. Do you remember Sean Collins – went off to Bermuda?'

'No.' Michael's voice remains dismissive.

'Well, DBL poached him from their own subsidiary in London – like a father stealing from his child's money box. Sean wants the sort of business you do; he wants it badly. DBL's stake in Wetthards is a sideshow, that's all. Conflict between their operations is helpful to them; live-round training keeps the troops sharp.'

Michael moves off the settee and turns off the television. 'So how do we get access into Lloyd's?'

'They own stakes in several Lloyd's broking firms. We can get into Lloyd's under their umbrella.'

'What about Templeton?' Michael pinches his fingers together. 'What about Richards-Riley? What's he going to say? Dietrich will pick up the phone–'

'And Richards-Riley will tell him what happened,' Mac says. 'That Wetthards wanted to use your methods, but that you wouldn't go along. He won't say anything detrimental about you. I'll fix it. Trust me.'

Over the next ten days, Lisa struggles with a problem she can't fix: Giles. He is neck deep in the quicksand of despondency. On Friday morning, when he complains – yet again – that he feels 'really bad' she strokes his shoulder and, for the umpteenth time, suggests he sees a doctor.

As soon as Lisa closes the door to the apartment that evening, before she calls out to him, she can smell it. Vomit. With her heart thumping, she races through the rooms until she sees one of his carpet slippers protruding oddly from the bathroom, hanging half on, half off, his foot. On the white tile floor, Giles is naked. He lies on his front with his face turned sideways; dried sick surrounds his lips and sticks to the stubble on his chin. In front of his mouth a congealing pool spreads under his head into his wiry hair.

She kneels on the floor and feels him breathing. 'Giles, wake up.'

Staggering to the telephone, she presses the push-buttons with dead fingers. It takes three attempts for her to tap out 999 correctly. Relieved that the ambulance is on its way, but worried by her own answer, 'I don't know how long he's been unconscious', she moves rapidly, with shallow breaths, unaware of the smell of vomit now, backwards and forwards between the living-room window and Giles. Unmovable – at least by her – and unmoving, Giles remains insensible on the bathroom floor. Her eyes search the dark street below for the ambulance.

Upright on the drinks cabinet in the living room, nagging at her memory, is an empty whisky bottle. It troubles her that she can't remember whether it was full the previous day. As she picks it up, the tips of her fingers brush against a smaller bottle: a brown paracetamol bottle. Seeing it is empty, she stumbles back. She falls over Giles's briefcase, which lies open on the living-room carpet, pulls herself to her knees, looks inside, picks out the contents and numbly slumps into an armchair. When she has finished reading the formal-warning letter from Giles's company and the notice from the Magistrate's Court, she replaces them in their envelopes and puts them on the drinks cabinet – next to the whisky.

In the hospital, with Giles asleep, Lisa mutters prayers to the God she wants to believe in. Her breath comes in stabs; her pulse bangs in her head, and her sweat grows cold. One hour of this, next to her husband but alone, is enough. At eight o'clock, Lisa searches her pockets for her car keys. They aren't there, just a spare key to the apartment that a kindly ambulance man reminded her to take. Realising her car is still outside the flat, she sniffs in the familiar hospital air, extracts a ten-pence piece from her purse and walks to the public phone in the corridor to phone her brother.

According to the monotone message on Peter's answering

119

machine, he isn't home. And she can't bring herself to speak to his machine. The clank of a dropped bedpan disturbs the sterile stillness of the corridor as she rummages for another coin.

Sitting cross-legged on the floor, her handbag at her side, Josie examines Michael's bookcase again and notices *On Death and Dying* by Elizabeth Kubler-Ross and a hardback report from the Institute of the Study of Conflict. As she peers through his books, she listens to the faint patter of water from the shower upstairs.

'The reservation was for eight o'clock; we're late,' she calls to Michael, knowing full well he can't hear her. 'You're living proof that men take longer in the bathroom.'

In truth, she is pleased he is taking the trouble to look his best. She runs a hand across the gossamer Diane Frès gown she has is borrowed from the boutique she works in. She isn't a material girl, but she feels special in the fabulous frock. And it suits the upmarket eatery which she is treating him to.

He disappointed her earlier by suggesting they meet at the restaurant. Like he was busy. Or doing something beforehand. Seeing someone perhaps. No, Michael wouldn't double time her. Or anyone else, come to think of it. Falling in love can hurt. 'Get a grip,' she tells herself.

The telephone rings; it jolts her out of her thoughts. She rises, walks over to it, raises her hand above the receiver and, on its fifth ring, answers it.

'Is Michael there?' a young woman's voice asks.

Josie swallows. 'Er...um...can I tell him who's–'

'Would you tell him it's Lisa?'

'What's the big fuss? I only had two paracetamol tablets,' Giles says.

'It's not just that. Giles, please. Talk to me.'

He doesn't, and by Tuesday everything is normal, or so he states. The Christmas lights in the High Street darken Lisa's mood further. She grinds her teeth and drives home through the evening streets, holding the top of the steering wheel tightly with both hands. On entering the apartment, she sees Giles filling a glass in the kitchen.

Lisa shakes her head. 'Giles, I got a five-page letter from the

Inland Revenue today. The questions are about expenses. They must be confusing me with someone else – trips to Paris, restaurants I've never been to. Obviously, they think there's something wrong. They enclosed a copy of a letter from the National Insurance people that was sent to me in August. I'd never seen it before so I phoned them. They said they'd had an acknowledgement. From you. What have you done?'

Giles downs a large gulp of whisky and water, and Lisa scans her eyes around the room. Peering back at her from the built-in fridge, the Pears Soap Baby magnet reminds her of the conversation with her mother the previous day. 'I'm not even sure if I want children, Mum,' she'd said. 'I've got everything I ever dreamed of. A smart flat – in Highgate no less – a career, and the man I love as my husband.' The same man who now glares at her.

'What I did was to keep your accounts,' Giles says, breathing alcohol into her face. 'You could have done them yourself. But no. You wanted me to. Save you the bother. Don't have a go at me. Lisa, it's me you're talking to – not the Revenue. I see the stuff you put through your expenses: shoes here, perfume there.'

'That's no excuse for you to–'

'I don't need an excuse. You knew I ran some bills through the company. It saves tax. And who spends those savings? You do. They can't do this; it was an ambush; I'll write to my MP. It's the project with that friend of Michael's, Templeton. That's the real problem. Another of your cash transactions.'

'That's not true; they haven't even asked about it. These queries run from when we got married to last year.'

'It's Michael who's twisted this around in your head. Isn't it? How dare you discuss our private life with another man – if you can call him that. So I had a little too much to drink, so what? I'm under a lot of pressure. He's fixated on you; he gives me the creeps, ringing you at the office, seeing you behind my back. And you're encouraging him. Go to him if you want him – leave me alone.'

Lisa's head droops as she listens to Giles's outburst. 'He wanted to help; he only gave me a lift back from the hospital – just calmed me down. You frightened me. I thought you were– My Mum's dying, and I needed someone to talk to. That's all.'

'Well, you've got my permission to speak to him again,' Giles snaps.

He leads her into the main room, picks up the telephone and

holds it towards her. 'Tell him,' Giles says, 'that it's best that the two of you don't have any more heart-to-hearts for a while.'

'Giles,' she pleads. But she dials Michael's number.

Beside the octagonal table in Jeremy Templeton's office stands a paper shredder with a solitary string of tinsel Sellotaped around the top of it. Perhaps, by way of complaint about the lack of other Christmas decorations, one of his staff has stuck the tinsel there. Or perhaps Templeton put it there himself. Bizarrely, next to the shredder, a small pile of impersonal Christmas cards, stripped naked of their envelopes, await execution. At the front of the table is an address list, a few pages long, to record the identities of the victims.

Jeremy Templeton answers the knock on the door himself; there is no one else in the underwriting office. The early morning corridor is noiseless. Rosy from the cold air outside, Mac's cheeks have a healthy glow.

'I think I'm getting the flu,' he says brightly.

'I wasn't going to get too close. What do you want, Mr Mac-Intyre?' Templeton asks, as if Mac doesn't have an appointment.

They sit intently, as chess players do, opposite one another at the table. Mac places his slipcase on top of the cards.

'You told Cedric Richards-Riley that it would be falsifying the accounts to go along with Michael's scheme.'

'Um, I'm sure I didn't use the word "falsifying". Let's be nice about it, the ideas were unacceptable. And he made it quite clear that the scheme wasn't his brainchild. Yours perhaps? Don't take me for a fool; I know about you two.'

'What's it matter? That's not the reason you rejected it,' Mac ventures. 'Fact is, you've already done everything you can to move losses and premiums around. It's not enough, is it? This isn't about one year's profits, is it? With Lloyd's three-year system of accounting this is about two, or even three, underwriting years, isn't it?'

'Who told you that?' Templeton barks.

'It's obvious,' Mac says, suspicion confirmed. 'I'll avoid the use of the word "manipulating" if you like. But the truth is you're – shall we say changing – the appearance of your results to a much greater extent than Michael thinks.'

'You're drumming in the dark,' Templeton says, dismissively.

'It's not important. But there's one thing I must know. Michael's still going on about it. I'll need to reassure him.'

'Reassure – yes, very droll,' Templeton interjects.

'The two million of business you give Wetthards,' Mac skips on. 'Why wasn't he told about it?'

'There's no mystery. The answer's very simple – even if he has trouble accepting it. He wasn't told because he didn't ask.'

'That's priceless.'

'Well, it's all much of a muchness now. You said over the phone that you're in a position to get Michael to arrange the business as I want.'

'Yes,' Mac says, 'but I need something from you in return.'

'What do you want?'

'DBL are going to back a new business I'm forming – with Michael. They'll ask Wetthards, and perhaps you, about him. I want glowing reports on him from you and Richards-Riley.'

'What!' Templeton snorts. 'Why should I even consider...'

'Because you need his products.'

Templeton claws his nails across the table. 'Every prima donna is just a sore throat away from retirement. But it wasn't– Look, there's something I'd like you to tell Michael: I didn't ask for his dismissal. Tell him I'm sorry he was fired.'

'I'll blow him a kiss from you, shall I?' Mac says, grinning from ear to ear.

When Mac departs, he finds he has taken Templeton's Christmas card list with him. He stops by a pyramid of black, 'winter of discontent', rubbish bags and peers at the list. The ticked names confirm his earlier suspicion: Templeton is trying to save a few pence by limiting next year's greetings. Considering that, Mac doesn't feel inclined to waste his time by walking back.

The eleven-hour outward flight to San Francisco is crammed with Christmas travellers. Michael and Mac wear jeans; there are no suits sitting in the Economy section. Explicable by terminal boredom or senile insensitivity or both, the elderly couple across the aisle subject the duo to prolonged bouts of staring which Michael decides to try and stop. He nudges Mac, glances at the pensioners, and places his hand on Mac's knee.

'Never tried that.' Mac grins. 'Mind you, I–'

The pensioners avert their gazes.

'Don't tell me. Please, don't tell me,' Michael laughs, withdrawing his hand. 'By the way, how did you get the time off?'

'I'm unwell,' Mac replies breezily.

'Flu – lot of it about.'

'I didn't know you sniffed flu too.'

On long-haul flights they would normally stretch their legs in Business or even First Class, but today they are paying their own fares. The flight is fun; they enjoy the activity around them, read, watch the film and talk. Michael holds a silver die, weighs the cube in his hand, feels the numbers indented into it and rolls it on his seat tray.

'What's that?' Mac asks.

'It's a present from Josie.'

'I thought you two...'

'Yeah. I found it when I got back from Lisa's. Josie left it on the table; it was to be for Christmas. The little card said, "You always have a choice." But she'd crossed out the word "have" and replaced it with "had".'

Mac sighs. 'What are you doing with it?'

'Confirming I have no choice. If I roll a six, we'll do a deal with DBL.'

'And what if you roll a three?'

'Then I'll roll it again. The dice is always right, but not often first time.'

'Talking of having no choices,' Mac says, 'you're going to have to mend some fences with Templeton.'

Michael nods thoughtfully.

While they eat the main meal Michael appears to be dreaming with his eyes open, but then he smiles and leans to face Mac. 'Do you know, we're saving £49.52 per mouthful compared to First Class.'

Mac grins. 'Oh, that's good. I'll tell my bank statement all about those savings when it arrives. I hope the figures you give Dietrich sound less dodgy.'

Chapter Eighteen

'Just cut it out, Mac. I've had enough; I'm tired.'

'There wasn't any need for you to bring a suitcase. We'd have been out of there half an hour earlier if–'

Michael bangs his hand down on the stretch Lincoln's back seat. 'Yeah right, your suit's in my case. Remember? It wouldn't fit in your overnight bag.'

'OK, sorry,' Mac replies, shamefaced. 'I guess I'm a bit on edge.'

'Me too. I'm nervous about what Wetthards have said to DBL.'

'Professor Dietrich wouldn't have sent the car for us if Richards-Riley had told him that animals run away whimpering just at the sight of you,' Mac says. 'I've told you: I've fixed it.'

The shimmering Lincoln pulls up at the entrance to the Hotel Donatello. As they step from it, the light from the mid-afternoon San Francisco sun dazzles Michael.

And the fact that the receptionist won't accept his credit card stuns him.

She glides her lithe arm through the air as she explains that DBL are paying, 'Professor Dietrich sends his best wishes.'

After checking in, intending to simply drop his bag off, Michael goes to his hotel room. But, enjoying the luxury as his shoes sink into the carpet, he wanders round. Sniffing the anonymous air-conditioned cleanliness, he springs on a sofa, fiddles with the cardboard come-on for Pay-per-View films, then follows the polished stair rail upwards to another sitting area and two large beds. A tired craving to pull back the starched sheets claws at him, but he resists it. Compromising, he lies on the nearer bed, stretches his arms and yawns. Resetting his watch back seven hours makes him aware of the time that he has kept Mac waiting in the lobby. He goes down.

The two of them stroll out into Post Street, towards the cable car route. They reach a clutch of tourists waiting at an intersection just as a cable car, with advertisements stuck to it like large refrigerator-magnets, approaches. Because the cable car is full, they stand on a metal platform to its rear holding onto the white rails. Leaning back, with only his hands and feet inside, Michael inhales the fresh air; it has the smell of a clean city; it hints of the sea. They travel up and down the steep hills of San Francisco, past the side of Chinatown, and disembark at Fisherman's Wharf where the cable car rotates on a large circle of metal-rimmed wood so that the car faces parallel tracks to go back up the hill. In no hurry, Michael and Mac watch as a long line of people moves forward to climb aboard.

In the bar overlooking the wharf, Michael takes a gulp of Miller Lite. It still feels cold when it reaches his stomach. He listens to the bar's music. The Christmas song lyrics, of robins, of snow on rooftops and of reindeer, contrast with the California sun. Lines of white-hulled fishing boats bob in the sea.

A few hours later, back at the hotel, Mac knocks on Michael's door.

'Can I have my pinstripe?' Mac asks, sheepishly.

'We've still got half an hour before Dietrich's due,' Michael says. 'Come in, let's have another beer.'

'No, I need to get changed,' Mac answers, very quickly. 'For dinner,' he adds, as if a further explanation is necessary.

'Be like that,' Michael says.

While Mac hovers just inside the room, Michael fetches the suit Grabbing it, Mac says, 'Well, you know what Liechtensteiners are like.'

'No, I don't,' Michael laughs. 'What's the population? Six?'

Actually, Michael knows Dietrich's *heimat* has 30,000 inhabitants. From his research, it seems Liechtenstein is a thimble-sized country run by misogynists. Women don't even have the vote. But Michael feels it would be wrong for him to give the principality the thumbs-down because of the way it elects to order itself.

'He speaks German, so he'll be here five minutes early,' Mac says. 'Meet you down in the lobby in twenty minutes.'

When Michael arrives in the foyer, he looks carefully at Mac. Mac can't hide his 'Class A' super-confidence.

'No jet lag?' Michael asks, plainly staggered. 'Christ! You brought your stuff through customs. Madness.'

'No–'

'You cunt. You fucking cunt, Mac. You didn't bring it through customs, did you? I did – it was in your suit.'

'Michael...' Mac starts.

But he stops. Michael's face looks angular; his features seem pointed. And a strange glaze, one that Mac last witnessed years ago, obscures the blue in Michael's eyes. Mac remembers the occasion very clearly.

It happened in Tottenham soon after Lisa married Giles. Michael was somewhere between dejected and despondent. And he wouldn't discuss it. Still children in men's bodies, Mac and Michael weren't looking for aggro; they were on their way back from The Spurs, eating hot dogs whilst cutting through a track between two of the area's concrete estates. Three skinheads, with Chelsea scarves tied to their wrists to indicate their paid-up membership of The Shed, cornered them. As Michael and Mac wore Doc Martens and silk Tottenham scarves, in a way that suggested affinity with the Park Lane Boot Boys, Mac knew there was going to be trouble.

Mac tried to back off, but Michael stood his ground – squared up to them. Everything happened shockingly quickly. After his two mates had scurried away, the largest skinhead remained – writhing on the ground. To the side of him, within his reach, was a Stanley knife: his 'tool'. Mac marked the man down as a builder, because of the way the skinhead had fought. Hard. And because of the knife, or rather its handle which, denoting personal ownership when tools lay around building sites, was painted yellow.

Hurt in the fight, cut above his eye, winded and with his groin aching, all Mac wanted to do was leave. But the fallen skinhead pulled himself up onto his knees and reached out to pick up his weapon. One final kick was necessary. Michael, who looked uninjured, delivered it. A penalty kick which knocked the man unconscious.

And that, Mac thought, should have been it.

But Michael picked up the knife, turned the prone body onto its back and squatted down on the man's chest. Mac's mouth went dry. Michael ran the blade a millimetre above the skinhead's cheeks,

127

from the corners of his mouth curving upwards. The blade touched onto the skin.

'A Chelsea smile,' Michael growled at the unhearing skinhead.

'For God's sake, Michael,' Mac yelled. 'Don't.'

Michael turned his head and looked at Mac as if he had never seen him before. The knife was clenched in his hand; his expression was one of cold fury. Whatever Michael had turned into in those moments wasn't the friend that Mac thought he knew so well. Staring at his fingers, Michael's brow furrowed. His palm sprang open and the knife fell from it.

'We'd better get out of here,' Michael said. There was no external threat, but Michael's voice was laced with fear.

'There's no excuse.' Michael's eyes remain opaque, impenetrable. 'You could've gone without for a few days.'

Visibly shaking, Mac sniffs and shuffles his feet.

'Sorry, Michael. I shouldn't have...'

'Don't ever set me up for a fall again. Ever. I don't just mean about the coke.' The angular features of Michael's face soften. 'This fence-mending you want me to do with Templeton, your previous chats with DBL – you aren't telling me everything. I don't mind. You can have all the rope you want. But don't forget: the noose is round your neck. I won't let you off again; I'll kick the fucking stool away.'

'Michael, please. I really am sorry; we'd better lighten up. This meeting with Dietrich is vital.'

A weighted silence follows.

'Hey,' Mac says. 'Did I tell you the one about this blind guy who walked into a shop swinging his guide dog above his head?'

'No.' Michael smiles as if nothing has happened.

'The shop assistant asked him what he thought he was doing and the blind man replied, "Just having a look around".'

Michael laughs. 'He could've answered, "I can't see that I'm doing anything wrong".'

Professor Dietrich is late; Michael and Mac stand side by side in the lobby. Michael's head droops downwards; coloured images float underneath his closed eyelids; he sways slightly. Feeling the presence of someone directly in front of him, he opens his eyes. Michael's neck muscles go into spasm. Professor Dietrich's cropped hair, mirrored sunglasses and double-breasted suit lend his powerful build an edge of groomed malevolence.

'I'm Ernst,' Dietrich says to Michael. 'Welcome to the Bay Area, Mac. Come, our carriage awaits.' Dietrich leads them out of the hotel to his limo where a uniformed chauffeur sits, bolt upright, at the wheel.

At the restaurant the maître d' fawns over their host, leads them to a centre table and lights the wick of a pewter lamp. The flame reflects in the polished silver and glasses of the place settings. Without asking for a wine list, Dietrich orders a bottle of German wine by name. He talks with pride, and at length, of its dryness and quality. As if the wine was from Liechtenstein.

'It's astonishing. Many people in England, and here in the States, think of German white wines as sweet. The reality's different. For example, Liebfraumilch. Outside the Mosel area, where it comes from, most Germans don't even know it. Germans drink mainly dry white, regional wines – better than French wines I think. Still, misunderstandings happen. Tell me about Mr Templeton, Michael.'

'That wasn't a misunderstanding,' Michael says.

A dull thud shakes the table, the glasses tinkle, and Mac's false laugh marks him as culpable. Michael guesses that Mac has tried to kick his shin, missed, and hit a table leg.

'Don't worry, Mac.' Dietrich takes off his sunglasses and eyeballs Michael. 'I hear from Wetthards that you're an honest broker, Michael. It's good. From talking with them it appears to me you weren't dismis– sorry, you resigned – just because of this Templeton business. It's also a matter of control. That's not to say that you were out of control – just out of theirs.'

No menus appear but, in line with Dietrich's evident expectations, food does. As they eat, the professor describes DBL then moves on to praise Mac's success in finalising the Swiss franc deal.

'It was a real achievement,' Dietrich says. 'But I heard that one of your brokers – Julian someone or other – had to be disciplined. Is that right?'

'Yes. Shame though, he was just a junior,' Mac replies.

'Well, as I say, misunderstandings happen. Anyway, to your health, Mac.'

They raise their glasses in Mac's honour.

129

As they feast on their desserts, Professor Dietrich questions Michael about his background and views. Dietrich savours the answers as if they are tasty morsels, repeating some of Michael's words, rolling them around his mouth.

Over coffee Dietrich changes the pace of the conversation, 'Your business plan's fine, excellent in fact. But we are, as you know, a shareholder in Wetthards. They say nice things about your professionalism, Michael, but their acclaim for – how did they term it – your IV method of reinsurance wasn't just faint. If it had a heartbeat, it would be buried by now.'

Mac opens his palm towards Michael, who says, 'Then why did they want me to...Look, IV deals are the cutting edge of a vast new field. Wetthards wanted to misuse them to evade tax. I don't want to attract the wrath of the Revenue.'

'And your methods are new?'

'No, I've been working on them for ten years. But now, they're ready.'

'Give me an example,' Dietrich says.

'OK. Let's say DBL want to take over Tricolour in France. Might cost – what? A hundred million. Although Tricolour's business is very profitable, it could take ten years for DBL to get their hundred million back. Meanwhile, how many other opportunities would DBL miss? But, with my methods of reinsurance, I can sell off the profit stream. Reinsurers might put up the whole hundred million in return for say...75% of future profits.'

'So I can buy Tricolour with its own money?' Dietrich asks.

'Don't get excited – just an example. Tricolour's bombproof. I'd need to look at the numbers on more suitable targets.'

'Another thing I can't fathom out, Michael,' Dietrich says, 'is your way of valuing companies.'

'It varies from case to case. In the last deal the main plank of the valuation was the inertia value.'

Mac cradles his chin, palpably puzzled; Dietrich blinks encouragingly.

'Inertia value is the profit that can be made by the company pushing up premiums regardless of the competition, relying on the fact that only two out of ten policyholders check out other prices each year.'

Dietrich wipes the corners of his mouth with his napkin. 'Sounds as if you can make money flow in any direction you want. So why wouldn't you help Herr Templeton?'

'This field's too important – too lucrative – to muck it up by getting involved in Mr Templeton's manipulative–'

'You've misunderstood, Michael,' Dietrich says. 'All Mr Templeton wants to do is look after the interests of his investors, to make sure his Names don't get sucked dry by your screwball government – Jim Callaghan isn't it?'

'He's the Prime Minister,' Michael says, 'but the Chancellor–'

'What's it matter?' Mac says. 'They're all the same, these Labour idiots. Can't even get the rubbish off the streets, or corpses buried.'

'Quite,' Dietrich says in a poor attempt at an English accent.

A waiter fills their cups with more coffee. Mac raises his eyebrows at Professor Dietrich who smiles, wryly. Michael sees the exchange and frowns at Mac.

'Templeton's business is not a condition?' Mac asks Dietrich. The apparent lack of confidence in Mac's voice doesn't trick Michael. It is a safe bet that, on this issue, Dietrich and Mac have compared cards beforehand. 'I know Michael won't...'

'No. I wouldn't have wasted your time by asking you to come out here, or mine in seeing you. I respect the fact that you won't do things you find, let's say, unpalatable. But, Michael, I'd like you to work through others – to assist. That's important to me. You can work through Mac, if you're both agreeable.'

Michael spills a drip of coffee on his Brooks Brothers shirt. 'I don't–'

'That's acceptable,' Mac interrupts, staring at Michael.

Extending his powerful arms, Dietrich says, 'Despite some reservations, I'd like to proceed. We'll be your backers; we'll take a majority shareholding. And we'll guarantee to buy out your interest in seven years' time. If your projections are right, you'll be sterling millionaires several times over by the time you're thirty-five.'

Michael's glistening eyes contrast with his otherwise stern expression.

Mac looks downwards onto the tablecloth. 'We had in mind just over a quarter of the shares rather than a majority.'

Professor Dietrich laughs. 'I've always admired the British sense of humour. We must have 51%. And you know it. There are all sorts of reasons: accountancy practice, access to Lloyd's...I won't bore you with them.'

'But with Cutesie's business,' Mac argues, 'we'll make a profit in the first–'

Dietrich puts his cup down. 'I should tell you: I've discounted Cutesie.'

'Why?' Michael asks.

The severity of Dietrich's demeanour provides no answer. Michael keeps his eyes politely, but persistently, fixed on Dietrich. Both he and Mac remain silent.

'Brokers tend to be optimists,' Dietrich says eventually. 'I don't expect all your optimism to be borne out. Frankly, I'm much more interested in Michael's connections to Home & Life. Michael?'

'What?' Mac says.

'Home & Life haven't promised me any business. Full stop,' Michael answers them both.

'They were your first client on these IV deals. You'd expect them to give you business in your new company...nah?' Dietrich asks.

Michael turns the corners of his mouth upwards to imply agreement, but doesn't answer. Instead, he takes a deep breath and returns the conversation to the negotiation, 'We might agree to 51%, but we'd need some heavy-duty protections. If you were unwilling or unable to continue as our backers, we'd want the right to buy out your interest for £1 – whatever the worth of the company.'

Professor Dietrich waves a dubious hand.

'And,' Michael continues, 'in order to provide real protection to us, no handcuffs in our employment contracts. Oh, and a provision so that Mac and I can sell our shareholdings to each other for £1, if just one of us wants out.'

Professor Dietrich moves in his chair, as if to rise. Mac intervenes.

'We'd be willing to use DBL Bermuda as a reinsurer. We could even offer them any IV deals before offering them elsewhere – first refusal. I know the president there, Sean Collins. He's ravenous for Michael's business. We've got the first deal, a management buyout, on the table. I'm confident.'

Michael mouths, 'You're confident?'

Ignoring the obvious disagreement between his guests, Dietrich signals to a waiter to come over.

'Our lawyers will contact you after Christmas to wrap up the paperwork.'

Professor Dietrich turns to the waiter who now hovers by his elbow, 'A bottle of Dom Perignon, please.'

As he enters the Captains' Room, Mac breathes in the rich aroma of coffee and relaxes his shoulders. He strolls to Richards-Riley's table and sits down before introducing himself.

Richards-Riley looks over his half-rimmed glasses at him. 'I know who you are, Mr MacIntyre. Jeremy Templeton says I must work with you.'

'Happy New Year to you in advance,' Mac replies ignoring the sourness of Richards-Riley's tone. '1979's going to be a vintage year.'

Cedric Richards-Riley gags; he looks ill.

'Are you all right?' Mac asks, feigning mild care. 'I think I'll have some toast. Fancy a late breakfast, Cedric?'

Mac takes his time catching a waiter's eye.

'Christmas Day was on Monday,' Richards-Riley complains. 'I've got just three working days to tie up as many deals as possible. Time's expensive.'

'Toast is reasonable, though,' Mac says as it arrives.

'Let's get down to it.'

Mac takes a bite of toast. A few crumbs fall onto the white tablecloth and he brushes them towards Richards-Riley.

'For God's sake,' Richards-Riley protests, patting his trousers.

'No need for us to work together.' Mac wipes his hands on a napkin. 'Wetthards can do it. I've got all the papers from Michael. The structure's as Mr Templeton says he wants. Happy Christmas,' Mac adds, passing over a folder.

'Why'd he give them to you?'

'Because I asked him to – nicely,' Mac says in an even, controlled tone. 'Oh, we don't want commission – this year.'

'I can understand Michael not wanting your new company to handle this. I can even understand you not wanting any commission – strange though it might seem. What I don't understand is why you asked Mr Templeton to give this business to Wetthards. Are you telling me everything? I don't want to seem unkind, but

133

Michael didn't show a great deal of interest in charity work when he was employed by us.'

Mac leans his head across the table. 'I'll tell you the reason, if you want. He thinks what Templeton wants to do isn't just wrong, but dangerous. Do you know what he told me? "Give it to someone you hate. Better still, give it to someone I hate. Give it to Richards-Riley".'

Richards-Riley scowls; Mac grins.

'You have the papers – should keep you busy. Still, perhaps you don't have to arrange it before December 31st. I wouldn't know.'

'These papers had better be complete,' Richards-Riley huffs.

'Or what?' Mac says. 'You've already fired him. If you need any help, I'll be happy to listen to a decent proposal. And if, as I think, Templeton needs an arrangement on another year, then we'll be talking again soon. It'll be your turn to give me a present – Christmas or not.'

The New Year resolution that Lisa makes is for Giles. While he sleeps on, she seeks out every whisky and red-wine bottle in the apartment and pours their contents down the sink. She leaves the empties on the draining board for him to find when he wakes. Job done, she runs a bath.

Lounging in the suds, she listens to a Gerry Rafferty cassette. She joins in a few words here and there, but her sing-along voice is too tenuous to sound happy. And, when she hears Giles' rapping on the door, she stops. Glancing at the little brass lock, she sees she hasn't closed it. She submerges her body under the water. Teeth bared, Giles enters. He stands above her, growls something she can't understand, and raises his fist over her cowering body.

Shaking his head, he lowers his arm. He doesn't hit her, but her body jerks all the same. Leaving the door wide open, he goes out of the room. She turns off the cassette, gets out of the bath, towels herself dry and puts on her underwear. Her bare legs tremble as she steps from the room. But, although she hasn't heard him leave, she can sense he has gone. In the kitchen, she finds her purse on the table. A few coins leak from the open clasp. The £50 that were in it will, she knows, buy reinforcements for his bottle army.

Directory enquiries give her the number of Alcoholics Anonymous who in turn provide her with the details of their support group for relatives and friends: Al-Anon.

She attends the next weekly meeting of the local group in the draughty room adjoining the church hall. The room has steel-rimmed windows and bare light bulbs. There, ordinary people, mainly women, some rich, some poor, some just like her, spill their sad tales. Intermittently, she listens.

'He used to be such a kind man. It started suddenly; he just stopped coming home at normal times. When he's there, he isn't – not really. He doesn't talk to the children. He won't allow any visitors in the house, even my parents. Sitting in front of the television, he just drinks. He hides the bottles in his study.'

The torrential flow of stories, one after another, of helplessness and despair, of attempts to help spat back into faces, sound all so different to Lisa. And all so the same. Still deep in pain, a few people have been coming for years. As a newcomer, she is asked last if she wants to talk. She shakes her head which rattles with the meeting's mantra: 'Let go and let God'.

After the Al-Anon meeting, Lisa goes straight to her mother's. The home-care worker, who comes in twice a day, has just left. Mrs Carter is in her nightgown. Her stomach is bloated; the gown sticks out in front of her as if she were pregnant. Hanging loosely from her emaciated bones, her skin is grey. It yields inwards when Lisa kisses her cheek. The community alarm is tied around her mother's wrist in such a way that she is unlikely to set it off accidentally again; Mrs Carter can't walk more than a few steps without becoming breathless.

On her mother's bedside table is her father's watch, a picture of him and his signet ring. The ring that Lisa had removed from her father's still-warm hand last year. It stings her, seeing it there.

Lisa sits on the bed, brushing her mother's sparse hair with a baby brush.

'Giles sends his love; he's sorry he hasn't been to see you lately. He's a bit under the weather – some sort of infection – and doesn't want you to get his germs.'

'Don't lie to me, Lisa,' her mother says, without reproach. 'There's no need.'

135

Of course, Lisa knows her mother is right. To pretend Giles wants to visit doesn't marry up with the in-law in-fighting that has been going on for years.

'I felt quite a bit better today.' Her mother's smile is all receding gums and long, cream-coloured teeth. The ghastly smile of the living dead: nature's cruel parody of a Halloween mask. 'Mrs Hammond came in and made me some tomato soup for lunch. I ate it all. I might not have to go into the hospice after all, though it does look very nice there. I'd like to meet some new people.'

'Oh, Mum. You are funny sometimes. Do you remember what you said when Michael and me–' She stops herself. Why Michael should come to her mind at this moment is a mystery to her.

'Did I tell you?' her mother tells her yet again, all excited, 'Michael sent me a Get Well card. But don't mention it to Peter, will you.'

Her mother's ambivalent attitude to Peter's accusation has never ceased to amaze Lisa. Mrs Carter loves her son to bits. But she still has a soft spot for Michael, the boy who – quite probably – tried to murder him.

'How was your day?' Mrs Carter asks. 'How's that interior design business of yours? You haven't said anything about it for ages.'

Lisa strokes her mother's forearm. 'Fine, Mum. Everything's fine.'

Chapter Nineteen

Two Months Later, February 1979

As they enter the cold modernity of Cutesie's office in King Street, Sydney, Michael feels a blast from the air conditioning and removes the dark glasses necessary to protect him from the February summer sun. Michael and Mac ride the mirrored lifts to the top floor, high above the street. There, they follow the bare legs of Donald White's secretary who leads them to his office. Donald puts both arms round Mac and bear hugs him; his broad frame squashes Mac as if he were a cuddly toy. Donald's tanned face glows as he lets go. There is no similarity between him and his daughter, except the scorching smile. Beneath it, Michael can sense an unease. Something is troubling Donald.

'G'day, you must be Mike. I'm Donald.' He grips Michael's hand.

'Nice to meet you, Donald,' Michael says. It is just as Mac has told him it would be. He has shortened Michael's name – without asking – but wants to be called Donald not Don.

'Megan and Mac have told me about you,' Donald says. 'But I reckon it's only fair to let a man, particularly a best man, defend himself. Real pleasure to have you here, Mike. We're going to enjoy spending some time with you and your folks, showing you around our beautiful city. I look forward to meeting your Mum and Dad at the barbie tonight. Mac's helping with the cooking so – eat first.'

The start of the business meeting is heralded by the entry of three executives in shirtsleeves. With traffic policeman waves, Donald signals for everyone to sit. Spreading themselves in pink conference chairs around a low table, they swap business cards by way of introductions. Donald looks at Mac's business card: *Joint Managing Director, DarIntyre Intermediaries Limited.*

'Oh, that's a shame,' Donald laughs. 'With the German connection, I'd thought you'd be tempted to name the firm MacIntyre und Darrett – MUD. Even that's better than MacIntyre and Darrett – MAD you'd be known as...'

Michael notices the humour in Donald's voice trail. Donald pauses, picks up the conch shell in the centre of the table and just holds it. The corners of his mouth turn down.

'I'm afraid I can't give you your wedding present, Mac,' Donald says, gravely. 'As you know, when Hurricane Tracy devastated Darwin on Christmas Day 1975 PSQC didn't sustain any loss – not one dollar. Yet Lloyd's still pushed up our premiums; it treats our business as if it's some sort of infectious disease. It's 1979; you'd think they'd understand by now. You know what our business is all about – we needed lower premiums.'

Visibly paler, Mac says, 'Needed? But you promised. I've resigned, formed a new company. You haven't given me a chance. We've agreed – you'll come over to London and explain to underwriters personally. The previous brokers should've arranged this long ago. Donald?'

'The name given to us in Lloyd's, Cutesie, is an insult.' Donald's eyes narrow. 'My company's called the Pacific Sea Quake Consortium or PSQC. Not Cutesie. How dare they? We're accused of being too smart – too cute – just because we want some fair treatment. The Consortium's exposure to Australian catastrophes is minimal. We're owned by a large collection of postage-stamp-sized companies in the Pacific and the Indian oceans. Buying reinsurance wholesale, in one lump, was supposed to be cheaper. It should've been.'

Michael looks at the other PSQC executives, none of whom have spoken and all of whom sit forward on their seats. They seem embarrassed to be there and anxious to leave. Mac presses his head between his hands.

'When we saw Professor Dietrich in San Francisco,' Michael says, 'he told us he was discounting the commission we'd earn on your business–'

'Do you mind, guys?' Donald despatches his shirtsleeved colleagues.

Michael continues, 'That is to say, Dietrich expected us to get less business from PSQC than we budgeted for – less than you'd told Mac.'

138

'So I phoned you, Donald,' Mac beseeches. 'You said, "no worries".'

'Look, don't start imagining things. If I'd have known, I would've told you. I'm hardly likely to have postponed telling you this until now, am I? Just before you marry my daughter? You think I'd keep this from Megan? This conversation's just as tough for me as it is for you. Our shareholders have lost patience; they won't allow us to use Lloyd's any more. I'm not in a position to give you the business.'

'But?' Michael asks, appearing neither shaken nor stirred.

'That's the bad news, but the good news is we can still arrange a management buyout. In fact we must, or I'm out of a job. If we buy PSQC, we'll keep all the existing business. And we won't need the so-called help of Lloyd's, or any other damn leeches. We've got to find two hundred million dollars. Can you do it, Mike?'

Michael splays his hands. 'I don't know,' the gesture says.

'It's my dream,' Donald implores. 'Running my own business – it's what I've wanted all my–'

'I'll give it my best shot,' Michael says.

The barbecue is at the house of Megan's sister, Kelly. At Megan's suggestion, the twenty 'Englanders' meet together at Circular Quay, down by the ferries, an area which bustles with people.

Next to a candyfloss kiosk a seven-foot man stands stock still, painted from head to toe in two-tone glitter. His tie is shaped like a lizard's tongue. Michael throws a dollar bill into the man's hat and asks his mother to take a photo of him next to the green statue. After the photo, the giant bows and mimes to her to swap places with Michael. When she does, his tie rises up horizontally and a salacious smile spreads across his green face.

'I've never seen you blush so much, Mum,' Michael says fondly. 'It's going to make a great picture.'

She smiles at him.

'That wasn't funny,' Josie says to Michael. 'You knew that would happen.'

'How many times do you want me to say sorry?' Michael asks, still without actually saying it.

'Say sorry to your mother.'

'No, Josie, my mother isn't upset. Not at all,' he insists. 'Look,

Lisa called me; I helped her out. Your reaction – not returning my calls, not even speaking to me on the plane – isn't reasonable.'

'Oh, that's sorry is it?' Josie says, stalking off into the ticket hall.

From Circular Quay they journey out to Chippendale, to the suburbs of Sydney, on a double-decker aluminium train. Upstairs, oblivious to the world outside, Kathy Darrett and Julie MacIntyre chat. Surrounding them, looking out of the windows, are all the other guests from England. Except two.

Downstairs, Josie and Michael sit together facing in opposite directions. To Michael's acute embarrassment, he can overhear snatches of their mothers' twenty-six-mile marathon conversation. He knows Josie can hear it too.

'Is it selfish of us? To want to see them happy – together,' Julie MacIntyre says. 'Josie wants to be so strong, but she needs someone.'

'It's Michael's fault. That thing with Lisa – since he was a boy,' Kathy Darrett sighs. 'He just can't say goodbye to things gone. Or people.'

Fragments of the mosaic of his past fly into his head. 'Let go!' someone with peaked cap ordered him. But, aged nine, Michael couldn't. Grapple-hook hands tried to wrench his fingers from his dead mother's wrist. His little body went weird on him, and his eyes glazed over. He can't recall whose nose he hit when, in his first icy rage, he lashed out with his free fist. And he isn't sure whether his hold on his mother was broken before or after a nurse stuck a needle in his arm. But he is certain that he must be allowed to untie his own bonds, in his own time.

Ignoring Lisa's cry for help – and she was crying – would have been cruel. Josie should be able to understand that. He looks at her. Her knees are tucked together, away from him. The train rolls on.

Kelly, Megan's sister, runs a ball applicator of mosquito repellent along her skinny arms then shakes them wildly in the air to dry them. An acrid odour pervades the kitchen. Straggles of her curly hair fly in all directions. Mac, modelling a blue and white butcher's apron, saunters in with the herd of English visitors behind him.

'Ah!' she yells, stopping. 'Hiyah, I'm Kelly. You must think I'm mental.'

'Normally, it takes people longer to notice,' Mac says.

'I'm Michael; I've heard lots about you.'

'Some of it nice, I hope,' Kelly replies.

'All of it,' Michael says.

'Kelly has some very attractive attributes,' Mac says, patting her behind.

She moves out of Mac's reach and grimaces.

'Mac,' Michael says, wincing.

'Sorry, Kelly,' Mac says.

The human traffic jam behind Michael presses forward. 'I'd better move through.'

Outside, in the backyard of the old terraced house, the smells of the New Zealand shrimps sizzling on the barbecue fill the air. The packed garden is lit by orange lanterns that swing from a wire between the tree and a dilapidated shed. Michael swats at the evening air, fails to hit any of the mosquitoes he hears buzzing, and wishes he wasn't wearing shorts.

'You look like a table tennis player who's lost his racket,' Megan jokes.

Michael glances at her bronzed legs. 'And you look as pretty as a picture.'

Megan takes a swig from her 'tube' of Twoheys, straightens, and runs a finger over her chin. 'Now my Dad can't give him the business, Mac still wants to marry me, doesn't he?'

'Yes. What makes you think...?'

'Does he love me?'

'Second thoughts?' Michael replies, gently tilting his head.

Kelly escapes from the kitchen, takes a few paces forward, smiles weakly at Megan, takes Michael's elbow in her hand, and kills the conversation. Dead.

In a voice which is anything but jokey, Kelly says to Megan, 'Are you sure you don't want to marry Michael instead?' Megan's jaw drops. 'Well,' Kelly adds, 'while you make your mind up, I want to borrow him.'

Pulling Michael by the elbow, she leads him towards the end of the garden to where, she says, 'a friend I'd like you to meet' waits. But, even before they reach the fence, he knows there will be no one else there. In the darkness, she whispers.

'I don't know what to do; could you have a word with Mac?

141

He's drinking like a fish; he keeps putting his arm round me and patting my bum. Touching me.'

Across the other side of the world, Giles and Lisa sit next to one another facing the daubed make-up of Suzanne Price: Lisa's accountant – the accountant Giles found for her years ago. Hanging on the wall are aged photographs of Suzanne smiling with minor, mostly unrecognisable, celebrities. Lisa finds the smile, like every-thing else about Suzanne, nauseating. A smudge of gaudy lipstick from Suzanne's prolonged peck is still on Giles's cheek. Three times the size of Lisa's, Suzanne's office is large. Large and grubby. The carpet feels gritty under Lisa's shoes. Bobbing her head up and down, Suzanne talks at, not to, Lisa but focuses on Giles.

'I didn't need you to come in; I can sort it out with Giles. He's told me it's not a good time for you. However, you shouldn't have written to your MP. All he's done is pass your letter on to the Revenue – that's really inflamed them.'

'I didn't,' Lisa says. She turns sideways. 'Giles?'

'It doesn't matter who wrote the letter,' Suzanne continues. 'The damage is done. The District Inspector's involved now. He wants a meeting, but a stalling letter would be best. No investigation's been started. The compliance side has no teeth; they can't even make you answer their questions. It may well blow over in a few months. Let me draft it with Giles.'

Lisa rocks backwards and forwards in her chair.

'No. I want to know what Giles – with your help – has done. And I want to meet the Revenue to find out what they want.'

'What the Revenue want is very simple,' Suzanne says. 'Money. At the very least, you're probably going to have to pay them something to go away and leave you alone. But to suggest I've done anything, with or without Giles's involvement, that has caused this is neither true nor fair.'

Lisa looks at Suzanne and at the lipstick smear that remains on her husband's face; she feels her stomach turn. No, it's not possible. Suzanne is nearly forty; he can't be having an affair with her.

'Perhaps if I left you two alone for a few minutes...' Suzanne rises from her chair. 'I'll just go and powder my nose.'

Once she has gone, Giles asks, 'What's the matter?'

'Did you say that? I can't believe it.' Lisa gets up. 'I want this sorted out. I'm going to stay by my Mum's bedside at the hospice. Do you remember her? She was that middle-aged lady at our wedding; she wore a hat and sat next to you at the reception.'

In the hospice Mrs Carter is no longer able to swallow, mute machines stand idle and, although Lisa's chair is too low for her to hold her mother's hand comfortably, she doesn't want to move from the bedside to get a higher chair or disturb the willing nurses again. The only sound she can hear is that of the breathing which rasps from Mrs Carter's open mouth.

Covered with a layer of dried sweat, Lisa's face feels dirty. Her hair feels unwashed, and she wants to brush away the fur that clings to her teeth. In the corner of the room the contents of her bag spill out onto the floor.

Lisa's deathbed devotion is interrupted by the silent appearance of a chubby, black nurse. With no pity in her eyes, but with great care in her movements, the nurse wipes Mrs Carter's dry lips. Then she guides Lisa away from her mother, towards the window.

'I'll sit with your Mum for a while,' the nurse says in a hushed tone. 'You look as if you could do with a little break.'

'But my Mum. It could happen any–'

'No. We can't be sure,' the nurse explains, 'but it's more than likely that your Mum will live at least another few days.'

Lisa gulps, collects some toiletries, and leaves the room. Her eyes are still filled with tears when she returns half an hour later. Lisa starts to twitch. Draping her arm round Lisa's shoulder, the nurse nuzzles her and strokes her forearm.

A man with a gentle face comes into the room, introduces himself as a counsellor, and leads her from her mother's bedside to a small ante-room. She follows him numbly, neither willing nor unwilling to go. A quintet of practical chairs form a circle round a raised floral display. As she takes a seat, Lisa glances at the cross-stitched image of Jesus that hangs on the wall. Under the image, in brown thread, are the words 'Do You Not Know Me?'

'I used to believe in God,' Lisa says, 'when I was small.'

'I'm not a priest,' the man says in a voice she could sink into. 'But if you want to see one here – or just have one sit with your Mum – we can arrange it. There are Catholic priests, Protestant ministers, rabbis and others – all of them come...'

143

'No thanks,' Lisa says, tearfully.

The man passes her a tissue and holds her hand with the same tenderness her father used to. She wipes her eyes.

'I feel so guilty; sometimes I want my Mum to die.'

'Don't be,' he says. 'Some people feel that way; it's normal. Feeling guilty won't help you or your Mum; guilt is a very negative emotion. We can give counselling for a year after your Mum's died, now if you want. We can help. Death's very hard; we don't hide that. And the death of the second parent's usually worse on the children than the first. It cuts all links to–'

'I don't want counselling, but I haven't got anyone to talk to apart from Peter, my brother. And he's as upset as I am.'

He looks down at her wedding ring. 'Talk with Peter. When someone's dying those closest to them need all the support they can get, especially from each other. I see you're married.' She nods. 'And you can't talk to your husband? We could speak with him, if you want. Explain to him how his support could help you and your marriage, both now and later. We wouldn't criticise, or tell him anything you told us.'

Lisa sobs until she has no more tears to cry.

When she is calm she answers, 'It wouldn't help. Giles is– But it's not just him. I don't even know if I love him any more.'

The white canvas sheeting is pulled taut by sturdy poles. Under it, the registrar stands in front of Megan and Mac. Michael, to Mac's right, can see out from the Botanic Gardens to the panorama of Sydney Harbour below. A puff of warm summer air lifts the petals in Megan's hair. Her face is radiant.

'Do you, James Anthony MacIntyre, promise to love, honour and be kind to Megan for as long as you both live?'

'I do.'

Donald White and Michael hand over the rings. Alert and emotional, Michael sees the tear that escapes from Donald's eye when Megan and Mac kiss.

Michael and Mac clasp each other before the line-up begins.

'Married man,' Michael says, beaming at his friend.

'Yep,' Mac replies, grinning off-centre.

* * *

144

Dancing with Megan's mother at the reception, Michael hangs on her words and flatters her with bright smiles. But at every opportunity, from over her shoulder, he gazes at Josie. She turns her head away. At the end of the dance, Michael kisses Megan's mother on the cheek, offers her his arm and escorts her back to her seat. He walks over to the empty chair by Josie and sits down.

'Such a gentleman,' she stabs. He moves to leave, but Josie touches his knee with her palm. 'No, don't. I'm sorry.'

As he opens his mouth to speak, Josie raises a finger and puts it across his lips. 'Just dance with me, Michael.'

She rests her head against his shoulder as they dance. He feels the heady glow of the champagne and her warmth. Fearful of offending her, he moves his body backwards to break the contact. But, with a twinkle in her eye, Josie reaches round and pushes his bottom back.

'I won't be able to sit back down.'

'Then you'll have to dance with me until I let you go,' she says laying her head back down on his shoulder.

They dance. They talk. Talk until the last clatter of the tin cans tied to the back of the Rolls-Royce dies away. Then, under the cloudless night sky in which the stars seem so very different from those he sometimes glimpses in England, Michael takes Josie's hand in his and says, 'I've missed you–'

She interrupts, 'I felt so hurt. I knew about Lisa, but...' Pausing, she too looks up to the stars. She laughs, dirtily. 'One day, perhaps, you'll give me your soul. Tonight, I'll settle for your body.'

Chapter Twenty

Like birds of prey sharing a single branch, hooked to the box with claw-like hands, Richards-Riley and Templeton stand together. A young Wetthards broker passes by on the gallery, murmurs hello, dips his head and increases his pace. Richards-Riley turns to check for eavesdroppers. Satisfied, he clears his throat.

'Jeremy, we have a problem. Darrett's prepared the documents exactly as you said you wanted them. And the mechanics don't work. He told us that the deal wouldn't stack up and now, instead of fixing it, he's made sure it won't.'

'Just get hold of Mac. He can handle Darrett,' Templeton says in a voice that would make a sadist flinch.

'MacIntyre's in Australia, getting married. Some outback throwback no doubt; five generations of inbreeding might make a girl brainless enough–'

'And Darrett? I presume he's there too,' Templeton says.

'Back next Monday. Mac's not returning for weeks; we can't wait.'

'Well, what are you going to do? I seem to recall you're getting commission on this, Cedric. The phrase is "earn commission", isn't it?'

'Professor Dietrich's given me information about MacIntyre and Darrett's new firm. I'm going to ask Diddy to speak to Darrett and give him the witch's warning; they're friends, you know,' Richards-Riley says.

'But Diddy and I, we're not close.'

'Diddy's family – all part of Wetthards – he'll do as I ask him.'

'For heaven's sake, don't explain anything,' Templeton says.

'Oh, don't worry, Jeremy.' Richards-Riley produces a huge golden smile. 'I won't; he doesn't need to know.'

* * *

146

The black saloon carrying Lisa and Peter slows yet further then parks behind the hearse outside the crematorium. Yesterday was Lisa's 29th birthday; today it is her mother's funeral. Giles isn't with her. He follows in the car behind, as she has asked him to. Sitting back in the seat, she stretches out her legs until they meet the panel that separates Peter and her from the pall-bearers in front. She is surprised at the limited legroom in such a large car, surprised too that this crosses her mind now.

Holding tightly onto her brother's sleeve, she looks straight ahead, through the glass screen directly in front of her, out through the windscreen. The dual sets of glass make her mother's coffin appear remote as the undertakers lift it from the hearse. Climbing out of the saloon, her breath forms white smoke clouds in the bitter February air. Lisa hears a dog barking far away from the slow drum-roll of the mourners' footfalls as they shuffle into the grim building.

Despite her coat, Lisa shivers. In the crematorium, the dark wooden beams and grey stones exude an air of dampness which the perpetual twilight does nothing to assuage. Whilst she continues to grip Peter's sleeve, Giles puts his arm around her shoulders and whispers words of comfort in his deep voice. Lisa doesn't turn to him. She remains paralysed, trance-like in trauma; her face is drained.

A priest, who has never met her mother, speaks of Mrs Carter's life and her love for her family. Lisa notices him referring to notes on yellow A4 paper, the colour of which seems out of place. Then, from the front, with his voice shaking, Peter reads from the Bible, 'Love is patient and kind...'

Lisa's eyes sting as memories of her mother and father flood into her mind. Her father picks her up and throws her, as a squirming four-year-old, onto her bed while she squeals with laughter. Telling her little seven-year-old daughter to shut her eyes and hold out her hands, her mother kisses Lisa on the forehead and gives her a squidgy bag: her goldfish, Popeye. She is fourteen and her Mum and Dad are with her after the High School prize-giving, hugging each other, so proud of her.

Talking to her in excited staccato bursts, her father is teaching her to drive – in his much-prized Mini. On her wedding day, her mother, so smart herself, stands next to her at the bedroom mirror gleaming admiration at Lisa in her wedding dress. 'We'll always be

147

here for you,' her mother told her. But now they have gone, both of them. And they aren't coming back.

'...Love never ends,' Peter concludes.

Holding her elbow, Giles steadies her and Lisa joins in the second hymn. She sings loudly, hears her own voice and stops mid-verse. Looking blankly at the flowers on the steps in front of the coffin, she wonders who brought the carnations. 'My Mum doesn't like carnations. Didn't like carnations.' She has said she wants to speak, and she still does. Her footsteps echo through the crematorium when she walks to the pulpit. As she leans her outstretched arms against the lectern, the congregation watch and wait. She can hear the distant dog barking.

'My Mum...' she says, then nothing more.

Unable to go on, unable to move away, with tears pouring from her eyes, Lisa buries her head behind the pulpit, hides from the mourners and shakes. Giles cuddles her back to her pew. She feels her body tremble as he holds her.

'I'm here,' Giles says.

When the organ music resounds in the crematorium, Lisa pulls herself from Giles's arms and clings onto Peter. The rollers under the coffin begin to rotate and, with an agonising slowness, it inches forward. Finally, it disappears behind a velvet curtain. As the curtain closes, a whooshing sound of flames fills the building. At her father's funeral she learned that the coffin wouldn't go straight into the fire, but she still convulses as the noise erupts.

Back at her parent's house, in the 'best room', Lisa holds out an oval plate stacked with egg and cress sandwiches for the mourners. Although Lisa doesn't know many of the older people there, they know her. These strangers' condolences and tissue words are meant well, but Lisa really just wants to get on with serving the food. Giles helps himself to a glass of red wine, whilst talking in low tones with Peter about Lisa's birthday. Giles will make another day special instead. Lisa overhears their conversation in which, mannishly, they overlook her feelings. Celebrating yesterday's lost birthday, celebrating anything, is not what Lisa wants. No happy horizons, please. She just wants to be allowed to be sad. Avoiding eye contact with anyone, she peers at the framed letter from

Hinchley Grammar School, which still hangs above the bureau, reading it as if for the first time. Giles pulls up next to her.

'I can't stand this much longer,' she tells him.

She means him to understand that she isn't just talking about the wake, but her meaning is lost on him. She lets him take her by the hand upstairs. He lies her on the double bed in her old room and spreads a blanket over her. Unlike the single bed of her childhood, the double bed crowds the modest room. Flock wallpaper covers the walls and a broken accordion lies on the floor. He strokes her hair.

'I'm sorry. I'm sorry,' he says.

His words remind her of the only previous time he was in this room with her, on a Christmas Eve, more than a decade ago. Then, after Michael's unexpected visit, they waited until the house slept and, as today, she let Giles take her hand and lead her up the stairs. His lovemaking had been too brief. But he was gentle. Afterwards, he told her he was sorry. Then too, he said it twice.

Giles turns the door knob. 'I should...'

She finishes the sentence for him, once he has gone, 'get some more wine.'

Sitting up, she looks out through the leaded-light windows. The winter skeletons of the climbing roses flaunt their thorns against the backdrop wall of grey cloud. As the front door bangs its own frequent farewell to the mourners, the number of voices downstairs lessens. And, after a while, Lisa lies back down to descend into an uneasy sleep.

Michael enters through the trademark green door, clambers down the steps into the lower part of Wheelers, and sees Diddy, toying with the red and white enamel of his Lloyd's cufflinks, across the restaurant.

'You look well,' Diddy greets him.

'You too, Stephen,' Michael replies in a stilted voice. It is always difficult for him to use Diddy's real name. 'Nice of you to invite me – not often I get written invitations from Lloyd's underwriters.'

Although Diddy smiles, Michael sees the contradiction writ large in Diddy's features. Diddy's lips seem happy enough, but his eyes look dead and done-for.

A waiter rushes forward with menus but, despite the appetite-teasing aromas of lobster, Dover sole and asparagus, Diddy and Michael put the menus to the side and order spicy Virgin Marys. They sip their drinks slowly.

'How was Mac's wedding?' Diddy asks.

'Excellent,' Michael replies.

'And Josie, Mac's sister. Was she there?'

'Honestly, this market. Is my love life common knowledge?'

'No,' Diddy replies with a laugh. 'Wetthards debriefed me.'

Michael runs his teeth over his bottom lip before responding. 'You're edging towards the point, like a barrister, asking questions to which you know the answers. You did invite me,' he adds, meaningfully.

Diddy grips the edge of the table, leans forward and says, sounding worried, 'Don't worry. What I'm going to say isn't market gossip. Wetthards told me. I was sorry to hear that Cutesie won't be giving you the business they'd promised.'

Michael raises his eyebrows and tilts his head.

'I feel awful having to be the one to tell you that Wetthards know this,' Diddy continues. 'But they do. And better you hear it from me than Richards-Riley, eh? Have you advised DBL yet? Are they still prepared to back you?'

Grateful that his tan hides his deep unease, Michael replies, 'We'll obviously be talking to DBL...when Mac gets back from his honeymoon.'

Diddy's cheeks redden. 'You know that saying in the London Market, "When you're hot, you're hot. And when you're not, you're not." No one likes a loser to handle their business. To win new accounts it's always helpful to have a bundle to begin with. What are you going to do?'

'There's other business we'll get from Cutesie,' Michael responds. 'The commission on that's higher. But, yes, we don't want news of our losing–'

'Regardless of how our lunch ends today,' Diddy says with a natural smile, 'I'll use my best efforts to stop Richards-Riley using it to...'

'Thank you,' Michael says.

Brandishing a pad, a waiter pulls up to the table. 'Ready, gentlemen?' Diddy nods.

'Five minutes,' Michael replies, shaking his head.

'Cutesie have no links to Wetthards. May I ask how they came by this information?'

'You can ask, but I don't know. I really don't,' Diddy says. 'Look, I haven't invited you here to issue threats. I've got a favour to ask, as a friend.'

'What do you want me to do?'

'Would you please assist Jeremy by casting your eyes over the contract documents? Wetthards seem to have got the impression that you've spiked the deal. It's important. I wouldn't ask...'

'Stephen, if Templeton gets his deal it's bad for you. Hell, you're under the same syndicate manager. And – I'm not exaggerating – it'll be the beginning of the end for Lloyd's as we know it. There are those who believe – and I'm one of them – that you'll be the next chairman. Surely–'

'Look, Michael. I'll be frank with you, I don't know all the details. But one thing I can say is that Jeremy Templeton's as straight as a die. Neither he nor I would do anything to put the reputation of Lloyd's at risk.'

Michael looks down at the menu. 'I don't feel very hungry.'

At home, on the first Tuesday in March, Michael listens to Richard-Riley's bare-knuckle phone call whilst twiddling with the toggles on Josie's coat. Last time she wore it, he called it her 'Paddington Bear outfit'. He wishes he hadn't. She looks so sweet in it, but since his remark it has rested, out of favour, by the side of the bookcase. Michael likes her mess, though he never tells her; that might encourage her to seek out his endurance level. Honeymoon over, surrounded by a pile of Josie's clothes, Mac is wedged into the settee puffing on a cigarette.

Michael holds the handset away from his ear, but Richards-Riley's voice remains very much audible.

'Damn you, Darrett. You've had the Templeton papers two weeks now. You promised Diddy you'd look at them.'

Michael balances the receiver under his chin. 'I know how concerned Jeremy is that everything's tickety-boo this time around. I'd hate to get it wrong,' he says, not bothering to cover his naked sarcasm. 'I'll telephone *you* Thursday,' he adds.

He puts down the phone and looks over at Mac. 'The thought of giving Templeton a deal that actually works is vomit-making,'

Michael says. 'I'm only doing the revisions to buy Wetthards' silence. The longer I delay in passing them over, the smaller the chances of us being short-changed and the higher the possibility of Templeton deciding to emigrate to Transylvania.'

'Give me the Templeton papers; I'll hand them over next week.'

Michael laughs for no apparent reason. 'Guess what? In the bumf Richards-Riley sent over, it says who Wetthards have used as the reinsurer. I'll give you a clue: they're based in Paris. No? Bigger clue? I'm closer to them than Wetthards are, or ever will be. The reinsurer's Tricolour. You know, I could...'

'Don't even think of it,' Mac says, pushing aside Josie's clothes. 'Is Josie staying here?'

Michael props himself on a packing case, four of which still act as pedestrian-calming devices around the room. 'She has her own place.'

'Asking you questions is like playing peekaboo,' Mac jokes.

Michael frowns. 'We must tell DBL that we don't have Cutesie's business. I'm not sure I can arrange the management buyout. Wetthards know we've lost the core business, and if we don't tell Professor Dietrich, they will.'

'Not once I've given them your papers.'

'Richards-Riley's gratitude has the shelf life of milk in August,' Michael says. 'Expecting Wetthards not to tell Dietrich is–'

'Let them. Donald White will be over in April. He'll tell anyone who wants to know that he'll be giving all Cutesie's business to us. And it's true.'

'Yeah, but not honest. Truth and honesty aren't even kissing cousins,' Michael says, repeating a phrase Josie threw at him a few days before.

Mac stubs out his Marlboro in a tinfoil cupcake holder.

'And the honest truth is going to come out,' Michael continues. 'We don't have the business we promised DBL–'

'Dietrich told us that he'd already discounted the Cutesie business. Come on, Michael, you were there.'

'Yeah, discounted,' Michael says. 'You think he meant discounted to zero? You think he would've gone ahead?'

'Richards-Riley, Templeton and Professor Dietrich were all cooked in the same wok,' Mac says. 'They think a scruple is something you pop into your mouth on a long car journey. Just so long as we make profits, DBL don't care how. We will. Tell me, how are negotiations with DBL going?'

'Dietrich's lawyers don't know whether it's Mayday or pay day,' Michael says. 'They keep arguing about all the wrong things – commas and colons that sort of stuff – not a clue about reinsurance.'

'Sounds a scream,' Mac chuckles.

At the end of the new company's first week of operations, Michael lingers over the morning walk from Moorgate Station. He sits down on a bench in the bijou park at Finsbury Circus, facing towards the bowling green. Drinking a cappuccino from a paper cup, he peers into the centre of the trumpets of the daffodils to his side. Dusty pollen covers the fronds.

After a tedious negotiation, Michael has hammered out a do-able deal with DBL's grammarian lawyers. DBL have signed it. So has Mac. Taking his silver die from his pocket, Michael rolls it in his hand several times. He gets a six and, with that confirmation of his decision to add his signature to the documents, rises.

They have leased half of the fourth floor of an office building in London Wall. Michael enters the ground-floor reception, raises his chin, and breathes in the scent of polished chrome. Two nubile women sit inside a circle of brushed steel in the middle of the reception, dealing with a flow of suited visitors, messengers and telephone calls. To the side, in front of a leather sofa, the pink of the *Financial Times* stands out amongst the neat piles of magazines.

Up in their new offices, Mac is interviewing a woman in her early thirties who wears a stylish trouser suit. She has been personally recommended to them by contacts in the market. Entering, Michael shakes the clammy hand she offers.

'As Claims Manager you'll have long hours, constant pressure and – if you're a masochist – fun,' Mac tells her. 'In a few years we'd want to see a Claims Director on the board. We'd like it to be an internal promotion.'

'Another soul purchased with promises,' Mac says after she has left. 'And talking of promises, I told Dietrich you'd sign by the end of the week.' Mac puts an arm up, shielding his face.

'You had no right to tell Dietrich that,' Michael says.

'Oh come on, Michael. You've been faffing around far too long.'

'You expect me to sign by Friday,' Michael says. 'What's wrong with today?'

Grinning, Mac rushes away. He returns with the documents, in triplicate.

When his signatures are dry, Michael says, 'DBL have got something to lose now; they've put in the capital, funded the lease on this office, and if they withdraw we can buy them out for £1. I'm not going to allow Wetthards to keep sticking a gun in my ear. You're going to tell DBL that we've lost the Cutesie business.'

Mac shakes his head. Michael lifts his. 'If you don't, I will.'

Mac's secretary can't do dictation, can't work the word processor properly and types only 20 wpm. But he has hired Melissa anyway. As she wobbles into his office, with one earring caught up in her pineapple hairdo, he ogles her thighs.

'Do you want me to wear longer skirts, Mr MacIntyre?' Melissa asks.

Mac shifts his marauding eyes to her breasts, prominent under her low-cut blouse. 'No, Melissa, I like stockings. Call me Mac, it's more...personal.'

'You asked me to let you know, Mr – sorry, Mac – when DBL's offices in San Francisco were open.' Her smile displays a small chip in one of her upper incisors.

'Thank you, Melissa.'

'We've got a problem, Ernst,' Mac tells Dietrich. 'Cutesie's unable to give us its existing business. But they're very interested in looking at the management buyout; the commission on that is much higher.'

Professor Dietrich laughs. 'I knew you'd lost the core Cutesie business. Of course I did. Who do you think told Wetthards? We've got connections all over the Pacific region. I knew before Donald White did; DBL haven't backed you for this one account.'

'Why did you tell Wetthards?' Mac asks. Shuffling a stapler around his desk, he waits for an answer.

'I think you know,' Dietrich replies. 'I told you; I told Michael. I thought I'd made it very clear to him: I want Mr Templeton to get his deal. Oh, while you're on the phone – the Cutesie management buyout. I'd like you to work with us, Mac. When Michael starts to put together details, I want copies of everything.'

'I don't think– Look, I can see where this might lead,' Mac says irritably. 'You'll use the information – launch a pre-emptive strike.

A management buyout minus the management? Michael won't wear it.'

'Don't be silly, we won't tell him. Between us we managed not to let him know how he came to leave Wetthards just at the time you wanted him–'

'I've just married Megan. Donald White's my father-in-law; it would destroy him. I can't–'

'Destroy him?' Dietrich says. 'You don't swallow that rubbish about him and his technicolour dream, do you? Take it from me, only one thing interests Donald White and that's control. He couldn't care less about the money, and he doesn't give a monkey's about his colleagues – or you, except insofar as you keep his daughter happy. He's a power freak, and he's overdue to short-circuit. If you're holding his hand at the time, you'll get burnt. At this stage, Mac, we just want to look at the papers. That's all. Nothing odd about it. We could make it...in your interest.'

'Exactly when', Mac asks, 'did Donald White know that he couldn't give me the business he'd promised?'

Dietrich stonewalls, shifts the subject, and ends the conversation.

Chapter Twenty-One

'Lorry loads of post are dumped in here every day. Even waste tips are emptied. But here nothing ever comes out,' Mac says, without a hint of humour. 'We're supposed to be partners. You shut yourself in this room. And do what? Donald White's coming next week, and I need copies of your work on Cutesie.'

The outer office is tidy and organised, but in the conference room they have to tread water in the inland sea of paper which floods the floor, sloshes over the table, and laps up onto the window sills.

'The Yorkshire Ripper claimed his eleventh victim yesterday,' Michael replies.

'What?'

'Well, that's the tenth time you've asked me. If you're holding some sort of competition, you're losing.' Michael gestures around the room. 'Virtually all of this is Cutesie.'

Picking up the file closest to him, Mac says, 'Virtually all Cutesie? What's this then? "Home & Life" this file's headed. Is that the business with what's-his-name...Cantwell? The business that Professor Dietrich seems to know about, but I don't?'

Michael simply smiles.

'Just tell me, will you?' Mac asks.

'There isn't much to tell. Home & Life would like to give me some more business. I'm just trying to find them a reason – easier said than done. When I was with Wetthards, I was close to getting a really major order; they must have told Dietrich. Sooner or later, Samson Cantwell will be important.'

Heaving a pile of folders onto the floor, Mac clears a space on the table.

'And...what's the position with Cutesie?'

'To move that forward, I need to go to Paris. After that, I'll have something to show you.'

'No, Michael. I know why you want to go to Paris: to see Tricolour. We gave our word to Dietrich that DBL Bermuda would get first refusal.'

'You might have. We didn't. It's not part of our final agreement with them, and I don't trust DBL.'

'It's obvious you know you can do Cutesie now, otherwise you wouldn't be wanting to fly off to Paris,' Mac says. 'DBL Bermuda must get first shot. If Dietrich feels you've shafted him–'

'That's not very likely,' Michael says, amused at Mac's choice of words. 'And if it's all the same to you, I'd like to keep my sex life private. I am seeing your sister.'

Mac doesn't laugh. 'Michael, I need the Cutesie papers now. I've got to meet Dietrich in Brussels on Friday. I wouldn't have to keep him up to speed – but no, you said he had to be told that we'd lost the core Cutesie biz. You made the bed. Now I've got to fucking lie in it.'

'All right,' Michael says, seeping reluctance.

Perched on high heels, Melissa struts in as Michael fishes out the folders. 'Do you want anything?' she asks Mac.

Mac leers at her. 'Um...fancy lunch?'

'What, again?' she replies. 'Yes, please.'

Watching them leave, Michael feels a sordid shiver run down his spine. The sway of Melissa's behind suggests she is soon to be nude. And the ink on Mac's marriage certificate isn't even dry. Still, Michael muses, Megan must have known that Mac and monogamy weren't made for one another.

On the first day of the new tax year, Lisa glances down at Suzanne Price's shiny nail polish. Surrounded by pre-war furniture, sitting on mismatched chairs, they wait in the poky Revenue office.

'I have advised you', Suzanne says, 'against proceeding with this meeting. We aren't prepared. The Revenue will understand; they're obliged to take into account your personal situation. And goodness, your Mum's just died, Giles is ill–'

'If you'd taken care of my interests instead of screwing my husband...'

Suzanne slaps her, hard. And leaves.

There are no pictures on the duckweed-coloured walls to take Lisa's mind off the pending meeting, just a fire escape notice screwed to the door. As if someone might steal it, Lisa ponders ruefully. By the time the young PAYE compliance officer and his boss enter, she has had time to contemplate her position. But not positively.

'I strongly suggest you appoint an accountant,' the District Inspector says.

His body language is stern. Next to him the young compliance officer has his eyes wide open; he seems to be pleading with Lisa not to undergo this trial. His aftershave is more persuasive; she wants to run away to avoid it. Crossing her legs under the table, she scrapes against the wood and ladders her tights. She winces.

'I'll appoint another accountant...when I know what you want.'

The young officer talks in general terms about how meetings such as this are conducted. With apprehension, Lisa surmises. Twiddling a pencil behind her back, she listens. The District Inspector takes his glasses off.

'We have an interesting case coming up. Investigation's been going on over three years. That's an interior design company too – funny that. We couldn't agree a settlement with them, so we're having to prosecute.'

The District Inspector stops – not pauses.

Without intending to, Lisa snaps the pencil. She withdraws the halves from behind her chair and places them together in front of her.

'What we want from you', he resumes, 'is a full disclosure and an agreement to settle any tax due – with interest and, of course, fines. We aren't the moral police; we don't like to condemn or prosecute where we can avoid it.'

Lisa can see pity in the younger man's face. 'I understand there's been a death in your family,' he says. 'Are you sure you want to proceed today, without an accountant?'

The District Inspector doesn't wait for her to reply. 'I'm not suggesting any wrongdoing,' he says in a tone which belies his words, 'but if there's anything you need to tell us, then please do so within the next few weeks. I have to caution you that the consequences of telling us only half the story can be unfortunate. Get an accountant. Take professional advice.'

Lisa stares at the duckweed walls.

'Meanwhile,' the District Inspector growls, 'I'd like some answers to get an idea as to the depth of any problems. Let's start

158

in the tax year that ended yesterday. Your tax returns haven't been made yet, therefore you're not facing any problem – yet. You were paid a large amount of cash from a Mr Templeton. In your cash book you report it as being seven and a half thousand pounds, but...'

'It was seven and a half thousand,' Lisa states, trying to retain a calm facade.

'Was it? I see there are numerous cash settlements. Is this normal in the interior design business?'

'Some of the clients insist,' she replies, unconvincingly.

'Do they?' he bites at her. 'Two years ago, let's see. A pair of carpet slippers. Was that expense wholly, exclusively and necessarily incurred in the performance of your duties? A subscription to a woman's periodical? Is this a home telephone bill?'

'I can explain.' But she doesn't.

'Let's move back to two invoices from three years ago. There's a hotel bill from the George V – that's in Paris, isn't it? Apparently, you stayed there between May 2nd and May 5th. However, on May 3rd another invoice shows you had lunch in the West End of London. Did you fly back for lunch and then return? Explain that.'

'...I've never been to Paris,' Lisa says, her chin shivering.

The shrill ringing of the fire bells ends the interview. Although on her exit it is clear that there is no fire, she feels that she has every reason to be alarmed.

Not wanting to return to her office, Lisa drives home. After collecting the mail from the box in the downstairs hallway, she shifts the key in the lock to her apartment but, in the process, drops the post. It lands in a heap on the mat. One letter, with the multicoloured logo of her husband's company on the back flap, stands out. Closing the door she calls to Giles, but he doesn't reply. She rips open his letter, feels the thick wove between her fingers, then unfolds his dismissal.

Having lived through the Blitz, Lisa's mother knew what to do in a crisis and she'd passed this vital information on to Lisa. Make tea. The china mug Lisa drops a tea bag into has a child's painting of a sunny day on it. Leaving the letter by the sink for Giles to find, she trudges, holding the tea, to her bedroom. She sits on her side of the marriage bed and looks out of the window. The spring sunlight highlights the ranks of tulips which sway majestically in the breeze. Lisa pulls the curtains on them and hides herself under the duvet.

When she wakes, it's dark. Her stomach rumbles and her eyes remain open, staring but unseeing, heavy with sleep. She reaches out for her mug but, feeling the coldness of the tea through the china, withdraws her hand. Hearing Giles sneak open the bedroom door, she turns on her bedside light and sees him peeking in.

'Giles, we need to talk.'

He stands in the doorway, silhouetted by the main lights from the apartment. 'I can't now. Do you want some tea, anything to eat?'

'No, Giles. I want to talk...' She starts to cry. 'Please,' she whimpers.

Giles lumbers over, climbs up on the bed, holds her in his arms and breathes whisky into her face.

Mingled with sobs, words burst from her in a torrent, 'Everything I care about is ruined. I can't bring my Mum back, but I do want my husband. You have to talk to me, Giles. What have you done with that bitch accountant? You have to tell me. We've got to sort it out. Who did you take to Paris? Was it her? What are you going to do about your job? And when are you going to stop drinking? I can't cope without you. Please come back – please, Giles.'

Holding her as she sobs, Giles says, 'I'm sorry about your Mum. I'm so sorry about Paris. Please forgive me. I'm not well.'

Lisa pushes his hands off her shoulders. 'Forgive you? I want to know who she is; I want to know everything. You can't do this to me – not any more – it's not fair. You've got to stop drinking – now. You're not well! What you're really saying is, "I'm an alcoholic. I can do whatever I want".'

The rude beeping of the alarm wakes Michael at five; he has offered to give Mac a lift to Heathrow. He has to go there in any case, to pick up an American visitor coming in from Boston, but Mac's flight out is much earlier. The offer was made in a weak moment, a worried one. Because Michael is concentrating on Cutesie, the new company's business production is suffering and expenses must be held below budget. However, Mac's new house is only fifteen minutes from Heathrow – hardly a huge minicab

160

fare. And to add 'insult to idiocy', as Michael described his offer to Josie the previous night, the extra cost of parking will negate the purpose.

Josie lies next to him. Trailing a numb arm across her, he silences the urgent clock. Sleepily, he kisses her tousled hair and stumbles into the bathroom. He looks through half-open eyes into the mirror. It has six bulbs in brass holders on either side, like something from a theatre dressing-room. Splashing cold water on his face, he smiles back at his haggard reflection and raises circus ringmaster hands out in front of him.

Showered, he plods back into the bedroom and dons his suit while, cross-legged on the bed, Josie grins at him.

'Any chance of a coffee?' he mutters.

Wearing only her mischievous princess smile, she waltzes downstairs.

'How can you be so happy this time of day?' he asks. But she has gone.

The smell of fresh coffee wafts from the kitchen. Scratching the top of his head, he stomps in.

'I'm late – have you seen my car keys?'

Still naked, on tiptoe, holding his keys above her head, she says, 'Tell me you love me.'

Mac is on foot, heading for the Grand Place. In his hand he carries an oversized Jiffy envelope. Nearing the centre of Brussels, he weaves in and out of side streets, passes the English bookshop which is hidden amongst patisseries and delicatessens, looks up to the spire he is using as a compass and enters an alley. It is lined with restaurants. Sprouting from them, tables and chairs bring the flow of pedestrians into single file. Oysters, lobsters, eels and crayfish, lying on ice at the front of the restaurants, beckon him. So, experimenting with three languages, does a man with a thin moustache. Mac chooses not to understand.

In front of him, twittering and chattering, a column of twenty Brownies frolic along the cobbles holding onto a blue string. The Pied Piper leader who pulls the front of the string looks round to check that the Dobermann-faced woman at the rear hasn't allowed any of their charges to let go and wander off, stringless. Following the Brownies into the Grand Place, he stares up at the pageantry

161

of gold-dusted crests on the ancient building to his right. He goes inside a café, which smells of waffles and wood, and makes his way through the well-dressed tourists, upstairs. It is less crowded there, and he sees Professor Dietrich at the far end.

'Today's Friday. Must be Belgium,' Dietrich greets Mac. 'It's been a long week. Atlanta, New York, Amsterdam, Berlin and now Brussels.'

They don't shake hands. Placing the envelope by the side of his chair, Mac takes a seat. A waiter shambles over to their table. Dietrich orders mineral water; Mac asks for a citron pressé. Both speak French to the waiter; Dietrich's French is fluent; Mac's is halting. Thirsty, Mac takes a gulp of his drink as soon as it comes. The sugar round the rim of the glass gives a deceptive sweetness to the first taste, a sweetness that is soon washed away by the violence of the lemon juice.

'Donald White's my father-in-law,' Mac says. 'I hear what you say, but it would break him; my wife would never forgive me.'

Dietrich smiles. 'I'm not a careless man. I stalk my victims first and, although I've never met him, I know Mr White better than you do. He'll stiff you and your partner, tell your lovely wife it wasn't his fault and buy her a trinket or something.'

'Then there's the money,' Mac says. 'Using Michael's methods, our commission on the management buyout will be two million dollars. Why should I–'

'Is that for me?' Dietrich asks. He leans forward and points at Mac's envelope. As he does so, his Mafia-like double-breasted suit bulges.

'Are you carrying a gun?' Mac asks, poker-faced.

'Quit jerking around. I don't like being made fun of,' Dietrich says, sourly.

Mac's grin emerges. He takes another sip and draws his cheeks inwards.

'Just give me the papers – and keep them coming,' Dietrich says. 'If the deal stacks up – just before Cutesie is in a position to make the management buyout – we'll move in. DBL will make the kill and you can feed on the corpse. Even after the costs of firing the existing managers there's enough meat for everyone.'

Mac lights a Marlboro and drags on it thoughtfully. 'What's my...?'

'Five million.'

Mac lets out a low whistle then shakes his head. 'If Donald White suspects.'

'If,' Dietrich says. 'Yes, if before, during or after he suspects anything then Michael can make the denials convincing. It won't be hard for him, providing he doesn't know the truth. You're very resourceful, Mac. Your wife will never know.'

'Donald's family.'

'I didn't answer your question the other day,' Dietrich says. 'Your dear father-in-law knew he couldn't deliver the business he'd promised you. He knew it before your engagement party.' Mac swallows the remainder of his citron pressé and looks into Dietrich's eyes. 'Despite the fact you didn't invite me,' Dietrich continues, shrugging his shoulders as if he has been snubbed, 'I know when it was.'

'Come on, Ernst, you're based in San Francisco. So when did Donald know?'

'Last year. Shortly before his daughter – Megan isn't it? – flew over to London.' Dietrich sips his water. 'It's now or never, Mac. We do have other sources of information. Five million or nothing – the body bag for the management buyout is already unzipped.'

Mac stubs out his cigarette, reaches down and picks up the envelope.

The following week, Megan smiles broadly as the Qantas passengers straggle out of the customs hall. Donald White emerges trolley-less and drops his massive briefcase, suit carrier and duty-frees onto the floor of Heathrow's arrivals lounge. Putting her arms round her father, Megan kisses him on the cheek.

'You look amazing,' he says.

'And you've developed a moon tan, Dad,' she replies. His skin is pale.

'Spending too long stuck in the office, that is.'

He picks up his briefcase which looks heavy, very heavy.

'What's in the briefcase?' she asks. 'Bits of Ayers Rock?'

'Believe it or not, the only thing in there is the information package Michael couriered out to me. Only finished reading it on the plane.'

Talking constantly, she carries his other bags through the terminal, up an escalator, and into the covered footbridge leading to the short-term car park. He climbs into the front seat of Megan's bright red hatchback, and she slams the doors on the dank smell of the concrete complex. Pirouetting in and out of the rush hour traffic, she taps her fingers on top of the Fiesta's steering wheel in time to the breakfast show music of Capital Radio. He dozes.

Megan parks on the double yellow lines by the railings in London Wall and watches her father heave his briefcase out of the rear.

'OK if I leave the other bags with you?'

She nods, grinning from ear to ear. 'Sure.'

'It's great to see you so happy. Thank you for collecting me, Megan.'

'Collecting you – you make yourself sound like a suitcase. Do you want me to find a parking space and come back when you've finished your meeting?'

'No, it could take a long time.' Donald's normal smile is missing.

'What's wrong, Dad?'

They sit in the conference room, which has been nicknamed 'the paper factory' by the staff. In preparation for the meeting, Michael has tidied the papers into piles. Messy piles though; the room is still a tip. But now it is a decorated tip; Michael has pinned two enlarged photographs to the wall.

'It's my duty to explain how this buyout will work,' Michael says, 'so you'll understand if it doesn't.'

While Michael drones technical jargon, clouds of tiredness drift across Donald's face. Mac too appears disinterested in the mechanics; he props his head up with his hands.

'Can we cut to the chase, Mike?' Donald asks.

'The cost of the management buyout of Cutesie – sorry, The Pacific Sea Quake Consortium – is two hundred million. Through reinsurance I can get hold of two hundred and fifty million. You and your colleagues pick up the difference: fifty million dollars. Oh, plus small change.'

'I understand that,' Donald interrupts. 'Do you think I spent the flight watching reruns of Skippy? You can get us a hundred million – not fifty. You've set lower premiums for policyholders. Who are you to tell us what premiums to charge?'

164

Mac's head shoots up; his eyes flit from Donald to Michael.

'Have you seen the new pictures, Mac?' Michael says, apparently ignoring Donald's outburst. Rising, Michael strolls round the table to the photos.

The two photographs are of the same city street. The one on the left is mundane. Bricks and mortar. Ordinary people doing ordinary things. But the picture on the right shows the same street flattened as if a grumpy giant has come along and stamped on it. A corpse lies in the middle of what must be the road.

'You recognise these photos, don't you, Donald?' Michael says. The skin above the bridge of Donald's nose creases together. 'Well, I'll tell you,' Michael continues. He runs his hand across the photo of wreckage. 'This is Port Darwin after Hurricane Tracy. Nine-tenths of the city was destroyed. Sixty people died that Christmas Day.' He points to other picture. 'Reinsurance can't bring them back, but it can pay for the rebuilding. It can stop it happening again. This photo is what all three of us do for a living. See it. Cyclone-proof new buildings. Next time the wind whirls in Darwin, all that'll happen is that a few fences get blown over.'

'What do you think we are? Oxfam?' Donald says.

'No, this is strictly business,' Michael insists. 'Lower premiums mean more customers. Your market share will increase. And more people will buy insurance. Hell, in many places where you're operating, only a tenth of the houses are protected. I need some strong arguments to get reinsurers to back this. The fact that the management would like to trouser all the money, rather than invest it, won't wash.'

'Donald, you told me the buyout will give you what you've wanted all your life,' Mac contributes smoothly. 'And fifty million is a lot of money.'

'I appreciate what thoroughbred pros you guys are,' Donald says, 'but I'll tell you what's a lot of money: that's your commission. It's too high.'

Michael strokes the air with open-palm gestures. 'Mac and I, we're risking our careers to get this done for you. Our firm won't be able–'

'Balls!' Donald blurts out. 'Do I have to listen–'

'And reinsurers pay our commission, not you,' Michael reasons.

'How do you come to that conclusion?' Donald asks.

'It's a fact,' Michael says. 'Just like your car insurance, the commission's included in the premium. You're getting fifty million; I don't understan–'

'If we reduce your commission,' Donald shouts, 'then reinsurers give us more – more of our own money.'

'It's not your money – at present it doesn't exist,' Michael counters in an even tone. 'We're making that money for you. You'll get twenty-five dollars for every dollar of commission. Two million is modest.'

'Modest? This is a few months' work. My colleagues will only agree a hundred thousand. Forget the two million; you're being – I hate to say it – greedy.'

'Greedy?' Michael asks icily, without raising his voice.

Michael's chin shifts forward of its own accord. It is the first sneeze of Michael's cold anger attacks. But he has made a deal with his devil. Verbal violence is permitted. He hesitates and then releases a valve inside.

'What do you think we are, Donald? Some sort of shoeshine boys?' Enough. Reset to reasonable. 'I've spent months on this already; we've got staff here, heavy overheads. And we expect a fair reward for taking the risk that it might not work out.'

'Fair?' Donald sneers.

'Fair,' Michael shouts. 'You pick up fifty million, argue the toss about wanting to double it, and quibble about the commission. And you call us greedy. You're not my kith and kin. As far as I'm concerned, you can get right back on the plane.'

'Donald, you're tired,' Mac offers.

Chapter Twenty-Two

Supper is a subdued affair that evening, all small talk and big silences. Mac can't find much to chat about with Donald. Or Megan. And he doesn't give a pimp's promise whether it seems polite; as soon as the meal is finished he suggests that Donald goes upstairs. Goes to bed. Goes away. Megan's lower lip trembles, but Mac ignores her obvious distress and asks her to get some coffee. She says she wants to clear the air. So would he, but in a different way. An irritating tinkle, kicked over the hedge from next door, bounces around the dining room. Mac would like to take a sledge-hammer to their neighbours' wind chimes. Above him a crystal chandelier twinkles. That too he loathes.

Their first marital argument starts with the lace doily which she slides under his coffee cup, explaining that it will protect the lacquered surface of the dining table. Objecting, he moves the cup off. Back onto the table.

'It's already got a saucer,' he says gruffly.

'That's a bit childish,' she replies under her breath.

He hears and adds, 'It wasn't even hot when you served it – nor was dinner.'

'What's wrong, Mac? Tell me.'

Mac surveys the room which Megan has spent vast amounts of money decorating. None of it feels as if it belongs to him. The chandelier, the table, the quagmire feel to the carpet, the smell of the exotic flower arrangement and the gaudy but expensive wallpaper. Nothing. Except Megan, beautiful Megan. And he now knows – well, strongly suspects – she has lured him into marriage. That knowledge rankles him.

'It's your bloody father; he poleaxed Michael and me again today. If he doesn't back off, I'm going to take him down.'

167

'He's my Dad,' Megan says.

'And you're my wife.'

After twelve hours' sleep, Donald White looks refreshed; his fire of a smile has returned. Conversely, Mac seems jaded. The three men sit at the dining room table that Megan has just cleared. Cleared without a word.

'Is Megan OK?' Michael asks Donald and Mac.

'Fine,' Mac grunts.

'Fine,' Donald agrees. 'It takes her a while to wake up in the morning – don't you think, Mac? She was looking forward to seeing you, Mike. She'll be better in half an hour or so. When she was at home she needed two alarm clocks.

'Sorry about yesterday. I was tired,' Donald continues. 'I'll go along with the fifty million. I can see the logic, and it's more than I can get elsewhere.'

Michael senses the breakfast breakthrough must be inched forward, but obviously of a different opinion, Mac steams in with: 'And you'll agree our commission?'

'I shouldn't have said "greedy",' Donald apologises. 'It was insensitive of me, but you know what we're like down under – not afraid to call a spade a shovel.' He turns to Michael. 'You were pretty blunt yourself, Mike.'

Michael looks across at Mac who rises, paces over to the patio doors, and stares out into the back garden.

'But we have got a problem with your commission,' Donald continues. 'It's not just down to me; I'll need to talk it through with my colleagues. Then I'll come back to you. We'll work it out, as friends do, Mike...as family do, Mac.'

Michael wears his negotiator's face; Mac continues to gaze at the patio.

Donald produces another burning smile. 'I understand you're going off to Bermuda in the first week of May, Mike. I'll try and get a proposal that you'll be happy with before you go. Alright?'

The following week, Richards-Riley telephones Mac. So they can't be seen through the twitching curtains of the London Market, so news of their meeting doesn't filter back to Michael, Mac suggests

168

they meet in the coffee bar of the Great Eastern Hotel. Close enough to Lloyd's. Far enough away.

Late for the meeting, Mac feels foolish as he wanders in and out of the wrong entrances before finding the main one. Through the door to the left of the hotel reception, sitting high in his chair in the otherwise empty bar, Richards-Riley waits. Mac can see his impatience from the tilt of his chin. Without saying hello, Mac sits next to him on the couch. Pointedly, Richards-Riley looks at the three empty chairs around the table and moves up.

'I was wondering when you'd call,' Mac says grinning. 'You're going to give me my Christmas present.'

Richards-Riley peers over his half-rims. 'You don't know what I want yet.'

'Quite right, Cedric,' Mac says, enjoying calling Richards-Riley by his forename – certain it will annoy. 'You might just want to chat,' Mac adds. 'Let's avoid politics and – if you don't mind me saying so – you don't look big on religion.'

Richards-Riley ignores the sarcasm. 'We need some assistance. In the strictest confidence, your guess that Mr Templeton was interested in changing the appearance of more than one year's accounts was correct. We need to move a loss forward. We'd thought we could use the basis that Darrett gave us, so kindly. But it needs further amendment.'

'Nothing wrong with moving a loss forward,' Mac jokes. Richards-Riley's golden glint appears. 'Look,' Mac says, seriously, 'whilst I don't share Michael's prissy attitude to moving profits to save tax, this is different. Moving a loss forward is more than irregular, it's almost inconceivable. Jeez, if investors find out, the outcry will result in a lynch mob.'

'For the record, Mr MacIntyre, in the special circumstances the Templeton syndicate finds itself, I see nothing amiss.'

'Really?' Mac says with a caustic laugh.

A pneumatic drill starts up outside; Richards-Riley pulls his watch from his waistcoat pocket in a 'we are wasting time' gesture.

'Can you get Darrett to provide us with an amended version?' Richards-Riley asks. 'Without telling him why?'

Lighting a cigarette, Mac nods.

'If you can,' Richards-Riley says, 'then our lawyers can set you up an Anstaldt, in Liechtenstein. It's a discreet sort of trust. We'd be prepared to pay for its set-up costs and make a payment of

£25,000. It's up to you whether you declare it on your tax return; I understand most people forget.

'Actually, we would mind if you declared it,' Richards-Riley contradicts himself. 'The Inland Revenue seem to have the impression that these sorts of trusts grow in clusters. And we don't want them sniffing around, old boy. Obviously, we wouldn't want to force you to reduce your tax burden. If you'd prefer, we could make you out a cheque. But we can't pay cash.'

'I'd prefer the Anstaldt. It sounds more beneficial. Oh, I don't want the papers coming to my office, or even my home. I'll give you a call to let you know my secretary's address. She understands me.'

'Personally,' Richards-Riley says, 'I find it refreshing to deal with someone who's so easy to understand.'

Over an hour late, eyes sunken into her head, arms drooping at her side, Lisa is tired when she unlocks the door to the apartment. Yesterday, Giles had made an effort and bought her the red roses which now stand proudly on the window sill.

But today, in lieu of hello, Giles says, 'Shit.'

'The traffic was unbearable,' she mutters as a reply.

Giles folds his body in two. His chest shakes and a muscle spasm jolts his arm upwards. She knows the problems: stomach cramps and other withdrawal symptoms. Afraid she will get the same truthful answers as most days over the past week, she doesn't ask him how his day was.

'And the client was worse than unbearable,' she adds. Giles scowls at her. 'The woman looked down her Chelsea nose at me,' Lisa goes on, 'pulled faces at my suggestions, and – with a lollipop-coloured finger nail – flicked away the plans it took me three days to prepare. Let her keep her gold-plated taps and ghastly floral lampshades.'

Standing by the empty drinks cabinet, Giles bares his teeth. 'Dear, dear. You poor little thing. My giving up drinking was your bloody idea; the least you can do is be there for me, just once in a while.'

'It will get easier, Giles,' she says. 'You're right, I shouldn't have complained. Sorry, but I must get the accounts done. I'll need a hand – ten minutes?'

170

'Alright,' he concedes, grumpily.

Half an hour later, she calls to him from the dining room. A petulant child, he flops down opposite her in front of the stacks of ledgers, invoices and accounts which cover the table. She explains that, starting with the previous year which they might remember more easily than earlier ones, they have to work through the invoices and receipts. In addition to the present year, there are six years that she has to examine. Looking carefully at each invoice, she asks questions which Giles answers in monosyllables. He shifts in his seat frequently.

'Have you got haemorrhoids?' she asks.

'Do you think that's amusing, eh?'

'I'm not–'

'This whole tax business – it's Michael's fault,' Giles spits. 'That man Templeton – he's under investigation. You're getting dumped on because of the connection. Michael introduced you.'

She ignores the venom and closely peruses an invoice from a London hotel. Check-in was at noon; check-out was three hours later.

'This is one of yours too, isn't it?' she says, raising her voice. 'Is this the same tart you took to Paris, or another whore?'

She gets up from her seat, places the palms of her hands on the table, supports herself with her arms, keeps her chin raised, and looks out of the window towards the spangled glow of the street-lights. When she turns to face him again, he too rises. As if to walk away. And she loses what remains of her temper.

'How could you put the receipts for your adultery through my company?' she shouts. 'You disgust me. You cheat on me. You cheat on my business. You cheat on every–'

Crack! Giles' fist crashes into her jaw. Lisa's head recoils. Putting her hand to her lips, she feels the stickiness of the blood. It dribbles onto her fingers. Lisa's eyes bulge like those of a fish on the end of a hook. She runs her tongue across her teeth and tastes the bloody saliva that cloys in her throat. The smell that fills her nostrils makes her retch.

With jerky movements, she replaces her palms on the table. Two drips land on the surface. Pressing her hands down, she locks her elbows to prevent herself from swaying and stares at him.

Giles bows his head. 'I'm sorry.'

'No, you're not really sorry. But I am. I want you to leave. Now.'

171

When the front door to the apartment slams ten minutes later, she unlocks her elbows, falls back into the hard chair, puts her hand to her mouth again and feels the wound. Inside her mouth, one of the back teeth feels loose. Seeking comfort, she lets her mind drift back to her childhood pretending, as she pushes her tongue against the molar, that it is a milk tooth. She basks in the happy recollections of parental Tooth Fairies who slipped sixpences under her pillow and took the tiny teeth to join their white friends in a secret jar at the back of her father's bedside cabinet. The memories fade as the stark throbbing of her bleeding gums intensifies.

Looking at the red roses on the sill, she shakes her head and sleepwalks across the room to the telephone. Peter picks up his phone before it completes a ring. Her cut lips sting as she talks. After putting down the phone, Lisa drops to her knees, bends her head and curls up into a hedgehog on the carpet. When the doorbell rings she shudders, but then realises Giles would use his key. It is her brother.

As she waits in Casualty, Peter tries to cradle her but the public display of affection unnerves her. She pushes him away. Garlanded with Out of Order tape, a television is chained to the wall. Apart from a drunk, who stares back sullenly if they look over, the chairs around them are empty. On the floor, right in front of Lisa, is a day-old newspaper. Margaret Thatcher's picture, arms raised in victory, beams up at her. 'Where there is despair, may we bring hope,' the headline reads.

'I think we can get away without a stitch. Anyway, no lasting damage,' the Indian doctor tells her. 'I'll ask the nurse to clean it up a bit.'

He scratches his bald pate in consternation and casts an astringent look at Peter. 'Would you wait outside while I speak to Lisa?' he asks, accusingly.

'He didn't hit me,' Lisa says.

'You walked into a door, did you?' the doctor says, brusquely. He sweeps out with his white coat-tails fluttering behind.

* * *

172

Even when it finally comes, Lisa's sleep is interrupted by bouts of tears. Soothing her, in and out of her room each time, Peter holds her until sleep returns. At daybreak, on the fridge door, with one corner under the Pears Soap Baby magnet, Lisa finds a note addressed to 'Strawberrylocks', a nickname he gave her as a child. 'Phone me when you wake. All love, Peter.'

First though, Lisa telephones an emergency locksmith. The man who arrives wears blue overalls and looks like an airman. She shuts herself in the bathroom and asks him to call her when he has finished. Forty minutes later, the new main lock and deadlock fitted, Lisa stands in front of him, holding her purse, trembling.

'Sixty pounds, madam.'

The swelling from her mouth makes it hard for her to talk, but she tries. 'I know I didn't ask the cost in advance, but...' The locksmith flexes his handlebar moustache and seems to mock her with a smile. 'Would you have had the gall to ask a man to pay such an inflated price?' she manages, as she passes him the money.

'I've been promoted to manager of the whole shop,' Josie exclaims.

Michael hugs her; he adores the bubbles of her enthusiasm and is careful not to pop them. The 'whole' boutique, the place where Josie has worked since she moved to London, is small and employs, including Josie and the Saturday girl, just four people. Still, it is in Hampstead and the job makes her happy. Telling Michael of what she might do with her new power, she plays with the possibilities, leaps up from the settee and then bounces back down again. Michael tickles her ribs. Laughing, she sprawls on to the beige carpet.

'You know I've got to go to Bermuda on Monday,' he says.

She kicks her feet out behind her. They touch the last remaining packing case in the room: the 'table' on which the television sits. Her dress rides up her legs, revealing her thighs. In a burlesque impersonation of a slave owner, with his hands on his hips, he rises and stands above her in his shirtsleeves.

'You didn't tell me,' Josie says. 'You're always going away, but not this time.'

Encircling one of his ankles with her hands, she stops him from moving.

'Why do you always arrive at the airport hours before you have to? Is it because you like to get away from me?'

'What makes you think that?' he says struggling, not very hard, to get free. 'I missed a flight once.'

She tightens her grip and levers herself up into a sitting position by his feet. Looking down, he can see inside the top of her dress; she isn't wearing a bra. As normal, she arouses him.

'If you let me go,' he says, 'I'll get some Moët so we can celebrate.'

Released, Michael springs into the kitchen and returns with a bottle of champagne. When he prises it open, the cork flies across the room and settles on the top of the bookcase. Michael pours the champagne into the tall glasses which Josie holds. Some of the liquid runs down onto her hand. Setting the glasses on top of the television, she licks her fingers.

'Too good to waste?' Michael asks.

'So am I.'

'I'm not a gangster. And if I was I wouldn't waste you, Josie.'

'That's not what I mean. Ask me to move in with you, Michael.'

'You have moved in. All your things are here.'

'There's lots more things. Ask me anyway.'

'Please fill up every space in the flat.'

'Is that the best–'

Michael loops his arms behind her shoulders and silences her with a deep kiss. He tastes the champagne in her mouth.

In Bermuda, as he descends the steps of the plane, the humidity hits Michael in the chest. A young mother and her toddler blow kisses from the observation deck down onto the thin stream of passengers trailing from the plane to the airport building. The kisses land on the man in front of Michael who, blushing, returns one.

The speed limit in Bermuda is 20 mph, but the taxi drives even slower, which gives Michael the opportunity to gaze out of its open windows. Coming in and out of sight, behind lush vegetation speckled with pink cottages, the bright blue water of the Atlantic hugs the shoreline. Flanked by the vivid flowers of the hibiscus, the narrow roads, travelled more by flimsy mopeds than cars, twist.

On Tuesday morning, inhaling the perfumes of the oleanders,

Michael walks the hundred yards from his hotel in Paget to the ferry stop. He sees the little boat chugging its way across the calm waters of Hamilton harbour towards him. As he climbs on, the other passenger greets him cheerfully. The man wears a cream silk jacket, a yacht-motif tie, beige shoes, canary-yellow Bermuda shorts, and socks. Long socks, almost up to his knees. To complete the outfit, he carries a briefcase by its handle. So foreign, so very British.

Once in Hamilton, trying not to look like a tourist, Michael follows the directions he has scribbled on a creased bit of paper. Along the way, during his five minute walk to DBL's office in Church Street, he passes a red pillar box, a white-gloved policeman in a British uniform, and a Kentucky Fried Chicken restaurant.

Six-foot-three Sean Collins, the President of DBL Bermuda, towers over Michael as they shake hands. Sean has adopted a more conventional hairstyle than the drunken barber one with its zigzag fringe he was famed for when working in London.

'Mac's in the States,' Michael says. 'He sends his love.'

'Always a queer comment from him,' Sean retorts. 'Anyway, you're the organ grinder on these IV deals.'

Beaming, Sean shows him through to a room where a bean-counter in Bermuda shorts and a woman with a sycophantic spray-on smile introduce themselves. On the conference table, next to the white china, steaming coffee waits.

'Always a pleasure to see a London Market broker,' Sean says with a laugh, '...leave the island.'

'If DBL don't want my business – plenty more piranhas in the pool.'

'I heard you were stroppy,' Sean says. 'And that you'd refused to promise us first refusal?'

'I wanted the option. But I'm here, aren't I.'

Sean breaks into a higher-pitched voice, 'Is this your first visit to Bermuda?' Michael shakes his head. 'Well, then,' Sean continues, 'you should know that the pace of business here is slower than in London. But many of our deals are larger. How was your flight?'

They talk for over two hours, about the flights to and from London, about Michael's hotel, about Bermuda, but not about business.

'And how can we help you, Michael?' Sean asks, eventually.

'The Pacific Sea Quake Consortium, Cutesie – do you know it?'

175

'Used to underwrite their business, years ago, back in London. So?'

'Cutesie want a management buyout,' Michael says. 'We need $250m.'

'Big number. Got any papers?'

Michael produces a single sheet from his inside pocket and passes it across. Smiling, Sean holds it between his thumb and forefinger.

'I see London Market presentations are as substantial as ever.'

'Everything you need to know – at this stage – is on that bit of paper.'

'When did you say you fly out, Michael?'

'Tomorrow.'

'Dinner tonight, then – Fourways Restaurant. I'll send a car. Seven-thirty?'

The lighting in Fourways is subdued, and the pianist plays to perfection supported by the choir of tree frogs whose chirrups drift in from outside. At the table next to Sean and Michael's, a rich gourmet dines alone. Michael takes the last spoonful of his strawberry soufflé as Sean Collins orders coffee.

'Brandy?' Sean asks.

'Why not?' Michael replies. He looks quizzically at Sean who, by turning up on his own, has cut the pretence that his colleagues are involved in the decision.

'We can live with the basic deal, but it's going to need some refining,' Sean says. 'The management's profit seems a bit steep. Fifty million?'

Michael smiles, confidently.

'But we can manage it,' Sean concedes. 'I need all the paperwork – urgently.'

Michael swills the brandy round in the bottom of the glass.

'And I need you to sign an agreement', Michael says, 'that the papers I'll give you will be treated in the strictest confidence, and that DBL Bermuda will be responsible if any of the information is misused by any other member of the group.'

'What do you mean "misused"?' Sean asks. 'That's ridiculous.'

Michael knows that Mac is keeping Dietrich up to speed. Hopefully, from Michael's viewpoint, this can be done without

Mac passing over any copies. But, in case that happens, knowing it might, Michael wants to protect himself against DBL encouraging another company to mount a takeover.

'Then sign it,' Michael purrs.

'We don't normally sign agreements like that. Besides, they're notoriously difficult to enforce,' Sean replies.

Michael hands him a two-page agreement and a covering letter from one of the UK's top legal firms. The agreement is clear: if any part of DBL is involved in a bid which puts the Cutesie management under siege then DBL Bermuda will be liable. Michael's instructions to his lawyers were, 'I want the agreement airtight. If, for example, DBL New York were to find the same information in a lock-up garage in the Bronx, that's DBL Bermuda's problem.'

'This one's enforceable,' Michael says. 'And I do need it.'

'You don't trust us, do you?'

'I trust you, Sean. It's not personal. I just don't want any accidents. No signature, no information. No information, no business.'

Raising an arm, Sean calls for the bill.

'The information's in my hotel room,' Michael offers.

'Why do I get the feeling I'm going to regret signing this?' Sean says.

But he pulls out his Mont Blanc.

Chapter Twenty-Three

Three days later, trapped in traffic, Dietrich's progress is slow. Dietrich knows the driver of the yellow cab is lost in New York's grid system; the driver wouldn't be wrestling with a road map otherwise. The streets are long and straight; a native New Yorker could find his way from Times Square to the Twin Towers blindfolded.

'How can anyone fail to find the World Trade Centre, one of New York's greatest landmarks?' Dietrich complains in fluent Spanish as they enter another one-way street. 'Stop here! You'll need to open the trunk; my money's in my case.'

Without leaving his seat, the driver presses a switch to open the boot. Dietrich climbs out, collects his bag and marches off without paying. He hears the driver shouting expletives at him, but Dietrich is sure the cab can't reverse against the traffic. And he is certain that the driver doesn't deserve to be paid. Finding another one a minute later, Dietrich finally reaches the World Trade Centre. In the express lift to the upper floors, the popping of his ears makes the whole foul trip even more intolerable.

Deep inside the polished chrome offices of DBL's New York offices, he is shown into the empty boardroom. It is bad enough that he has had to come all the way to New York, but now his over-promoted vice-presidents are keeping him waiting. Few describe Dietrich as a friend. Those that do are misguided.

Hands behind his back, Dietrich walks around the room and peers at the bold swirls of the nineteenth-century bond certificates. They are housed in modern frames. The bonds imply an illustrious history that DBL doesn't have; the frames a bright future which Dietrich is sure it will. Yesterday's illusion is tomorrow's reality.

Sixteen mahogany chairs surround the table. One by one, Dietrich picks them up and places them in a pile against the far wall. The stack's shape resembles a bonfire. He doesn't want to waste time. Vertical vice-presidents are not verbose.

Fifteen minutes later, the door inches open and a trio of executives slink in. Dietrich sees the astonishment in their faces as they survey the new seating plan. He stares at them while he waits for their tardy colleagues.

Idiots. They knew Dietrich had let the worst lawyers in London loose on the documents which brought MacIntyre and Darrett into DBL's den. True to form, the lawyers agreed papers which contained no provision to force Darrett to use DBL Bermuda. Dietrich didn't protest. It was all part of his plan. But now DBL Bermuda and DBL New York are, in concert, dancing to the wrong song.

Two more executives shuffle into the room.

'This Cutesie business!' Dietrich launches his opening salvo. 'You must be mad. DBL aren't putting up two hundred and fifty million Australian dollars – two hundred and fifty million lira for that matter – what's the point?'

'Tell DBL Bermuda to sail on,' Dietrich continues. 'The profit on Cutesie – what sort of name is that – is pathetic. Tell DBL Bermuda no. You should be interested in making money, not giving it away. DBL aren't going to pump in millions of dollars to inflate the bloated ego of Cutesie's President. Donald White's a clown.'

'Michael Darrett put this deal forward to our guys in Bermuda,' a woman with a New Jersey accent says in palpable disbelief. 'Pardon me, but isn't his partner Donald White's son-in-law?'

'I'm not here to play Happy Families,' Dietrich says. 'Mr MacIntyre, White's son-in-law, is providing us with the inside track. With a buyout, the corks round the management's hats will twirl to the tune of a fifty million dollar profit. Throw the management out, and DBL grab the profit.'

'Bermuda will go ape,' one of the suits ventures.

'Who the fuck cares?' Dietrich says. His features relax. 'That said, I don't want Sean Collins to know we're carving Cutesie up. Just tell him you need a bigger profit. Spin out the negotiations. Meanwhile, I want you to set up a company in Panama. Don't bother getting it a licence as a reinsurer – just leave it simple. Name it in honour of Mr MacIntyre: Entire Reinsurance SA.'

'Oh, that's good,' the woman with the New Jersey accent says. 'If anyone catches on, it'll be down to him.'

'Yah,' Dietrich agrees. His lips curl into a smile. 'But nothing will go wrong.'

On Tuesday May 14th, a week after Michael's visit, Sean Collins tries to reach him. It is noon in Bermuda. An hour later, at six o'clock in London, Michael returns the call. Sean Collins is at lunch. It is Thursday before they speak.

'Sorry about the telephone tennis,' Michael says.

'Well, we're both used to it,' Sean replies.

'I don't think it would be as bad if you didn't take four-hour lunches and alternate days off.'

'That's rich, that is: being lectured on work ethics by a London broker.'

'I'll have you know, I've been in my office by ten every day this week.'

'By ten, eh? Am I impressed, or what?' Sean says. 'Anyway, the reason I'm phoning is that I've got a problem with the Cutesie deal. As you know, it's a biggie. We needed New York to work with us. At first they were all over us, but now they've reprogrammed their adding machines.' Michael detects the edge of scepticism that has crept into Sean's voice. 'Price is too low, apparently.'

'So that's that,' Michael says, unmoved.

'You said you had other markets, so I guess you're not going to be much bothered. I've been asked to get better terms from you, but I won't mess you around. If you move the price, you know where we are.'

Without knocking, Mac enters as Michael replaces the receiver. The conference room, which Michael has turned into his primary office, is surprisingly tidy. Much of paper forest has been felled, and the clearings reveal the aged-pine table top. But, in the corner, four squalid snowdrops decorate the carpet – cigarette butt evidence of Mac's frequent visits. Mac lights a Marlboro with his Cartier lighter.

'We have to do something about those cleaners...or you,' Michael says. 'You used to smoke from time to time. What's it now, two packs a day? More? There's no ashtray in here, Mac.'

'Oh, don't nag. You can't blame the cleaners for wanting to get out of this room double quick,' Mac says. 'And I'll leave when you

180

tell me who was on the phone just now – was that Sean Collins? Problem?'

'Not really. Bermuda have backed out; so I'll go and see Tricolour next week. No worries, as Megan would say. Sean said that New York won't play. Strange though, this business is ideal for DBL. New York's told Sean that the price looks wrong. But that's crap.'

Mac grins, disarmingly. 'You sure? You can't spend much more time on Cutesie. We're heading for a loss. Don't do this trip to Tricolour. If DBL think the terms are wrong, I'll go back to Donald. He is my father-in-law...'

'What? We'd get stuck in the mud of a negotiation which would take months. Tricolour will agree it on the spot. Don't you want to get the Cutesie deal done?'

'Course I do,' Mac says. He takes a long drag on his cigarette. 'But Donald hasn't agreed the commission. And this isn't some crusade, Michael.'

A twinkle appears in Michael's eye as he toys with the thought of teasing Mac about the stakes. He could say this buyout means lower premiums for policyholders, that the price of insurance is almost like a tax, and that they are putting money into every community that Cutesie operates in. Or he could argue that he was sparing the careers of its employees. But, up close on individual deals, save-the-world sentiment spins away. That just leaves Michael's stubborn streak. Oh, and...

'We've got two million reasons to press on,' Michael says. 'All of them fold. Even if push comes to punishment, we'll get paid.'

'I think we're flogging a dead horse,' Mac says, flicking ash onto the carpet. 'By the way, Templeton won't agree that you've done a proper job with the reinsurance mechanics. He needs greater flexibility. I'm preparing a memo for you.'

'What's the problem with the work I've already done?' Michael asks.

'You don't want to know,' Mac replies.

'If you tell me I don't want to know,' Michael's stern expression cracks into a smile, 'then I don't want to know.' He drops the smile. 'And if it's so awful that you can't tell me, then I'm not doing it.'

Mac licks the ends of his fingers and squeezes the glowing stub of his cigarette until it glows no more. 'What do you call a broker

181

with a clear conscience?' he says. 'I'll tell you: poor. Look, we've gotta keep Dietrich sweet until we make a profit.'

'I'm sure you can stall Templeton for a while,' Michael stalls.

'Alright,' Mac chirps, seemingly well satisfied with a rain check on a maybe. 'How's it going with my sister? I hope you two children are still happy in the sandpit.'

Michael's smile returns, and he opens his mouth as if to reply.

Cringing, Mac withdraws. 'No, sorry I asked. Please don't tell me. I really – really, really – don't want to know.'

Hunched in garden gnome postures, Lisa and Peter sit at the table. Piles of ledgers, invoices and accounts are scattered in front of them. Sitting in Giles's chair, Lisa stares at the parched remains of the three-week-old roses on the window sill.

'Peter, can I ask you a big favour?'

'A triple cornet-sized favour?' Peter laughs. 'Ask away.'

'You know I hate to be alone. Will you move in with me for a while?'

'One condition,' Peter agrees, instantly. He points at the papers. 'You have to let me help you.'

'Oh, thanks,' she says. 'But I think I may be beyond your help. I telephoned the District Inspector. He told me – well, made it clear – I have to get an accountant. He's given me to the end of next month.'

'What happens if you don't?'

'The Revenue will raise assessments based on estimates – plus penalties and interest which together may double the amount. Surprisingly, he was very nice about it. But he's already given me time enough and can't see any progress.'

'You could appeal.'

Lisa looks mournfully across to the drinks cabinet and, avoiding eye contact with Peter, continues in a monotone voice, 'He said I stood little chance of winning – one of his previous employees works as the adjudicator's assistant. He didn't spell it out, but there's no point in me complaining. If I don't pay, they'll prosecute me. I might have to go to prison.'

The sound of a can, bullied by the wind outside, carries into the room.

'You won't go to prison, Lisa. Put it out of your mind. I'll find you an accountant, someone you can trust. But we've still got this Templeton problem.'

'He paid me £7,500. The Revenue say they aren't allowed to give me an explanation, but they obviously think he paid me more. And now even Mrs Templeton won't return my calls. I'll have to sort it out with the tax office.'

'With the tax office? Michael can sort Templeton out – he did introduce you to him. Just pick up the telephone. He'll be delighted to hear from you.'

'The trouble is, even after all these years, I still care for him. If I telephone him, I'll just hurt him again. Last time I phoned, Giles was standing over me. I told Michael I didn't want to see him for a while. The time before that his girlfriend answered. Anyway, I really don't want him involved in this,' she says despondently. 'You're not to...'

'All right,' Peter says.

On Friday afternoon, in the conference room, Michael's head swims as he looks at the figures. Often, he has to drink at lunch. *In vino veritas* is the axiom, but Michael believes 'in beer banknotes' is a better motto for a business producer. Even so, the alcohol makes him tired. He swings his neck from side to side, hears little clicking noises, and yawns. His thoughts drift aimlessly before they settle on something Mac said yesterday. The conversation seemed innocuous at the time. It started by Michael teasing Mac about his lopsided grin and moved on to the less than serious topic of other people's lip pigments and pearly whites.

But, he remembers, Mac said, 'Four gold teeth. I think Richards-Riley's dentist has got a day job as a jeweller.'

Not lots of golden crowns, but four. Michael scratches his chin; to the best of his knowledge, Mac has only met Richards-Riley once. That was when Mac handed him over some papers on Templeton. And when Mac last talked about the rollover Mac said that Templeton, not Richards-Riley, had requested revisions. So, Mac being in Polo-swapping proximity with Richards-Riley sniffs a bit.

He wanders into Mac's empty office. Scanning the room, he notices a shirt hanging from the inside of the door – a hangover from Mac's single life when he would come straight into the office, hungover.

183

Snuffling for secrets, Michael bends right over the desk. In the top drawer he unearths Mac's diary, his spare car keys and, strangely, a list of addresses headed 'Xmas Cards'. But he doesn't get a chance to look at it for long; a perfumed weight crushes him against the desktop. Melissa, dressed to thrill, leans over him, presses her breasts into his back and reaches a hand round to fondle the front of his trousers. Startled, Michael clasps his legs together. But that traps her forearm, and she just carries on groping him. He struggles upright.

Melissa's lower jaw drops. 'I'm sorry. I thought you were...'

Tugging down on her skirt, she turns towards the door and stumbles into Mac who is coming in. She falls against him like a tramp with a meths habit. Mac laughs loudly and, with not a glance at his rainy-day lover, shuts the door in her face.

'We could share her if you want. She goes like a train, complete with whistling noises and steam,' Mac says, in between laughs.

'I didn't...' Michael gasps. 'She just...'

'I believe you,' Mac winks. 'Melissa's very...affectionate.'

'What about Megan?'

Mac forces a grin. 'All right, Mr Goody Two Shoes. Megan's perfect, but I don't think she'd be into sausage sandwiches.'

'That's not what I–'

'Look, Megan wants babies. The smell of discarded nappies and sick on my lapels – it's not my speed...'

Michael raises his eyebrows. 'Your speed – good one. I've been wondering why you haven't been sniffing lately. Moved onto speed, eh?'

'No, and I haven't used coke for ages. I promised Megan,' Mac counters.

'Ages! And what's a nostril of white powder compared to this stuff with Melissa? I can't believe that you and Megan don't–'

'I don't ask about your love life. Okay, so I won't make the finals of the world's best husbands,' Mac defends.

Mac strolls round to his side of the desk and perches on a corner. 'What's a Christmas card list doing in your office in May, Mac?'

'I don't know – been there ages. It's Templeton's. I picked it up by mistake and didn't give it back. He was shredding Christmas cards at the time – nice man.'

He tosses it over to Michael who, without explanation or conscious thought, holds onto it.

'You going to tell me what you were searching for?' Mac says.

Michael pulls up a chair and plumps down into it. 'Why do you keep your spare car-keys at the office?'

'Because I do,' Mac says. 'Come on, Michael. What were you looking for?'

'No telex from Donald White yet?' Michael obfuscates. 'He told us that he'd have a word with his colleagues and get a compromise off to us before I left for Bermuda. It's been weeks now.'

Mac shakes his head.

'Home & Life phoned me yesterday,' Michael continues. 'I'm seeing Samson Cantwell the week after next. Get your father-in-law to play ball before I do something he regrets.'

'What's Samson Cantwell got to do with the price of fish?' Mac asks.

Michael crosses his legs and leans back. 'Donald White hasn't agreed our commission.'

'So? Home & Life will never agree to a takeover of Cutesie. Hostile takeovers are too messy for grand old companies such as Cantwell's.'

'If Donald White insists on a party,' Michael says, 'then I'll find some presents for him to unwrap.'

'Wait for Donald's response, would you?' Mac asks.

'Didn't say I wouldn't.'

'And while I'm at it – leave Templeton alone.'

Michael raises a half-smile. 'If he kicks my kennel once more– are you up to mischief with Wetthards? 'Fess up, it's good for the soul.'

'Don't be a muppet,' Mac replies.

Michael's blue eyes focus on his. Mac changes the subject, 'You seen your mate Patrick Coughan recently?'

'Not recently. Why?'

'He's in the paper today, been made Financial Editor of the *Protester*. That's a rabid magazine – makes me want to climb a tree.'

'They like to expose things,' Michael says. 'Melissa might like it there.'

When Michael comes out of Mac's room, he glances at Melissa and, unusually, goes into his own office. From there, he can watch her. Although her mascara is smeared and it is obvious she has been crying, there is something else he sees in her expression –

185

wrath. She fumbles with her Tipp-Ex bottle, gives up trying to open it and walks over to Mac's fireproof filing cabinet. Unlocking it, she ransacks two folders and, watched by Michael and her colleagues, woken from their work by Mac's earlier laughter, marches over to the photocopier. Her gait is fierce. But an hour later, when she has finished the copying, she looks drained. She makes the short walk back to her keyboard seem like a gangplank. Teasing his fingertips down his cheek, Michael tries to work out what she has just done. It looks like a spiteful act.

'One Perrier and a pint of lager,' Peter says to the barmaid, loudly.

'There's no need to shout,' she replies.

She's right. Apart from a grizzled man who gazes into space, Michael and Peter are the only patrons. The atmosphere between the two of them is even less jovial. Still, Michael knew when Peter phoned that it was about Lisa, so he didn't hesitate to agree to the meeting. Sunday at noon, over a pint, like friends.

'I need your help, or rather Lisa does,' Peter says.

'How is she?'

Peter scrapes his foot around the rim of a hole in the lino. 'Not too good,' he replies after a pause. 'I think Lisa told you that our Mum had cancer. She died. Now, Giles has...problems. I'm staying at Lisa's place.'

'With her and Giles?'

Peter looks into his Perrier. 'No.' Michael hears the ticking of the bar's coach clock in the ensuing silence. 'The thing is,' Peter resumes, 'she's undergoing a tax investigation. She didn't want to ask; she doesn't even know I'm meeting you.'

Michael smiles to encourage Peter to continue.

'It's not the only problem, but it would be best if Lisa's tax could be dealt with in one swoosh. Mr Templeton has told the Revenue, perhaps in a VAT return, that he paid her more than the £7,500 she actually was paid.'

Michael gulps a mouthful of lager before replying. 'He told me it was fifteen.'

'Lisa's certain it was seven and a half. It's not the sort of thing she'd forget.'

'I see,' Michael says.

'You do believe her, don't you?'

'Course,' Michael replies without any hesitation. Lisa wouldn't lie about something like that. 'I'll ask Jeremy Templeton to confirm it was £7,500.'

Michael offers his hand to add wordlessly, 'Consider it done.'

'Thanks,' Peter says. 'I'll give you a lift home if you want. Islington's pretty much on my way.'

The traffic lights turn amber and Peter brakes hard to stop. Michael is puzzled; most people would have driven straight through. Looking over his shoulder, Michael sees a police Panda pulling up behind them, but he still finds Peter's action strange. After all, Peter has only been drinking mineral water.

A Vespa scooter draws alongside. Glancing across at it, Peter stalls. With beads of perspiration forming on his brow, he turns the key and stamps his foot down on the accelerator.

'You'll flood the ignition,' Michael says.

Opening the passenger door, Michael gets out. He pushes against the front wing, rocking the car.

'You can't stop here!' a constable calls.

Waving an unwarranted thanks to the police, Michael jumps back in and the engine starts.

'The alternator was jammed,' Michael says as they draw away.

'You know about these things, don't you?'

It isn't so much what Peter says, it the way he says it that annoys Michael. He hears it as a clear accusation.

Michael replies in a calm voice, as if he is talking about the weather, 'That was a long time ago. I was ten years old when you crashed on your scooter. You still think I did it, don't you?'

'You've never said you didn't – all these years.'

Turning left, then right, Peter stops outside Michael's house.

'Do you want to come in?' Michael asks, making it clear with his tone that he has something to say.

Peter shakes his head. Michael stays in the passenger seat, rooted.

'In Cubs you not only watched while I was bullied and teased – you joined in. You even gave me that nickname I hated: "Crater". I don't know why you did it. You were seventeen; I was ten. Did you say sorry? No. You know why you want it to be me, rather than your teenage driving? Guilt.'

187

'Michael, can we end this?'

'No, you started it. You had a broken arm and a damaged scooter. Big deal. Was I sorry? No. Was I going to deny it? To you? So you'd start your own brand of bullying again? Anyway, you wouldn't have believed a denial. Not then. Not now. You think my parents would have let me get away without giving them an answer?'

'You never once told Lisa, "I didn't do it".'

'She never...' His voice fades. Aged ten, Michael wondered whether Lisa had cobweb doubts clinging in the corners of her mind. But she never asked, and he had treasured that trust in him. 'Does Lisa think I caused your accident?'

Cringing, Peter says, 'Of course not. Look, sorry, Michael. It was a long time ago. And I'm grateful that you are going to help Lisa out. Thanks. Oh, there's one thing I meant to warn you about: Giles is blaming you for him and Lisa splitting–'

'Kindred spirit? See a lot of him, do you?' Michael says. He gets out of the car and bangs the door closed.

That evening, cool against Michael's skin, the outside air blows in through the landing window Josie likes to keep half open. He gallops down the stairs with a huge white towel wrapped around his waist. Lolling on the settee, she waves her hands in the air to the music of the Electric Light Orchestra.

'They're in the bathtub again, Josie,' he says.

'What are, precious? Nasty spiders? Would you like Auntie Josie to come and wash them down the plughole?'

'Not spiders. Toenails. Your toenails.'

Josie giggles and runs off, up to the bathroom. She appears halfway down the stairs a few minutes later. Nude.

'Would the gentleman care to bathe now? His servant will wash him.'

Relieving the white tiling that covers the bathroom walls, a thin row of Villeroy & Boch tiles depict multicoloured fish swimming in crystal waters. Recently recoated, the enamel of the Victorian bathtub gleams. She kneels by the side of it, facing the brushed-nickel taps, gently pressing down onto Michael's scalp as she massages the conditioner in. Lounging in the suds, Michael laps up the pleasures of being pampered. Her fingers chase through his

188

hair. She cups water in her hands and pours it over his head. Clearing the strands at the front, she strokes his brow and touches his closed eyelids with her fingertips.

'I'm tired,' she purrs, sounding anything but. 'I think I'll go and have a rest.'

Lying back, he lets his head slip under the water to pretend that he will stay in the tub a while longer. But, as soon as she leaves the room, he comes to the surface with a rush of bubbles, steps out of the bath and pads himself dry.

A sword of light from a chink in the bedroom curtains cuts the room in two. Standing in the doorway, he smiles at Josie who is squatting on top of the duvet. He notices that, even in that posture, her stomach is taut.

'Hello,' she says, grinning pointedly at his erection.

He steps across the beam of light, glides onto the bed and draws his hand across her cheek.

'If you're tired, you'd better lie down,' he says.

She grins at him and, slowly, stretches her body out on the bed. Leaning down, he kisses her on the lips. They dwell over the kiss and he brings his body to lie on top of her. Coiling her calves around his thighs, she moves rhythmically under him. But he knows she isn't fully aroused, and he makes no attempt to enter her. Besides, out of the corner of his eye, he notices her fumble an arm towards the bedside table. They keep his condoms in the drawer. Michael finds latex sex a turn-off.

He kisses her earlobes, inches his torso down the duvet and moves his attentions to her neck, her shoulders and then her pert breasts. But his erection fades, as he feels no response from her. Instead, she is fiddling with a condom. Trying to remove the foil.

'No, don't,' he says. 'Just relax.'

Sliding further down the bed, he buries his head between her thighs. At first, she seems unmoved but he persists and, when she starts to sigh, he allows himself a private smile and feels his desire rise up again. Around them, feminine and masculine smells copulate. He can feel her body temperature rising as she grinds against his mouth. Gasping, she places both of her hands on top of his head and pushes down on it. He slips his forefinger into her and enjoys the sensation of her inner muscles contracting as she shudders to a climax.

Smiling, he climbs on top of her. Her mouth forms a frown, but her eyes grin at him. She unfolds her hand and holds the opened condom so he can see it. He doesn't take it from her.

'Michael,' she says in what he perceives as a soft rebuke.

He shifts as if to roll off her, but she pushes her pelvic region up and impales herself on him. Mesmerized, as one, they rock until he pulses deep within her.

Afterwards, with him still inside her, they rest together.

'I could go on the pill,' she says, touching his face.

'You don't want to though, do you?'

'Who says?' she replies. 'I'll tell you what I don't want. I don't want you to marry me just because we have an accident.'

'Eh?' Michael says.

'I can't wait for you to ask,' she says. 'Will you marry me, Michael?'

Chapter Twenty-Four

Jeremy Templeton doesn't question him about it, and Michael knows why not. It is neither the time nor the place. But Michael shouldn't be in the members-only toilet. Having never been challenged, he often uses it. The shoe cleaning machine saves him a job at home, and neither that nor the wooden clothes-brushes are available in the substitutes'. Besides, Michael hates the word; logically or not, he has never thought of himself as a substitute. And as he won't invest in Lloyd's, or pay an extra fee, that is how he is classified.

Judged by its mahogany toilet seats, chequered tiles, and the mosaic crest on the floor, the toilet harks back to the 1930s. But the long urinal with its knee-high glass splashback, and the beach-hut cubicles which stretch out towards the horizon of the far wall, are 1960s sanitary chic. The images are mixed, blurred; the surfaces are spotlessly clean.

At one of the middle washstands, in front of the mirror, Michael brushes his seemingly immaculate jacket, while at the next sink Templeton dabs his hands with a cotton towel. Templeton acknowledges Michael with a nod and moves away towards the washing bin to dispose of his used towel.

'Jeremy,' Michael says, stopping him in mid-step. 'Would you hang on a second? I've got those papers.'

Bending, Michael retrieves the slipcase lodged between his ankles. He opens the brass poppers and extracts a large Manila envelope which, with a knowing glance, he passes to Templeton.

'I didn't think you were–'

'We told promised Professor Dietrich that we'd...'

Michael leaves the sentence unfinished. He doesn't tell Templeton the main reason why he has suddenly cleared some space in his conscience. Michael agrees that two wrongs don't make a right.

191

But he accepts that, sometimes, one wrong and one right cancel each other out. And stopping the heavy-booted tax men from tramping on Lisa's flowers is right. Besides he has constructed the new deal with care; it won't prejudice his IV deals.

'I won't insult you by asking if this will now work. I'm grateful,' Templeton says, bestowing a rare smile on Michael. 'It was some time ago, but did Mac pass on my message?'

'What message was that?' Michael asks, hesitantly.

'I wanted you to know that I didn't ask for your dismissal.'

Michael hides his incredulity and for a few minutes they converse like distant cousins at a wedding. Or a funeral. Neither smile again.

Then, when Michael feels the time and, strangely, the place is right he says, 'Can I ask you a favour? You remember Lisa, the interior designer? Would you give her the short letter she has asked for?'

'Sorry,' Jeremy Templeton says, 'I can't do that.' He clasps the Manila envelope to his chest.

'I'm off to Paris tomorrow,' Michael replies.

'I don't see what that's got to do with anything,' Templeton snorts.

As he clings onto the rail of the elevator at Charles de Gaulle airport, the airline breakfast turns in Michael's stomach. The escalator has no steps, but travels upwards like a vast, silver conveyor-belt. It pulls at his calf muscles. Still tired from the early start, cramped flight and perilous taxi journey, Michael arrives at Tricolour's offices. Its severe, monolithic exterior belies its dramatic interior. Sunlit stainless steel girders criss-cross the ceiling and, creating an impression of movement, ocean-going yacht-sized sails jut out from the walls.

Clouds of smoke hide Monsieur Amiens when Michael is shown into his space-age office. A hand extends from the fog and squeezes Michael's in a vice-like grip. The urbane face of Amiens emerges. His nose is strong without being large; his hair is curly without being messy; his lips are full without being fat and a briar pipe protrudes from his mouth at a forty-five degree angle. He is the only Frenchman Michael has ever met who smokes a pipe.

As usual, they play linguistic charades; they speak in French until Michael's inattentive schoolboy grasp of the language is tested well past its limits. Shrugging his shoulders, in a way only the French can seem to manage, Amiens smiles. Michael grins back and Amiens switches to English, starting the conversation from scratch. His accent is heavy.

'Good to see you, Michael. You're a famous man here, in our offices. These IV treaties – we're very keen. And this Cutesie business is good. No?'

In front of him, covered with pencilled comments, the Frenchman has the typed details of the Cutesie deal. Michael has couriered the papers to him in advance.

'Your firm is eager too, eh. Your partner, Mac, called half an hour ago.'

'Really?' Michael replies.

'He wanted to be sure we had the presentation. I say to 'im yes and that it is – how do you say it – fulsome. He sounded surprised; he said you normally enter discussions with just one bit of paper. "Horses for courses," I told him.'

'Swill for swine, meat for lions,' Michael says. 'He doesn't know you well.'

'No kidding, he was really pushing – trying to sell the deal. Normally, I would reject an offer where the broker appears desperate. But it looks good, eh?'

'Well,' Michael says, 'I think it's worth a read. I'll ask Mac not to...'

'Thank you,' Amiens says. 'One thing intrigues me. On page one you state the client as being Cutesie's management, but on page eight...?'

'Cutesie haven't agreed my commission,' Michael replies.

'If we're the reinsurer, we pay your commission. I have no problem with it. Sure, it's two million. But the deal is big, eh? Why did you tell them what it was?'

'I know many brokers don't, but I always disclose commission,' Michael says. 'Yes, you pay us. But you take it away from the client. It comes out of their pockets.'

'But how does that affect who the client is – perhaps my English?'

'Your English is perfect. At the airport, I asked the taxi driver to bring me here. He did. So I paid him. I'm taking Cutesie's management along the route they've asked to travel. But if they won't pay the fare, I'll drop them in the middle of nowhere and find another customer. And complete the journey.'

Amiens sucks on his pipe, engulfs himself in fog and chortles, 'So if you make your client disappear in a cloud of smoke, exactly the same business remains.'

Six places at the elegant table mean four more handshakes from Tricolour executives. Each clasp is as fierce as Monsieur Amiens's. Michael wonders whether such handshakes form part of Tricolour's management training. Saying little over drinks before dinner, Amiens's underlings look at him for permission to speak even when asked direct questions by Michael. A waitress, dressed in a lace costume puffed out at the back by a bustle, uses silver tongs to serve Michael with crusty bread.

'I think you already know', Amiens says, 'that we are the reinsurer on the Templeton business on which you put together the mechanics. Monsieur Richards-Riley told me yesterday that you 'ave improved the scheme, but I don't understand why you aren't the broker.'

'I wouldn't want my firm's reputation smeared if there's a scandal.'

Keeping his own expression neutral, Michael watches Amiens's mannerisms carefully. But it isn't necessary, Amiens's shocked reaction is to speak in his native tongue. '*Oui, mais*, pardon.'

Amiens reverts to English, 'Monsieur Richards-Riley said you were very much in favour of the scheme – or perhaps implied. But he is a gentleman, no?'

Feigning incomprehension, Michael peers at Amiens.

'I felt a...personal obligation to assist Templeton,' Michael explains. 'But you should understand that Templeton isn't just rolling a bit of profit forward. It's more complicated than that. Templeton wants to hide losses. New investors joining Templeton's syndicate are picking up the cheque for the previous diners. If they understand the bill, they'll complain. A lot.'

A waiter enters, carrying a wine bottle with an odd tenderness as if it might detonate if dropped. He bows. Holding the bottle out in front of him, with one hand on the neck and the other supporting the base, he parades the label round the table. By historical accident, Tricolour own a vineyard. Deep lines crease Amiens's brow as the sommelier departs.

'Michael, I'm troubled by what you've said. However, although the contract documents aren't signed, we're already committed. And Monsieur Richards-Riley...' Amiens says, beginning a voluminous regurgitation of Wetthards' technical arguments.

Slivers of seafood mousse, surrounded by a sauce suspiciously close in taste to raspberry jam, are followed by maize-fed chicken. Doubting the chicken was fed much at all, Michael is still hungry at the end of the meal.

Finally, Michael coughs a polite request to interrupt Amiens. 'I think we all know, on reflection, that Richards-Riley's reasoning is gobbledegook.'

Amiens's colleagues look on like rabbits caught in headlights. They fiddle with buttons, pull ear lobes, and tap fingers on the tablecloth. Michael sips his wine.

'Anyway, why is this with Tricolour?' Michael asks. 'Why isn't it arranged with DBL Bermuda?'

'Most of it goes from us to DBL Bermuda. We channel it through.'

'Like a sewage pipe,' Michael mutters. 'Oh, really,' he says, more audibly.

Monsieur Amiens wipes at the corners of his mouth with a serviette, turns to the other executives at the table, and says, 'We must review our position.'

Having flown straight back from Paris the previous evening, Michael is somewhere between exhausted and asleep when he comes out of Moorgate station at 8 a.m. To rid himself of the bitter taste in his mouth, he stops off at the tobacconist's to his left. When he emerges, sucking on a Trebor mint, he feels his shirt collar tighten inexplicably and looks around.

The road is choc-a-block with traffic. Motorbike couriers, immune to injury according to their driving, hurtle through the narrow central gap. A pair of pigeons nibble at a discarded bun by the cashpoint. Michael stops; he sees Richards-Riley and Templeton, on the opposite side of the road, scowling at him.

A man with black teeth and pitted skin clutches Michael's sleeve.

'Give us twenty quid, guv,' the man threatens. 'It's nothing to you.'

Michael stares across the road then turns to the tramp whose dirty fingernails claw at his suit.

'Twenty pounds?' Michael asks. 'Not spare us some change? Uh...?'

Although Michael smells the halitosis and sees the venom in the reply, he can't hear the words. He tries to fend the man off, but the beggar yanks further on Michael's jacket and reaches into the inside pocket where his wallet is. The tramp's filth-ridden hair presses into Michael's face.

Michael feels his chin jut forward, but he fights back his rising anger. Using no more force than necessary, he grasps the man's wrist and twists it until he feels the weight of his wallet return to his suit jacket. Tightening his lock on the man's hand, he pulls it out of his suit.

'Who sent you?' Michael demands.

A glob of saliva shoots past Michael's ear as the tramp rants incoherent abuse instead of answering. The man tries to flee, but Michael holds firm and they heave, like one man tug-of-war teams, in opposite directions.

Losing, the tramp crashes into Michael. An insect jumps from the man's donkey jacket into Michael's eye. Michael staggers backwards and free-falls, into the road, in between two cars frozen by the congestion. Looking up, he sees the tramp running away and Templeton still scowling. But Richards-Riley is brandishing a huge golden glint. Smiling right into him. Michael struggles to his feet, pats the grit off his trousers and stares across the road again. Templeton and Richards-Riley have gone.

Michael throws open Mac's office door. The shirt inside it swings like a hanging man, and Mac's Pirelli calendar falls off the wall.

'Templeton and Richards-Riley just set some hobo on me,' Michael says stridently. 'They were both there, watching from the other side of the road, outside Moorgate station. What were they doing there? I don't believe in coincidences.'

'It's not a coincidence,' Mac says. He stands up and paces furious circles around the room. 'They must have been on their way here; they're waiting downstairs in reception. I just got the call. They were due here at 8.15. They're early. You're early too; you're not supposed to be here yet.'

'What on earth?'

'I'm surprised you didn't run into them. You've gotta get out of here, otherwise they really will lay into you.'

'I'm not afraid of them,' Michael says.

'Well, I'll be scared for both of us, then. And our firm. Let me handle this. You came up the back way, right? Go back down it. Quick, I'll explain later.'

Richards-Riley and Templeton won't accept the seats Mac offers them and remain erect, predatory.

Mac leans back in his chair. 'I do like spring mornings.'

'We just saw Darrett brawling in the street,' Richards-Riley says. 'Is he here?'

'Are you sure it was Michael?' Mac asks, disingenuously. 'If he saw you,' Mac adds in a voice that almost slides out, 'then he might think you paid someone to attack him.'

'Perhaps we did,' Richards-Riley booms. Templeton looks aghast. 'Don't disillusion him,' Richards-Riley continues in a lower voice. 'There's plenty of homeless looking for handouts. God knows, he deserves a good thrashing. It's a disgrace. Darrett told Tricolour – over a glass of their frightful wine, no doubt – that Jeremy's business is detrimental to the interests of Lloyd's. How pompous – from that little upstart. The deal was pretty much done and dusted; now Tricolour have withdrawn their support. Darrett's birth was anal.'

Templeton says nothing. He doesn't have to, his flaring nostrils speak for him.

Waiting for the next verbal baton charge, Mac rises, strolls across the room, picks up his calendar, replaces it on the wall and returns to slouch back into his chair.

'That's better,' Mac says.

Richards-Riley folds his arms across his chest. 'Try to see things from our viewpoint. DBL Bermuda will move into pole position; we can do without Tricolour. But Michael mustn't cause any more

197

aggravation. You've got the papers on the Anstaldt. However, we haven't paid in the £25,000 yet. If Michael bites our hands, you get no food.'

'We all eat from the same bowl,' Mac says, summoning a contained smile. 'It's your fault. You told Amiens about Michael's involvement, and Amiens asked him about it. Well he would, wouldn't he? I know it's easy to be wise after the event, but this reminds me of those American mobile-home owners you see each time there's a bit of wind, standing there dumb as tent posts. "Oh, yes, Mister," they say into the cameras. "That's the third time we've seen our lives blown away in five years." Why don't they move? And why don't you', he lashes out with a laugh, 'be more careful in future?'

When Melissa enters with coffee, Mac's visitors become genial and take their seats. Mac sees Templeton try to draw a smile from her. He fails.

'The best way to attract a woman is to open your wallet and think of England,' Mac observes once Melissa has gone.

'Where do people like you and Darrett come from?' Richards-Riley snaps. 'Are the papers Michael's prepared sound?'

'Yes,' Mac replies, shrugging. 'Oddly enough, he was proud of the work. Even more strange was the fact that he changed his mind about doing it over just one weekend. I didn't have to push him. He pretty much volunteered to do it.'

'So why did he torpedo our deal with Tricolour?' Richards-Riley asks.

'It makes no sense,' Mac agrees, looking straight at Templeton.

Seeming to Mac to be somehow guilty, retaining his right of silence, Templeton drinks his coffee.

'I'll give this Judas his coins', Richards-Riley hisses to Templeton as they leave, 'and nail Darrett up.'

Mac overhears the comment and winces.

On Friday of the same week, Michael and Mac sit together at an empty box waiting to bend the ear of an underwriter across the aisle. A wisp of cigarette smoke blows in front of Michael's face; the plumes around the room mean it is 4.30 p.m. Michael doesn't need to look at his watch. In nicotine-deprived unison, smokers ferret in their pockets. The activity of the room slows as the ground-floor doors swing their well-heeled cargo out towards the wine bars.

'Just stop it,' Mac says. 'Firstly, the only reason I phoned Amiens was to help. It's preposterous to even think I tried to screw up your meeting. Secondly, it's absurd for you to believe that Richards-Riley or Templeton set someone on you. They wouldn't even speak to someone so careless as to get himself homeless. And lastly, if you'd been there, when they came into the office, the cleaners would still be trying to get the bloodstains out of the carpet.'

Michael persists, 'I'm just saying–'

'Cancer stick?' a broker interrupts, offering Mac a No. 6 and sitting down opposite them.

'No thanks, Trev,' Mac replies, lighting a Marlboro.

'Too late to run away?' Michael says to Mac.

Trev, aka Slimeball, produces a slimy smile and slides a hand through his hair which has benefited from a bountiful dollop of Brylcreem.

'Heard a good one yesterday,' Slimeball says. 'What did the backward dyslexic say to his mother when he took his first step? Look, Mum, I can wank.'

Slimeball laughs raucously at his own joke.

'You're sick,' Michael says.

'I've got a funnier one,' Slimeball rasps. 'You've lost the Cutesie account.'

Mac gives Michael a look of critical dismay, a look which Michael endures in silence. Standing up, Mac clenches his fists and grinds his heel into the soft leather of Slimeball's shoe.

'If you repeat that bit of malicious gossip, I'll hire someone to break your legs.'

'So it's true then,' Slimeball says, recovering his foot.

'Bugger off,' Mac spits.

'Once the rumour's reached that far down the food chain,' Mac states once Slimeball has limped away, 'we've no chance of damping it down. Fuck it, our chances of winning new biz are reduced. Wetthards must've leaked it, and we both know why: your tête-à-tête with Amiens.'

'In a couple of weeks the market would've known in any case. Cutesie's annual negotiation is overdue, and we aren't out there banging the drum.'

'The news needn't be out yet. It's your fault,' Mac accuses.

Michael smiles winningly. 'Does it really matter?'

Mac frowns. 'S'pose not. Slimeball really winds me up.'

'Wetthards! It's tit for tat. Time for another tat.'

The balding underwriter they have been waiting for finishes underwriting and rises, ready to leave. Michael and Mac stroll across, cutting off his line of escape.

'Not the two of you together,' the underwriter complains, sitting back down. 'Can't it wait until Monday? Don't you have anything to do this weekend?'

'Won't take long,' Michael soothes.

'My dentist always tells me it won't hurt,' the underwriter retorts.

Michael and Mac share a smile and begin their double act.

All day Saturday, Josie and Michael romp through the verdant countryside of the Cotswolds. Bathed in the rays of the May sun, each village is more breathtaking than the last. Michael drives while Josie looks out the window at the thatched roofs, peeping flowers and manicured lawns. The Alfa Romeo purrs into Chipping High Street, and Michael parks outside the market square.

'Chipping Camden's my favourite village,' Josie says, stepping out of the car.

'You've never been here before,' he laughs.

'I know what I know,' she giggles.

And she does. The gentle giggle hides strong emotion. And she is a strong girl. Strong enough to insist that he waited until tonight to give her a considered answer. Boys can be so blind. He hasn't noticed her 'it doesn't matter anymore' attitude to contraception, or heard her being ill in the morning. She is strong enough bring up their baby on her own. She is so strong she could cry.

Holding hands, they amble along the gentle curves of the seventeenth-century street. Little has changed here in the last three hundred years. They stop by a crooked window that probably wasn't a rectangle when the first lime bedded the craggy bricks around it. Pitted but smooth, the glass is of different thicknesses within the same pane. Each pane bows so that, looking into the shop, the view is distorted. And the distortion itself is beauty. Josie squeezes Michael's hand. The suspense is agony.

'You haven't answered my question, Michael.'

'Yes, we can go to the embroidery shop,' Michael says. His face is straight, but his eyes are alight. 'I'm told it's excellent. I didn't know you were interested.'

She smiles back, as best she can.

'You okay?' he says. 'We did say tonight. But if you–'

'No, it's fine.'

Later, behind the imposing doors of the Cotswold House Hotel, the cosy restaurant is busy and the manager takes them to the table at the far end where, with a nifty bit of sleight of hand – not lost on Michael – the manager removes the 'Reserved' sign. The table overlooks the twilit garden where a stone path vanishes into a tunnel of topiary. To Michael, it looks like the start of a maze. The tables, covered with apricot cloths, decorated by vases of country flowers, are several feet apart.

Inside his trouser pocket, Michael feels the contours of the ring box that he has kept for ten years. There was just one occasion, shortly after Lisa's marriage, when he was tempted to part with it. He had dangled the box over a storm drain. But he couldn't let go.

'I have,' they both start to say at the same time.

Josie draws a breath. 'You first,' she says.

'You asked me to marry you.'

The black pupils of Josie's eyes hide all but the merest fraction of the irises' green colour. Her lips are slightly parted, expectant. She appears more attractive to Michael than ever. He pulls out the velvet box.

'My answer is yes. Yes, please,' he says.

Opening the box, he reaches across the table and kisses her, tenderly, on the cheek. He places the ring in her hand. Three small diamonds, encased in white gold, glisten in the candlelight. Putting it on, she leaps up and hugs him. He gazes at her, sees only her, but he can sense the other diners are watching. Sitting back down, Josie stares at her newly decorated finger.

'That's not your engagement ring,' Michael says. Josie's brow furrows. 'I want us to choose that together,' Michael explains. 'I thought we might go down to Brighton. There's a little area there, The Lanes – lots of cobbles, coffee shops and jewellers. It'll be romantic.'

'Yes, that would be...fantastic.'

'I love you,' Michael says.

Tears stream down Josie's face. An approaching waiter turns back.

'Oh, Michael! I've waited such a long time to hear that. I know it's obvious that you love me; it's been clear for months. Why couldn't you say it before? Now you've said it, I want you to keep on saying it. Every day. Again and again.'

'I will,' Michael coos.

'Is this the ring you wanted to give Lisa?'

'Are you offended?'

'Offended? No, not really. I want us to go and pick out a ring together. And I know why you gave me this one, Michael. It comes from your heart, not your bank account. It tells me what I wanted to hear: you've made a clear decision.'

'I have; I love you.'

'But I don't want Lisa's ring, sorry.' She takes it off and passes it to him. 'I want you to throw it away.'

'Okay, I will,' he says, palpably hurt.

'You don't understand women very well, do you?' she asks, softly.

'Guess not,' he replies, recovering his smile.

The waiter returns, bowing slightly. 'May I offer you an aperitif?'

'Would it be possible', Michael asks, 'to have a couple of Kir Royales?'

'Certainly, sir,' the waiter confirms, jotting down the order.

'What's that?' Josie asks Michael once the waiter has gone.

'Champagne and crème de cassis – that's a blackcurrant liqueur.'

'I shouldn't be drinking much,' Josie says. She twiddles her fingers.

Michael peers at her. 'You are upset about the ring, aren't you. I only...'

'No,' Josie says. 'No, really. I'm not. I have another question to ask you. Do you want to stay in Islington...after we have children?'

'Er...That's the sort of thing', Michael says, gently, 'we'd– we'd discuss when–'

'We have talked about children. You do want them, don't you?'

'Well, yes. But...'

'Michael, I'm pregnant.'

Chapter Twenty-Five

The standing lamps over Jeremy Templeton's cubed table seem to Michael like the smaller white sisters of Belisha beacons. They shine down on the Reuters reports that he skims through whilst waiting for Templeton to finish his phone call. An obscure Welsh politician with a penchant for posturing, Neil Kinnock, has been named as shadow education spokesman. And, inside Vienna's magnificent Hofburg Palace, US President Jimmy Carter and ailing Russian leader Leonid Brezhnez have signed the SALT-2 arms limitation treaty. 'A victory in the battle for peace,' Jimmy Carter trumpets. Michael is uninspired but, for Lisa's sake, he tries nonetheless to end hostilities.

Tersely, Templeton terminates his telephone conversation.

'No further interruptions, please,' Templeton commands his secretary. He turns to Michael. 'I'm pleased you accept that I had nothing to do with that attack on you,' Templeton says, in a conciliatory tone. 'I think it was just one of those things...'

Michael examines Templeton's interlaced fingers.

'You say Cedric Richards-Riley was there before you,' Michael probes, 'and that you'd just joined him when I came out of the tobacconist's.'

'Really, Michael. Please. I can't imagine that Cedric...let's move on. I'm sorry Wetthards leaked the news of the Cutesie business into the market. Still, no real harm was done. And I've already forgotten what you did to us with Tricolour. You're quite right: we should put all this behind us.' Templeton manages a smile. 'I appreciate the business you showed me today. Some of it was... rather good.'

To Michael's despair, Templeton begins a long speech on the nature of relations between underwriters and brokers. As it continues, Michael scans the office looking for something, anything, of interest. Apart from the lamps, the office is Spartan. Perhaps, Michael muses, once upon a time, there were plants. Until Templeton talked to them. Finally, Templeton ends his monologue.

Michael resists the urge to pat the inside pocket of his jacket in which, as insurance against Templeton refusing his request, a copy of the Christmas list nestles.

'I'd like your advice, Jeremy,' Michael says. 'If business goes well, then I'll be looking to make an investment. Is property a good idea at the moment?'

'Oh, that's it. You're here about that damn girl, aren't you? Look, I paid her £15,000. If she says any different, then she's a liar.'

'You told me you paid Lisa fifteen thousand, and I'm not questioning that,' Michael soothes. 'Trouble is, she's told the Revenue it was seven and a half. Obviously there's a mix-up.'

'There's no mix-up.'

'It would be of great assistance if you could provide her with a short letter to say that you paid her £7,500,' Michael says.

His negotiator's face reveals not a trace of emotion.

'Sorry, Michael.' Templeton gestures towards the door.

Michael glances at the Robert Carrier recipe and crumbles the hard-boiled egg yolk on top of the spinach soup. The book is new; Josie has given it to him as an engagement present, or a heavy hint. Still, he likes cooking and there is nothing on the box that Wednesday. Recipe-free cuisine is more fun for Michael, except when it comes to actually eating the food. Josie has told him she thinks concoctions like Spam curry form part of a deliberate ploy to ensure he stays free of culinary chores and that, yes, she would like him to cook at least once a week.

Turning off the main light, he takes the soup through to the main room.

'Da...na,' he announces.

'Food,' she exclaims.

He places the bowls down, kisses her cheek, and lights the candelabrum. It is far too large for the table. She laughs.

'Delicious,' she says after the first spoonful. 'By the way, I haven't told Mac that he's going to be an uncle. It would be nice if you told him, don't you think?'

'Sure. Guess what? I've made fruit fiesta for the main course.'

Michael sees her face pale and her body tense.

'No, it's nice,' he says, astounded.

'Look,' she yells, pointing at the window that faces directly onto the street.

Michael can't see much of the face that is pressed against it, but the man's eyes brim with undiluted hatred.

Michael flies out of his seat, opens the front door, races out into the mews, hurtles around the corner and stops. The street is empty. His footsteps echo as he walks this way and that, checking between parked cars and peering into dark corners.

'No sign?' Josie asks on his return. Michael shakes his head. 'I can't be sure,' Josie continues, 'but that frizzy hair – those sort of bulging eyes. Yesterday, just before you got back, a man knocked on the door.'

'You didn't tell me,' Michael says, sitting back down.

'Well, he just stood there – really angry looking – but he didn't do anything. He asked me, "Who are you?" As if he lived here. I shut the door; he went away. I thought he'd just come out the pub...'

'What, was he drunk?'

'Not really drunk. He'd been drinking, though.'

'I don't know who it was,' Michael says. 'But I'm not putting up with it.'

The next morning, Michael takes the train, in the opposite direction to usual, out to the suburbs. From Enfield Chase station, he walks down Windmill Hill, crosses by the church and gazes at the picturesque canal. The eighteenth-century cottages in Gentleman's Row provide a welcome contrast to the pigeons and pasta palaces which give the town a gritty, urban feel. Summer drizzle drifts into his face as he waits at a cluster of pedestrian lights.

Just before Enfield's other station, Enfield Town, he goes into the little shop packed with military memorabilia. Flags, uniforms and medals adorn the walls. He smiles when he finds what he is seeking: a First World War bayonet. Declining the vendor's persistent offers to wrap the weapon, he puts it in his briefcase.

He takes the overground to Liverpool Street, rings Richards-Riley's office and, discovering he is out of the office, strolls to

205

Wetthards' offices. The commissionaire doesn't challenge him, and he zigzags through a series of back stairs to the fire door just outside Richards-Riley's office. It feels odd in his ex-employer's offices, but Michael's heartbeat is normal. He remembers what his mother used to say to him about spiders when he was small. 'They're more afraid of you than you are of them.'

He knows Wetthards' offices. The toilets, photocopier and stationery supplies must have been positioned by someone who thought the staff should get some exercise whilst at work. Patiently, he peeks through the little window at the secretary. After a few minutes, she pulls her cardigan together and traipses off.

Michael enters Richards-Riley's office and, without turning on the lights, closes the door behind him. Wandering over to the desk, he opens Richards-Riley's diary. There is a nine o'clock meeting, at a client's office nearby, inked in. It is half past ten; Michael knows Richards-Riley will be back soon. Moving Richards-Riley's cracked-leather armchair so that it faces the credenza, he switches on the picture light. It highlights the bloody First World War scene of the murder of a wounded German prisoner and gives Michael enough light to work by. The click-clack of the secretary's typing resumes.

At the back of the credenza is a neat row of books. Michael hauls three blue annuals forward, thumbs to the pages that the investors in Templeton's syndicate are listed, and draws the Christmas card list out of his jacket. He hums, very quietly, whilst cross-referencing the two lists. The annotated address list will allow him to contact Templeton's Names.

Finishing, he places the tomes back, turns the chair round and scrutinises the picture on Richards-Riley's desktop. A woman in tweed with crow's feet and expensive teeth is wrapped around a younger version of herself. Michael presumes they are Richards-Riley's wife and daughter. He leafs through Richards-Riley's diary, jots down Richards-Riley's home address and peruses the 'contacts' section. Only one entry has no surname by it: Cecilia. She must be the daughter. Cecilia lives in Oxford.

When he hears Richards-Riley's voice, Michael moves to a visitor's chair and takes the bayonet out of his briefcase. The door yawns; the lights flick on. He toys the weapon around in his hand, holding it by the blade. It isn't sharp; he doesn't cut himself.

'What the...!' Richards-Riley hisses.

'Close the door,' Michael orders icily.

Richards-Riley hesitates; Michael rises, walks over and slams the door.

'Darre– Michael, have you gone insane? How did you get in? Are–'

'I've got a present. Just for you.'

Michael leans forward and pokes the bayonet handle at Richards-Riley who, seizing it, flings it onto the carpet by Michael's feet.

'My secretary will have called security–'

'If you want me to explain why I'm here to anyone else, I'll do so. Loud and clear. I think you'll want this meeting to remain private.'

Richards-Riley sits down in his armchair and exhales deeply. Michael points to the back of Richards-Riley's family photo.

'I never knew you had a daughter,' Michael says. 'Nice place, Oxford. I was planning on going there with my fiancée. But she's a bit jittery at the moment. It can be like that with girls, can't it? If they get frightened.'

Richards-Riley flushes. 'You steal into my office brandishing a weapon, and then you threaten my daughter.'

'There are no circumstances in which I'd hurt Cecilia.' Michael pauses. 'But someone's trying to scare Josie. The day before yesterday they came to my home. My home! Yesterday evening they did it again. Last week, I was attacked. You stood there and watched. You smiled.'

'Look, I–' The telephone rings. Richards-Riley snatches it up. 'No, everything's fine. Just ask the security people to wait outside.'

'Michael,' Richards-Riley continues, putting down the phone. 'I know nothing about anyone coming to your house. Goodness me, man. That thing with the vagabond was...'

'Was what?' Michael asks.

'Unfortunate. I shouldn't have smiled, but I didn't ask him to attack you.'

'You spoke to him, though. What did you say to him?'

'He was pestering me; you can't expect me to divulge more than that. But these other goings-on – I'm at a real loss.'

'If I find out any different, I'll visit your home. Presuming that won't be necessary, I'll accept a small token of atonement from Templeton.'

207

'Jeremy wasn't–'

'I want Jeremy Templeton to provide my friend with the letter she needs.' Richards-Riley looks nonplussed. 'He'll know all about it,' Michael adds, rising.

'I'll speak to Jeremy, but I can't force him.' Richards-Riley jabs his index finger towards the bayonet. 'What is that, some sort of symbolic warning?'

Smiling, Michael picks it off the floor and hands it over to Richards-Riley.

'It's a paperweight,' Michael says.

The following day Richards-Riley repeats Templeton's refusal to supply the letter, stoking Michael's growing anger. Rather than blow off steam in senseless telephone tetchiness, Michael arranges to meet an old school friend. Michael wants privacy for the meeting. It doesn't matter if they are seen – Lloyd's people won't recognise the editor of *The Protester* – as long as they aren't overheard.

Hidden in the backstreets off Cornhill, five minutes from Lloyd's, the George & Vulture is perfect. It teems with dealers and wheelers who sit in rows on wooden benches from centuries past. The smells are mixed: bubble and squeak, chunks of steak on the griddle, beer and scrubbed floorboards. Michael and Patrick share a table for four with two young brokers whose voices are drowned by a hundred resonant others. There is privacy in the noise. They order red wine and mixed grills from the waitress with stout legs who waddles from one table to another memorising orders.

'Been to any good stranglings lately?' Patrick asks.

'Not this month – not a broken bottle in sight.'

Looking at one another, face to face, they jabber, interrupt, joke and poke fun. Schoolboys again. Their red wine conversation twists down narrow valleys and up onto golden peaks before Patrick asks for the destination.

'...but you must want something, Michael; you always have a purpose.'

Guarding his words, Michael tells him a watered-down account of the Templeton business and of Wetthards' involvement. Michael is a bystander in this version; he plays no role in the design.

Patrick tilts his head. 'Is that it? There are four hundred Lloyd's syndicates.'

'Four hundred and four, actually,' Michael teases.

'Whatever, it's not news that one of them manipulates its results a bit. Every public company paints its financial statements to present the picture it wants seen.'

Catching the waitress's eye, Michael points to their empty wine bottle and mouths a thank-you as she acknowledges his order.

'It would certainly be news to Names who were on Templeton's syndicate last year. Most of them wouldn't mind a loss. With a decent accountant they could recoup it all – every single penny – from the Revenue.'

'You sure?' asks Patrick.

'Yeah. In fact, due to a quirk in our toytown tax system, some Names would get a 102p rebate for each £1 of loss. And the others would just take the loss on the chin. But all of them would want to know what had happened. All of them would *need* to know that.'

'Why?' Patrick asks.

'Why! You're asking me why?' Michael takes the bottle of red from the waitress with a smile of thanks. 'If anything goes wrong. Templeton will leave his investors in limbo. The tail of liability could take decades to sort out. This could ruin his Names. Utmost good faith, pah.'

'No investor's lost money yet; I still don't think it's newsworthy. This might happen – that could occur. It's airy. Besides which, to print the story would suggest that Lloyd's is plagued by dishonesty.'

'I'm not saying that, but I'll give you a quote if you like.'

In readiness, Patrick pulls out his notepad.

'I thought reporters used Dictaphones these days,' Michael says.

'Background noise would be too– Anyway, that quote?'

'One Lloyd's underwriter has spread uneven results to mitigate the unfair tax burden that would otherwise fall on the investors,' Michael says. 'The Lloyd's establishment isn't aware of this, nor would they have any reason–'

'Stop it,' Patrick says putting his pad away. 'Tell you what, if I can get a defensive reaction from the Chairman of Lloyd's, I've got something. I can see the column headline: "Lloyd's Denies False Accounting".'

Michael flinches; he wants a delayed action fuse not a suicidal, kamikaze leak. 'In order to be fair, why don't you phone around first? Speak to Templeton and Richards-Riley if you want. Ask them how they'd feel if you discussed this with Lloyd's elder statesmen.'

'You're using me, Michael. I have got a job to do. You're giving me half a ball; it won't bounce. I'll only make the calls if I can use your name. And, I must warn you, the wasps will fly at the stick in their nest.'

Michael smiles a deep, contented smile.

That afternoon, while Michael works undisturbed in the paper factory, the wasps fly. They leave their first stings on Post-It notes around the telephone in his office. When he emerges from the conference room just after five, he peers at the messages and blows air through his teeth in a silent whistle.

'Isn't it wonderful to be so wanted,' he says out loud, to himself. 'It warms my heart – all the love and care the market provides – a harvest festival of goodwill.'

But the call from Diddy is unexpected.

While Michael waits to be connected, he looks at the two photographs that sit on his desktop. Lisa and Josie. He reaches out, removes Lisa's photo and puts it in a drawer. It is the one of her in her wedding dress. The one, he thinks, that should never have been there in the first place.

'Thanks for returning my call,' Diddy says. 'I have a problem. Last week my deputy made a mistake: he underwrote a piece of Algerian earthquake business. I've told all of my investors that we don't accept quake. I asked your broker to allow us to retract our agreement, but he tells me it's not possible. Please, Michael. If I have to go back to my Names, it won't look very professional.'

While Diddy appeals for clemency, Michael holds his mouth over the speaker and hails his secretary. She fetches the broker who trundles in with his slipcase; Michael claws at its contents, trawls the slip from its folder and spreads it out.

'Diddy, I have the business in front of me. I'll ask our broker to let you off. I'd like to show a bit of goodwill.' Michael presses his tongue against the inside of his mouth. 'You're part of Wetthards.'

'Thank you. Mind you, you're going to need all the friends you can get. Heavy-duty people want to get their pliers on your

210

toenails. Richards-Riley's called an emergency board meeting about your bringing the press in to win an argument against Templeton. Something about a friend of yours – a young lady? Lisa?'

'Um. There's been a bit of a misunderstanding. Lisa's an interior designer. It's about a single invoice. Templeton says he paid her £15,000; she says it was £7,500. The tax people are giving her grief. She needs a letter. I did ask him pretty please nicely.'

'If Templeton's told you he's paid her £15,000 then he did,' Diddy says.

'I'm not part of the Spanish Inquisition; I'm not saying he didn't,' Michael says, dwelling on the word 'saying' long enough to make his meaning clear. 'Look, I've known Lisa since primary school. She wouldn't lie about this. And you know how I feel about Templeton's reinsurances.'

'Everyone who knows of them does.'

'Are they honest? Do you approve?' Michael asks. 'Come on, you'd rather run naked across Lord's cricket pitch than fix up an oddball deal like Templeton's for your own syndicate. Do you really feel that Templeton is still as straight as a die, or does he give the truth a coat of paint once in a while?'

'No comment,' Diddy comments.

'I haven't given the journalist enough information for him to run with the story. But I want the invoice, and I did lay down business sacrifices before asking Templeton. Real jam. And as for Richards-Riley, if you only knew– In any case, Lisa's a friend and she needs my assistance.'

'What a gallant hero. I hope you're wearing your armour,' Diddy says. He pauses before adding, 'Thanks again for your help.'

Chairing the meeting, Richards-Riley surveys the boardroom and decides, patriarchally, that it is in dire need of refurbishment. The blind that shields the room from the main office looks like the shower curtain in Hitchcock's *Frenzy*. With its clerks' chairs and carpet tiles, the room is far from an advertisement for Wetthards. Nor is the disunity of the discussion.

'Michael's actions seem reasonable to me,' Diddy says. 'I get the impression that he feels entitled to payback. Have you done him some new wrong?'

211

Richards-Riley rues the day he promoted Michael and, even more, the day he banished him. Looking at Diddy he remembers: Diddy warned him that Michael Darrett would neither forgive nor forget. But that was after the deed. Richards-Riley ignores the question and raises his eyes to the stark ceiling.

'Darrett's got some silly notion in his head that we had him attacked,' Templeton replies on behalf of Richards-Riley. 'It's nonsense, claptrap. Just an excuse for his own dreadful behaviour. This is blackmail.'

'Not blackmail. Bribery, Jeremy,' Diddy says, drumming his manicured fingers on the table and opening an A4 Black & Red notebook. 'Michael brought you jam, and you took it. He thinks you paid this young lady £7,500. If so, give her the letter. If not, don't. I'm not suggesting that you do anything improper.'

'Neither am I,' Richards-Riley says. 'But I don't see why you won't give Darrett this letter. After all, you did pay her £7,500. Twice. Give her two letters if it makes you feel any happier.'

'I paid that woman £15,000 and that's that,' Templeton says. 'If I now say I paid only £7,500, I'll have to pay tax on the difference. I'll only be able to claim £7,500 as an expense.'

'Why would an interior decorator be tax deductible?' Diddy asks.

'My Mayfair property is a business proposition,' Templeton explains.

'You have a conflict of interest, Jeremy,' Richards-Riley snorts, 'which interferes with your role as underwriter for the syndicate. Your personal tax affairs are nothing to do with our business.'

'How can you possibly take Darrett's side?' Templeton asks.

'This has got to end,' Richards-Riley says. 'Give her the letter, Jeremy.'

'I feel most uncomfortable,' Diddy protests, banging his notebook shut. 'A business deal all wrapped up in silence? An allegation of assault? A colleague into property development? And now, albeit under protest, you're going to provide a false invoice? I want the minutes of this meeting to record–'

'This meeting has never happened,' Richards-Riley interrupts. 'There'll be no minutes. Thank you for coming.'

Diddy rises; Richards-Riley and Templeton remain seated.

'This is unreal,' Diddy says as he reaches the door. 'I see you intend to carry on without me. I do trust that nothing – I repeat nothing – you're doing will undermine the repute of Lloyd's.'

Templeton looks askance, Richards-Riley offers up appropriate astonished assurances and Diddy departs.

'MacIntyre's supposed to keep Darrett in order, but he hasn't,' Richards-Riley says to Templeton. 'We'll deduct £4,000 from what we're paying him. That'll be most of your tax. You're in for the rest. Get the letter to her, quickly.'

Templeton pulls himself to his feet. 'If Diddy knew we were paying Mac to babysit Michael, he'd–'

'Well, he doesn't know,' Richards-Riley says. 'And neither you nor I are going to tell him, are we?'

There are just the two of them left in the office. It is so late that even the vacuum cleaners have gone to sleep, so quiet that Michael can hear Mac's telephone call.

'No way,' Mac says, raising his voice. 'He did what?'

'You're charging me £4,000 because of that!' Mac shouts, before slamming the phone down.

'Problem?' Michael calls out.

'Just the builders,' Mac grates.

'Enough fun for one day?' Michael asks, packing up his brief-case. 'Coming?'

In the elevator, as they travel down, Mac stands close to Michael. Mac's fists are clenched and his face is two inches from Michael's. Michael examines Mac until he backs away.

'I don't know why you're teed off with me,' Michael says as the lift doors lurch open. 'They're your builders. Cheer up. I've got some good news...Uncle.'

'Uncle?' Mac asks as they step into the foyer.

Disarming Mac with his smile, Michael nods. Mac stops and turns to face Michael, bringing him to a halt too. And, for the first time ever, Michael sees Mac's eyes fill.

'As prospective brothers-in-law go, you aren't too appalling. Say hi to Josie from me, will you?'

'I thought you'd be pleased,' Michael says. 'While I think of it, I'm seeing Samson Cantwell tomorrow – you know, Home & Life. I'll arrange a dinner, with him and his wife, at the Ritz. Can you and Megan make the 20th of July?'

'I think so,' Mac says, warmly.

Mac follows Michael, through the revolving doors, out into the street. As they walk past the sandstone buildings and into Finsbury Circus a bird dropping grazes Michael's sleeve.

'Can't let the birds...walk all over you,' Mac laughs. 'Oh, are you bringing that flatmate of yours to the Ritz?'

'Yes. And I'll tell her you called her that. Her stomach is still flat.'

'Ho ho,' Mac says, deadpan.

Shortly after eleven, when she hears Mac's key in the lock, Megan turns off her bedside light and pretends to be asleep. A dull thud and a muttered curse tell her that he has bumped into one of the 'tank traps' – builders' toolboxes that litter the battleground house. Breathing deeply, she reflects on her right to be tired.

The builders call her 'luv' and leer at her when they think she isn't looking. Even their leching is better than their sullen lack of thanks for teas, patronising 'you're a woman' explanations of their cowboy practices, and puerile attempts to rip her off. They wanted £300 to secure the banister on the landing, but she has foxed them. A two-inch bracket and a little fresh plaster got that job done for £30.

She isn't surprised that Mac is late, rather at how early he is; his nocturnal meetings and business dinners often go on past midnight. Sometimes she wakes up and talks with him over a glass of wine. If he welcomed her doing so, she would do this every time. But often, when he is late, he pushes her away with the rough fingers of offhand words. So, when he comes into the bedroom and dumps his clothes by the side of the bed, she just mumbles a sleepy goodnight.

Megan wakes when Mac does but, like the night before, feigns sleep. Listening to him enter the walk-in wardrobe and plod out of the bedroom, she continues her dead-lions game. She considers getting up to make his breakfast, but some of his early morning moods are like wet days at the seaside.

When the front door slams, just after seven, she knows that she has an hour before the builders descend to inflict another day of constant banging and banal radio stations. In and out of the bathroom inside fifteen minutes, she dresses quickly in the most unattractive clothes she can find. Rushing around the house, she puts masking tape around the internal doors to try and contain the ever-present dust. But at eight-thirty the telephone rings, and she knows before she picks it up that it will be the builders. At least once a week they moonlight off to even better-paid botching, giving her an excuse that would insult the intelligence of a goldfish. She calls their explanations 'my gran died again apologies'.

The builders don't disappoint her, but the upside is that she has the house to herself. And a chance to catch up. She starts in the bedroom. Mac's suit lies, like a discarded school uniform, in a crumpled heap on the carpet. It is her job to take it to the dry cleaners. Like she is his personal servant or something. She empties the coins from his trousers, hoists up the jacket and pats it. In the inside pocket, she finds a sheaf of papers tied together with pink ribbon. It is the same type of ribbon she saw around the folders when they bought the house. Lawyers' ribbon. Normally, Mac's business papers are of less interest to her than a year-old edition of *Anglers' Weekly*. But that ribbon.

She unties it. The first page reads: 'Heads of Agreement. Proposed Takeover of the Pacific Sea Quake Consortium by Entire Reinsurance Company SA, Panama. Prepared on behalf of Entire Anstaldt, Liechtenstein.' Megan's lips draw inwards. This is not what her Dad wants. And she knows it.

Chapter Twenty-Six

The steely eyes of the giant portrait stare down at Michael. The power of the man who, 170 years before, founded Homeworkers Assurance Company fills the ancient room. After a series of mergers, the name has changed to Home & Life. But the traditions of the company, buried deep in its corporate soul, are still embodied in the portrait.

'Good weekend? I thought it might be nice for us to meet here,' Samson Cantwell says, from the head of a table the size of a swimming pool.

The word 'nice' plays in Michael's head; the discreetly elegant head office of Home & Life is not just nice, and the word does scant justice to the Telford Christie Room in which they sit. Everything about the room, from the rosewood edging of the oak parquet to the crafted cornices, speaks of old money. It looks so solid.

Solid like Samson Cantwell who has the granite features of a Roman statue. Mid-forties, grey at the temples with forceful, dark brown eyes, Samson is the perfect face for any boardroom photograph. 'Overseas Operations Manager', his business card reads. But a manager of Home & Life has more weight than ten Michael Darretts. His ambition for further power pervades the vast room. Those who have ever stood in his way can vouch for the fact that Samson is destined for the top.

'Why bring this deal to me, Michael? Why so generous?'

'Once the management of Cutesie have completed their buyout they'll need to develop. Obviously, the easiest new sales come from existing associations and theirs are special. Wonderful pocket-sized companies in the Pacific and Indian oceans. Combine Cutesie's connections with your know-how and product range and you'll both reap excellent profits. Cooperation with Cutesie is in your commercial interest, and theirs.'

216

Samson narrows his eyes. 'Friendly cooperation?'

'Yes,' Michael says, with a trophy-winning smile.

'Some cooperation arrangements are about as friendly as Viking war parties,' Samson says. 'Have you got a hidden agenda?'

'I appreciate that Home & Life isn't big on conflict,' Michael reassures him. And, knowing UK insurers are slower than sloths on Mogadon, he adds, 'At this stage, I just want confirmation that you'll give the proposal serious consideration.'

'Sorry, even that will take us a while,' Samson says. 'September?'

It takes Megan two hours to prepare the stuffed quails, but she enjoys it. With the builders out of the house, she has her kitchen back. Surrounded by duchesse potatoes and oven-roasted peppers, it is a glorious meal. And so it remains for thirty minutes; an hour after Mac has promised he would be home. He knows she is cooking something special; she telephoned him earlier.

A further hour later, baking on a plate in the oven, Mac's food withers. Without bothering to get a wine glass, Megan pours a glass of Australian Chardonnay into a tumbler. Sipping it in the morning room, perched on Mac's carver chair, she retreats into dark thoughts about the papers she has found.

The crunch of gravel under Mac's Mercedes announces his return.

'It's been a long day,' he says when chided for his lateness.

Rising, Megan gives up his chair. He slumps into without saying thank you, and she stands under the archway, between the kitchen and the morning room, waiting for a further explanation which he doesn't provide.

Megan bites her upper lip. 'I came across some papers in your jacket.'

'Are you searching my pockets?' he asks, lighting a Marlboro.

'Don't twist things around. You left your suit on the floor; I took it to the dry cleaners. Suits don't look good if you clean them with papers inside. The papers aren't about the buyout my Dad wants. One section's even headed "Early Retirement of Donald White". Dad talks about retirement as if it were a terminal illness. What's an Anstaldt?' Megan finds her voice rising against her will; she wants to stay calm. 'And what's that Panamanian company, Entire Reinsurance? It's a play on your name, isn't it? Entire – MacIntyre?'

217

'You don't understand,' Mac says.

A loud crack from the oven signals that Mac's plate has given up on him. But Megan hasn't. Still feeling somewhat uneasy about ensnaring him, she doesn't want a prolonged fight. Despite a spate of recent arguments, he is still Mac – exciting in and out of the bedroom. Above all else, she wants his children. Without a word, she goes into the kitchen, turns off the oven, and returns with an onyx ashtray. Taking a deep breath, she produces a smile which says as much as her words.

'Then you explain – make me understand.'

'Nothing's happened – probably nothing will. I don't want to do anything that's against your father's interests. You know that, Megan. It's not me or Michael doing things to him; it's the other way round. Your father still hasn't agreed our commission. Look around you...all of this is from loans.'

Her eyes grow hostile. 'That isn't an explanation,' she cuts in angrily. 'I didn't ask for this big house. Michael doesn't seem to need–'

'You didn't ask for this house? Who do you think you're kidding? You picked it out just like you did the ring on your finger. My partner cost us £4,000 yesterday; we need the money.'

'Tell me about the papers. Please, Mac.'

'Not now. I'm tired, and I'm going to bed. Sorry about the dinner.'

Megan finishes her wine, slowly.

The Ritz hotel suite that Michael has booked has been transformed into their private restaurant for the evening. There is no evidence that it has ever been anything but a dining room. Starched linen, flower arrangements, and serviettes tied together with fancy braids, add to the air of perfection.

Michael feels Josie's foot tapping his ankle under the table. Looking up, he sees her stifle a giggle and point her eyes at his shoulder. Tiny specks of glitter have fallen onto Michael's jacket from her diamanté evening gown. Smiling, he squeezes her knee under the table.

Elizabeth Cantwell guffaws; her laugh contrasts with her appearance. Sleek and slender, plainly used to being spoilt, with oblong Asiatic-like eyes, she reminds Michael of a Siamese cat.

'Normally,' Elizabeth says, looking at her husband, 'the people I meet on Samson's business dinners are as desiccated as packet coconut. But – if you don't mind me saying so – you're rather jolly hosts.'

Michael sees Samson wince at the clear suggestion that Michael, Josie, Mac and Megan are loveable members of a lower caste.

'I'll take that as a compliment,' Michael says. 'Then again, Mac and I have skins as thick as coconuts.'

'Shall I compare Mac to a summer's day,' Megan laughs. 'No, a fresh coconut – perhaps it's the hair.'

'I don't think', Josie chips in, 'we want to discuss body hair over dinner. Well, perhaps we do – but not in front of our guests.'

'Tell me, Megan, what business are you in?' Elizabeth asks, over coffee.

'The baby-making business. Just starting out. Doing the ground-work...or bodywork. Mac married me for my mind, but I wed him for his looks. They're too good to lay waste to in one generation; they need to be recycled.'

Mac chokes on his vintage port.

In the taxi, on the way back to Islington, Josie asks Michael, 'Samson Cantwell barely said a word. Was I too...?'

The taxi hurtles round a corner, pressing them close together. He moves to kiss her lightly on the cheek but, jolted, his kiss is harder than he intends and ends up on her eyelid. They laugh.

'You did very well, and he enjoyed it. So did his wife – a lot. She'll want to see us again and that means – cynical or not – he's going to be doing more business with us. I'm going to invite them to Monte Carlo in September, for the annual reinsurance confer-ence. I've arranged for our company to rent a villa nearby, at Cap d'Ail.'

Fluttering her eyelashes, Josie asks, 'Am I invited to Monte Carlo?'

'Oh, damn.'

'What, you didn't mean to tell me?'

'It's not that – something else. You must come, get the time off work. The way we do it, it's more social than anything else. Or, like tonight, it seems that way on the surface. Lie around the pool – eat food from the markets all cooked for you.'

'Tough life. I don't know how you hack it. What's the "damn" for?'

'Samson did say something. I had a conversation with him; I asked him how he was getting on with the proposal I've put to him on Cutesie. He told me it was very interesting. It's just gelled.'

'Interesting? That's good, isn't it?' Josie asks, above the squeal of the taxi's brakes.

'No. Where Samson comes from interesting means awful, but he said "very interesting", which is worse. Then again, he was probably just pulling my chain.'

'Why would he do that?'

'He thinks I'm not telling him everything; thinks I've got a hidden agenda.'

'And have you?' Josie asks.

'Of course,' Michael laughs as the taxi rushes forward again.

It is just a shadow that Michael glimpses as the taxi reaches the mews.

'Drive on,' he instructs the driver, firmly. 'Stop after the pub.'

'Stay here,' he tells Josie as he charges out. Adrenaline surges through his system; his muscles tense; his chin juts forward and the blue-eyed boy becomes an opaque-eyed hunter.

Sprinting forward, with the natural movement of a greyhound in full flight, he races to the carport. He sees the shadow slink backwards into the darkness as, without slowing, he dashes into the mews.

Michael stops a few inches in front of the cornered man. A hurricane of aggression tears through Michael's mind, but he controls it. Growling rather than panting, he advances further and blocks the stalker into the corner by the back gate. The man has frizzy, uncombed hair and bulging eyes which stare back at Michael. Michael is certain they are the same eyes that shot hatred through his living room window. But now, trapped in the dark corner, they are filled with fear.

'You want to see inside my house again?' Michael says. 'You'd better come in.' The man shakes his head and presses his back against the gate. 'I'm not asking you,' Michael rasps. 'I'm telling you.'

Taking his keys out of his pocket, he shepherds the man to the front door, opens it and, pushing his prisoner inside, turns on the lights.

220

'You're Lisa's husband...Giles.'

'I'm...er,' Giles replies.

'Take a seat,' Michael says, shoving Giles towards the sunken settee.

The wind slams the door. Michael lowers himself onto his haunches, inside Giles's personal space, and locks his eyes on Lisa's husband.

'I'm going to tell you this once,' Michael says. 'So listen carefully. I've heard you and Lisa are separated. I'm not sorry, and I couldn't give a flying fuck whether you believe me or not, but, however badly I wanted Lisa, I always respected your marriage. Now, I love someone else. You're scaring her. When I've finished, you'd better run away. You come near me again, you'll regret it. But if my fiancée ever sees you again, I'll turn what remains of your scummy life inside out and upside down. By the time I've finished, you'll wish you were dead.'

Josie enters; Michael stops talking. And, before she can even close the door, without meeting either of their eyes, Giles scampers away.

'I asked you to stay in the taxi,' Michael says.

'It's my home too. Who was he?'

Michael winces. 'He won't come back again.'

'Who was he, Michael?' Josie repeats.

'Lisa's husband.'

'I thought this thing you had for Lisa was over,' Josie says.

'It is,' Michael replies, forcefully.

In Virginia Water, the plumbers have been partying with jointing compound, and the en suite smells sour. Rather than use it, Mac waits outside the upstairs bathroom from where he looks down from the top of the stairwell at the regal red carpet runner that waterfalls down the treads onto the parquet below. He rests his hand on the banister. It moves fractionally, and he resolves to speak to Megan about the builders' incompetence.

Megan comes out of the bathroom in her bra and pants, puts her arms round his neck and kisses him. He feels her tongue explore his mouth and tastes her toothpaste.

'Mm,' Mac says. 'I just need the loo. Then I must make one quick call.'

'Don't be long,' she says in her bright Australian twang.

Using the dining room phone, he reaches Professor Dietrich in San Francisco.

'I've got a problem, Ernst. Michael's up to something. You know Donald White's playing hardball on the commission?'

'Yah,' Dietrich says.

'I think Michael's found a route round Cutesie. You know how tight he is with Samson Cantwell of Home & Life. I believe Michael's planning a management throw-out of his own if Donald doesn't agree to pay up. That means DBL would get into a takeover battle. Expensive and messy they are.'

'You believe? You think? Any concrete information?'

'No, but I know Michael.'

'Calm down, Home & Life hate conflict. They won't go head-to-head with DBL. Listen, don't lose your nerve, we're ready. Ideally, we'll make our move at the last moment. That way no white knight can come along and ruin everything. But, if we have to, we can gobble Cutesie up earlier. Just focus on the five million, Mac.'

Mac puts down the telephone and climbs the stairs, grinning.

The hiatus of holidays leaves the Cutesie and Templeton sagas drifting in the open sea of uncertainty. But on August 20th, when Mac returns to the office bronzed but brassed off, he pushes open the door to the conference room.

Mac slings a letter in front of Michael. 'What the hell is this?'

'Welcome back,' Michael says.

'Well?' Mac demands while Michael reads it.

'It's a letter I asked Jeremy Templeton for,' Michael says, innocently.

Mac tuts. 'Yes. For that bitch Lisa.'

He throws down a second letter, like a gauntlet, onto the table. 'And read this one. Templeton's no longer prepared to accept any of our business. Don't try and pretend it's a coincidence.'

'We don't need him,' Michael says, rising from his chair.

'You should have told me about Lisa's bit part,' Mac smoulders. 'You owed me that much.'

'Yeah, sorry,' Michael agrees, and massages Mac's temper with the balm of questions about his holiday with Megan.

Melissa brings in two coffees and an ashtray. Her legs are bare;

222

her skirt barely covers her panties. And Michael sees her eyes flash a lewd invitation to Mac.

'For all I care, you can nuke Templeton now,' Mac says, brushing Melissa's knee as she struts out.

'Samson Cantwell and his wife are coming to Monte Carlo,' Michael says, changing the subject. 'By the way, has Donald White put forward any proposals on the commission yet? That man doesn't know a good deal from orange peel.'

'No,' Mac replies.

'I wish Samson Cantwell would get to grips with the friendly cooperation agreement. Once we can surprise your father-in-law with that bolt-on bonus he should be Mr Generosity. He'd bloody well better be.'

'He hasn't been big on gratitude so far,' Mac says. He strides out of the room after Melissa, taking his coffee with him.

Michael shifts a pile of loose papers and finds the telephone.

'Patrick!' Michael says. 'What's happening? I thought you were a top investigative reporter. In your last edition you ran a story about those East German families making their curtains into a hot air balloon and sailing over the Berlin wall. That's not what your readers want.'

'We always run a human interest story or two. That one had political connotations. I know why you're phoning. Templeton's a no-go. The Arctic chill of the responses was intriguing, but there wasn't enough in them to run a story. Have you got any further information?'

'I just wanted to check that you spoke to the Lloyd's Chairman, or some of the other elder statesmen, about Templeton's deals.'

'Michael, there was steam coming out of the telephone. Ugh, that man Templeton. In the circumstances I–'

'Patrick, if he was a bit upset, doesn't that tell you something? It's just a few calls. I can give you their names and extension numbers.'

'If that's what you want,' Patrick says. 'It's your funeral.'

Michael's hand shakes as he phones Lisa; he tells her he wants to pass over the Templeton letter personally. But there is more to it than that; he must see her to check she is all right. And, he has decided, to tell her goodbye.

When she opens the door of the apartment, Michael takes a step backwards. He doesn't mean to let his shock show, but his image of his beautiful Lisa jars with the defeated woman in front of his eyes. Most of her hair is trapped inside her dressing gown; the rest straggles about like stray snakes. Her fingernails are bitten, and she has put too much perfume on.

'Come in,' she says. 'I'm sorry, Michael. I didn't expect you until seven.'

'We did say six,' he says softly, pecking her cheek as he enters.

She is flustered and, although it isn't his home, he walks ahead of her into the kitchen and switches the kettle on. He glances at her gaunt body.

'Don't tell me how I look,' she says. 'I know.'

'You look fine, Lisa. Really fine.'

Really Fine offers him a broken smile. 'Do you honestly think I look okay?'

'You do. Sorry about your Mum.'

'I know. Thanks. I think we're out of milk. Black all right?'

He nods. She rubs her mouth and looks around the kitchen vacantly before retrieving two mugs from the draining board. They take their coffees through to the dining room and sit down at the table where a single iris is arranged, as only a man could have, in a jam jar.

'Peter's moved in,' she explains, pointing at the flower. 'He's being an angel: keeping the place tidy, doing most of the cooking – even picks up the iron from time to time.'

Michael looks at her; he can't tell her goodbye. Not when she is like this. His mouth moves, but no words come out. He thinks back to halcyon days when she was his Wendy and he was her Peter Pan. And he has been stranded for years, a little boy in Never-Never land, waiting for her to come back. He stares at her, lost in his memories. His eyes cloud with tears; he lifts his chin to fight them away.

'For Christ's sake, Michael,' Lisa says. 'Please don't feel sorry for me. That's the last thing I need. I'm getting better, pulling myself out of this depression. I'll do it.'

'Course. Oh, before I forget.' Michael passes over the Templeton letter.

'Thank you very much,' she says reaching across to stroke his arm. 'The accountants can settle everything now.'

'It's right, isn't it?' he asks when she opens the envelope.

He squeezes his fingers into a fist. He meant to say 'alright' not 'right'. To ask her if the letter was right. Not to ask if she has lied.

'The letter's fine,' she replies as she reads it. She looks up; he sees a trace of hurt fly across her face. 'And, yes, it's right.'

He smiles a request for forgiveness. 'Are you able to work at the moment?'

'Not yet,' Lisa says. 'My GP says I should, but I want a holiday first. Peter can't get the time off, and I'm not going away on my own. That would be miserable.'

'The Monte Carlo conference is in two weeks,' Michael says, knowing even as he is saying it that he shouldn't. 'We've got a private villa. Come out and get some sun for a week. You really should take a break before starting work again.'

'I don't know; you've done enough, Michael. What about Josie?'

'I'll talk to her,' he says. 'I'm sure she won't mind.'

Reaching a hand across the table she presses the ends of the fingertips against his. 'You're the kindest man I've ever known.'

Michael blushes. 'I–I–must be going. Josie will be waiting for me.'

The benign August air that floats through the open windows of Michael's house contrasts with Josie's hoar frost tone that evening.

'Lisa? You want Lisa to come to Monte Carlo? Why? So you can sit around staring at her in her swimsuit, making me feel like a skunk? What were you thinking? That I wouldn't mind? I do. It's bad enough that you're seeing her again.'

Michael shifts on the settee to face her. 'Her brother asked me to help her. I wasn't sniffing around her back door hoping she would throw me a bone. If you saw the state she's in, you'd understand. She's depressed, hurt, confused. I had to help. And now I want to say goodbye to her.'

'Say goodbye?' Josie gets up and paces to the bookcase. 'And take a week doing so. One for the road to see if you can exorcise your obsession with her?'

'Sorry? Is that what you want me to say? Well, I'm not sorry.' Michael bats back the tears. 'I need to tell you some things I've never told anyone before.'

'Well, no one's stopping you,' Josie says, placing her hands on her hips.

'When my real Mum died I sat on the floor alongside her holding her hand for like five, perhaps six, hours–'

'I know that. And I am sorry. But it's got nothing to do with this.'

'It has,' Michael interrupts. 'It took every adult in that room and a hypodermic needle to wrench me away from her. It was the first time I had one of my rages. Look, I know I'm not perfect. And I've never asked you before to make allowances, but I need to say goodbye in my own time.'

'I want you to talk to me, but right now you're making this worse. Don't you see what I see. You still loved your mother. You still love Lisa too. For God's sake, Michael. We're supposed to be getting married. I'm carrying your baby.'

'She hasn't even said she's coming yet, and you'll be with me in Monte Carlo.'

Michael's empty eyes look away and a two-minute silence descends. He wants her to comprehend that he doesn't have a choice.

'It's a choice, Michael. If Lisa says yes, then I'm not going to come anywhere near Monte Carlo. You go...if you want to. Spend a week with her there. But ask yourself a question first. Will I be here when you get back?'

As Josie runs from the room, he realises that she doesn't know the answer either.

Chapter Twenty-Seven

Before slamming the front door, Mac gives Megan a civil kiss on the cheek – the sort of kiss you would give an aunt. That Tuesday, a week after the Neanderthal builders have driven their last white van back to the depths of Hounslow, Megan is back in her routine. And that includes getting up early on Tuesdays.

It is all very well for Mac to tell her to telephone in the evening, when it is cheaper, but her father is either in bed or in the office when she attempts that. It is the opposite end of the day in Australia. And if she rings at weekends, Mac hovers over her looking at his watch and drawing blood with his barbed wire requests for her to be brief. So, with him out of the house, she pads upstairs to call from the extension in the bedroom.

In order to make the room snug, and the call more of a treat, she clears up first. After making the king-sized bed, she picks up Mac's Y-fronts – and his shirt. A strand of hair clings to the cotton. It is too light a shade to be either hers or Mac's, so she sniffs the shirt. It smells of perfume.

Sitting down on the bed, she doesn't move for twenty minutes. Eventually, she clambers downstairs for her quick-fix alternative to shopping therapy: Blue Mountain coffee. But this morning even that velvet taste does nothing for her, and she treks wearily back up the stairs to phone home.

'Hello, Dad,' she says, trying her hardest to keep her voice normal.

'What's wrong, Megan?' Donald asks.

She can't bring herself to tell him. 'I just wanted to hear your voice.'

'Everything OK between you and Mac?' he probes, softly.

'I don't know, Dad; I just don't know,' she replies. Her voice shakes.

227

'I'll see you in a couple of weeks in Monte Carlo,' he consoles her.

The line goes silent; then her mother talks to her. Although soothed by the lullaby of her mother's voice, Megan doesn't tell her either.

When Mac returns from the City, he finds the front door bolted. He knows she is inside; the house is lit up like a Las Vegas casino, and he can feel her presence. Setting his briefcase down, he raps on the Edwardian knocker. But she doesn't answer.

'Oh come on, Megan. I can do without your tantrums. What is it now, did I forget to thank you for putting my Weetabix in a bowl this morning?'

He stomps around the gravel path which moats the house to try the back door. That too is locked. After crunching his way back to the porch, he bangs on the knocker again and again.

'Megan,' he shouts.

'Go away!' her voice tells him from just behind the door.

'What's the matter? Come on, open the door.'

'Go to the slapper whose cheap perfume I smelt on your clothes.'

'Megan, you're imagining things. Please, let me in.'

In large red letters, outside the door, the mat reads, 'Welcome'. Mac blots out the message by sitting on it. Calculating that she is more likely to forgive and forget a denial than an admission, he assumes that interwoven in her suspicions are the papers she has discovered in his jacket. His mind races. He thinks about those pants-down politicians who, regular as motorway pile-ups, stand hand in hand with their wives outside their besieged houses. Helped by their instantly forgettable faces, those adulterers and their ambitious wives can slide back into their comfy mutual dishonesty. All they have to do, Mac considers, is to be unselfish and not confess.

The evening air stills; the neighbours' wind chimes take a nap. And, for a while, he lets the silence talk for him.

'I love you,' he asserts after ten minutes. 'I'll wait until you're ready to see me.'

'Then you'll get cold,' she replies.

He pulls himself up and faces the door.

'If it's still those papers, I'll sit down with you and explain.'

228

'You'll only lie to me. You can explain them to my Dad.'

An hour later, she opens the bedroom window and throws his travel bag out. It sails over the gravel and into the roses.

After fishing the jetsam out of the flower bed, he calls, 'I want to talk.'

'Talk then. This is as close as I want to get,' she says from the open window, twenty feet above him.

'I didn't–'

'What do you take me for? All those late nights when I couldn't reach you in the office. My friends asked me to come out to the South of France for a couple of weeks – do you know what I told them? I couldn't possibly come without Mac. You didn't have the same decency; you came without me.'

'Let me in.'

'No, I'll meet you in Monte Carlo. I need some time away from you. Perhaps I'll bring a special friend or two.'

The smell of sex pervades Melissa's Stoke Newington apartment. Her broken bra lies, like a dead seagull, in the middle of the room. One of the sheets is crumpled underneath Mac. The other trails, tangled like a sail ripped from its rigging, from the corner of the bed.

'They were fresh this morning,' Melissa says, unknotting the sheet.

'Next, you'll be telling me that you change your knickers every day,' he jibes.

'I hope that was a joke,' she says, bitterly. 'Sometimes, Mac...'

Shrouding herself in the sheet, she covers her nakedness. He hears her lock the bathroom door and looks around the room. On the work surface, by the cooker, the half-bottle of champagne he brought lies, discarded, on its side. In use, serving its purpose, the black and white television, with a wire coat-hanger aerial, brings the sounds of a *Panorama* studio discussion into the room. Mac gets dressed.

When she comes out of the bathroom, her face is puffy. She wears a silk kimono, which might look expensive were it not for the deviant threads fringing the hem.

'I'd do anything for you,' she says, sitting down next to him on the bed. He pulls on his brogues. 'I hate it in the office,' she carries

229

on. 'Some of the girls snigger at me. And that old git in the post room. It's like he's taking my clothes off with his eyes. You do care for me, don't you, Mac?'

Sighing, he gets to his feet. 'My wife knows. It's over.'

She peers down at her hands. 'You just had to do me one last time. Is that it? You bastard.'

'Sorry,' he says. '...Sorry you feel that way.'

'I hate you,' she shrieks.

He walks out of the door and closes it behind him.

At eleven the next morning, Melissa stands, sagging at knees, in the conference room, waiting until Michael finishes a row of figures.

'Just got in?' Michael asks.

'Can I put this down?' she says and, without waiting for a reply, drops a huge Twinlock drawer file, bulging with photocopies, onto a free chair.

'I'm leaving,' she says. It is more of a plea than a statement.

She is standing awkwardly, as if in pain. Her black top hangs unevenly on her shoulders; her face is bloated and blotchy. Looking at her, Michael knows that Mac has spat her out.

'Take a seat,' he says. He uncrosses his ankles and straightens in his chair.

'What's this?' he asks, gesturing to the Twinlock file.

'Have a look.'

Skimming through the papers on the Anstaldt and Cutesie, he feels his mouth fall open as he comes across a copy of a memo from himself to Mac. In it Michael details the number of PSQC jobs that will be saved. A copy of Mac's Post-It note to Dietrich is photocopied over the memo. 'Fuck this for a game of soldiers!' Mac has scrawled. Michael hides beneath a smile which, he is aware, seems a bit inappropriate.

'Will Mac know I have these?' he asks.

'Not unless you tell him. He doesn't know I have copies.'

Michael nods a thank you at her. She starts to cry; he pulls a handkerchief from his pocket and passes it to her.

'Melissa, you're on a month's notice. You don't have to work it. If you want, we could give you a termination payment. That would be tax free.'

230

'Thanks,' she says dabbing her eyes. 'Will you give me a reference?'

'Well...' Michael starts. His eyes drift between the aluminium bin in the corner and the Twinlock. 'Yes, I'd be pleased to. Obviously, as you worked for Mac rather than me, it'll be sort of a standard one. Is that OK? Do you know what you're going to do now?'

'I've no idea,' she says. 'I could ask you the same question. Would you walk me to the lift, Michael?'

Guiding her through the gauntlet of 'good riddance' glares, he can't help feeling sorry for her. But he doesn't blame the eyes that judge her. She looks like a late Saturday-night hooker passing early-morning Sunday worshippers.

'Take care,' she says at the lift.

'Bye,' he replies.

Unable to concentrate, he meanders out of the office and into the little park by Finsbury Circus. Sitting on a wooden bench, he watches the men bowling on the green. They are kitted out in white, with aprons and butcher's hats. Dappled sunrays percolate through the rhododendrons behind him.

Michael jogs through a series of displacement activities. He runs his fingers through his hair, blows his nose, tightens his belt and looks at his watch without seeing the time. And then, just as he expects, it hits him: an avalanche of icy anger.

'Stay calm,' Michael mutters, like a lunatic talking to himself.

He sits there, static and stoic, while the storm of evil emotion passes. When his vision clears and his skin slackens, Michael stamps his feet on the ground. He has been sitting there for so long without moving that they have gone to sleep. Taking his silver die from his pocket, he shakes it in his palm until he gets a six. Decision confirmed, he walks back.

When Mac returns from the market, Michael follows him into his office, closes the door behind him and takes a seat.

'Samson and Elizabeth Cantwell are going to join us in Monte Carlo,' he opens with a deceptive smile. He extinguishes his smile. 'But you're not. Not till the end.'

'Why?' Mac asks, rising from his chair.

231

'Because you're off to the States. We have to put down markers for the accounts we've targeted there, go and see the clients. Gotta be done, Mac.'

'Yeah, sure, but not now. It can wait. Donald White will be in Monte Carlo. We're fucking partners; you don't give me orders.'

'If you won't go, I'll have to. I've thought this through. If both of us are in Monte Carlo for the whole week, it'll let Donald have time for his type of grinding long-game. A short, sharp confrontation will work better. All the Europeans we need to see at the Monte Carlo conference are my connections. And the States needs a push. You're going,' Michael says, pointing his finger at Mac. 'I had a strange conversation today. Is there anything you'd like to share with me, Mac?'

'Did Melissa...?' Mac asks. He paces circles around his office, licking at his lips and flitting his eyes here and there – like a prisoner bent on escape might walk round the exercise yard.

'She's resigned,' Michael says.

'It's a bit of a mess. I dumped Melissa last night. Megan smelt some perfume on my clothes and wouldn't let me in the house.'

'Is there anything else you want to tell me, Mac?'

'No,' Mac snarls, 'isn't that bad enough for you?'

Michael knows the only reason Josie has started decorating the living room is so she doesn't have to talk to him about Monte Carlo, or rather doesn't have to talk to him at all. So, on Friday, he decides not to use his key and rings the front doorbell. Michael holds red roses behind his back; they are nestled between tiny blooms of gypsophilia, encased in cellophane and bound together by a ribboned bow.

Brush in hand, she answers the door. In her wake, on the newspaper which lines the floor, is a trail of white footprints. Wrapping himself around her, and her brush, he flourishes the flowers from behind his back to behind hers. He doesn't care about the paint splodge that sticks to the lapel of his suit; his hug banishes all signs of Josie's anger. She smiles a huge smile and, tidying her hair with her free hand, gazes at him.

'I can't believe that I'm such a sucker,' she says. 'Bought by a few roses.'

'There's thirteen. That's more than a few.'

232

He dashes upstairs, sponges the emulsion off his jacket and changes into old jeans and a faded T-shirt. Then, offering only 'won't be long' and 'wait and see' explanations, he disappears out of the house. Twenty minutes later, he returns to give her a second surprise: a Chinese takeaway.

They sit on the newspaper, cross-legged, by the base of the battered ladder, surrounded by tinfoil cartons and evidence of their clumsiness with chopsticks. The conversation is of practical things. The real talking is done by Michael's 'I didn't mean to hurt you' face. Josie stretches out her little finger and rubs a paint spot off the bridge of Michael's nose; Michael interprets her touch as accepting his apology. He tears off a corner of newspaper and cleans her finger. Tenderly, he takes her hand in his fist, draws it up to his mouth, and kisses her fingertips.

'About Monte Carlo...' he says. 'Lisa probably won't come.'

Above them, the bare light bulb flickers.

'You could retract her invite, Michael.'

'I couldn't do that.'

'Why not?' she asks.

He could tell her that he would feel dreadful doing so. That would be true. Wouldn't satisfy Josie. Or he could tell her that he would forever blame himself if he didn't help and something happened to Lisa. Like with his real mother. But that might suggest his love for Lisa lingers on. He stays silent; Josie pulls her hand free.

'I meant what I said,' Josie says.

When Lisa wakes up on Wednesday morning, she opens the window. A squirrel darts across the lawn and into the dahlias. She smiles at the sensation of the air on her skin. Busying herself, she bathes, blow-dries her hair, puts on a little make-up, vacuums the apartment, cleans the bathroom and washes the dishes. The apartment is spotless by the time she picks up the telephone. And she feels fine – really fine.

'Michael, is the offer to stay at the villa still...?'

'Of course.' He gulps. 'I wouldn't withdraw an invitation.'

'Then I'd love to come.'

* * *

233

Dietrich summons Michael with a Gestapo phone call. At ten o'clock that Saturday morning, the day before Michael is due to leave for Monte Carlo, he arrives at Dietrich's flat in Hans Place.

'He'll be with you in a minute,' the Asian girl says as she shows him into the lounge.

Her lipstick is an aggressive shade of red. Jet black hair frames a face which, like the concave stomach she flaunts by leaving her blouse undone, seems pre-pubescent but far from innocent. Glossy and exotic, she looks like an extra from a Bond movie.

Wandering around the room, he shudders as he examines one of the display cases. Two giant stag beetles are suspended, horn-to-horn, in a combat neither lifeless insect can now win. The acre of polished floorboards is bare but, incongruously, two Turkish rugs hang on the walls. In one corner, a Japanese wedding cupboard is equally out of place next to a word processor. Michael notices the machine isn't plugged in, which is the same way he has come to feel about the man who enters the room: Richards-Riley.

It is now clear to Michael that the link between DBL and Wetthards is a marriage of connivance. Michael suspects DBL has overpaid for the block of shares it owns in Wetthards. But, as Michael knows, DBL exacts interest on its debts. Richards-Riley has to deal with DBL's multifarious loose ends in London.

'I thought–'

'Well he's not here,' Richards-Riley says. 'Professor Dietrich called me yesterday afternoon. There I was, enjoying a peaceful round of tea and biscuits, and his voice exploded down the telephone line. He's up in arms about questions to Lloyd's raised by your mucker – Patrick something or other – the editor of *The Protester*.'

Michael sits down at the table. 'What are you doing here?' he says.

'If it's any of your business,' Richards-Riley replies, circling raptorially around the table, 'I often stay here. Professor Dietrich's asked me to talk to you. For crying out loud, Michael. These are your products; these problems are entirely of your making. Who are you to say that Mr Templeton can't use them? There's no copyright on ideas. We offered to put the business through you; proffered you a handsome commission on it. You turned us down; we went round you. Can you blame us?'

Michael notices the constant use of the words 'we' and 'us'.

'Helping Mr Templeton was something you agreed with Professor

Dietrich,' Richards-Riley launches his next salvo. 'You failed to keep your word. Worse, you deliberately tricked us. You gave us a plane that wouldn't fly. Then you took one that did – off to Paris – and trashed our business. DBL are angry. So is Jeremy Templeton.'

'What are they going to do...uh?' Michael says with an expression of stone. 'Have some tramp attack me on the street?'

'We've been over that, Michael,' Richards-Riley spits. 'Just hear me out; this is serious. Professor Dietrich says he's considering dumping his association with you. You'll have no access to Lloyd's.'

'If DBL do that, sir,' Michael replies, 'I'll buy them out for £1. Have they forgotten that's in the agreements? We place less than one-tenth of our business into Lloyd's. Frankly, if that market is going to the bad then I want no part in it. If DBL want to withdraw, I'm powerless to stop them.'

Richards-Riley bares his teeth. 'Going to the bad! You tried to blackmail Templeton into providing a false invoice to one of your friends. Then, when you failed to get it through irrational argument, you called in the press. I hope you're not going to insult me by denying it. No story's been printed – I doubt it ever will be – but your conduct remains outrageous. You have the barefaced audacity to accuse a highly esteemed underwriter of wrongdoing. It's you who is wrong, Mr Darrett. You're risking the reputation of that fine syndicate, of Lloyd's, and of my company – ruining your own in the process. Wetthards, Templeton, me and you, we're all linked by our connection to DBL. Play the game.'

Michael's expression hardens to granite.

'Do Lloyd's know what Templeton's done?' he asks.

Richards-Riley continues, but his tone softens, 'They do now. Yesterday I got another telephone call. I'm not going to tell you who it was from. Discretion's needed, and you've shown precious little of it. Lloyd's have requested that Mr Templeton and I come in to discuss these deals with them. But I've been asked to let you know in the clearest terms that you should have acted in a different fashion.'

Michael looks at Richards-Riley's predatory face.

Richards-Riley purses his lips. 'That meeting will take place next Wednesday. And beforehand, early next week, you must apologise to Mr Templeton. Professor Dietrich is in London the week after, and you'll say you're sorry to him. And, at the same time, Michael, you must apologise to me.'

'Excuse me,' Michael says.

He brings out his silver die and rolls it on the desk until he gets a six.

'Is it any wonder that some people would like to see your head impaled on a stick?' Richards-Riley says.

'You told me to play the game. Count me in. I'll beg Professor Dietrich's pardon, but I can't kiss and make up with Mr Templeton next week. What am I supposed to apologise to you for anyway? For not French kissing you after you fired me?'

Richards-Riley's craggy fingers dance frantically through the air. 'Professor Dietrich demands it.'

'I didn't say I wouldn't, but I can't – not next week. I'm in Monte Carlo.'

'There's something you should know, old boy,' Richards-Riley says revealing the golden glint of his sadistic smile. 'Jeremy Templeton didn't ask for you to be dismissed. Quite the contrary, he berated me for doing it. It was Professor Dietrich who suggested I terminate your employment. Though, I must admit, I was only too happy to oblige.'

'Professor Dietrich? I hadn't even met him at that time.'

'No, you hadn't. But Mac had. Work it out for yourself. It's high time you grew up and recognised just who your real friends are.'

Chapter Twenty-Eight

All Michael can see is headlights coming from the wrong side of the road. Dribbles of sweat run from his temples, and his shirt sticks to his skin like cling film. Seeking relief from the humidity, he opens the window. Mediterranean air and diesel fumes waft in. The drive from Nice airport to Cap d'Ail is a half-hour straight run; all he has to do is to follow the signs. And it is Sunday; the traffic isn't heavy.

If the car didn't veer to the left each time Michael brakes, it would be easy. Easier still if Michael could keep his mind on the driving. No tears from Josie that morning. No goodbye kiss. 'I love you,' he'd said, and he meant it. Her response was just a 'how could you' look, and he knows that she meant it too.

Darkly, Michael reflects that he should have returned the car the moment he realised it had faulty brakes. But the owners of the villa arranged the rental through a friend. It was free. Returning unwanted gifts is something Michael finds vexatious.

Four storeys high, the ancient villa towers above him as he parks in the courtyard alongside Samson's BMW. After turning off the engine, his hands stay glued to the top of the steering wheel. His heart pulses double time. Spooked, he climbs from the car into the unlit courtyard and mounts the eighteenth-century steps leading to the double doors. They creak open, and a cascade of light decorates their distressed paint. But no one stands in the doorway. Not a sound. Hesitantly, he walks into the vampire's lair. Despite the light from a chandelier high above him, the horror-movie illusion continues.

'Hello?' Silence.

Jittery, he passes the bottom of a vast spiral staircase and enters a room the size of a conference hall. A door on the far side of the room squeaks. Michael jumps.

237

'Hi,' says a voice as American as apple pie.

Relieved, he moves towards the girl's voice.

'I'm Danny; you must be Michael. I'm in the middle of cooking. I saw you coming.'

'Lots of people think that, but not many say it,' he replies.

Kneading dough, on a butcher block worktop that fills the middle of the kitchen, she treats him to a toothpaste-advertisement smile that makes him more conscious of his sweaty clothing and matted hair.

'You need a drink,' she says, fetching two Heinekens from the icebox.

Too quickly, he gulps down his can. Danny's hyena laugh, at Michael's attempts to rid himself of hiccups, is less attractive than her lithe body.

'Megan arrived with her friends in time for lunch. They're friendly,' Danny says. 'Samson and Elizabeth Cantwell came this afternoon – just after Donald White. He looked pooped. Worse than you.'

'Thanks.'

'Lisa got here an hour ago; she's gone to bed – they all have. Mac's not coming until Wednesday; that's right, isn't it? Now you. Lisa tells me you're single.'

'I'm engaged,' he asserts, between hiccups.

On the patio, to the rear of the villa, Samson's voice is brighter than the early morning sunlight. 'Monday morning – best part of the week,' he says to Danny.

Pea-sized grapes hang in bunches from the wooden trellis that covers the patio. Secured by hemp loops, the intertwined stems of the vine climb up the vertical supports. Under the cast-iron table top, dragons' hindquarters encroach their claws onto the quarry tiles. From the house wall, next to the kitchen window, a pigmy gargoyle enjoys the antics of the merry-go-round of visitors with grotesque amusement.

Whilst Danny lays the table, Samson gropes her with a look of unadulterated lewdness. Seeming responsive to the strong aphrodisiac of Samson's power, she pampers him with a smile, pulls her stomach in, and accidentally brushes past him.

'No Elizabeth?' spoilsport Michael asks.

'Won't see her till noon.'

Danny brings out some warm croissants and a pot of coffee. Samson devours the croissants, and Michael kick-starts his mind with caffeine.

'Will Home & Life accept the friendly cooperation proposal on Cutesie?' Michael asks, bluntly.

'Yes, Elizabeth and I wouldn't have come otherwise. It would've been too embarrassing. My board have approved the proposal. Actually, they're very excited about it. We need to tie up the details.'

'Excited, not interested?' Michael teases.

'Very funny, Michael. I've also got that letter you asked for that confirms that we won't use any of the information provided on Cutesie without your permission. But you don't appear to be charging us any commission. Have I missed something?'

'No,' Michael says, smiling.

'At Home & Life we like our pipers paid. No commission, not even for the introduction? Indulge me, Michael...elucidate, um?'

Michael grins. 'Over breakfast?'

'I didn't start this discussion,' Samson jousts.

'Much as I'd like to take your money, I can't accept fees from both you and Cutesie. That would create a conflict of interest.'

'So you'll be charging them extra commission?' Samson asks.

'No,' Michael says. His face provides even less of an explanation.

'Your business is a mystery to me.' Samson quizzes Michael with his eyes.

'And to me sometimes. One thing about it is simple: work. I've got twenty-two appointments with reinsurers in Monte Carlo today. This conference saves us a fist-full of plane tickets. I'll sit around the pool for the rest of the week – people will come here. If you want, you can come with me into town this morning – come back when you've had enough. The girls will look after Elizabeth.'

'Do you want me to take the BMW?' Samson asks.

'Great,' Michael says, with relief, thinking of his wretched hire car.

Amid the chaos of the main square, Samson finds a parking space and, although it is only inches wider than his 7 Series, reverses into it without any difficulty.

239

'Luck like that normally only happens in films,' Michael says.

'Luck? Skill. Still, I'm not nervous about driving here,' Samson taunts.

Michael hasn't spoken of any such fear, but he knows that Samson shares his ability to translate the subconscious Morse code of messages tapped out by human movement and speech.

'You'd be nervous in my hire car,' Michael defends.

'That would depend on how you drove.'

They walk across the square to the open-air café decked out with canopies like a wedding reception marquee. Businessmen sit at every white tablecloth. Some sip espressos and peck biscuits, others laugh too loud, but most huddle and whisper over papers. In groups of threes and fours, the men market their unseen goods to one another. None seem quite sure who is buying or who is selling. Amongst them, stamping their heels into the male bastion of reinsurance, is a sprinkling of firm-faced young women. Visible stitching on jackets and soft leather shoes advertise mainland Europeans. Contrasting sharply, some of the British contingent wear their 'London is the centre of the universe', home-and-away kits of pinstripe suits and black brogues. A man carrying a handbag and a cardboard sign with his name on it mills around the edge of the café.

Hailed, taxi-style, by the arm of his first appointment, Michael and passenger pull up at a rear table. Obviously lost by the frenetic speed of the introductions and jumble of words, Samson rubs the side of his face. On the other side of the table, two Italian businessmen gabble statistics and launch into a sales spiel for their company. Taking no notes, Michael retaliates with a pitch of his own. The seeds of the discussion don't germinate, and the Italians depart. Leaving Samson to guard the captured table, Michael charges off. He returns a couple of minutes later with two Austrians to repeat the dance.

By the time of their fifth rendezvous, as the conference itself is known, Samson seems shell shocked but amused. A squadron of executives descends, pepper nearby tables with their requests for spare chairs, and dive-bomb the cloth with business cards which show them to work for different companies. But they all represent the same German firm. Michael knows all the men: a Colombian, a South African, a New Zealander, a Frenchman, a Dane, a Pole,

240

and their leader, a German. Samson adds their cards to the deck building up in front of him.

Without explaining Samson's presence, and ignoring the customary aperitif conversation, Michael digs into the main course. Looking around the table, he grins. 'As I'm so popular, may I presume that you got my package on Cutesie and want to proceed.'

Jury-like, the men stare at him. The German nods, almost imperceptibly, at the South African.

'I'm very much looking forward to meeting Donald White on Wednesday,' he says with a heavy Afrikaans accent. 'Tell me, Mr Darrett, have you sorted out your little problem with Cutesie?'

Although he isn't actually grateful, Michael mouths a thank you to the man for not committing a breach of etiquette by mentioning commission in front of Samson. But Michael wants the conversation to be opened up. So, knowing evasion will ensure the men won't let the subject drop, he doesn't answer.

'Oh yes, Wednesday. If you could let me know, by say Tuesday night, how many of you are coming. Bring your trunks. Stay on after lunch.'

The South African seems bemused, but the German leader's normally bland face cracks into a smile. '*Aber*...Michael. That is, as always, very kind. But please answer our question. The problem with Cutesie – you will solve it?'

'A problem?' Michael replies. 'My presentation mentioned a problem with Cutesie agreeing the commission? Surely not.'

'Of course not,' the Dane cuts in, speaking for the first time. Michael notices Samson looking sideways at him, palpably aghast at the aggression.

'The news is all over Europe,' the Colombian pipes up. 'You know how the market works. This is a big deal and we keep our ears and eyes open. Don't–'

'Michael, please,' the German intervenes with polished politeness. 'Neither we nor any other reinsurers will be happy if you withdraw. We need a level of comfort.'

Michael smiles enigmatically.

'My wife gave me an English phrase book for my birthday,' the Frenchman says, joining the attack. 'I love them; they're so funny. We don't know Donald White from a bar of soap – is that how you say it, Monsieur Darrett?'

'You could,' Michael laughs. He hasn't heard the phrase before.

'And you could provide an answer,' the Pole fires at Michael.

Michael picks his words as carefully as mushrooms in the forest. 'My company won't resign because of a dispute over commission.'

The New Zealander mutters a mild curse, but the German silences his colleagues by chasing a hand downwards through the air. 'There's a lot of work involved in this, Michael. Convince us to spend the necessary time on it. Realistically, what are the chances of the deal falling through?'

'Tell me,' Michael asks, 'do you think my commission is greedy?'

'No,' the German says emphatically.

'Then you'll get the business,' Michael says.

The seven men leave with the same flurry as they arrived.

'Welcome to my world,' Michael says to Samson in the short lull that follows.

Samson scratches his head and asks, 'Would you mind if I retired from the fray in time for lunch back at the villa?'

'Of course not; I'll take a taxi back. Spend some time with Donald – the two of you can plan how to work out your cooperation together.'

'You don't want to be there?' Samson asks, looking nonplussed.

'No,' Michael says. 'I trust you.'

Michael returns at five and changes into his bathers. Self-conscious, he potters barefoot down through the kitchen where, dressed in a bikini, Danny is preparing some Pimms. Coquettishly, she reaches out and prods his stomach; he complains light-heartedly. The afternoon sun remains bright. Carrying the tray of drinks, Michael squints as he exits onto the patio.

Donald White and Samson Cantwell are engrossed in conversation, but break off when Michael appears. Placing the tray down, Michael makes dwarf talk about Donald's trip while holding his hand in a duellist's shake.

'Whenever you're ready,' Donald replies, in answer to the handshake.

'I'd prefer to wait until Mac's here,' Michael says, transferring two glasses of Pimms from the tray to the table. 'Enjoy.'

Lisa and Megan wave from the poolside. Michael is only a few yards away from the pool when he notices that all but one of the women are topless. On the first lounger, reading a paperback, Elizabeth Cantwell takes off her film star sunglasses.

'Give me a kiss,' she says, as if she is the hostess rather than a guest. Balancing the tray in his palm, he touches her cheek with his lips.

'Good luck,' she says with a sexually greedy smile.

'With what?'

'Whatever it is that my husband thinks you're planning.'

'Planning's not a great strength of mine – Josie's having a baby.'

She raises her eyebrows. 'Oh, isn't that lovely. Where is Josie?'

'She's not coming, I'm afraid. It's a shame–'

'I remember that – not being allowed to travel in early pregnancy.'

'Dreadful,' Michael says, placing a Pimms by her side.

'Give me your address later; I'd like to send her a note.'

Uncomfortably aware that her feline eyes are making a tour of his body, he tilts his head at her and runs his teeth over his bottom lip. Standing there, holding the tray in one hand, he feels like a performing seal.

'It's OK, Michael,' she laughs. 'I'm just seeing how your body hair compares to other coconuts. Am I seeing you at your best?'

'No,' Michael replies. 'I look better with all my clothes on.'

Released by her smile, he walks towards the palm tree under which Megan and Lisa lie on loungers. With them are Megan's two friends whom Michael hasn't met before. All four are bare breasted. When he approaches with the Pimms, they sit up and a tomato-puree coloured blush engulfs Michael's cheeks. Passing over the drinks is an awkward feat. Straining his neck, he tries to keep his chin and eyes facing forward whilst pecking Megan's and Lisa's cheeks. The glasses on the tray topple dangerously. Exchanging cocktail-party handshakes with Megan's friends, he smiles nervously. Their breasts bounce around like over-friendly puppies.

'Surreal,' he says.

'Oh come on, Michael,' Megan giggles in her Australian accent. 'Stop being so terribly British. This is Monte Carlo; everybody sunbathes topless here.'

Megan moves up on her lounger and pats the space next to her. Having no choice, other than a gauche sprint back to his room, he sits amongst the girls and their music which resonates from a cassette player. When Megan's friends turn onto their fronts to sunbathe their backs, he expects some relief from his inner cringing. But one of them is wearing a G-string, and her bottom reminds Michael of the soft porn postcards Mac sometimes sends him.

Finishing his Pimms, as quickly as he dares without appearing rude, Michael flees to the safety of his room and tries to telephone Josie. There is no reply. He has no sooner lain back on the bed than the extension rings.

'It's Mac,' Danny announces and hangs up.

'Where's Megan?' Mac demands. 'A fortnight she's been away – traipsing around the Med. Not a single call. That American bitch says it's not convenient to talk to her.'

'Don't blame Danny. What's up?'

'Your bloody secretary has booked me into downtown Atlanta. I need two wallets to venture onto the street here: one to surrender going out, the other to be mugged of limping back. I should be outside the city centre; she shoul–'

'Well, whose fault is it that your secretary left? How's business?'

'Dreadful. This is a fool's errand, Michael. And you know it.'

'What do you want, Mac?'

'I want to speak to Megan.'

'Sorry, Mac. I can't force her.'

At seven, revived, Michael returns downstairs. He talks with Elizabeth Cantwell who sits on a stool pulled up to the butcher block in the kitchen, sharing an apparently cosy glass of wine with Danny. Lured by Lisa's voice, Michael saunters onto the patio where, as if for the first time, Megan introduces him to her friends. They are now wearing evening dresses and warpaint, pretty in the sort of way money can buy.

'Hello, Tamara. Hello, Lucinda,' Michael says, unsure who is who.

Their friendliness has that instant heat that can be turned on and off like gas.

Samson, like his wife, seems to Michael to find the role of guest difficult to adapt to; he holds court with a series of travel tales. Lisa smiles into Michael's eyes.

At the table, when Michael takes his first spoonful of chilled watercress soup, he notices that Donald White's large frame is tense. Donald's lower jaw sticks forward slightly, his lips are parted and his bared teeth are gritted together.

'...and the speed at which Michael gathered and gave information this morning was astonishing,' Samson praises effusively.

Michael watches Donald's irritation fester.

'...but one thing puzzles me, Michael,' Samson continues, 'why did no one talk about that hurricane – David, isn't it?'

'Well, it hasn't landed yet. Not in the States, anyway,' Michael says.

'You can never get Mike to answer a straight question with a straight answer,' Donald says, rapping his fingers on the cast-iron table top.

Breaking off a conversation with her friends, Megan says, 'Dad!'

'I am the client,' Donald replies.

Michael shrugs, smiles at Megan and Samson, and continues to ignore Donald. Tapping Michael's shin under the table, Lisa gives him a knowing smile.

'What are you up to?' she mouths.

Over crème brûlée, when Megan visits the bathroom, Michael strikes under the cover of a compliment.

'I like your sense of humour, Donald.'

'Thanks?'

'I've got a joke. I wouldn't have told this one while Megan was here, just in case. But I should tell you – not waste it. A few years back, Gough Whitlam went above John Kerr's head and rang Buckingham Palace. "Your Majesty," he said, "I would like Australia to be a kingdom, and for me to be King." "No," the Queen replied, "Australia is a country, and you are a"...', Michael pauses and turns to face Donald square on, '..."citizen of it".'

No one laughs, least of all Donald.

'Mac tells me that you never lie,' Donald says, breaking the silence.

He sips his wine before adding, 'Is that true, Mike?'

Michael switches on his negotiator's face. 'No.'

'So you're a liar.'

'No,' Michael insists.

Donald frowns. 'Both can't be true.'

'Does it matter?' Lisa intervenes. 'I imagine Pol Pot doesn't lie, but I wouldn't ask him to babysit.'

That inspires Michael. 'I tell lies in the same way other people do. A few weeks ago, I went to see a friend', he looks at Lisa, 'who was under the weather. I didn't bring grapes or daffodils; my gift was not to tell the truth. "You look fine," I told her. But to say that I'm a liar implies–'

'He's right,' Samson interrupts. 'London brokers of Michael's calibre don't tell lies in business. You just have to listen carefully to what he doesn't say.'

At the end of the meal, complimenting Danny on her cooking, Samson motions for her to pull up a chair between him and Elizabeth. Claiming a sudden migraine, Elizabeth says goodnight to everyone except her husband and Danny.

Manifestly jet-lagged, Donald White hauls himself from the carver chair. The blush wine, which has added to Donald's bad temper, has made Michael mellow.

'Sleep well, Donald.'

With conspiratorial smiles, Megan and her friends announce their departure to a nightclub. Blatantly as an afterthought, they ask whether anyone would like to join them. Samson pales and excuses himself upstairs. The Cantwells' bedroom window is two storeys above the patio, but their voices carry in the night air.

'I was just flirting; you flirt too, darling,' Samson says.

'You're totally insensitive sometimes,' Elizabeth shouts. 'And as for her...'

Frozen, Danny sits with Michael and Lisa. All are silent. And all exhale gratefully when the wooden thuds of the Cantwells' window shutters end their enforced eavesdropping. Danny goes to her bed.

Just the two of them are left: Lisa and Michael.

'You deliberately goaded Donald White, didn't you?' she asks.

'What makes you think that?' he counters, smiling.

'Because I know you,' she smiles back. 'It's so sweet of you to invite me. Josie's not here. Have I...?'

'If it's anyone's fault, it's mine. We're supposed to be getting married, supposed to be having a baby. But we just keep arguing.'

Lisa pulls her chair close and rests her head on his shoulder. 'It's all over with Giles. The divorce will take a while, but I'm certain. And you? Are you certain?'

But rather than answer he poses his own question: the one he has asked himself, over and over.

Freed by the wine, it gushes from him, 'Why didn't you marry

246

me, Lisa? Your wedding day – you in that white dress, full of happiness and life. That was the worst day of my life. Why did you have to ask me to watch?'

'I was wrong. That evening, before I went off to university, I wanted to give myself to you. But not like that. And before that there was...Peter's moped. I know we were children, but I thought you'd tried to...If you loved me, you wouldn't try and kill my brother.'

He pulls away from her and watches her casting her mind back. 'You never denied it – not once – and I know you, Michael. But you can't have. Not you.'

'Oh, Lisa.' His voice swims in sadness. 'Peter accused me of causing his accident. But not even he accused me of trying to murder him. You never asked me, and I loved you all the more for your trust. So you know, I didn't try and kill him.'

Lisa puts both her hands up to his cheeks and strokes the shadow of his stubble. 'I know that now. Perhaps it's not too late, Michael. Perhaps...'

He reaches out and takes her wrists in his hands as if they were injured birds. 'I love Josie, and I want the baby she carries. I've always loved you, Lisa; I think I always will, but you broke my heart. Every time I saw you...you broke my heart.'

Chapter Twenty-Nine

Neon lights strobe the smoke-filled nightclub, picking out random, sweaty faces. Gyrating to the hammer-drill music, the rich and could-be famous perform their versions of night-fever jiving. Megan shakes her hips and rolls her neck in an orgasm of exertion as she dances. Thrusting her bottom backwards and forwards, she enjoys the feeling of being ogled by the man in a cream suit at the bar.

When she wiggles back into a seat by her friends, he sidles up to her. Smiling at him, she takes a sip of champagne from her glass.

'Hi,' drawls Slimeball, 'my name is Trevor.'

Bare-legged, wearing an Australian flag T-shirt, Megan strolls into the kitchen around eleven the next morning. On a stool, by the butcher block, Michael scribbles notes whilst rolling his silver die across the wood. The aroma of freshly-ground coffee fills the room.

'Mac told me about that die,' Megan says. 'You use it to make decisions?'

'No,' he says, 'I use it when there are no choices.'

'There's always a choice. Where is everyone?'

'They've all gone to town. Back soon. How was last night?'

'Great,' Megan says. 'And loud – my ears. Oh, I'm off out tonight too.'

'With your friends?'

'They do have names,' she says. 'You don't like them, do you?'

'I don't know them – that's not fair,' he says, wondering why he has started this uphill conversation.

'Perhaps if you spoke to them. They're going to a different restaurant.'

'Oh?' Michael enquires.

'I talked to a broker at the nightclub last night; he's having dinner with a client from Argentina. The client's wife will be there; I'm going to make up a foursome.'

'Your Dad's here, and Mac's coming tomorrow. You're going on a date?'

'It's not a date. He's a real gentleman; he kissed my hand when I left.'

Moving to the percolator, Michael pours Megan a coffee and hands it to her by way of a reply. Or an apology. Even Michael isn't sure which.

'His name is Trevor Martinson,' she offers. 'He's coming over at seven; I'll introduce him...'

Michael pulls at his ear lobe. 'There's no need; I know him. His nickname in the market is Slimeball. It's not your hand he wants to kiss. Don't be naive.'

'I can look after myself. I'm still going.'

Michael thinks he may be able to persuade her but, from the courtyard outside, the polo field voices of Megan's friends herald their return. Retiring to his room, he retrieves a white book which lists where each of the rendezvous participants is staying. He telephones Martinson's hotel.

'Please would you leave an urgent message for Trevor Martinson. Mrs Megan MacIntyre's husband is arriving. She will not join Mr Martinson for dinner.'

When Michael trudges back down the spiral staircase, Donald White accosts him at the bottom.

'Mike, we need to talk before Mac gets here tomorrow,' Donald says in a voice as subtle as a steel-capped boot.

Donald leads him into the reception room. 'Do you know what an Anstaldt is?'

Gazing out through the gaps of the shutters in the vast reception-room, with his back to Donald, Michael answers, 'Yes. It's a sort of trust, sometimes used to...limit tax.'

'Megan tells me Mac's got one. He's hidden it from you too, hasn't he?'

Michael turns round to face Donald. 'I don't approve of the Anstaldt. It's tax evasion. Recently – I shouldn't tell you this but – Lisa's been in trouble with the Revenue. And once they get their teeth in...not worth it'

Diamond bits in Donald's eyes grind into him.

249

'So you know all about this,' Donald says. 'Megan thought–'

'Well, Megan thought wrong. I've even got copies.'

Within an hour the villa is alive again, and Michael welcomes four dark-suited lunch guests who all arrive at the same time bearing chocolates, champagne and, at no small expense in Monte Carlo, English newspapers. When lunch moves into the afternoon, none of the guests leave. Michael finds a spare pair of trunks for one. To make do, the others take off their ties and roll up their shirt-sleeves.

Everyone bar Michael relaxes. Flitting bee-like from guest to guest, he pollinates agreements to the Cutesie deal and introduces Samson to a Swiss man who asks elemental questions about the weather.

'Count us in for 25%,' the guest says to Michael before moving around the patio to say his farewells.

'What is going on?' Samson asks Michael.

Michael flashes his eyes towards the Swiss man. 'That's the Reinsurance Director of Bern & Luzern. He's just agreed to take a quarter of the Cutesie deal.'

'Obviously, my comments on Kent's rainfall were crucial to a decision involving tens of millions. Is it really that simple?' Samson asks.

'The larger the stakes,' Michael explains, 'the greater the import-ance of who you deal with – confidence is vital. I know that man; we've had other successful dealings. His decision must follow his instincts. He wanted to look you in the eye.'

'But I'm not the client,' Samson protests.

Michael swallows. 'He's spoken with Donald, and that went... very well. Your involvement with Cutesie is a facet he wanted to–'

With a ham actor cough Samson interrupts, 'My wife is a very perceptive lady. According to Elizabeth you're scheming. This deal with Cutesie is excellent for my company. I'm very grateful for your introduction to Donald, but...'

'Elizabeth told me it was you who thought I was planning something. I'm sticking with my knitting to get the job done, but it's hard. Donald White thinks I'm a liar; you heard him yesterday. And reinsurance is based on trust.'

250

'Well, in fairness to Donald, I also heard what you said to him. Home & Life want the cooperation deal to go through, Michael.'

'So do I.'

Work finished, Michael excuses himself, goes to his room, opens the armoire and retrieves the framed photo of Josie from his case. As he shuts the wardrobe it squeaks in antique annoyance at being disturbed. After staring at the picture for a minute, he telephones Josie in the shop. He thinks he can hear her voice behind the scenes, opting not to be there, but he doesn't plead. 'Just send my love.'

Picking up the phone again, he dials Diddy's direct line at Lloyd's.

'No, Michael,' Diddy says in a low voice. Michael can hear the noises of the underwriting room in the background. 'Don't force the issue. The business you objected to has been cancelled. It's as if it never happened.'

'It was arranged. You know it was.'

Diddy lowers his voice further so it becomes no more than a whisper, 'And now it isn't. Jeremy Templeton hasn't done anything wrong; he just thought of doing so. Impure thoughts might be a sin in a confessional box, but not on an underwriting one. Just say sorry and everything will go back to normal.'

'And what is normal?' Michael clips his words. 'Has Templeton told his Names the real results? Will he ever? Pound to a penny he's found another twisted path to avoid disclosure.'

'I'm assured that's not so, Michael.'

'One way or another, Templeton will march on. No harm done. Not many dead.'

'I wouldn't have put it that way,' Diddy says, 'but...yes, that's about it.'

'If I'm pushed out of the market before finalising a major deal, there's no way back for someone like me,' Michael states. 'After Templeton has my apology, putting me in the wrong by my own admission, DBL will fire me from my own company. Won't they?'

'I can't believe–' Diddy starts before seeming to choke on his words.

'I'll apologise. Best that way,' Michael says.

* * *

251

For the rest of the afternoon Michael lazes, next to Lisa, beside the pool. In the centre of the water two small twigs bob up and down, not quite touching. Michael points them out to Lisa.

'I think it's a courtship ritual,' she says.

'It's wasted. If they do get together, they're too wet to start a fire.'

Behind sunglasses, he stares at the curve of her hips, at the gentle sway of her breasts and at the triangle of cloth over her sex. Compelled to lie on his front, his back enjoys the sun and his mind revolves as comfortably as a hamster tied to its wheel.

On the other side of the pool, under the palms, Megan's friends talk with Elizabeth and Samson.

'It's hot,' Megan says and jumps in.

The twigs embrace.

She swims over to Lisa and Michael, rests her elbows on the poolside and, with a dazzling smile, calls him in. The sing-song notes of her Antipodean accent are child-like. The underlying 'play with me' message contrasts with her adult arguments as she rattles on about his back getting sunburnt, him having not been in the water all afternoon and that she feels he is ignoring her. When logic fails, she splashes him and brings Lisa into the conversation.

'I know when I'm beaten,' Michael says, rising.

Self-conscious, forbidding himself from checking if he appears decent, he dives in towards the far end. Away from her. But the pool is only twenty feet long, and when he surfaces Megan is next to him. Lisa moves to the side of the pool, lowers herself and submerges her feet.

After ducking down beneath the surface, Megan emerges with a mouthful of water which she squirts into Michael's face. It is a strangely sensuous act. With her hair dripping, despite her smile, she seems vulnerable. Protectively, almost paternally, without bringing their bodies closer, he links his arms round her neck.

'I love Mac so bad it bleeds,' she says, dropping the smile.

He tilts his head in understanding.

'He's such a shit,' she adds. Megan dips under the water and swims back towards her friends.

Easing herself into the pool, Lisa floats over to Michael. He watches her graceful movements and remembers how it was, all those years ago. She is still as beautiful to him as she ever was.

'Do you feel for Megan?' Lisa says.

'Did I what?' Michael laughs, intentionally misunderstanding.

Lisa puts her arms around his waist and pulls his body into hers. For the sake of appearances, although he is aware it wouldn't dupe a fool, he leans his head back. Her bare breasts nudge against his chest. Fully aroused, he presses himself against her.

'Well, I can tell one thing you feel for me,' she says, smiling.

Two of the lunch guests stay for dinner which Danny serves, at seven, on the patio. Flashing smiles, she exchanges quips with everyone except Samson. Michael watches Megan who is down in the shadows by the pool, tall in her heels, waiting for Slimeball's arrival. Amidst the discordant melody, of cutlery on china and of laughter, he hears the occasional noise of a bat swirling through the night air to take a sip from the pool.

Michael feels an urge to smash the gargoyle's permanent expression of sick pleasure when, eventually, Megan walks back up to the patio. Donald rises from the table. Holding her head high, she brushes aside her father's arms and walks through into the villa.

Half an hour later, Michael wanders away from the patio and picks daisies from the lawn. As the lawn is manicured and the flowers are closed, they are hard to find. The bouquet is tiny. He places the flowers in an egg cup, sets them on a tray, and raids enough food from the remains of the meal to fill a plate for Megan. The daises have begun to open by the time he knocks on her door.

She is sitting up in bed wearing a silk chemise. There are telltale blotches on her face from the careless removal of her make-up. A patchwork quilt, older than her father, covers her lower body.

'I've brought you something to eat,' he says.

He puts the tray on the bed. Little rivulets of tears chase down her cheeks. Resting an arm around her shoulders, he feels her body heave. Donald pokes his head around the door, but he goes away.

'I've never been stood up before,' she whines. 'It wasn't a date,' she contradicts herself.

Michael glances across to the sequinned evening dress, strewn across a chair.

'I shouldn't have said it was.'

'You can tell Mac it was a date, though. Is he having an affair?'

'No.'

253

She moves out from under his arm. 'Was he?'

'I know he has odd ways of showing it, but he loves you.'

'Answer my question...please.'

'How would I know, Megan? Look, when you got married...it was no secret. Mac's not chorister of the year; he never has been. And our lives – here an overseas trip, there a visit to a nightclub. I don't hold his hand. We–'

'You'd know if he was seeing someone.'

Michael tries to muster his thoughts. But, in thinking, he leaves a gap before answering that he knows is a month overdue.

'He isn't,' he says.

'I don't know why you're protecting him.'

'Megan, if there had been something, and it was over, would you really want to know? Or just be absolutely certain it was finished?'

'He doesn't deserve you as a friend.'

Michael lowers his eyes.

'I don't want to be here tomorrow,' she says. 'My Dad, Mac and you – it's going to be awful, isn't it?'

'It's just business.' He replaces his arm around her. 'Mac's desperate to see you.' She shakes her head. 'Your Dad', Michael continues, 'said you'd told him about the Anstaldt. You spend the money too, Megan. And your father doesn't know the whole story.'

'So what about the other papers?'

'I don't know what you've seen. Which ones do you mean?'

'Entire Reinsurance Panama? About my Dad being pensioned off?'

Uncharacteristically, Michael's body refuses his mind's standing orders to offer no clues. His arm tenses on her silk nightdress.

'Michael?'

'I can't discuss them with you...yet. There's no point in worrying.'

'And I'm a kangaroo,' she says seriously. 'I'm going back to London.'

'And your friends?'

'Can they stay?'

'I can't kick them out,' he says coldly. 'Can I let Mac know you'll be waiting for him at home – send your love?'

'What are you, Michael, a marriage counsellor?'

Michael looks away towards the door.

'Tell him', she says, 'if he screws around, I'll fuck off.'

He laughs from the pit of his belly. And, seemingly despite herself, she joins in.

When their laughter subsides, he says, 'I'll tell him that.'

He should go downstairs to his guests, and he wants to see Lisa. But he retires to his room to compose himself. He lies down and, in the swamp of his thoughts, is sucked into a fully clothed sleep.

Shortly before midnight, wearing a baby doll nightdress, Lisa steps into Michael's room and shuts the door. Despite the darkness of the room, she notices the picture of Josie on Michael's bedside table. She picks it up and replaces it, face down.

'It's me,' she whispers.

But he is fast asleep. Squatting down, she unlaces his shoes, slips them off and positions them, as she thinks Michael would himself, neatly on the rug. Bit by bit, she tugs down his socks, inches them over his ankles and then places them into his shoes. Dextrously, she releases his shirt buttons and pulls the shirt off the side of his chest. His chest hair is blond, clean – manly. She stops and, putting her palm on him, feels his heartbeat. Surely, he must wake up at any moment.

Continuing, she raises the deadweight of his hand in the air, eases the shirt past Michael's elbow and, very gently, draws the material underneath him to lift the shirt from his other arm. Then she pauses. He stirs in his sleep, and she drops the shirt on the floor. Lisa undoes the top button to his trousers, unzips him and inserts her hands inside the trousers just below his groin. Gradually, she glides them down over his knees and steps to the end of the bed. With a firm grip on the bottom of each trouser leg, she pulls by degrees, first one then the other, unhurriedly, until they are bunched around his ankles. Sliding them off, she lines up the creases and places them on a hanger in the armoire. She hovers above his body and touches her breasts.

Although he remains inert, she thinks she glimpses a slight movement of his eyelid. She can't be sure in the dark. But he wants her; she knows it. She can see his arousal building as the material of his underpants pushes upwards. He must be awake. She moves her hand lower, up inside her skimpy nightdress, between her thighs, and rubs against her sex.

255

'Michael.'

Crossing the room, she collects a blanket from the top of a wicker hamper. A floorboard squeaks beneath her. He stays asleep. After she covers him with the blanket, she put her lips to his cheek and strokes his forehead.

'You can wake up,' she says.

He utters a deeply sleepy 'thank you' and rolls over onto his side. Lisa hesitates, steps backwards, turns, switches out his light and leaves him, closing the door behind her.

Chapter Thirty

Donald and Samson spend Wednesday afternoon admiring each other's anecdotes, and Michael applauds them politely during the interludes with clapped-out comments such as 'oh, really'. He is catnapping; after Lisa's nocturnal visit, it took him hours to return to sleep.

'When's Mac due?' Donald asks, apropos nothing.

Michael shrugs and turns his head towards the pool in search of Lisa. Only Elizabeth sunbathes under the palms. Megan's friends have gone to see Megan off at Nice airport. At breakfast, Lisa asked if he had slept well, looked at him quizzically, and then vanished.

When Michael hears a car pull into the courtyard, he excuses himself. He opens the door to Mac and meanders with him into the reception room. Avoiding premature eye contact, Michael looks round the vast room. He sees it anew. Chasing round the entire ceiling, the stucco border depicts a medieval hunt in which a wild boar suffers a dozen different deaths. Three silk rugs cover most of the floorboards and divide the room into sections. The first section has a banqueting table on which there is just one object: an incongruous modern telephone. On the far side, separated by a delicate table on which crystal decanters and glasses sparkle, a pair of chaise longues overlook the courtyard.

Michael walks to the middle section where two oversized armchairs face each other in front of the hearth. Letting out a low moan which tallies with his long stubble and sunken eyes, Mac slouches into the nearest chair.

'Can I see Megan first?' he asks hoarsely.

'No,' Michael says, flatly.

Michael notices Mac is trying to summon anger but, after eight flights in six days, he can only rustle up mild irritation.

257

'Why not? If it was the other way round, I wouldn't–'

'She's gone. She left a message, "You screw around; I'll fuck off".'

Mac lolls forward, defeated. Michael sits down opposite him.

'You told her,' Mac says.

'Why would I do that?' Michael asks icily. 'Guess?'

'I dunno,' Mac says. Patently horrified, he gapes at Michael.

Michael's lips are thin, his cheeks draw inwards and his lower jaw juts forward.

'Let me pin the tail on the donkey for you. I know about the Anstaldt – Doctor Templeton I presume. I know about the Cutesie management disposal and Entire Reinsurance. Panama – exotic location that. When Melissa left, she gave me copies of the papers. What's the matter, Mac? Where's your famous grin?'

'I was going to share the money with you. I promise.'

'Yeah, right. I didn't tell Megan about Melissa, but when you go home tomorrow–'

'I'm going home tomorrow?'

'To see your wife. Start the antibiotics to cure the infection you've given your marriage – compassionate leave,' Michael says. He breaks into a cold laugh, too laboured to be real.

'For God's sake,' Mac croaks, 'what's so funny?'

Michael stops his sham laughter. 'You. It's fucking comical that you thought you'd get away with this.' Betraying an iceberg of anger, a quiver traces across Michael's lips as he mimes picking up a menu. 'Let me see, what's the dish of the day? Stealing wheelchairs? Loosening roller coaster bolts? Ah yes, delicious! Betrayal. Bit pricey at £25,000, but what the hell. Got to eat. Let's kick off with the kickback–'

'It's £21,000. I had to stump up £4,000 because Lisa...she lied, you know.'

'And I'm supposed to take your word on that? Dream on.'

'It is £21,000,' Mac mumbles. 'What do you want from me?'

Michael gets up and walks over to the banqueting table while he considers, yet again, what he does want. He doesn't want what Mac can offer: half the proceeds for teaming up with DBL to carve up Cutesie and half the money paid to Mac for acting as Michael's minder.

'Nothing,' he says.

'What?' Mac gasps.

'You heard. That's enough for now. You seem a tad tired. Go for a rest.'

'But we must speak with Donald–'

'He can wait. By the way he knows. Not all the details, but enough.'

'Can I have a drink?'

'You're supposed to ask for a cigarette before execution,' Michael says. 'Nothing to snort today, or have you started injecting? Were you on something when you had Wetthards fire me?'

'Michael, I–'

'When you get up from your rest, I'll deal with Donald.'

Leaving Mac in the armchair to have his drink, Michael rejoins the others on the patio.

When Mac comes out into the lobby, Lisa is on the bottom rung of the stairs. She is about to climb them and is cradling a cup of coffee in her hands.

'Hello,' he says, 'could you show me where I'm supposed to be sleeping? Apparently, I'm in the room next to yours. Lucky me.'

She twitches, spilling a dribble of coffee over the side of her cup.

Following her '£4,000 butt' up the stairs, he stays just one step behind her. Close enough, he hopes, to make her uneasy. In the poky room, he throws his bag on the single bed and knifes his eyes down her spine as she turns to go.

'You lied,' he says to her.

She turns and, crimson-faced, stares at him.

'About the Templeton money. You lied.'

'You're loathsome,' she says. 'Stay away from me!'

Donald White and Michael stand, gunslinger distance apart, in the reception room. Between them, Mac slumps in one of the oversized armchairs by the hearth. Breaking the silence, the grandfather clock in the lobby chimes seven times.

'I can explain,' Mac mutters.

With a machete gesture, Michael hacks off Mac's proposed explanation.

'There's nothing Mac wishes to explain to you,' Michael says.

'Then you do it. Go on, use your Vaseline vocabulary,' Donald snipes. 'What about Entire Reinsurance, Panama?'

'Mac owns no shares in Entire Reinsurance. It was formed, without his knowledge, by someone with a warped sense of humour.'

'Who?' Donald demands. 'It's DBL, isn't it?'

'Except for the reasons we agreed, I haven't given DBL any information about Cutesie,' Michael says, emphasising the nick-name Donald hates.

'Are you telling me that no alternative bid for PSQC will be made?'

'No, I'm not saying that. But I am saying that Mac won't benefit in any way if you do get swallowed up.' Mac retches into a handkerchief. 'And if DBL do make an unfriendly bid,' Michael continues, 'I'll do everything in my power to stop them.'

'Your power?' Donald says. His voice oozes sarcasm.

'The same power that brought you Samson Cantwell,' Michael retorts.

'And what's your bite on that deal?' Donald demands.

'I'm surprised Samson hasn't told you. On the friendly cooperation agreement our commission is sod all less ten. Zero.'

'I don't believe you.'

'Well, that's your problem. That's the second time you've called me a liar. As if I'm going to lie to you about something so easy to check up on – do me a favour.'

Sitting down on the other side of the hearth to Mac, Donald says, 'You're still my son-in-law. Have I really misunderstood so badly?'

Michael ignores Donald's attempt at appeasement and pulls the trigger. 'What about the commission, Donald?'

'My colleagues–'

'Your colleagues?' Michael huffs. 'I was in your offices, before the wedding, remember? Or were you out fishing? You're trying to tell me that those same humble subjects who barely spoke in front of their monarch, King Donald of the Kingdom of Cutesie, are calling the shots, eh? You,' Michael stresses, 'are the President.'

'Mac...Mike,' Donald says in a subdued voice. 'I'm sorry, but I can't go along with anything higher than I suggested in London.'

260

Forcing back an urge to physically attack him, Michael says only, 'I understand.'

Danny's star-spangled voice calls, 'Dinner.'

They sit on the patio at the cast iron table. The ladies wear evening dresses, but all the men, except for Samson, sport shorts. He is dressed in a sober suit.

When Danny is in the kitchen, Elizabeth looks directly at her husband and explains to Michael, 'I don't want Samson to feel young and frisky again this week.'

Michael hasn't invited any reinsurers for dinner. Although there are eight people, the table seems half-empty. In the middle of it a candle flickers; its life is precarious; even the smallest gust threatens to snuff it out.

'What a glorious week so far,' Elizabeth says.

'I wouldn't know,' Mac says, killing that conversation in its pram.

Michael isn't sure whether it is Tamara or Lucinda who blurts out, in a nasal voice, 'Mac and you must be very well paid to afford all this.'

'It's our company's money, not ours,' Michael replies. 'We should be very well paid, for the risks we take. I've just dedicated, for example, seven months to a single project, and I've got no guarantee of any reward. Meanwhile, the company's been haemorrhaging money. We've got twenty staff – lots of other costs too.'

'Is this the time–' Samson interjects. Or starts to.

'I know it's rude, but can I ask how much money you get if it goes ahead?' Megan's friend asks.

'The deal's large. If it goes through, our client will make enough money to buy a small country and the morals of all its inhabitants. But my company will have all the money it needs...to buy a can of Fosters,' Michael says, with intentional indiscretion.

Donald snarls. Samson scratches his chin. And Mac sweeps his hair back across his forehead. A slight wind blows out the candle on the table. No one tries to relight it, and a tombstone heaviness descends. Tilting his head, Michael looks at Lisa. She seems to understand; she shepherds Elizabeth and Megan's two friends into the villa so that the men might fight in peace. Clearing the bowls of half-finished desserts from the table, Danny pulls a face which Michael reads as a sign of her disappointment at the lost appetites for her afternoon's work.

'You've agreed the commission, Mike,' Donald says.

'No, I haven't,' Michael insists.

'You said, "I understand". You agreed.'

Michael shakes his head gravely. With a sigh, Mac lights a Marlboro and blows a wisp of smoke up into the night air.

'The point Michael's making is entirely valid,' Samson says in a smooth, 'this sherry is my favourite', voice. 'My board understand, from me, that this deal will be finalised. But, as is evident, that doesn't mean it's agreed. You're a fair man, Donald, can't you settle on a sum that will satisfy Mac and Michael?'

Moving forward on his seat, Mac obviously wants to talk. But Michael stares him back into the oblivion of disgraced silence. Danny brings more wine from the kitchen and fills Mac's empty glass.

'Donald's a fair man?' Michael says to Samson, incredulously. 'He told me this buyout was his dream. So when he came to us – months back this was – saying he had a problem with our commission, I trusted him to come up with a compromise. Since then he's dorked me around.'

Michael can see it is just a question of time before Donald erupts.

'I've had enough,' Michael mouths when Danny holds the bottle over his goblet, but he mouths it to Donald.

'If Mike weren't so greedy and hadn't tried to cheat me–'

'For the record, Donald, I've never tried to cheat you. Nor will I, despite everything.' Michael switches his negotiator's face on. 'You, sir, have called me a liar and a cheat. On that basis, it's impossible for me to continue to represent you as your broker. I resign.'

Mac grinds out his cigarette purposefully. Michael knows Mac had been due to make £5m; now he can expect nothing.

Samson opens a palm towards Donald.

'I'm sorry, Mike. I went too far,' Donald says, softly.

'Reinsurance is about trust, Donald. You don't trust me, and I don't trust you anymore. It's that straightforward. Whilst I can't work for you, I'll keep my earlier promise.'

'What earlier promise?' Samson asks.

Mac recovers enough to say, 'We said we'd–'

Before being cut off by Michael, 'Try and protect Cutesie if DBL make a hostile bid – without any payment for our services –

in the same spirit as we made the introduction between Cutesie and you, Samson.'

'The commission's paid by the reinsurers,' Samson says. 'It is not up to Donald. If the reinsurers are happy, then you must go along with it, Donald. Sorry, but if you want us involved, I must insist.'

'Mac and I can't work for Cutesie,' Michael says. 'But – and I know this sounds odd – I still want the management buyout to proceed.'

'I've said I'm sorry,' Donald says. 'I'm also sorry that my apology hasn't been accepted. I need the buyout; you both know I do.' He turns to Samson. 'The two of us can reach an arrangement. We don't need Michael. I can finalise the loose ends directly with the reinsurers. If Home & Life are in concert with us, they'll be relaxed enough.'

'Home & Life would like to persevere, but we won't if you object, Michael,' Samson says.

Tightening his lips to make his displeasure yet clearer, Michael weighs his words, 'You must do as you see fit.'

Far away, a car hoots in the Mediterranean night air.

Michael's features reveal no emotion. 'You've seen how the reinsurance market works, Samson. It's complicated. Do you really fancy Donald's chances of pulling off an agreement of this magnitude? There is another way. You can become the client; Home & Life can use the deal I've lined up and insert new management into Cutesie. Like a management buy-in. You'll get a much better deal that way.'

'That's outrageous,' Donald argues.

'I must stop you there, Michael,' Samson says firmly. 'You indicated earlier that there was a takeover threat to Cutesie. Takeover battles are a complete anathema to the management of Home & Life. Sorry. If you won't be the broker, then we'll have to take our chances on Donald getting the reinsurance up and running. I'll need board approval but...'

Mac downs the contents of his glass, and Donald takes a sip from his.

'Please, Donald, have some more of our wine,' Michael criticises.

'Don't be like that, Michael,' Donald says. 'Just because you've lost out. You know what I think–.'

Dropping his bland expression, Michael interrupts, 'I couldn't give a wallaby's dropping what you think. I'm a professional, and

I've put a huge amount of work into the Cutesie buyout. I want this project to succeed. And I think you'll fail.'

'So you won't mind if we try and arrange things without your or Mike's involvement?' Donald asks Mac.

Heaving himself from his chair, Mac growls a sabre-toothed acceptance.

'Michael?' Samson asks.

'I'll leave you to it, gentlemen. Goodnight,' Michael says.

Michael leaves Donald and Samson to rekindle less grievous negotiations.

'Good night,' Mac says to Michael in the lobby. His sunken eyes portray an entirely different, hostile message.

After Mac has wound his way up the stairs, Michael steps into the empty reception room. Lisa and the others have gone to bed. Moving to the banqueting table, he picks up the telephone, lets it ring for several minutes and then tries again. On the third attempt he raps his knuckles down on the table. Josie, his fiancée, has taken the phone off the hook. He gets the engaged signal.

Half an hour later, guessing she will have replaced the receiver, he rings again. She answers it immediately.

'It's midnight. You're still up?' he asks.

'I'm busy packing, Michael. I'll talk to you when you get back. Bye.'

That is the entire conversation. He turns the lights off and walks to a chaise longue. Collapsing into it, he gazes out to the courtyard.

At two, he is distracted from his brooding by the voices of Samson and Donald on the stairway. Their conversation seems to be muted. Perhaps they have found a route forward. Perhaps not.

A selfish cacophony of creaking floorboards, banged doors and flushed toilets interrupts the stillness. After waiting until all is silent again, he goes up. Lisa's door is ajar and, as he passes it, he looks through the crack. The night light glowing by the side of her bed seems to be sprinkling glitter on her hair, and he can see that she is wearing men's pyjamas. Pushing his palm against the door, he opens it a further inch and moves his foot forward. But he doesn't go in.

Back in his own room, Michael gets undressed and levers himself between the taut sheets which feel crisp against his naked skin. The villa slumbers.

Overtired, and having drunk more than a bottle of red wine during the evening, Mac wakes just three hours after having gone to bed. He can't return to sleep. Throwing on his Levis and an old jumper, he plods out of his room to go downstairs.

He stops on the half landing and loiters at Lisa's door. Grinning off-centre, he eases it open to view her form under the bedclothes.

'I've paid for you, bitch,' he whispers. 'You owe me £4,000 of service. And I don't need an interior decorator.'

Chapter Thirty-One

Mac steals into Lisa's room, closes the door and turns off the night light. Waiting for his eyes to adjust to the darkness, he sniffs the air. He breathes in the scent of her sleeping body. As her form comes back into focus, he watches her move to the melody of her breathing. Curled up, she slumbers on her side.

'Debt collector,' he whispers.

She doesn't stir. After taking off his jumper, he undoes the stud of his jeans and drags them off. Erect, Mac takes hold of the top of her continental quilt. He jerks the duvet from the bed with a single movement.

'Is that you, Michael?' Each syllable is sleepily slurred.

Throwing himself on top of her, Mac pushes Lisa onto her front and, with one hand, squashes her face down into her pillow. Using his larger body weight and superior strength, he crushes her beneath him and grinds himself against her backside. He knows she can feel him through the thin material of her pyjama bottoms. Not just hard, brutal. And he can feel her.

She is thrusting back. He eases the pressure on her head.

'Oh, Michael,' she murmurs.

Teeth bared, Mac would like to hurt her. But he can see the advantage of waiting. Sliding his free hand under her body, he carefully undoes a button of her pyjama top to gain entry and then massages her breasts. Her skin is soft, yielding.

'That's nice.' Her voice still hasn't woken up.

Trailing his hand lower, he unties her pyjama cord and tugs her pyjama bottoms halfway down her thighs. He climbs further up her back and uses his feet to manoeuvre the material down her calves and off, over her ankles. Lisa is exposed.

'Let me turn around,' she says. 'You're starting to frighten me.'

Mac knows that at any moment she will realise it is him. He

266

pushes himself between the crevice of her buttocks. Her head twists under his hand; her resistance feeds his lust for carnal cruelty.

'No,' she says. 'Not like that. I'll scream. I mean it.' She is screaming.

Michael jolts awake and throws himself out of bed, nude. He stands there listening to the noises of the night: an owl's hoot, the wind testing the villa's shutters, and the rustle of leaves. But there are no sounds from inside the villa. No one snores. No floorboards creak. He lies back down.

Lisa's shriek rends the air: 'Get off me, Michael!'

He flies out of bed.

Lisa feels him grasp her hair, wring it and submerge her head back into the pillow. As his anvil hand weighs down on her head, Lisa feels the contours of the pillow's feathers against her lips. He is trying to force himself between her clenched buttocks, but her muscles are rigid. Her heart pistons faster and faster. Her dry tongue sticks obscenely out from her mouth, rasping into the pillow. She can't breath. Summoning every bit of energy, she struggles beneath him. But he is too strong.

And she hears Mac threaten, 'If you make any more noise...'

The instant she realises it is Mac, her body becomes covered in a thin film of cold sweat. Her pulse throbs in her forehead; her limbs defy her willpower's command to resist and, gagged by the pillow, she can't call out for help. With no escape, she feigns unconsciousness.

'Easier now, bitch. I'll wake you up for the best bit,' Mac whispers.

Spitting venom, he wrenches her pyjama shirt off. Two buttons spin to the floor. Savagely, Mac manhandles Lisa onto her back and stuffs part of the shirt into her mouth. She drops the pretence of unconsciousness and stares hatred into his frenzied eyes as he gropes her.

'I paid £4,000 to Templeton for your lie,' Mac growls. 'Open your legs, slag.'

She feels him kick his knee up between her thighs, prising her legs apart. But then she hears Michael call out her name from

267

somewhere inside the villa, and she knows that all she has to do is to keep Mac off. Just for a minute or two. Desperate, a trapped animal, Lisa lashes her arms about blindly. Fighting again, she scissors her legs back together.

She hears rushing footfalls from the stairway. Another few seconds. Feeling Mac try to ram himself between her closed legs, she knots her calves together, pulls the material from her mouth and, screeching, rakes her fingernails down his cheek. They are short and don't draw blood.

He padlocks her wrists with one hand.

Michael can hear the noises coming from inside Lisa's room as he hurtles onto the half landing. Stark naked, he crashes in. Throwing the door back against the wall, he flings himself across the room and dives feet first into Mac's side. He lands just under the ribcage. With a grunt, Mac falls off the other side of the bed. Michael rises and, silently, without looking at Lisa, walks towards Mac's crunched-up form. He holds his hands out in front of him, horizontally. It is as if he is carrying an invisible box, or as if he is going to strangle Mac.

'Don't, Michael!' Lisa shouts.

Elizabeth races in and rushes to Lisa. The two women wrap their arms around each other to form a single protective unit. Opaque-eyed, Michael stands there, nude, whilst the room fills with guests. All are in various states of undress. Crawling on his hands and knees, Mac reaches the far wall and props himself against it.

'It wasn't Michael,' Lisa says and moves her head towards Mac, directing all eyes to him.

Woodenly, one of Megan's friends picks up the quilt and passes it to Elizabeth. She drapes it over Lisa.

'We should call the police,' Elizabeth says, but Lisa shakes her head.

'Can you get him out of here, Samson?' Elizabeth says, with a cursory roll of head towards Mac.

Whilst Samson lifts the offender from the floor, Megan's two friends shamble out of the bedroom. Without any force or words, Samson takes Mac's elbow. He starts to lead him away, but Donald takes a firm grip on Mac's shoulder.

'Why?' Donald asks, with a dark frown.

Mac's head faces downwards; his body is limp; his penis is flaccid. Picking up Mac's clothes, Donald follows Samson out.

Michael views the movements around him, but feels as if he is watching from somewhere else. Watching himself. He feels calm, but the face he sees has glazed eyes and angular features. He knows it is a macabre illusion; you can't see your own face. Perhaps it is a memory from a mirror, or just a weird response to shock. Whatever it is, Michael wants rid of it.

'Michael...' Elizabeth says, pointing her eyes at Michael's body.

Michael regains control of his mind and moves a fig-leaf hand to protect what remains of his modesty.

'I'll be back in a minute,' he says.

Dressed, Michael returns to find Lisa, now swathed in a white bathrobe, rocking back and forth in Elizabeth's arms. He kisses Lisa's forehead. Easing out of Elizabeth's embrace, she pulls him close to her. He remembers a hymn that they sung together as children at Sunday school. And, lips shaking, he tries to sing it to her. His singing is broken, disjointed, and she cries in fits and sobs. When he stops, she cradles his face between her hands.

'Please, sing some more,' she says. But he doesn't.

Elizabeth leaves. Once Lisa and Michael are alone, he lies with her under the duvet. Although he is fully clothed, he feels her heart pounding under her robe as she clings to him. He looks her in the eyes; the blind eyes that saw him as a rapist. Lisa had called out for him, Michael, to get off her. He doesn't want to ask her, not then, but the nosebleed of a question dribbles out regardless.

'Why did you think it was me?'

The question hangs in the air, and she pulls away from him. Glancing at her, he sees that her skin is even paler than a few moments previously and that her eyes bulge. It seems to him that she just can't bring herself to hear her own explanation. Lisa gets out from under the quilt, sits by the window and peers down at the courtyard below. When Elizabeth returns with three cups of tea on a tray, Michael rises from the bed and takes his tea with him down the spiral staircase.

In the reception room, Donald sits by the hearth in one of the huge armchairs. He sips Scotch. Tear marks stain his cheeks. Finding the decanter, Michael leaves his teacup and, pouring one for himself, joins Donald in the other chair. Better than tea.

'He's asleep,' Donald says.

Michael doesn't reply. 'I'm leaving tomorrow,' he says after a few minutes.

'What about your meetings?'

Michael shrugs, rises and strolls over to the window facing out to the courtyard. 'What meetings?' he says. 'I came here to finalise your business.'

'I'm – I'm sorry...I've got no right to ask, but will you tell Megan for me, Mike?' Donald asks, almost begs.

Michael walks to him and holds Donald's forearm. Taking the empty glass from Donald's trembling fingers, he pours two more small whiskies. The grandfather clock chimes four.

'No. I'm sorry, Donald, but no,' he says, handing Donald his drink.

He can see Donald understands. But still, Megan has to be told. Otherwise at some dreary cocktail party a so-called friend will vomit the, 'I didn't want to be the one to tell you, but...', news onto her dress.

'I'll go to London – not the telephone,' Donald says. 'Megan will be very wounded. Mike, it's my fault. If you knew–'

'Mac tried to rape Lisa; that's not your fault. Not at all.'

'I must tell you something, Mike. Before Megan and Mac were engaged–'

'You think I don't know?' Michael says.

Head bowed, Donald rises and offers Michael his hand. Michael takes it.

'No hard feelings?' they ask each other without moving their lips.

'No hard feelings,' they agree by holding the grasp for five seconds.

After Donald goes to his room, Michael stares into space, mulling over mundane details. If he calls the hire car company, they will collect their death trap. And he can take a taxi to the airport. But he will end up waiting around the villa for hours. Or he can fix the brakes. It is something to do rather than staying slumped in a chair downing alcohol.

Intense, upstairs, Lisa focuses on the lack of movement in the courtyard. Elizabeth sleeps on the bed. Earlier Samson poked his head round the door to say goodnight to his wife.

'You're in safe hands,' Samson told Lisa. 'Anyone who tried to attack Elizabeth would be out of their–'

'How dare you?' Elizabeth interrupted.

But it is clear to Lisa that Samson meant it as a compliment of sorts. Elizabeth is an effective guard, asleep or not.

Around five, someone comes out of the double doors and into the courtyard. He opens a car bonnet. Although the figure appears blurry in the dark, the blond hair is distinctive – at least to Lisa who watches from her window. It is Michael.

At six o'clock, Elizabeth shoots up with a start.

'What's that noise?'

'Mac's car,' Lisa replies, absent-mindedly, from the window. 'I guess Mac's going home. Good.'

And then a searchlight inside Lisa's head lights up, in lurid detail, the association between her peep-show suspicions and Michael's earlier actions in the courtyard. The brakes. Taking a long drawl of oxygen, she hurtles, past a wide-eyed Elizabeth, down the stairs and charges into the reception room. Michael paces by the hearth.

'Lisa?'

'I saw you, by the cars, in the courtyard, Michael. Tell me the truth.'

'You think I tampered with Mac's car? I was fixing mine.'

'I don't care about Mac. You went into the courtyard with no tools. No tools. No spanner, no wrench, not even a screwdriver. Tell me the truth, Michael!'

'Of course there were tools; they were in the boot. I used them.'

'That doesn't matter,' she says, gulping. 'I know, Michael.'

'Know? I didn't touch Mac's car.'

'Not Mac's car. Peter's scooter. You caused his crash, didn't you?'

'No.' Michael touches his upper lip with the tip of his tongue.

But he must have. Otherwise her teenage rejection of him was wrong. And her whole life could have been so very different. So very happy.

'You just wanted to frighten him,' Lisa implores. 'Hurt–'

'I've answered your question,' Michael says, shaking his head.

They don't speak. He has to be lying to her. She wants him tell her that he understands why she had to ask. And she wants him to admit it. So she can forgive him. And she would. She takes him by

271

the hand and leads him to an armchair where she snuggles her robed body into his. For comfort, warmth. But no. Bare metal in the snow, icy cold. Not hate, not rejection, just numb.

'Did you lie about the Templeton money?' he asks.

'Yes,' she says. 'I'm so sorry.'

His eyes offer no forgiveness. They tell her emphatically that he wants to be elsewhere, with Josie. She searches for healing words, but the only ones that come to mind mimic the worst of his wry barbs.

'We should both try and get some sleep,' he says, prising himself free. And she hears his words as goodbye. Goodbye for good.

Danny serves breakfast on the patio at eight for Samson, Elizabeth and Michael. Surprisingly, their conversation is normal and their behaviour – nearly normal. Nearly. Michael notices Samson's eyes on Danny's derrière. But Elizabeth doesn't object. And, oddly, Samson's gaze lacks any sexual content.

Over freshly-squeezed orange juice and poached eggs, they swap notes on cities visited and restaurants dined in.

Then Michael sees Elizabeth nod to her husband, Samson blink approval and her lips chew on some unformed words.

'Why won't Lisa involve the police?' Elizabeth asks, eventually. 'I would.'

Michael looks down onto the quarry tiles where the breeze plays five-a-side with a team of eucalyptus leaves. Elizabeth coughs and Michael replies.

'I can't say.'

'Why can't you say?' Samson asks. 'Because you don't know, or because she wouldn't want it?'

In lieu of an answer, Michael presses his lips together.

'If she changed her mind, you'd give evidence. Wouldn't you?' Elizabeth asks. 'But you know she won't.'

'I don't think she will. Once Lisa's made up her mind...'

'Home & Life', Samson says, 'are a very conservative company, Michael.'

Michael replies, 'I understand.'

The overseas manager of Home & Life wipes an imaginary bead of sweat from his forehead. Knowing that Samson's company is

272

allergic to scandal, Michael understands that they can't deal with Michael's firm because of Mac's behaviour.

'Thanks,' Samson says.

'For what?' Michael asks.

'For making that so easy for me.'

A solitary swan flies through the clear skies overhead.

'You're going today?' Elizabeth enquires.

The extra, unspoken question is the one that Michael answers, 'Oh, please. You must stay.'

'Thank you, Michael,' Elizabeth says with a smile.

Breakfast over, Samson and Elizabeth scrape their chairs back on the tiles and leave Michael with the gargoyle, and its unsettling grin, as company. Michael leaps from his chair, tears it from the wall and hurls it onto the tiles where it smashes into a dozen unsmiling bits.

'Can't we go a bit faster?' Mac says to the driver of the black cab.

'Listen, mate...' the taxi driver threatens, but he looks in the mirror and pauses. 'Are you alright?'

'Yeah, I'm OK,' Mac replies.

'I'll do me best, mate. Traffic's...you know.'

Mac settles back into the seat. It smells faintly of vinyl and urine. Opening the ashtray and the window, he decides to ignore the 'No Smoking' sign.

'Can't you read?' the cabby complains.

'Sorry,' Mac replies, but he makes no attempt to put it out.

Blocking the road, the taxi screeches to a halt outside Josie's Hampstead boutique. Mac fishes in his pockets for the right fare.

'Oi, not so much of a hurry you're in now. Where's my tip?'

Mac staggers into the shop.

A few dresses, unsullied by price labels, are elegantly draped over the centre-piece arrangement: a tea party of sleek nymphs frozen in bronze indifference. On the walls, an array of delicate scarves adorn the severed necks of blank-eyed sculptures. Mac can't see a cash register anywhere in the shop, and only one single rack of clothes contradicts the impression that the place is an art gallery.

'You look like you should be in casualty,' Josie says.

Her colleague peers at the unlikely customer.

'I thought you were in Monte Carlo gorging on Beluga and quaffing Buck's Fizz,' she says. 'So you've finally decided to come and see where I work. I was just off to lunch. Do you...?'

'No...er,' he slurs. 'I need to get home to see Megan.' He swivels his head from side to side. 'Nice place. Something I must...'

'What is it, Mac? Do you want a seat? You look dreadful.'

'It's Michael. He's turned on me. He's going to say some– I don't want you, or Mum and Da–' Sober, he sways drunkenly. 'Whatever he says, it's not true.'

'Is Michael back too? Where is he?'

'I don't know how to tell you this, Josie. The last time I saw him was in Lisa's room, and he was–' She talks over the top of him as he says, 'naked.'

'What! You bloody moron. You're just trying to hurt me.'

'Naked,' Mac repeats.

'I don't believe you.'

Back at his house, the chandelier tinkles when Mac stumbles into the dining room. He picks up the note from the lacquered table, but doesn't read it immediately because under it – indented into her favourite piece of furniture, as if she doesn't care any more – are the marks from Megan's writing.

'Gone to pick my father up,' Megan's note reads.

Chapter Thirty-Two

Seven o'clock and all is not well with Michael. When Josie told him she was packing, he presumed that she meant her things. Bereft, feeling like a stranger on foreign soil, he stands in the centre of his living room. Nothing of his remains in the room, even the television has gone. The new furniture might have come straight from a Habitat catalogue. On the wall, where his bookcase was, hangs a sampler with a picture of a cream house. Three words are embroidered above the sampler's alphabet: 'Home Sweet Home'.

Hearing the shower running, he calls out and waits. Exhausted, it takes him a while to work out the obvious: she couldn't have arranged this within a week; she has planned it in advance. But he knows he can't win an argument and desperately wants to avoid one. When Josie sweeps down the stairs, her expression is as uncompromising as a force-nine gale. The long, tiresome journey and missed sleep register on his contrite face.

'You've made some changes,' he says. 'Looks good.'

'All your things are in the small bedroom.'

Although he knows from her demeanour it won't work, he starts to recite the pre-cooked meal of a mini-speech. It lacks conviction.

'Did you think up that rubbish lying in her bed, afterwards?' she interrupts.

'Please, Josie. It's over. She's out of my system.'

'Out of your system – pumped out into her? And now you've decided that whatever you had was gone, you think you can come back to me and tell me...what?'

'That I love you; that I want us to be together,' Michael says.

'That's why you invited Lisa to Monte Carlo, is it? Get out!'

Michael knows this is the pivotal point; he knows she expects

275

him to say that this is his home, and he knows if he does she will leave. Leave with her furniture. And their unborn child.

'Okay,' he says, 'but can we talk first. Josie, I don't want to lose you.'

He sees his agreement more than surprises her; her lower jaw drops. Folding her arms, she sits down on the new settee. With a hangdog look, he joins her.

'Mac came to the shop today,' she challenges him. 'He told me that the last time he saw you, you were in Lisa's bedroom – nude.'

Despite his tiredness, perhaps because of it, Michael laughs – neither controlled nor contrived, but fits of laughter.

Visibly unnerved, she says, 'Stop it.'

But, unable to stop, he carries on for another minute before gritting his teeth and pulling himself back to sanity.

'I didn't kiss Lisa, let alone sleep with her.' Michael tries a smile.

'Tell me, what did happen then?' Unfolding her arms, she stretches out a hand into the space between them on the settee. 'Tell me again, Michael. Tell me that you weren't in Lisa's bedroom.'

'You don't want to know everything, Josie.'

Her solitary hand remains on the settee.

'Don't patronise me. I asked you a question.'

'I was in her bedroom. But–'

'But what?'

He reaches out to touch her hand, but she withdraws it.

'I was there because Mac tried to rape her.'

She gives him a look as if he has slapped her face.

'Mac can have any girl he wants. Why would he? I don't know what to believe any more.' She softens her voice. 'Why's he scared of you, Michael?'

'He has no need to be frightened – not of me. Look, he's my brother too; we were just born to different parents.'

'I need time to think. Please go. Take some clothes; go to your parents.'

'Josie, please.'

'I'll call you on Monday.'

When he hears Megan's hatchback on the gravel, Mac comes out of the house. Stepping forward, he waves tentatively to her and her

276

father. He expects her to park next to his Mercedes, as normal. But she doesn't. Glaring directly at Mac, she simply uses the rear of his car rather than her brakes to stop. Even at low speed, the crunch is loud. Broken glass from the coupling cars ejaculates messily onto the little stones underneath.

Donald tumbles out of the Fiesta; he is unharmed, but seems dazed, as if he would like to be somewhere else, anywhere else, away from the carnage of the confrontation. Hesitantly rounding the Fiesta, Mac opens Megan's door.

'Are you alright?' he asks.

Ignoring him, she gets out of the car and marches into the house. Mac follows her. In the middle of the hall, she stops, turns and digs her heels into the parquet with conspicuous malice.

'What do you want?' Mac pleads.

'What do I want?' Megan replies with a castrating sneer. 'I want a divorce.'

On Friday morning, Michael strolls past the rostrum and peers into the Casualty Register: a book the size of a church bible which stands on an aged pedestal. Oblivious to the pinstripe soup of brokers around him, he reads the huge copperplate swirls detailing maritime mishaps. He isn't indulgently wasting time, but rather calming himself before mounting the marble steps up to the gallery to see Templeton.

Disregarding the scattered line at Templeton's box, Michael manoeuvres himself into Jeremy Templeton's line of sight and then, once he is sure Templeton has seen him, clutches his slipcase firmly and makes as if to walk away. Rarely, except for fireside chats with new investors, do Lloyd's underwriters break off while underwriting. But Michael knows Templeton craves revenge – and wants to see the white flag of an apology before taking no prisoners – sorely enough to deviate from his normal discipline. Templeton stops the broker he is talking with in mid-sentence, rises from his pew and nods at Michael. Walking towards the lifts, they find a clear space by the rail where they can talk in private.

'I thought you were going to apologise next week,' Templeton says. 'I may face disciplinary action–'

'I haven't come to apologise about that. But I have a genuine apology to make about Lisa and the invoices. Willingly or not, I understand Mac's taken care of most of your extra tax liability. But you still have some, and I'll pay it. Sorry.'

'You didn't know?'

'No. If you're prepared to leave things there...'

'Thank you for that, but I'm not. I want–'

'Don't ask me to do that. You haven't said sorry for passing Mac backhanders, or for anything else. I don't want you to. We're even.'

'No, Michael. As a result of your actions my Names will have to find hundreds of thousands of pounds more tax.'

'It would've been tax evasion,' Michael says. 'It was wrong.'

'Wrong? You're wrong, about all of this. I was just trying to look after my investors. All of this conspiracy nonsense is in your imagination. Why'd you do it? And while we're at it, I didn't give Lisa that work because she was the cheapest. I gave it to her because...because, Michael, I respected you. If you said she was competent, then she was.'

'Respected me?' Michael says, staring down towards the rostrum. 'Ten years of my work, you tried to steal. What sort of respect does that show? And why did you keep pushing me? To cheat on taxes. So can you really blame me for believing Lisa rather than you, uh?'

'What is it with you?' Templeton replies. 'It's not just me you're at war with, it's everyone you think had a better start in life than you did. You had a decent upbringing; I know you did. It was just different, that's all. Why do you hate us?'

'It's not us and them. Right now it's just me and you. I don't hate you, but I loathe the way you've tried to use me.'

Around the men, above the noise of names called from the rostrum, is a din as deafening as a prison canteen. But all that Michael hears is silence.

'Can't we just leave it?' Michael asks out of the blue. 'You know what'll happen to me if I apologise to you. How long do you think I'd last? A week?'

'Less,' Templeton says. 'But I'll have my apology all the same.'

'Please, Jeremy, don't force me into a corner,' Michael says.

'Or what?' Templeton snarls. 'Are you threatening me again?'

Without warning, Michael walks away.

He steams through the ranks of the chinless foot-soldiers, down into the bowels of the Lloyd's basement and to the public phones there.

While Michael waits to be connected to *The Protester*'s editor, he taps his fingers on his slipcase in which the primed gun of Templeton's Christmas card list is holstered.

'I've decided,' Patrick Coughan says instead of hello, 'that we will run an article on Templeton. Pretty small beer though. You're holding out on me.'

'Oscar Wilde said there are two tragedies in life: getting what you want, and not getting what you want,' Michael says, obliquely. 'Templeton insists on an apology. I'm going to give you the full scoop, so I can say sorry about something.'

'And?' Patrick says. His voice is impatient; Michael can hear the maelstrom of newsroom activity in the background.

'I've got a list of all of Templeton's investors.'

'So?' Patrick says. 'Come on, Michael. I'm really up against it today.'

'I've cross-referenced it against addresses. Most are ex-directory, but I've got hold of enough telephone numbers for you to–'

'Bingo,' Patrick says. 'Even after deleting their expletives, I should get some juicy reactions. Drop it over, will you? And gimme the technical gubbins on how his deals work; I do know you had something to do with them. I won't publish your name – promise. I need it Monday morning latest. You do understand this will destroy the man, don't you?'

Before Samson and Elizabeth leave Monte Carlo on Friday morning, Samson gives Lisa a lift into town. Both he and his wife offer to come along, but Lisa declines politely. She wouldn't mind companionship, but she doesn't want chaperones gifting her their time out of charity.

At the café, sipping an espresso, she watches the last dances of the rendezvous revellers swirl around her. Most seem to have departed and she imagines that many of the others have retreated to drink fruit punches and frozen yoghurts on hotel sunloungers whilst topping up their tans. She sits there for over two hours, interested but isolated.

By the time she returns, after lunch, only Danny remains with her at the villa. Lisa spends the afternoon lying in the dappled shadows by the edge of the water, watching the Mexican waves of the palm leaves cheer the breeze.

279

It is four when, wearing blazing-yellow hot-pants and a bra-like top guaranteed to annoy the good residents of Monte Carlo, Danny bounces towards Lisa. 'I'm missing a couple of ingredients; I need to go and pick them up,' Danny says. 'OK with you if I leave you alone for an hour?'

'Sure,' Lisa replies, automatically.

When Danny's gone, Lisa tries to raise a smile.

'I guess I'd better get used to being alone,' she says above the gentle lapping of the water.

The hallway in the Darrett's house is a much used, much loved room in itself. Above the dado rail, the motley souvenirs on the polished shelf tell visitors more about the family's life and loves than could be played out in a month of evenings at the gramophone club.

From where she sits without her glasses on the hall seat, glued to the telephone, Michael knows his mother can only see the mementoes directly opposite her. A Victorian doll jostles for pride of place with a pair of Delft clogs, a stein and a framed picture of Michael, their adopted Adonis, dancing with Josie at Mac's wedding. Michael peeks downstairs and sees his Mum fondling the picture as she listens to Julie MacIntyre.

At least, he presumes it to be Mac and Josie's mother. Whoever it is, for Michael the call is both painfully embarrassing and compelling listening.

'Um...I know,' his mother says. 'Oh, poor Josie...Is she?' The one side of the conversation that Michael can hear is fragmented, broken up by silences the lengths of pieces of string. 'No, you're right. We can't interfere. Well, yes...that too. There must've been an almighty argument between Mac and Michael. I don't know what it was about though. Exactly. Normally, I'd be thrilled to have Michael stay – we don't see enough of him – but I haven't seen him so out of sorts since he was ten. No. Apart from driving to the office to collect some papers, he's done nothing all weekend. Hang on, Julie. He's coming downstairs. I'll find him another errand.'

'Mum, please,' Michael complains, softly.

'Make your Dad some tea, will you? He must be parched,' she says.

Mr Darrett takes the mug that Michael brings him in the garden, leans on his fork and looks into Michael's eyes.

'Josie will forgive you. You'll get back together.'

'Lisa never forgave me.'

'Well,' his father says, meaningfully.

'Dad...' Michael says. His voice evaporates in the September air. His father puts down the tea and turns the earth.

On Monday morning, Michael enters his company's office where, all the busier for being watched, shirtsleeves and blouses scurry. Despite the usual all-revealing light and the everyday tip-tap musak of terminal keyboards, a dark eve-of-storm atmosphere pervades the fourth floor.

Mac rushes to him. 'They've been waiting half an hour.'

'You look terrible, Mac. Who is "they"?'

'Professor Dietrich, Templeton and Richards-Riley. All your favourite people are in the conference room. Just say sorry, Michael.'

'Did it work for you?' he snaps. 'And you had something to be sorry for.'

Mac flusters and looks down. 'Michael, I– Anyway, where've you been?'

'You'll find out. Let's get this over,' Michael says, opening the conference room door.

The paper factory is clear of files – Michael has collected them over the weekend – but it is full of people. From one end of the table, a B-movie gangster in his black double-breasted suit, Professor Dietrich mutters a greeting. Or a curse. Either way, Michael isn't bothered. He pulls a chair out but, holding the predatory stare of Richards-Riley, stays upright.

'Good morning, gentlemen,' Michael says. 'Is this a social call?'

Templeton's tight lips advertise that he isn't in the mood for Michael's flippant sarcasm. With a toss of his head, Richards-Riley signals to Dietrich.

'Do you need me?' Mac asks.

'Yes, take a seat,' Michael says. 'Has everyone got coffee? We'd hate–'

'You know why we're here, Michael,' Dietrich says. 'Apologise!'

'Apologies have much more meaning when they're personal.

281

Are all of you sure you don't want to speak to me individually?' Michael asks, smiling.

'What's wrong with you, Darrett?' Richards-Riley hisses.

'Here we go then,' Michael says. 'First apology: I apologise that if you, Professor Dietrich, proceed one centimetre further with the Cutesie management throw-out, I'll cripple DBL for misusing privat–'

'You can't prove–' Professor Dietrich starts.

'Perhaps I can't prove that Mac gave you inside information, perhaps I can. I've got copies of all Mac's papers, letters and notes. And, by using the name Entire Reinsurance Panama, you haven't exactly made your position easy to defend. But, whatever...Cutesie can hold DBL Bermuda responsible; Bermuda agreed a binding confidentiality agreement.'

Templeton interrupts, 'I know nothing about Cutes–'

'DBL do. That brings me to my apology to you, Mr Templeton. This morning I gave my journalist friend the full story. Everything. Right now he's working the phones contacting dozens of your investors. Those he can't reach can read all about it. Still, nothing to worry about...'

'On top of the prospect of disciplinary action!' Templeton splutters. 'Nothing to worry about? Damn you!'

Out of the corner of his eye, Michael sees Dietrich and Richards-Riley exchange glances. Dietrich runs a finger across his throat.

'Sorry, Jeremy,' Richards-Riley says to Templeton.

'What?' Templeton almost spits at Richards-Riley. 'Are you telling me that I can't ride this little squall out, that you're going to drop me as underwriter for my – *my* – syndicate? Thirty years I've–'

'Mr Templeton,' Professor Dietrich says, 'this sort of in-fighting is exactly what Darrett wants.'

'Sorry, Jeremy,' Richards-Riley repeats.

Templeton's face flushes and he bangs his forearm down on the aged pine of the conference table. 'Cedric, let me be clear: if you try and force me out, I'll take the whole of Wetthards down with me.'

Although Michael finds this threat difficult to digest, he knows he must plough on. 'I have yet another apology.'

'You jumped-up tosser, Darrett,' Richards-Riley says. 'I've had as much of your so-called apologies as I can stomach.'

'I apologise to anyone in this room with an Anstaldt. Because, on my way in this morning, I dropped off a letter to the Revenue advising them of Mac's. It tells them how he came by it, and who helped him set it up. Some tax inspectors are suspicious people; they might think that the reason for a trust in Liechtenstein is tax evasion. Arguing that your local building-society branch is over a mile away may not be persuasive. I hope anyone who's got one has declared it on their tax return.'

Richards-Riley doesn't hold his gaze, but to his surprise Templeton does.

Stifling what he feels is an inappropriate pang of conscience, Michael addresses Templeton: 'I gave you a chance to avoid this.'

'How can you live with yourself?' Templeton erupts. 'I didn't have you fired. But no, you didn't want to hear that. I didn't lie about the invoices; Lisa did. But no, you wouldn't listen. I wasn't trying to hide anything from my investors – just protect them.' He lowers his voice. 'And, no, I don't cheat on my taxes. But you–'

'Quit whining, Jeremy,' Richards-Riley says. 'You knew what was going on. You notice what you want, when you want.'

Templeton claws Richards-Riley with a look of distilled disgust. 'How dare you talk to me like that,' Templeton says.

'There's nothing illegal about using an Anstaldt,' Dietrich says, seemingly proud of his country's contribution to the world economy.

'They're used to avoid tax,' Michael says. 'And to accept improper payments.' Michael locks his eyes on Richards-Riley. 'Whose money's in yours?'

'There is an explanation,' Richards-Riley says, without offering it.

'No doubt there is,' Michael says. He turns to Templeton. 'But not an innocent one. You wouldn't be able to bring Wetthards down if there was. I don't suppose I'll ever find out how much money's been taken, or who's wallet it's been lifted from. And I'm not even sure I care anymore.'

Richards-Riley glares at Michael over his half rims.

'Give me a pound, Mac,' Michael says.

Mac extracts a creased note from his back pocket and passes it over. 'Uh?'

Grasping Mac's pound, Michael says, 'Congratulations, Mac, you own my entire shareholding.'

Richards-Riley's golden glint appears when, in open-mouthed rage, he shouts at Professor Dietrich, 'Fire him!'

'Not yet,' Michael says. 'I've got a last apology: I won't, under any circumstances, do business with anyone in this room again.' He swivels to face Mac. 'And that includes you.'

Out of steam and unemployed, Michael turns to leave.

Unabashed, Mac grins off-centre.

Chapter Thirty-Three

Bitter. That is what Michael spends Mac's pound on. Downstairs in the Wine Lodge, Michael murders his second half-pint while he kills time before his meeting with Samson. Despite the short notice, Samson has agreed to see him.

The cathedral ceiling of the foyer throws back the echo of his footsteps as he enters the gilded splendour of Home & Life's offices. Samson himself comes to reception and grasps both of Michael's hands in a double handshake.

'Sorry to hear your news. Let's go up,' Samson says.

When they get out of the ancient lift on the top floor, they pass a suit of armour from a bygone century. Samson guides Michael through hushed corridors furnished like antique galleries to his office. They sit in two Windsor chairs, upright and polite. Solicitously, Samson's prim secretary places coffee in front of them. While Samson expresses condolences for Michael's newly unsalaried status, Michael plays with his spoon and watches the ripples revolve.

'I haven't told my board yet,' Samson says.

'You still want to proceed?'

'Yes, but there are problems. Cutesie don't have much time, and Donald wants to take Megan home. He says he can't do the reinsurance. He's spoken to a few of the people you introduced him to in Monte Carlo. They've told him that Hurricane David's heading straight for Florida and there's another, Hurricane Frederick, following on. Apparently, they're too busy to structure something. And Donald seems to be giving up so easily...'

'He doesn't know these people,' Michael says, 'and they don't know him. They're just fobbing him off. I could–'

'I shouldn't be talking to you about this. Not only have you resigned as Cutesie's broker, but I can't deal with you because of Mac.'

285

'I'm no longer tied in with Mac; when I resigned, I sold my shares. There're no restrictions on me. I'm forming a new firm; it won't be a Lloyd's broker, but...'

Samson tips forward in his chair and smiles wanly.

'I still can't move ahead; we'd get into a takeover battle with DBL. That's not the sort of thing that Home & Life enjoy.'

Summoning his negotiator's face, Michael says, 'But DBL have decided not to proceed with the takeover.'

'Why would they do that?' Samson asks.

'DBL's Bermudan operation signed a confidentiality agreement. I've made it clear to Professor Dietrich that it'll be enforced,' Michael says. 'DBL will back off.'

'Are you sure? Absolutely certain, Michael?'

'Yes, sir.'

Samson smiles, though Michael isn't sure why. Perhaps at the answer. Or perhaps because Michael has employed the mode of speech he uses in Lloyd's. Used to use in Lloyd's.

'You become the client; I'll get the deal done,' Michael says.

'And Donald?' Samson asks.

'You'll need to share the fifty million with Cutesie's management. How you split the money is down to you. And I'm not going to insist on Donald being bundled out of the back steps. I'd like him treated fairly.'

'What?' Samson exclaims. 'You're just going to leave it there? After the way he was prepared to drop you, take months of your work and pay you nothing?'

'Yep,' Michael says.

'You are a sod sometimes,' Samson laughs. 'You know jolly well that he's due an early bath.'

'Just don't drown him in it,' Michael says, seriously.

Samson drinks his coffee in a single gulp before breaking into a huge smile.

'So Cutesie's a deal. One detail though, Michael: your commission.'

'You know my commission.'

'That's decent of you. My wife told me you'd find a way forward. I fancied a bet as to whether you would try and up the ante, if you did. But both of us wanted to wager on you not getting too greedy.'

'Would you have paid more if I'd asked?'

'No,' Samson laughs. 'I wouldn't. Two million is a vast amount of money. You don't even have a partner to share it with now.'

'Um,' Michael says, unable to raise a smile.

In Virginia Water that evening, the argument ricochets off the expensive wallpapers.

'I wish you were dead,' Megan shouts.

'You spoilt bitch,' Mac bellows.

She slams the master bedroom door and locks it.

He hammers on it with his fists.

'Dad, help me!' Megan shrieks above the clamour.

The staircase spirals downwards, twisting in a half corkscrew. Looking down it, Mac sees Donald put his foot on the bottom tread.

'Go away, Donald,' Mac warns and resumes his pounding. 'Open the door, Megan.'

Mac leans against the banister. A gap appears in the lining paper that covers the makeshift joint to the wall. Pattering down the staircase, a hard rain of plaster clinks against the polished-steel urn on the half landing.

Pivoting his weight on the banister, Mac brings his feet up to the door handle and presses it down with his shoe. With a mighty shove, supported by his arms on the banister, he breaks the lock and forces the door ajar. He catches a glimpse of Megan, using her body weight, banging it shut. The banister creaks ominously and a cube of cement drops on the urn, knocking it down to land at Donald's feet.

'Piss off,' Megan yells. 'You're not coming in. I'm only taking what's mine.'

'Open the fucking door!'

'Stop him, Dad,' Megan screams from within the besieged room.

On the rail, Mac arches forward again.

'Careful, Mac. The banister...' Donald calls out, bounding up the stairs.

As Donald reaches the landing, Mac kicks out at the door with both legs. But the attempt is met head-on by a thud of equal energy from inside. The door stays closed. Something has to give. It is the banister.

Feeling the banister buckle behind him, Mac pulls himself for-

287

ward. Fifteen feet down, the top rail lands first. A surge of sonic shock rattles the windows as it hits the bottom of the stairwell. The noise echoes in Mac's head as he struggles to keep his balance. A dozen spindles smash on top but stay joined, forming a horizontal picket-fence just off the floor. Arms flailing, he turns his head in time to see the spindles settle.

'Mac,' Donald gasps.

Mac topples backwards and plummets into the cavity. His back-bone hits the spindles, fracturing the middle ones. Dazed but unscathed, Mac lies in a hammock of broken spindles. He hears the bedroom door open, Megan and Donald whisper gravely on the landing. And then he sees them, hand in hand, peering down at him over the edge. Looking back at them, Mac grins off-centre.

'You almost killed yourself. You idiot,' Megan says.

He rises and dusts off his clothes. 'No such luck,' he says. 'Someone up there likes me.'

Megan negotiates the debris on the stairs. 'To think...I wanted your child. This is all just some fucking game to you. Before I leave on Wednesday, I'm going to tell your parents, Josie...everyone... about the things you've done.'

'They won't believe you,' Mac replies, retreating to find his car keys.

'Today,' the *News at Ten* presenter intones, 'British Leyland announced that the production of MG cars will cease.'

Michael can hear the television news clearly from the hall seat where, opposite the photo of himself and Josie dancing Down Under, he sits waiting for the telephone to ring. Waiting for Josie to keep her promise: to phone him today, Monday. It's getting late. Perhaps she isn't going to call. He guesses dinner was around seven, so he has probably been sitting by the phone two or three hours. It is difficult to tell. It seems an eternity until he hears the last news item: 'And finally'. He doesn't listen to it very carefully. Something about a pig-carrying contest.

He picks up the telephone, cradles it in his hand and touches the dial. Closing his eyes, he shakes his head and puts the phone back on the hook. Yearning for the oblivion of sleep, he drags himself upstairs and into the bedroom. His bedroom. He stands there in that room with the bittersweet memories of his boyhood rushing at

288

him. All that misplaced guilt. All those innocent games. The agony and ecstasy of learning how to love and be loved. But he must have been away for those lessons. Because he isn't getting anything right.

When he does start to undress, his movements are lethargic, seemingly painful, almost arthritic. He tries to take his shirt off without undoing the cuffs, but has to pull it back over his head and start again. Before removing his trousers, he sheds one sock and is just about to take off the straggler when he hears the phone. Wearing only boxer shorts and one sock, he springs up and vaults down the stairs.

Mrs Darrett beats him to it. 'Hello, dear...yes, he's right here.'

'Michael,' she says.

'Josie,' he replies, hardly daring to breathe.

'All of your things in the spare bedroom...'

'Do you want me to come and collect them?'

'I want you to come and help me put them back; they don't belong there. They miss you Michael, and so do I. Our baby wants you back too, I can tell.'

Chapter Thirty-Four

One Month Later, October 1979

Propped up against a nest of pillows on the double bed, seven months pregnant, Josie repeats her question: 'Well, how did it go?'

'What?' Michael replies, peevishly.

'Don't be like that,' Josie says. 'Do I have to spell it out? How did your meeting with the Chairman of Lloyd's turn out?'

'Sorry,' he says. He smiles at her. 'I know he's Chairman,' Michael answers, 'but he's still a human being. Diddy gave me a bit of a hard time about the press and that, but he was OK. I don't think Lloyd's will find against me. Besides, I'm out of Lloyd's. I think that's why he suggested we met in his club; he knew I wouldn't fancy the risk of walking into Lloyd's and finding some kangaroo court waiting for me.'

'And?' she presses, reaching out for another kumquat from the over-sized bowl of pregnancy-fad titbits. The fragrance of exotic fruit fills the room.

'The club was alright, if you like that sort of thing. Old fogeys with bifocals peering into out-of-date copies of *Country Life* – I didn't apply for membership.'

He stops talking and turns his attention to undoing his shoelaces, as if he has told her everything.

'Michael!' she says, throwing the tiny orange at him. The sounds of Josie's 'Greatest Hits' cassette intrude into the room from the bathroom. He presumes that she has left the machine on by accident, like she often does.

'From what Diddy let slip,' he says, 'it seems Templeton and Richards-Riley will probably end up with a slap on the wrist. Perhaps a month's suspension, who knows. But Templeton's syndicate is closing down, and Wetthards is holed beneath the waterline. Oh,

290

he did tell me that DBL are going to be required to divest of – sell off, that is – their interests in Lloyd's brokers. Including Mac's company.'

'And? What about Mac? You are going to help Lloyd's by telling them what happened, aren't you? I know he's my brother, but–'

'What reason have I got to hold a grudge? I got the whole commission on the Cutesie buyout,' Michael says. 'Those shares I gave him in the company, they're not worth anything. When DBL sheds its interests in Lloyd's brokers, Mac won't have a job. It doesn't matter what the Lloyd's inquiry does.'

'He hurt you, Michael. Covering up for him is lunacy; we both see him for what he is now. And you must let your feelings out...'

Michael grits his teeth. Sister Sledge is chanting the chorus of 'We Are Family' from the bathroom, *ad nauseam.*

'I've got to turn that music off,' Michael says. 'It's doing my head in.'

He troops into the bathroom, silences the cassette, fills the sink with cold water and immerses his face into it. As he dries himself, the lights that surround the bathroom mirror show no mercy. He has not been sleeping well, and the charcoal pouches under his eyes are prominent. Sighing, he traipses back into the bedroom.

'You take it out on other people,' Josie continues where she left off. 'Do you know how irritable you're becoming? This anger inside you is choking you; you've got to release it. You're not a child any more; trust yourself. God knows, everyone else does. I do.'

'Josie, stop it will you?' He throws himself face down on the bed.

'Sorry,' she says, stroking his hair. 'I love you.'

He rolls onto his back, gazes up at her and offers her a weak smile. The best smile he can muster at that moment. But she grins at him, as if they haven't been arguing. An unsettling feeling of annoyance descends on him. Again.

'Oh, quick, Michael. Feel there.'

She lifts her negligee and presses his head onto her bulging stomach.

'If it's a boy, he'll be a better footballer than you were,' Josie says. 'Then again, from what I remember of your skills, if it's a girl...she'll be better.'

He tuts a childish objection.

'It was a joke, Michael,' she says. 'A joke?'

He doesn't reply; their minor disagreements merge into one furious silence.

'Can't we get married before the birth?' Michael placates her after a while. He knows the answer, but he is also aware that the question is always welcomed. 'Apparently, that's sort of a tradition in some parts of the world.'

He lifts himself up and sits next to her. She puts her arms around his neck and kisses him full on the lips.

'It's not proper to get married to someone you've known for under a year,' she says as she draws away from the kiss.

'You've known me since you were six weeks old,' he replies, stroking her abdomen. 'Is it good etiquette for the bride to breast-feed at the reception?'

She snatches the pillow from his side of the bed and hits him round the head with it, softly. Clubbed by the feathers, he throws himself off the bed, leans against the wall and remains there, motionless, with his eyes open.

'My decisions will always be obeyed,' she says in a Dalek voice. 'It will be in March so I can have a big wedding and my legs won't resemble Herbert the Hippo's. Besides, our mothers agree with me so – on a show of hats – you're outvoted.' He stays lifeless against the wall. 'I hate it when we fight,' Josie continues. 'Let's go out together tomorrow night. There's a new restaurant that–'

Michael draws in a sharp intake of breath. 'Sorry, did I forget to tell you? I'm off to Amsterdam in the morning.'

'Oh, Michael. I wish you'd tell me in advance.'

'I'm only away a night,' Michael says, apologetically.

'Mum says Mac's off to Munich tomorrow,' Josie says. Michael knows full well that Josie is trying to provoke him into venting his spleen, by reminding him that Mac's business life is carrying on as normal. 'I suppose you'll be at the airport two hours early, as usual,' Josie adds. 'Mac never gets there until thirty minutes before.'

'Well, he only lives fifteen minutes from Heathrow. I hate rushing for flights. Do you want me to be more like your brother?' he asks with a smile.

'That's better,' Josie says. But it isn't. Not for Michael. It is worse.

* * *

Michael needs to be at the airport at nine o'clock; he has set the alarm for six. But, at four o'clock, his legs swing out of bed and his torso follows. Android-like, he cancels the alarm and goes into the bathroom where, from the mirror, his alter-face stares back at him. His chin juts forward, his cheeks are hollow and his eyes are opaque. Ice-cold anger courses through his veins.

Dressing on the landing, he stuffs a spare pair of socks and underwear into his jacket pockets. He doesn't need a briefcase for this trip; he has a one-page presentation to make. If he needs a fresh shirt, he can buy one. A briefcase would be an encumbrance; he might forget it somewhere and incriminate himself. Not taking it is a calculated act. But, in his conscious mind, he has never planned to murder Mac.

When he is otherwise ready to leave, he goes back into the bathroom and hunts in the cabinets amongst the ugly remains of half-finished beauty products until he finds his tinted glasses. Putting them on, he looks in the mirror and adjusts the smile of his alter-face. He glances at Josie on his way out. She is fast asleep.

Driving at just over the speed limit, he reaches Finsbury Circus just before five and parks the car in one of the deserted bays. He fishes his gloves out of the side pocket. As he puts them on, he remembers that Mac gave him those gloves as a birthday present a few years back. His chin juts further forward. Grown men giving each other birthday presents. Ridiculous.

He retrieves the keys to the London Wall offices from his pocket. The keys he has forgotten to return. At least, he thinks he forgot. He is momentarily shocked by the alternative, but it does not matter now. He enters the offices and goes straight to the fourth floor. After memorising the flight information for Mac's Munich trip, he looks in Mac's desk for the spare car keys. He will need Mac's Mercedes after the deed. He finds the keys in the top drawer, just as he expects to.

Michael drives his Alfa Romeo straight to the airport and arrives at Heathrow's long-term car park three hours before his flight, just after six o'clock. There is plenty of time to do what has to be done. He checks that the date and time on the car park ticket are legible, places it carefully into his wallet, puts his tinted glasses on and takes the shuttle bus to Terminal 1 surrounded by grey-skinned heart-attack candidates.

Although he knows it is too early to check in, he strolls over to a British Airways desk. Accepting the refusal, he flirts with the girl. She is plain. Not his sort.

'I can take rejection from someone as pretty as you,' he gleams.

As he speaks, he listens to himself. He has the sensation of being outside his own body. All-smiles schizophrenia, the sane part of him sees his behaviour as. It isn't the first time he has had this out-of-body feeling. But in earlier episodes he had quickly regained control of his mind. This time, his doppelgänger isn't so easily deterred. Everything the other person inside him says sounds corny. But she laps it up; Michael's handsome features allow him to get away with murder.

Once he is sure that she will remember him, he wanders off to WH Smith and buys a copy of *The Times*. The till receipt, like the car park ticket, is timed. Just to be safe, he walks around the shop, puts *The Times* back in the pile and picks up the distinctive pink of the *Financial Times*. He pays for it at the opposite till. That receipt he leaves on the counter.

At six-thirty, still two and half hours before his flight, he climbs into the back of a taxi. The driver doesn't look at him until, speaking from behind the FT, Michael states his destination: the train station at Virginia Water. He rolls the words out with an upper-class accent, enough to create an impression without laying it on with a trowel. Fifteen minutes later, he manoeuvres himself out of the taxi and, standing close to the window so that the driver can't see his face, pays. He adds a modest tip. Nothing memorable. Outside the station, he drops the FT into a waste bin.

He has the opportunity to think during the five-minute walk to Mac's house, and ticks items off an incomplete mental checklist. Yes, Mac will vanish. Everyone will have their own theory as to what has happened, especially in Lloyd's. He lets the imaginary voices of the Captains' Room cynics loose in his head. 'Perhaps he's in prison, or torturing some under-age girl in a damp cellar.'

To relieve the tension, he avoids treading on the lines between paving stones as he walks along. It reminds Michael of the games he played with Mac and Josie when they were children. Games like Hide-and-Seek. He has several ideas as to where to stow Mac's corpse If the body were ever to be found then, whilst he might keep the police in flat-footed ignorance, Josie would suspect him.

Josie will suspect him anyway, but it isn't that realisation that causes tears to form in his eyes. It is an emotional cocktail of anger and joy. Joy, that the red-hot nastiness of normal anger surging through his body is melting his murderous, icy wrath. The mist clears from his eyes, his chin recedes and cheeks fill out.

He takes off his glasses and cries tears of euphoria as he bathes in the vindictive vision of a less than lethal revenge: the extraordinary pleasure he can extract from explaining to Mac that not only will Mac not be best man, but that he won't be invited to the wedding. More malicious acts come to mind. He can provide the final rusty nails to ensure Lloyd's nail down the coffin of Mac's career: tip the police off about where Mac stashes his cocaine, and expose all of Mac's misdeeds. Hundreds of them. Michael's thrilled. Thrilled that they are just thoughts. His thoughts. Not things he has to do. Choices.

And, as he turns on his heel, he knows – he doesn't know why, but he just knows – that this evil anger has left him. Left him forever.

THE END